"YOU DRIVE A HARD BARGAIN," HE SAID, EXTENDING HIS HAND. "CLEAN SLATE, AVA?"

Her fingers were warm and strong as she slid them over his palm and shook. "Clean slate, Brennan."

For a second, they sat there, fingers entwined and eyes locked together, and Brennan wanted nothing more than to lean over the console between them, to kiss her fast and deep and not stop until they were both completely out of air and common sense.

Get it together, you jackass! Ava was about to interview him for a tell-all in the paper, which was the one thing—the *only* thing—he'd managed to avoid when his life in Fairview had come flying apart at the seams. He needed to pin every last ounce of his composure firmly into place in order to keep his past in the past.

Putting his mouth on hers would ruin him.

All Wrapped Up

KIMBERLY KINCAID

ZEBRA BOOKS
KENSINGTON PUBLISHING CORP.

http://www.kensingtonbooks.com

30 7478 298

R

ZEBRA BOOKS are published by

Kensington Publishing Corp.
119 West 40th Street
New York, NY 10018

All Kensington titles, imprints, and distributed lines are available at special quantity discounts for bulk purchases for sales promotion, premiums, fund-raising, educational, or institutional use.

Special book excerpts or customized printings can also be created to fit specific needs. For details, write or phone the office of the Kensington Sales Manager: Attn.: Sales Department. Kensington Publishing Corp., 119 West 40th Street, New York, NY 10018. Phone: 1-800-221-2647.

Zebra and the Z logo Reg. U.S. Pat. & TM Off.

First Printing: October 2015
ISBN-13: 978-1-4201-3771-2
ISBN-10: 1-4201-3771-9

eISBN-13: 978-1-4201-3772-9
eISBN-10: 1-4201-3772-7

10 9 8 7 6 5 4 3 2 1

Printed in the United States of America

This book is for the men and women who gear up to bravely run into buildings when all others run out.

Words cannot express how humbly grateful I am for your courage and your willingness to sacrifice.

ACKNOWLEDGMENTS

If writing a book is a group effort, then bridging to a new series is a total team event. I can't think of anyone I'd rather have on my side than the following people.

First things first—I have to thank the Kiss of Death chapter of the Romance Writers of America for setting up the tour that started the firefighter-hero/heroine ball rolling. Thank you for putting my feet on the path.

To the men on C shift at Atlanta Rescue Squad Four, Engine Six, and Quick Six, especially Captain Williams, George, Jenks, Jason, Peter, and Clark, who didn't bat an eye at having a romance author with lots of questions ride along for a whole twenty-four hours—your patience, professionalism, and willingness to show me how things are done made this book possible. Any mistakes or liberties taken are my own, while all the knowledge belongs to you. Y'all know how to get it done like a boss!

To retired firefighter Jon Bartholomew for his expertise on back injuries and physical therapy timelines, and to Dr. Sajjad Khan for the medical advice regarding narcotic substance abuse rehabilitation protocol, your guidance was instrumental in getting the finer details on the page. Also, to the lovely Dana Carroll, without whom this book would still have no title. I am so grateful.

To Alyssa Alexander, Tracy Brogan, Robin Covington,

and Avery Flynn, who read this book in various stages and always asked for more (even when it was in the ugly-baby stage!), there are not enough words to thank you sufficiently for your encouragement and friendship.

To my grandfather Ted and my father-in-law Bob, both of whom proudly served fire companies, I cannot think of finer heroes to use as role models. You are both missed beyond measure.

To my unbelievably supportive daughters—Reader Girl, Smarty Pants, and Tiny Dancer—your excitement at watching me living my dream, even when it's hard on you, is what keeps me going. And Mr. K. . . . well, I'm pretty sure you know that without real-deal love, there are no books about real-deal love. Just like without you, there's no me.

Lastly, to my incredible readers, who have laughed, cried, ooohed, and aaahed with every Pine Mountain love story. I promise, while the journey may be shifting, it is far from over! I cannot be a writer without amazing folks like you, asking for the stories that need to be told. Thank you for being the biggest part of this girl's happily ever after. I love you all!

Chapter One

Nick Brennan's boots sounded off against the neat stretch of pavement in front of his apartment, and he inhaled a deep breath full of frozen air and screaming back pain. He'd learned to cope with an extended and somewhat brutal version of winter upon moving to Pine Mountain two years ago.

The pain was a little more difficult to swallow, but then again, the snap, crackle, and pop running the length of his spine was more rule than exception. After nearly two and a half years, Brennan had learned to suck it up and lock it away.

After all, there were worse things than blowing out a couple of vertebrae. Not to mention worse ways to deal with the pain.

Brennan stuffed back the thought, popping the locks on his Chevy Trailblazer and sliding into the well-worn driver's seat. The Double Shot's staff schedules weren't going to write themselves, no matter how much his back creaked like a hundred-year-old staircase, and he needed to get to work, stat. Brennan might've closed the bar last night, and yeah, the four before it too, but his friends Adrian and Teagan needed all the help they could get.

With business booming under the new management of the burly head chef and the owner's daughter, busy shifts were a foregone conclusion, especially around the holidays. Not that Brennan minded. All that work kept him moving forward, and that was a good thing. Because going back?

Not an option.

The handful of country miles between his apartment complex and the small-town bar and grill started flashing by in a late-morning slideshow of snowy pine trees and mountain backdrops, and Brennan cracked his window to take another deep breath despite the December chill in the air. Dwelling on the past and the physical pain that went with it only spelled trouble, and he forced the muscles in his shoulders and back to unwind as he slid more air into his lungs.

Wait . . . was that smoke?

Brennan's pulse catapulted into go mode, his heart triple-timing it against his sternum even though he refused to let his movements follow suit. With his senses at Defcon One, he methodically scanned the narrow road in front of him from shoulder to shoulder, scooping in another lungful of air as he lasered his focus through the bare trees to the sky overhead.

Fuck. Definitely smoke. Enough to mean very bad things.

And it was getting stronger by the second.

Brennan swung the Trailblazer around a familiar bend in the road, whipping gracelessly into the parking lot of Joe's Grocery. His palms went slick over the steering wheel as the building came into view past the tree line on either side of Rural Route Four. Black smoke funneled from the far end of the clapboard building near the roofline, billowing with enough density to kick his oh-shit meter up another notch. Fueled by nothing more than pure instinct and hard-edged adrenaline, Brennan threw his SUV into PARK and laid waste to the distance between his sloppy parking job and the front entrance.

"Joe!" Relief uncurled in his chest at the sight of the store's owner standing outside the front door, despite the obvious panic on the older man's face. "What happened? Are you hurt?"

"No." Joe shook his head, eyes glassy and breath puffing around his face from the cold. "Caleb and I were stocking produce when all of a sudden the fire alarms started going berserk. I did a quick look for people in the aisles, but by the time we got Michelle from the register at the front and told everyone to get out, smoke was all over the place."

Jesus. Something must be burning back there, and *fast*.

"Okay. If everyone's out, we need to move away from the building and call nine-one-one." Brennan turned toward the opposite side of the parking lot, where the two college-aged kids on Joe's staff stood alongside a smattering of shoppers, thankfully all far enough from the building to be out of harm's way.

For now, at least. Fires could turn on a dime and leave nine and a half cents change, and the smoke now steadily pushing at the expanse of windows on Joe's storefront was thick enough to make Brennan twitchy.

Right. Time to go. "Come on." He turned to lead Joe across the parking lot, ready as hell to let the Pine Mountain FD have at the building so he could get out of there and slide back into the shadows, when an ungodly scream stopped him cold.

"Matthew? *Matthew!*" The woman belonging to the noise came hurtling around the corner of the building from the back, her head whipping from side to side in a panicked search.

"Whoa!" Brennan looped an arm around her waist to stop her midstride as she angled herself toward the front door. "You can't go in there."

"My little boy!" She struggled against his grip, turning to fix him with a wild-eyed stare. "He was in the bathroom, but I can't find him. I think he's still inside. Please, you have to let me go!"

Realization punched Brennan's gut full of holes. "Ma'am, it's not safe inside. You need to wait for the fire department."

"No." She shook her head, vehement. "No, I don't see him anywhere. He's not out here. I'm going back inside!"

For a split second, the entire scene froze into place. Black smoke, foreboding and malicious, pushed from any exit it could find. The heat pouring off the building, demolishing the chill of winter from twenty feet away, was a clear-cut sign of a large, active fire within. Brennan's brain screeched at him to restrain the woman and fall back, to let the fire department arrive and secure the scene, to *not* act impulsively in a way that could cost him everything. Again.

But then he caught sight of the propane tanks Joe sold in the summer, lined up in a chain-link storage locker against the side of the clapboard building, and he was done thinking.

"Joe, get my cell phone out of my truck and call nine-one-one. Tell them you have an active fire with reported entrapment. Round up everyone on the outside and stay as far away from the building as you can until they get here. Go now." Brennan flipped his keys to the older man, scanning the grocery store for the best strategic point of entry. Damn it, despite all the possibles, this still had *spectacularly bad plan* written all over it.

He turned toward the woman, purposely slowing his words and movements so he didn't spook her further. "The last place you saw Matthew was the bathroom in the back of the store?"

"Y-yes," she sputtered. "When the alarm went off, I looked all over, but I couldn't find him. I thought . . . maybe he got out another way, but . . . oh God. He's only seven. You have to help him. *Please.*"

Serrated echoes of a different voice yanked at his chest from the depths of two and a half years ago, stealing the breath from his lungs and cementing his body to the asphalt.

You don't have time for this. Your only job is to get this kid. This. Kid. Right fucking now.

Before Brennan could register the movement, the past was gone and his boots were crunching over the frost-encrusted gravel strip leading to the side of the building. The bathrooms were in the back of the store, and he needed to start there and work forward. Just because Matthew's mom hadn't seen him there didn't mean he *wasn't* there, and it was the last place the kid had been for sure. With the fire alarm going full bore and the building full of smoke, they could've missed each other, and at seven, Matthew had to be terrified.

Probably enough to hide.

Jacking the neck of his long-sleeved thermal shirt up to cover his nose and mouth before zipping his black canvas jacket tight, Brennan clattered to a stop by the side door, marked EMPLOYEES ONLY. Although it was ajar, he laid a quick hand on it to assess the temperature, relief splashing through him at the relatively cool feel of the steel panel. This had to be where Matthew's mom had exited the building.

Calculating his surroundings with every move, Brennan swung the door open and stepped inside the space, squinting hard against the thick curtain of smoke issuing up from the floor.

Christ. Until it had a place to go, this smoke was going to be a major roadblock. He needed to find Matthew. Yesterday.

"Matthew!" The acrid air scraped a path into Brennan's lungs, but that didn't stop him from crouching down low and drawing in another ration of breath. "Call out, buddy! I'm here to help."

But the bathrooms and the small office beside them turned up empty, and Brennan banged both doors closed behind him in an effort to isolate his search field and contain some of the heavy smoke. The heat had gone from zero to unbearable in about three seconds flat, and between the sweat stinging his eyes and the smoke clogging his path, visibility was pretty much nil.

Nope. No way was he leaving without this kid.

"Matthew!" Swiping an arm over his brow, Brennan tried again, the bellow burning in his chest as he called out over the clanging smoke alarm. "I'm here to get you out!"

The only answer was the incessant bell and the soft, underlying *whoosh* of unseen flames that told Brennan he needed to haul ass unless he wanted to die trying.

Pushing forward, he bent even further for breathable oxygen as he quickly checked the employee break room and made his way toward the main section of the store. Despite the high overhead ceiling, the normally wide-open space was cloaked in hot, soot-filled air and thin stretches of orange flames, and Brennan coughed hard against the sucker punch rattling through his lungs. Fully on his hands and knees now despite the bite of the linoleum through his jeans and the screaming tightness in his back, he forced Matthew's name past the charred taste of smoke in his mouth.

Process of elimination told him the boy had to be somewhere in this room, so Brennan shuffle-crawled toward the wall to start a strategic search. Yes, he needed to move as fast as possible, but speed wouldn't matter for shit if he missed the kid altogether. Starting in aisle one, Brennan clambered down the smoke-obscured rows, instinct thrumming through him as he shoved past metal shelves and cardboard displays. The first four aisles turned up empty, each one hotter and more smoke-laden than the one before it, and damn it, where was this kid?

Brennan sucked in a raw breath to call out again when a deep chill of fear plucked down his spine.

What if Matthew *had* gotten out safely? What if the boy was outside, right now, wrapped up in his mother's arms, while Brennan was trapped inside?

What if history was cruel enough to repeat itself?

The barely there sound of a cough sank hooks into every inch of his attention, and he whipped toward it without pause. "Matthew?" The word flew past cracked lips, and Brennan crawled forward as fast as he could, searching wildly. "Call out, Matthew! I want to help you."

"I'm here."

The wavering reply sent a shock wave of relief through Brennan's chest. A set of saucer-wide eyes blinked out from an oversized shelving unit half full of cases of water, and holy hell—Brennan never would've seen the boy hiding there if he hadn't paused for that brief second.

"Hey, bud. I'm going to get you out of here, but we've got to hurry." He didn't want to frighten Matthew any further, but they'd been running out of time since the minute Brennan had crossed the threshold.

"I want my mom," the boy said, coughing over the words, and Brennan instinctively pulled the collar of Matthew's shirt over his nose and mouth to match his own.

"I want to get you to her." Brennan calculated the distance between their location and the front door in his mind, weighing it against the return trip to the back of the store. The front door was the fastest route out, for sure.

Just as long as it wasn't blocked.

"Come on." Brennan stomped on the thought and reached for Matthew, who thankfully slipped from his hiding spot to crawl next to Brennan on the floor. Other than looking tearstained and terrified, he didn't appear to be hurt, which was a huge mark in the win column. With one economical move, Brennan swung the boy to his back, and even though his muscles seized in pain from the added pressure, he aimed himself full-on at the exit.

"Hold on as tight as you can, okay?" He stabbed his boots into the linoleum in a wide stance, balancing Matthew's weight with the need to stay as low as possible. Between the smoke and the tall shelving on either side of them, visibility was limited to only a few feet forward, but Brennan still covered the space with confidence. He'd memorized all the exits by his third trip to Joe's, and by the sixth time, he could find the front door with his eyes closed.

Some instincts were sewn in forever.

Brennan rounded the corner at the end of the aisle, sweeping his gaze in a lightning-quick one-eighty before tipping it upward. Flames sparked like bright orange pinpricks through the haze of black smoke, covering a huge section of the far wall, and what little breath he had left shot from Brennan's lungs, making him dizzy. *Shit*, this fire had moved fast, changing the game with each passing second. Which meant he was only getting one chance at the door.

And dizzy or not, he needed to take it *now*.

Locking his hand over Matthew's interlaced fingers to make sure the boy had a solid grip, Brennan gave all he had as he stood and pumped his legs toward the door. Clips of daylight showed through the window, peppered with flashes of red and white. His muscles played chicken with his lungs, each daring the other to give out first, but he thrust the burn of both from his mind and ran.

Ava Mancuso flicked a glance at the GPS coordinates for her latest story assignment, absolutely convinced she was in hell. Or at the very least, purgatory, because honestly, she'd been floating between both at the *Riverside Daily* for the past five years.

And the only thing she had to show for it was an extremely high tolerance for grunt work, and a standing prescription for antacids. Double strength.

"Whoa. What's the matter with you?"

Ava blinked back to the reality of her tried and true Volkswagen Jetta just in time to catch the concern-tinged gaze of her coworker, Layla Ellis, as she turned toward Ava from the passenger seat.

"What makes you think something's the matter?" Ava plastered a smile over her lips, her voice mired in cynicism even though she tried to keep it neutral. Layla had been a photographer at the *Daily* for nearly as long as Ava had been a reporter. Or at least, Ava would've been a reporter if her tyrant of a boss let her out from behind her laptop to actually investigate a decent story.

One screwup four and a half years ago, and Gary had

never let it go. All Ava had ever wanted to do was tell real stories about real people. Not in that overblown sensationalist way so many other reporters adopted instead of digging deep to do their jobs, but respectfully. Truthfully. With power and emotion.

Instead, she was consistently assigned to cover events like the Riverside Turnip Festival, all because the source for her first big story had spun more fairy tales than Walt-freaking-Disney.

Layla lifted one white blond eyebrow over the rim of her glasses, rooting through the camera bag perched across her lap. "Ah, let's see. For starters, your sarcasm is thick enough to spread on a cracker. And secondly, no offense, but right now you're wearing a face only a mother could love. So what gives?"

Ava's gut gave up a healthy yank, but she lifted one shoulder in a bored shrug to temper it. She wasn't about to admit that her mother hadn't even loved her face when she was born, and anyway, Layla knew all about Ava's work-related misery.

Her personal life? Not so much. As in, not even a little, not ever.

Ava opened her mouth to deliver a tart reminder that they were on their way to cover the Pine Mountain Elementary Math Bowl, but a sudden blast of lights and sirens glued the words to her throat.

"Holy shit, hang on!"

Ava swung the Jetta to the tightrope-thin shoulder of Rural Route Four just in time to avoid being sideswiped by a convoy of not one, but two fire trucks marked PINE MOUNTAIN FIRE DEPARTMENT, followed closely by an ambulance. *Jeez*, they were hauling the mail. In the five years she'd lived in the Blue Ridge, she'd never seen anyone take the sharp twists of Pine Mountain's main road so fast or so furiously.

With that much manpower, this emergency wasn't a garden variety burned pot roast. Heck, even those barely happened in teeny-tiny Pine Mountain. Whatever this was had to be substantial. Gargantuan.

Newsworthy.

"You okay?" Ava asked, sliding a glance to Layla's spot in the passenger seat.

Her friend nodded, although her knuckles flashed white over her camera bag from the sudden swerve. "Uh-huh," Layla said, but her acting performance sure wasn't going to win her any Oscars.

"Good." Ava stole a deep breath, taking a second to wrestle her pulse back out of the stratosphere before pulling back onto the road.

"Where are you going?" Layla pointed to the GPS that was currently squawking at Ava about her missed turn, but no way in hell was Ava going to the Math Bowl now. She gripped the leather-wrapped steering wheel with enough determination to make her knuckles sing.

"I'm going to find out what that's all about."

Layla pulled back in shock, her shoulder thumping softly against the Jetta's passenger door. "Are you sure barging onto the scene of an emergency is such a good idea?"

"I'm not barging. I'm investigating. I want a Pulitzer, not a spot with the paparazzi," Ava said, tipping her chin toward the stretch of road in front of them. She followed behind the ambulance at the rear of the convoy, calculating a respectable distance and then adding two car lengths just to be sure. While she had ambition to spare when it came to working a story, there were some boundaries she refused to cross. "But I'm not passing up a chance to prove myself with a first-rate story, either. Something huge is going on out here, and it just fell into our laps. I'll be damned if I don't at least find out what it is."

The red and white strobe lights cut a painfully bright path through the smudgy gray shadows of the bare trees overhead, and a quick, relentless chill rolled down Ava's spine at the sight of the fire trucks rounding the bend ahead of her. The image of a dark-haired, darker-eyed firefighter recruit flitted across her mind, knocking her heart against her ribs with an involuntary jolt.

Meeting a guy like Nick Brennan had been the last thing Ava had expected that summer after college, when she'd finally punched her one-way ticket out of Philadelphia and the upbringing she'd give anything to forget. But between his easygoing demeanor and his chocolate-smolder gaze, Ava'd never had a chance.

On second thought, meeting Nick Brennan had been the second to last thing she'd expected seven years ago.

Letting herself fall in love with him? Yeah, *that* had been the first.

The ambulance in front of her let out a sharp *whoop* as it barreled into a particularly tight angle in the road, slapping Ava back to the here and now. This was no time for a sap-happy jaunt down memory lane. As much as she might wonder what had become of the sexy firefighter-in-training, the past was meant to be left behind. Her parents were living proof that love could go as rotten as month-old milk, and no way was she going down that road.

She'd already walked away from it once.

"Do you smell that?" Ava's senses sharpened over the pungent scent of smoke filtering through the vents in the Jetta, and she swung her gaze from side to side, squinting to gather details from either side of the asphalt.

"Yeah," Layla said, craning her neck to look out the

passenger window. "Something is on fire, and whatever it is, it's close."

The thin, gray haze that Ava had chalked up to road dust was becoming unmistakably thicker by the second, and she did a mental tally of the buildings in the immediate area. Nearly everything in Pine Mountain was located either at the plush mountain resort or on Main Street, where her brother's bakery stood. The only three things on Rural Route Four large enough to require such a drastic response were that bar and grill she'd heard about but had never been to, the apartment complex where her brother Pete used to live, and Joe's Grocery. Judging by the amount of smoke clinging to the air around her car, whichever one of those was closest was the one on fire.

And Joe's Grocery was just around the bend.

"There!" Layla exclaimed, pointing to a clearing in the thick trees lining the road. The fire trucks whipped through the near-side turnoff for the grocery store, and Ava jerked her car to the gravel-lined shoulder of Rural Route Four.

Slinging off her seat belt and shouldering her bag, she thrust her feet onto the thickly wooded side of the road. "Okay. I'm going to get as close as I can to figure out what's going on, maybe see if I can talk to any witnesses to get a story."

"Right. I'll try to get as many shots as possible, but I'll probably need to move around a bit. It depends on the barricades," Layla said, already in motion at Ava's side.

"Just be careful. I've got my cell if you need me."

Police cars blocked the far entrance to Joe's, but they must've just arrived since the side where Ava had parked was still clear. Layla stopped to take a few quick photos of the outlying area, but Ava slipped through the snowy pine trees at the perimeter of the building, pulling her coat around her with a shiver. Her pulse hopscotched through her veins as the smell of smoke invaded her nostrils, prompting an unbidden cough from her chest. She flipped her cell phone into her palm and flicked the microphone icon on the screen, intending to dictate the facts from the outskirts of the area.

But the scene was so utterly surreal, she knew in an instant that any words she'd choose would fail to capture it.

The far side of the tall clapboard building was completely covered in black smoke and angry orange flames, and one of the freshly arrived fire trucks jerked to a halt in front of the blaze. Firefighters jumped down from both sides of the truck, scrambling to cover the scene with brisk, calculated movements. While the flames hadn't seemed to reach the side of the store closest to where she stood, smoke plumed from the windows and roofline in a way that said they were damned close. The telltale shimmer of extreme heat blurred outward from the building, and smoke lifted heavily from the roofline, rising up to paint the sky overhead with fat smudges of foreboding gray.

Sweet Jesus. This fire was *huge*.

A heavy metallic *clang* rattled in Ava's ears, and the brisk back and forth between firefighters as they readied the hoses and ladders for immediate use nailed her purpose back into place. She recorded a quick assessment of the scene, describing the details in her cell phone even though they were indelibly printed in her brain. A small group of bystanders lined the outer edge of the property, one of whom was a college-aged young woman who looked nothing short of distraught as she watched the firemen prepare to fight the blaze. Ava's heart squeezed against her ribs, and without thinking, she stepped closer and put a hand on the girl's shoulder.

"Are you okay?" she asked, and the girl turned, her eyes brimming with tears that she was clearly trying to fight.

"Oh! Uh, yeah. No. I don't know." The tears wobbled on the girl's dark lashes, and she tugged at the hem of her cheerful red apron embroidered with the words JOE'S GROCERY. "We were just inside like ten minutes ago, and the fire seemed small. But now it's really bad, and . . ."

"It'll be all right, Michelle. I promise." A pretty blonde in a chef's jacket put her arm around the girl, squeezing tight, and Ava split her gaze between the two of them.

"My name is Ava Mancuso, and I'm with the *Riverside Daily*," she said to the older woman, whose damp brow and disheveled ponytail told Ava she'd probably been inside Joe's when the blaze started.

"Bellamy Griffin," the woman said with a nod.

Ava gentled her voice over her next words. "Can you tell me what happened?"

"I'm not sure, really. Everything went so fast. One minute I was grabbing some extras before work, and the next, the whole back of the store was full of smoke." Bellamy's eyes skated over the scene, her shaky exhale puffing around her face in the cold. "I thought everyone got out, but then Kitty Wilson rushed out in a total panic without her son, and Brennan ran back inside—"

"Hold on." The name pricked hard at Ava's ears, but she shook it off in favor of the realization rocketing down her spine. "Somebody's still in there?"

"Yes. A little boy got separated from his mother. The manager from the bar and grill up the road went in to try and find him before the fire department showed up, but now they're here, and"—Bellamy lowered her voice, turning toward Ava so the young woman still standing close by couldn't hear—"no one's come back out yet."

Ava pulled in a breath, and the acrid taste of smoke landed hard in her mouth. Instinctively, she narrowed her stare on the front of the store, her heart thumping a steady pattern against her sternum as she edged close enough to feel the heat churning off the building.

And then the main doors burst outward in an explosion of sound and movement, and a dark-haired man wearing nothing more than jeans and a winter jacket came flying out from behind the glass and steel with a child latched firmly to his back.

In an instant, the scene erupted. Paramedics swarmed forward in a rush of rolling gurneys and portable equipment, while firefighters closed in on the front of the building, knocking out windows to create an escape route for the smoke and closing in on the entryway with the hose. Miraculously, the man who had rescued the child sat upright on the gurney, appearing more irritated at the attention than injured from the fire. He fit into Ava's line of sight for just an instant, leaning forward to look at the boy safely cradled in his mother's arms.

Oh . . . God.

Absolute shock cemented Ava's feet to the asphalt, and despite the pulse now going ballistic in her veins, she'd know that dark-eyed stare anywhere.

Nick Brennan, the man she hadn't seen in seven years but had once loved with every last cell in her body, had just become the story of the decade.

Chapter Two

Although it took four hours' worth of medical tests and some extremely creative evasive maneuvering to get around the knot of local reporters clogging the lobby at Riverside Memorial Hospital, Brennan finally managed to break free just in time to pick up his Trailblazer, courtesy of the Pine Mountain PD. The smell of smoke, still heavy in the air though the fire had long been put out, had tugged at the back of his throat even from the far side of the parking lot, but he'd tamped it down with a controlled breath. The last thing Brennan needed was to linger on the past when he'd had such a crazy day, especially since he barely had enough time to clean up and get to the Double Shot for his shift.

As much of a pain as the doctors and reporters had been, they had nothing on his boss.

"If you ever pull a stunt like that again, so help me God, they'll be taking you to the morgue instead of the emergency department." Teagan O'Malley jammed her boots into the industrial kitchen tiles in the back of the restaurant, planting her hands over the hips of her jeans as she flattened Brennan with a merciless scowl.

Pulling the side door shut behind him, he shot a look at

the huge man standing behind her in the narrow galley kitchen, meeting the chef's storm-colored gaze with a silent *help a guy out*. But even though Adrian Holt was the closest thing Brennan had to a best friend in Pine Mountain, he was Teagan's fiancé first, and the guy just held up his hands as if to say *not it*.

Shit. Looked like Brennan was on his own for this one.

"Come on, Teagan," he said, shifting his weight from one Nike to the other. Christ, his back was screaming six ways to Sunday now that his adrenaline rush had trickled to a stop, and it took every ounce of his stoic willpower to blank the discomfort from his face. "You're a paramedic. You treated me yourself on the way to the hospital, and Dr. Russell spent ages poking and prodding me within a half inch of my decency. I'm totally fine. No big deal."

Her auburn brows hiked up toward her hairline as she swiped an apron from the neatly folded stack by the pantry, and okay, maybe *fine* wasn't going to stick quite yet. "You almost passed out from smoke inhalation because you ran into an actively burning three-alarm fire without assistance or protection, Brennan! Where I come from, that doesn't constitute fine. It constitutes bat shit crazy."

Of course she had to bring up that he'd gotten a little dizzy in the rig on the way to Riverside Memorial. But it wasn't as if he could admit to Teagan and Adrian that he'd been in that particular driver's seat before and he knew the light-headed thing passed quickly with a little O2. Eating a little too much bad air from time to time was just an occupational hazard.

Or at least, it used to be. Hell, he really needed to get a handle on this so they could forget about the fire and move on, stat.

Brennan grabbed the inventory clipboard from the shelf by the pass-through to the bar and scraped together a smile, because the alternative wouldn't get him very far. "And yet I've been called worse. Look, I get that it was dangerous—"

"It was downright insane," Teagan interrupted. "You have no idea how lucky you are that the whole thing didn't end up in disaster. All the guys at the fire house are ready to give you an earful. Don't even get me started on the blue streak my captain was cussing over the radio in your honor."

Not surprising, all things considered. But still . . . "There was a seven-year-old kid in there. What was I supposed to do?"

This time, his unspoken bid for backup yielded a look from Adrian akin to *he might have a point,* and finally, Teagan's irritation faltered.

"You're supposed to wait for the pros," she said, although the mention of the boy and the shared glance with Adrian took a whole lot of heat off her words. "I thought . . ." She paused, pulling in an audible breath. "I thought you were really hurt, okay?"

Shock rippled its way up Brennan's spine, chased quickly by a swift shot of remorse, but he caged both behind a mostly neutral expression. "I'm sorry," he said, softening his tone so she'd know he meant it. "I just got a little dizzy for a few seconds from all the smoke. But my pulse ox was nearly normal by the time we got to Riverside, and Dr. Russell even said I'm okay to work tonight as long as I take it easy. So really, I'm fine."

"You're a pain in the ass, is what you are," she grumbled, but the smile poking at the corners of her mouth was a dead giveaway.

"Thank you. Look, we've all had enough excitement for one day. What do you say I buy you a beer after our shift and we just get back to normal?"

But Teagan's response was summarily cut off by their sous chef, Jesse, as he entered the kitchen wearing a big old what-the-hell on his face.

"Uh, Brennan? A TV crew just pulled into the parking lot, and the upstairs phone has been ringing off the wall with people looking for you. Something about wanting the big story straight from the source?"

Brennan's gut dropped low enough to turf his kneecaps, and Adrian lifted a shadowy brow, finally throwing his two cents into the conversation.

"Better go somewhere else if you want normal, dude. Looks like we're gonna be fresh out for a while."

Three hours and a whole lot of avoiding the front of the house later, Brennan was out of options. Adrian and Teagan might've been able to get rid of all the nosy-ass reporters, but the Double Shot's dining room was still brimming with locals wanting to get a glimpse of their "hometown hero." The waitstaff had been steadily turning tables since they'd popped the front doors open at four o'clock, and if the volume and intensity of Adrian's gruff kitchen directives were any indication, they were headed for the weeds in both the back of the house and behind the bar, all before the dinner shift even got into full swing. Brennan's servers needed all the help they could get, and that meant he was going to have to take one for the team.

A *big* one.

Brennan shifted his weight in a move he'd given far too much play tonight, his cross-trainers squeaking against the well-traveled kitchen floor by the door to the bar. His back felt like a team full of ringers had used it for batting practice, and he pressed a palm into the throbbing muscles under his gray T-shirt with a grimace.

"Teagan catches you making that face, and pissed won't even begin to cover it."

God *damn*. For a big guy, Adrian's stealth was just not right. The fact that he didn't miss even the slightest trick wasn't lost on Brennan, either.

"I'm cool," he said, dialing his expression to a nice, controlled easy-does-it. Brennan nodded down to the three plates in Adrian's grip, snapping the corresponding ticket from the queue. "These going out the door?"

"Table nine." Adrian didn't let go of the plates, and although his words were clipped to the quick like always, Brennan caught the concern hiding beneath them. "You had a helluva morning. You sure you're straight?"

"Yup." At least, he would be when all this hype died down and he could slide back into the woodwork. Preferably with a heating pad and an extra PT session. "Absolutely."

"Good." The gravel in Adrian's voice returned with a don't-fuck-with-my-kitchen vengeance, and the thick, black tattoo on his forearm flexed as he passed over all three dishes in half as many seconds. "Because I've got six more just like 'em that need to go out the door on the fly. Let's turn and burn a little, yeah?"

"I'm on it." Balancing the plates over both hands and a forearm, Brennan shouldered his way past the swinging door to the dining room. The place was as packed as he'd ever seen it, with every available table occupied and standing room only two-deep at the bar. Teagan was a blur behind the stretch of mahogany and brass at the back of the restaurant, and whoa, even her father, Patrick, who owned the place, had slipped in beside her to help out. The air hung thick with noisy chatter and the *clink* of glassware and cutlery, the warm overhead light spilling down from the exposed wood beams of the ceiling just low enough to make the place cozy, even with the brimming crowd.

Brennan covered the hardwood beneath his feet in quick strides, sneaking in a breath of relief. If they were this busy all night, he should be able to avoid too much attention over what had happened this morning.

"Brennan? Oh my gracious me! It's *you!*"

Or not.

"Hi, Mrs. Teasdale. How are you tonight?" Brennan shifted to a stop in front of table nine, lifting up the plate in his left hand. "Tuna melt, as usual, right?"

The elderly woman's hand fluttered up to her throat as Brennan distributed everyone's dinner with polite efficiency. "Look at you, so modest! As if you didn't pull Matty Wilson out of a blazing inferno today."

"It wasn't nearly as dramatic as that. I'm glad Matthew's okay, but really, I just got lucky," Brennan said, hoping his smile didn't look as ill-fitting as it felt. Mrs. Teasdale might mean well, but Pine Mountain's small-town grapevine could withstand a nuclear apocalypse with a zombie invasion on top. The last thing he needed was to fuel the rumor mill.

"That's not what Kitty Wilson said," replied the woman next to Mrs. Teasdale. "She said you saved Matthew's life. Everyone down at the Main Street Diner has been talking about it. Why, you're a regular hometown hero!"

Brennan barely resisted wincing. "That's nice of you to say, but really, I'm just a regular guy."

"Nonsense," Mrs. Teasdale clucked, picking up a red and green paper shopping bag from the chair next to her. "We've made you a little something. It's just some Christmas cookies and a bit of my fruitcake to get you in the holiday spirit, but . . . well, the three of us old biddies have lived in Pine Mountain for a lot of years, and Kitty Wilson was born and raised here. We're just so grateful for what you did for her, and for Matthew."

"I'm just doing my job."

The words were out before he could trap them, and *damn* his deeply rooted instincts. Brennan ratcheted up his smile and gestured to the back of the restaurant. "I mean, I need to get back to the kitchen, ladies. Thank you for the cookies. It's, uh, really nice of you."

Before the hot seat he'd parked himself right smack in the middle of could spontaneously combust, Brennan bee-lined back toward the kitchen. He tried to make steady work of running plates and helping behind the bar, but after the four-thousandth mention of the fire at Joe's, he came perilously close to throwing in the towel.

"Another phone number for you, Brennan," Teagan said, holding up a bar ticket smudged with red ink. "But I've gotta tell you, if these girls start flinging their unmentionables around, I'm going to have to draw the line." Her sarcasm fell prey to the ear-to-ear smirk taking over her face, and Adrian met it with a gravelly chuckle as he hauled a tray of clean pint glasses to the slim stretch of countertop by the service alcove.

"Come on, Red. He pulled a kid from a burning building this morning. Give the guy a little credit."

"I don't want any credit. And I definitely don't want anyone's number," Brennan argued, snapping the caps off a couple of Budweisers and sending them down the bar. Damn it, he never put stuff like this to words when he'd been a firefighter. He sure as shit wasn't going to get gabby now that he wasn't. "In fact, don't you need help breaking down the kitchen?"

"Nice try." Adrian edged past him, refilling the glassware shelves behind the bar only a hair faster than Teagan could empty them. "But we're slammed out here. Jesse can handle breakdown on his own. Right now, we need all able bodies behind the wood. If I'm in the front of the house, you're in the front of the house. You feel me?"

Well, hell. The guy had a point, and it wasn't as if Brennan was a stranger to slinging drinks. Plus, as antsy as the crowd made him, a steady stream of customers at the bar would keep him focused and busy and in control.

Provided that none of them mentioned the words *rescue, fire,* or *grocery store*, he'd be money for the rest of the night.

"What can I get you?" Brennan placed a palm against the smooth wood of the bar, leaning in toward a middle-aged guy wearing a crisp button-down shirt and horn-rimmed glasses.

"Perrier with lime would be great." The guy paused, throwing a quick but thorough perusal Brennan's way. "Are you Brennan?"

His gut took a swan dive into a giant pool of suspicion. "Who's asking?"

"Mike Trotter, *Bealetown Bugle*. Got some questions for you, if you don't mind." The reporter whipped a recording device from his pocket, aiming it under Brennan's chin in a presumptuous thrust. "Tell me, what was going through your head when you ran inside that burning building today? Did you think you were going to make it out alive?"

Brennan dug deep for his calm, but damn, it took effort. "No comment."

"Come on," the guy tried again, closing in on Brennan's personal space a little further with the recording device. "This is the biggest thing to happen in Pine Mountain in years, and the public deserves to know the real story. Fire and Rescue hasn't released the boy's name to the public yet. Can you tell us if you know him?"

Brennan resisted the urge to pop off with a two-word directive a little harsher than *no comment*, but he lowered the man's drink to the bar with a heavy *plunk* instead. "Will this be it for you?"

"The stunt you pulled today drew some pretty serious speculation from one of my firefighter sources. Says that rescue you made is one in a million for a civilian. Do you have any training as a firefighter, Brennan?"

Adrian swooped in just as Brennan swallowed the bitter-edged *yes* burning a hole through his mouth.

"Do we have a problem here?" He unfolded to his entire six feet, five inches, crossing his arms over the cement wall of his chest with clear disdain as he stared at the reporter.

"I was just trying to get a story," the man sputtered, pulling the recorder back in a nervous jerk. Adrian's gaze narrowed to a thin-bladed stare, and he leaned halfway across the bar as the man's Adam's apple lifted over his shirt collar in a hard swallow.

"Get it somewhere else."

Brennan waited until the reporter had slunk off his bar stool before turning to cock his head at Adrian. "You enjoying yourself over there, Gigantor?"

"Maybe." But his satisfied smile marked the word as a massive understatement. "Look, I need reporters harassing my staff like I need a frigging prostate exam. Anyway, you're part of the crew. I've got your back."

The phrase sent a familiar ache through Brennan's gut, but he tamped it down. He might be strung tighter than a fistful of butterfly knots right now, but man, this was too good to pass up. "Aw, you're all hearts and unicorns, Holt."

"Uh-huh. And I can still turn you into paste if the spirit moves me," Adrian flipped back, his smile tripling in size. "Now can we tend some bar here, hero? Or are you gonna just stand there looking pretty?"

"Speaking of pretty," Teagan interrupted, reaching between him and Adrian to pluck a bottle of tequila from the back shelf, "there's a woman at the end of the bar who's asking for you, Brennan."

He bit back the urge to frown. "I told you, I really don't want anyone's phone number."

Okay, so he hadn't exactly dated anybody since moving to Pine Mountain, and yeah, it probably wouldn't hurt him to try, but Brennan wasn't interested in the kind of girl who'd go all starry eyed with rescue syndrome.

"Well, good, because she didn't offer it," Teagan said over her shoulder, filling two drink orders at once. "All she did was ask for you. For what it's worth, I didn't get an idiot vibe from her. She's down at the end of the bar, last seat."

Unable to curb his curiosity, Brennan aimed a covert glance across the room, but with the milling crowd, it came up about six people too short. A shot of unease rippled through his chest, but he locked it down before it could seep into his expression. This night had already lasted two weeks, the bar was still full to the rafters with people asking questions he didn't want to answer, and the ibuprofen he'd thrown back three hours ago had gone on a complete walkabout.

The last thing he needed was one more person with his name on her lips.

"Fine. But after this, if anyone else asks, I'm not here." Brennan stuffed his bottle opener into the back pocket of his jeans, covering the rubber floor mats behind the bar with a purposeful stride. One quick meet and greet, and he was going work-only for the rest of the night. He didn't care *who* walked in the door asking for him.

But then he looked up into a set of startlingly familiar green eyes, and everyone in the entire bar disappeared.

Chapter Three

Even though Ava had watched him covertly for twenty minutes before snagging a seat at the packed-to-the-seams bar, the sight of Nick Brennan standing right there in front of her made her heart go for broke in her rib cage.

"Ava?" Her name was nothing more than a shocked breath as it moved past his lips, but the word landed in her ears as if he'd shouted it at her.

"Hi," she managed, and great. Sign her up for the lamest opening ever. Ava straightened on her bar stool, forcing herself to look past Nick's decadently long eyelashes and the holy-shit expression plastered to his otherwise gorgeous face. "It's been a long time."

"It's been seven years," he corrected, blinking twice before taking a step back.

Oh God, maybe she'd made a mistake coming here like this with no warning. But trying to talk to him at the hospital had seemed downright rude, and if she waited until tomorrow, she'd lose her chance. She'd never expected the place to be so jammed, though. Ninety percent of the town had to be in the warmly lit confines of the bar, most of them clamoring for Nick's attention.

Ava made an attempt at a smile. "You look good."

Okay, so it was a massive freaking understatement, but come on. Nick's stare was still melted-chocolate sexy, although his dark hair was longer than the near crew cut she remembered, just enough to be casually tousled without going the full-on bed-head route. A closely trimmed goatee had replaced the boyish clean-shaven face in her memory, but if anything, it made him even better looking. Long, sturdy muscles pulled tight over his forearms as he braced his palms on the bar, triggering a long-buried spark in Ava's belly as he leaned in close enough for her to catch the brisk ocean scent of his skin.

"Thanks. You look—" Nick's words yanked to a stop, and Ava realized just a half second too late that the mother of all serious frowns bracketed his mouth. "Far from home."

"Oh!" The sudden change in both his expression and his body language peppered holes in her composure, torching the smooth, professional opening she'd practiced ad nauseam on the drive over. "Well, I, ah . . . I live in Riverside now."

That jarred a frown. "You do?"

"For the last five years," she said, pausing so he could respond with what he was doing so far away from his own hometown of Fairview, which sat just outside Richmond, Virginia.

But he didn't. Instead, he moved his hands from the bar and took a step back, reestablishing the distance between them. "So what brings you out to the Double Shot tonight?"

Ava scooped in a breath and went right for full disclosure. "I came to see you."

"Interesting change of heart," he said, his tone utterly unreadable as he flipped a couple of shot glasses to the three-inch strip of black matting on the inside rim of the bar. "Last I remember, you never wanted to see me again."

"That's not true." The pungent scent of bourbon sent a razor-wire punch to Ava's chest, and she held her breath to avoid another inhale as Nick filled the shot glasses with an expert flip. Damn it, she should've known putting herself within fifty feet of a bar would give her the sweats.

Just like she should've figured Nick might be less than thrilled to see her.

Ava swallowed. "Listen, Nick, I—"

"Brennan."

Now it was her turn to be surprised. "What?"

"I don't really go by Nick anymore." He slid the shot glasses a few spots down the bar to the guys who had motioned for them. His expression made the Great Wall of China look like a teeny little roadblock, but Ava refused to let it deter her. Story or no story, she'd left him without a good-bye seven years ago. She might've had damn compelling reasons for her actions—even if she'd rather stick an ice pick in her eye than admit them—but she still owed Nick an apology.

"Brennan," she said, trying the name on for size. "I know it might seem like I left because I didn't want to see you again, but that's not true. There were . . . complicated circumstances. But just because I didn't intend to hurt you doesn't mean it didn't happen. I'm really sorry."

"No sweat."

"No sweat?" Ava's brows took a one-way trip upward, and her shoulders met the back of her bar stool with a bump.

But Nick . . . Brennan . . . whoever he was just gave a shrug as he slid the frost-covered lid on the beer cooler in front of him to the open position, barely looking as he took out a bottle and uncapped it for the woman standing behind her. "Sure. Like you said, it was a long time ago."

Ava hesitated, uncertainty welling in her throat. Nick's

face was perfectly neutral, and even though his shoulders had gone momentarily tight beneath his dark gray T-shirt as he'd delivered the all-is-well, right now he was nothing but smooth movements behind the bar.

Stupid. Seven years had passed since she'd hastily stuffed everything she'd owned into a pair of beat-up suitcases and taken the sunrise ferry off Sapphire Island. Of course Nick had moved on and forgotten all about her. And anyway, that's what she'd wanted.

Even if, despite all her efforts, Ava hadn't been able to forget him.

"Right. It was a long time ago," she said, shaking off the thought as she buckled down. She'd come to the Double Shot for a story, and she needed to get to business. "You're obviously busy, so I don't want to keep you. I was hoping maybe we could talk after your shift, or whenever is convenient for you." Ava's instincts sprang back to life at the reminder of why she'd come, and she pulled a business card from her back pocket and handed it over.

Nick's gaze flashed, wide with undiluted shock before his grip went tight enough to bend the card stock between his fingers. "You're a reporter?"

She nodded. "I write for the *Riverside Daily*. What you did today out at Joe's Grocery was extremely brave. I'd like to write a piece about what happened. We could—"

"Let me ask you something."

He cut her off with such quiet intensity and precision that Ava's only choice was to reply, "What?"

"Do you still drink Arnold Palmers?"

Jeez. Nick might forgive, but it sure as hell looked like forget wasn't on his agenda. "Yeah."

"Good. Tell you what," he said, his expression going sharp around the edges as he methodically filled a pint glass first with ice, then with just the right ratio of lemonade to iced tea. "Drink's on the house, but it's the only thing you're going to get out of me. I don't talk to reporters. Especially not if they're you."

Before Ava could work through her shock to reply, Nick placed the glass directly on top of her business card and turned to walk away.

Brennan got four steps away from the end of the bar before he realized there was a zero percent chance this night wasn't going to strike him dead. Not to go all *Casablanca* or anything, but of all the bars in the Blue Ridge—hell, on the entire eastern seaboard, for Chrissake—Ava Mancuso just had to walk into his. Tonight. Looking for a fucking *story*?

There wasn't enough distraction or liquor in ten small-town restaurants for this.

"Jeez, Brennan. You okay?" The degree of concern glinting in Teagan's eyes was Brennan's first clue that his normally ironclad composure was unraveling like his grandmother's knitting, and he funneled every last shred of control into his inhale.

"Yup. We're low on Cold Creek's summer ale. I'm going to grab a case from the walk-in." Of course his back would probably dish up a whole lot of I'm-glad-you-think-so-tough-guy over hauling around anything heavier than a cheeseburger after the strain of this morning's rescue mission, but so be it. He'd come to terms with the fact that hurting went hand in hand with being busy a long time ago.

The pain kept him grounded, reminding him that he could do worse than hurting, and anyway, if he wasn't busy working himself into exhaustion, he'd have way too much time to think about things. Like how the burnt smell of smoke still lingered in his hair even though he'd washed it three damned times, or how he could still feel the weight of Ava's emerald green stare on his back from halfway across the bar.

Time to go.

Brennan crossed the narrow channel of space behind the bar in half as many strides as usual, the startling lack of sound filling his ears with relief as he pushed through the swinging door to the kitchen. Bypassing Jesse with a nod and a quick "hey," Brennan cut a hot path to the walk-in, not stopping his forward momentum until he was surrounded by three walls of industrial steel shelving and a whole bunch of cold, calm air.

Inhale. Exhale. Find control. Inhale . . .

Damn it, how had Ava Mancuso gotten even prettier in seven years?

"You look like shit, my friend."

"Jesus!" Brennan's head jacked around, his eyes stinging from the frigid wake-up call as they popped back open to land smack on Adrian's crossed arms and raised eyebrow. "You do know sneaking up on people is uncool, right?" He reached up to the shelf across from him to grab the case of beer that would keep him busy until Ava was good and gone from the bar, but Adrian stepped in his path, the door clicking shut behind him.

"And you do know that you're changing the subject, right?"

The words were all gravelly statement and left no wiggle room, but Brennan met them with a perfectly practiced and very blank stare.

"There's no subject to change. I'm fine." Getting into a pissing match with the guy wasn't usually on Brennan's to-do list, especially since Adrian was roughly the size of a small nation. But the last thing Brennan wanted was to pop the cork on all of his ridiculous emotions right now.

Which sucked for him, because Adrian didn't budge. "You're rattled as hell. You want to air this out, or do I need to send you home?"

"You can't send me home." Panic spurted in Brennan's chest, and he sucked in a breath of frosty air to dilute it. "The holiday season just started. The bar is slammed."

"Jesse just went out to cover the crowd and the over-flow. I don't want to replace you, but I will if I have to." Adrian waited, and when nothing but the low hum of the walk-in and his buddy's brows-up *what gives* passed be-tween them, Brennan knew he was the captain of a sinking ship. If he wanted to stay and keep busy, keep moving, and keep his shit together, he was going to have to earn it.

"Look, all these reporters just give me the shakes, all right? I'm not exactly a public-eye kind of guy."

Adrian hit him with a look that read *fair enough*. "That pretty woman at the end of the bar is a reporter?"

"Among other things," Brennan muttered, and damn it, he really needed to keep his big mouth on lockdown.

"Clearly, you know her." Adrian held up a massive hand to cut off Brennan's protest at the knees. "Before you try to argue, Teagan already told me the woman asked for you by your first name."

"So?"

"So, we've been friends for more than half a year and I didn't even know you *had* a first name. Come on, Brennan. I get that you don't want to take out a billboard, but be-tween what went down this morning and the way you look right now, you're torqued up to ten. I've got a bar full of people out there, some of whom are liquored up and all of whom want a piece of you. You don't have to talk about this, but you do have to be straight before I let you back behind the wood to deal with them."

Brennan's defeated exhale puffed around his face in the frigid air. "Okay. Yes, she's a reporter at the *Riverside Daily*, and yes, I know her. We used to"—*be madly, insanely, irreversibly in love*—"have a thing," he bit out. "It was a long time ago."

"Looks like you two did a number on each other." Adrian tipped his platinum blond head at Brennan in a clear bid for more intel, but screw it. Brennan wasn't getting away without at least telling him something, and maybe if he unloaded a little of what had happened, he could blow it off like the steam it was and get back to normal.

"It was the summer after college. Prime time to be young and dumb. I got a line on a job waiting tables at the beach resort out on Sapphire Island. You know, off the coast of Virginia Beach?" Brennan turned toward the open-air shelf at his side, straightening the cardboard cases full of beer against the metal grooves. God, Mason had been so freaking pleased with himself when he'd landed them both on the short list to work at the prestigious resort for the summer. Two best friends, one last hurrah before the fire academy, and a gorgeous beach town full of beer and bikinis.

Brennan cranked down on the memory and stuffed it away. Copping to his summer with Ava was one thing, but the rest of his past wasn't up for grabs. Not now.

Not ever.

"I met Ava on the first day there. She was part of the summer staff too, working as a hostess," he said, pulling a case of beer flush with the front of the shelf while Adrian fell into step straightening the cases on the opposite side of the walk-in. "I missed every single word the restaurant manager told us in orientation, but it was worth it. The way that woman looks in a pair of cutoffs should be a fucking felony."

Adrian chuffed out a laugh. "Sounds like love at first sight."

Brennan returned the laughter, only without any humor. "More like love is blind. We spent the entire summer glued together, and I thought we really had something. But the morning after our last shift, Ava packed her bags and took off. No good-bye, no note, no phone call, no nothing. She just disappeared."

"Ouch. Did you ever try to find her?"

Brennan's pulse kicked beneath the heavy cloak of his composure. "I was twenty-two and off my rocker for the woman. Hell yes, I tried to find her. But Ava was a ghost."

"Come on," Adrian said, turning from the shelf to nail him with a doubtful look. "Between Google and social media, nobody's a ghost these days."

"This was seven years ago, remember? Anyway, I did look for her, online and in person. Her roommate had no clue where she'd gone, and her cell had been disconnected. There was no trace of her, not even in her hometown. I looked everywhere I could think of, but nobody had ever heard of her. It was as if she didn't even exist."

Except in his memory, and there, Ava had been all too real. Glittering, bright green eyes, the brown-sugar smell of her skin, a smile so sexy and sweet he'd get half hard just thinking about it, the seductive, velvety sighs she'd make underneath him that took him the rest of the way there . . .

No. No more. Ava Mancuso was in his rearview, and he needed to slap a big, fat ROAD CLOSED sign over memory lane and reroute this shit, permanently.

"Anyway." Brennan cleared his throat, then did it again just to make sure his vocal cords got the message to put some extra indifference on his words. "After a couple of weeks, I figured she didn't want to be found. So I took the hint and stopped looking."

"And now she's here looking for a story?" Adrian jerked his stubble-covered chin toward the beer on the shelf in front of them.

Relief swirled in Brennan's gut at passing the I-really-am-fine muster. He hefted a case of summer ale from the rack, even though his back protested heartily under the sudden added weight. "Along with half the other reporters in the Blue Ridge. Too bad for them I've got nothing to say."

"Hmm." Adrian slid a case of beer of his own to his shoulder, flipping his tree trunk of an arm over the cardboard to balance it one-handed while he popped the walk-in handle with his other palm. "You tell her that?"

A tiny kernel in Brennan's subconscious flinched, but no way. He might've been a little colder to Ava than necessary, but she'd earned every frost-encrusted syllable.

"Yeah," Brennan said, following Adrian through the now-quiet kitchen toward the pass-through. He'd made it wildly clear he wasn't giving Ava what she'd come for, and she'd had plenty of time to gather her purse and her pride and walk out the door. Now, *finally*, Brennan could get on with his night and his life. "All I want to do is tend bar. I'm not interested in anything else."

Wait . . . had the crowd gotten even bigger in the ten minutes he and Adrian had been in the kitchen?

"Looks like you're gonna get your wish," Adrian half hollered over the wide expanse of his shoulder, and even then Brennan had to strain to hear him over the loud thrum of voices and music. He moved toward the alcove at the midpoint of the overly crowded bar, intending to get these beers on ice so he could start serving up drinks, stat, but Adrian stopped him midstride.

"You sure you're really good to go?"

Brennan nodded. "Absolutely." Christ, he was more than ready to loosen the death grip of this day with some good, old-fashioned, bone-numbing work.

"Good." His buddy stood to the height of his six foot, five inches, scanning the bar with a crooked smile before saying, "Because your reporter is digging in as hard as you are. And it looks like her drink is empty."

Chapter Four

After the fourth time Ava reread the same ho-hum line from the Pine Mountain Fire Department's press release on the blaze at Joe's Grocery, she gave in and let her eyes drift shut. Okay, so it served her right for letting her stubborn pride keep her ass glued to her seat at the Double Shot's bar until last call a mere eight hours ago, but come on. Her worth was on the line. She didn't care how much sleep she had to sacrifice, she was going to get this story.

No matter how many hard-edged, silent stares Nick sent to the end of the bar along with her drink refills.

And there had been a *lot* of them.

"Hey." Layla leaned against the flimsy entryway to Ava's cubicle, a stack of photo printouts tucked in the crook of her arm. "Did you talk to the hero guy?"

"Good morning to you too," Ava flipped back, arching a brow to take any potential sting off the words. She'd always admired Layla's propensity for cutting to the chase. Took one to know one, and all that rot. "I'm working on the, uh, hero guy. But nothing solid yet."

"Sounds like a tough source. I bet half the Blue Ridge wants a shot at him after yesterday."

Ava stiffened against the back of her creaky old desk chair. "I can handle a difficult source."

Layla winced and twisted the end of her white blond ponytail between her fingers, and great—here came the kid gloves. "Crap, Ava, I'm sorry. I didn't mean it like that. You're a great reporter. Gary's totally giving you the raw end of the deal with all these lame assignments."

"To an extent, I get it." Ava dialed down her voice to its lowest setting to avoid being overheard, because Gary's hearing bordered on superpower freakish. "I fully admit that I screwed up that first really big assignment he gave me by not double-checking my source."

Okay, so "screwed up" was putting it a bit mildly. But she'd been really gung ho to break her first meaningful story, and the allegations of misconduct in the workplace at a prestigious local law firm had seemed very legit. Until Ava's source admitted after the fact that she'd made up her story after an argument with her boss, and said boss had come within inches of suing the *Daily* for libel, even after they'd printed a front-page retraction.

And Ava had been at the bottom of the career ladder, with Gary absolutely convinced she couldn't properly work a source ever since.

"Still," she continued, leaning closer to Layla. "it's been long enough. Fact-checking myself to death and covering nearly nonexistent stories while my colleagues get the lion's share of great assignments isn't what I signed on for."

Layla transferred the photos in her arms to the corner of Ava's desk, sliding into the seat across from her and dropping her voice to a hushed murmur. "Look, Ava, don't get me wrong. I love working with you and don't want you to leave, but not all newspapers are run by managing editors like Gary. If he's still giving you crap assignments after all this time, maybe you should just move on to greener pastures."

A heavy ache settled in behind her breastbone, and Ava reached for the supersized container of Tums she'd been using as a paperweight. "I can't. Gary might be putting me through the wringer, but I've got five years under my belt here. If I go somewhere else, I'll lose my seniority and have to start all over again. Plus, it's not as if there are a ton of prime reporting jobs in the Blue Ridge."

"You've got a point there. The paper in Pine Mountain is even smaller than this one," Layla admitted.

"All I need is one chance—one big story to prove what I've got—and Gary won't have any choice but to give me more plum assignments."

"That's true," Layla said thoughtfully. "Even Mr. Royce would notice if you broke something huge and didn't get bumped up to some better stories, especially with newspaper sales kind of flagging lately."

Ava nodded at the mention of the *Daily*'s owner. "Which is exactly why I need to break this story on the fire at Joe's, no matter what."

Well, that was the main reason, anyway. Copping to the fact that she also didn't want to leave Riverside because her brother Pete lived a hop-skip away in Pine Mountain wasn't in Ava's game plan. After all, most people would find it utterly strange that she and her older brother went to such great lengths to stick together.

And explaining that it was a deeply ingrained survival tactic as the children of two raging alcoholics didn't really make for lively conversation.

Layla reached out to squeeze her shoulder, and the move anchored Ava back down to her overstuffed cubicle. "Okay. What can I do to help?"

Ava opened her mouth to dive into what she'd uncovered so far on the fire—and more importantly, what she *hadn't* been able to uncover on Nick Brennan—but her words fell prey to the sound of a very gruff, very irritated throat being cleared.

"You're late, Mancuso."

Ava's heart hit her breastbone, and she winged around in her cubicle just in time to catch her boss's trademark scowl right in the chest. For as often as Gary wore the expression, she'd swear it had to be permanently etched on his beefy face.

"But I've been here since nine o'clock," she said, twisting in her desk chair to double-check the time stamp on her laptop. Not even an extra slap to the snooze button was worth the beady-eyed wrath she'd incur for walking in at 9:08. And considering she was probably a dead ringer for a cast extra in a zombie movie right now, that was totally saying something.

Gary, however, was clearly unimpressed. "The weekly reporter's meeting was supposed to start in the conference room three minutes ago." He paused to give his gold-plated watch an exaggerated tap, crossing his arms over his considerable paunch as Ava's confusion multiplied.

"But that's not until noon." They'd done their weekly wrap-ups at lunch on Friday for the last five years. Ava knew, because she'd never missed a single one.

"Not today," Gary said, his frown traveling upward to land in a crease between his brows. "Now did you want to join the rest of us for the reporter's meeting, or are you in over your head with your copy edits?"

The question was laced with just enough suggestion that Ava's belly went tight, and she lifted her spine to its full height. "Nope," she said, not balking but not breaking their eye contact either. "Not at all. I'm ready whenever you are."

Giving Layla a quick nod, Ava grabbed the blue-fabric-covered notebook she'd been using to gather her research on yesterday's fire and followed Gary into the tiny conference room at the end of the hall. Of course, the other three reporters on staff were already seated at the four-person table, leaving her to drag a chair from the perimeter of the room and squeeze into a self-made spot. Part of her was irritated as hell to have to wing her way through this meeting two hours early, but Ava had learned ages ago to be prepared for anything as far as Gary was concerned. Ironically, it made her a better reporter. Provided she could actually snag an assignment of value, anyway.

Cue the segue.

"Right. Now that we're all finally here—" Gary's squinty gaze landed on Ava with all the subtlety of a hand grenade, but she met it toe-to-toe. She might be willing to prove her worth by working her buns off, but she wasn't anybody's rag doll to be tattered or tossed around at will.

Not anymore, at least.

"Let's get started," Gary continued, testing the limits of his desk chair as he pushed back to look at the group. "Where are we on this fire in Pine Mountain yesterday? We're losing sales to Bealetown by the week, and I don't want that jackass Trotter from the *Bugle* scooping us on this."

Well, at least there was one thing she and Gary could agree on. Mike Trotter was a dick and a half.

"Can't get scooped on a story that isn't there," came a wry voice from across the table, and Ava zeroed in on its owner. Of her three fellow reporters, she liked and respected Ian St. Clare the most, even though she knew Gary did too.

Ian pushed at his already rolled up shirt sleeves, shaking his head as he added, "Both the PMFD and the RFD are giving the standard just-the-facts press release pending investigation, but at first glance, it doesn't look like arson. As far as the rescue goes, the little boy's apparently fine, but his mother put out a statement at the hospital refusing all interviews. So that's a dead end."

Gary frowned. "Goddamn overprotective parents. What about the guy who ran in to save the kid, this hometown hero? Feel-good stories sell a shitload of papers, Ian. Tell me you at least talked to him."

Ava's heartbeat ratcheted all the way up despite her titanium-strength effort to stay cool. Just because she hadn't seen Ian at the Double Shot last night didn't mean he hadn't been in touch with Nick. And even though she'd seen Nick blow off all the other bids for attention last night, he hadn't left any doubt as to who his least favorite reporter in the Blue Ridge was at the moment. If Nick had spoken to Ian and given him information pertaining to the rescue, Ava was screwed. Yes, she was desperate for the story, and oh *hell* yes, she'd do nearly anything to get it, but scooping an in-house reporter was hugely frowned upon in journalism, not to mention being a bitch move of unrivaled magnitude. But if Ian hadn't made any headway with Nick, there was still a chance she could land this story.

Please, God . . . this is my big chance to prove my worth as a real reporter.

"He hasn't returned my calls or e-mails," Ian said, and Ava exhaled in a *whoosh* of relief. "As far as I can tell, the guy's not talking to anybody at all. I've been watching local outlets, but word on the wire is his favorite response is *no comment.*"

"Come on. The guy—Brennan, right? He risks life and limb running into a fire, but doesn't want any credit for it?

No spotlight at all?" Gary snorted. "I need a freaking story here. Can't we lean on him?"

"We could." Something flickered behind Ian's eyes, and wait . . . was that unease? "But that hasn't really worked for anyone so far, and nearly everyone in King County has tried. I get that this fire is the biggest thing to go down in Pine Mountain in a while, but to be honest, unless it turns out to be arson, I don't think there's much of a story there."

Now or never.

"Actually, Ian, I respectfully disagree," Ava said, swinging her gaze between Ian's surprise and Gary's thinly veiled disdain. "I was on the scene at Joe's yesterday, and I've been taking a look at some of the facts. There might be more to the personal-interest part of this story than we think."

"More to the hometown hero than meets the eye, huh." Gary's brows folded hard beneath his receding hairline. "You got some kind of angle on the guy I don't know about?"

Ava's pulse pitched. Okay, so she was probably the only person who knew Nick had planned to become a career firefighter seven years ago, but her cursory search this morning had come up eerily empty, so she couldn't prove he'd actually done it. If she shot her mouth off with facts she couldn't back up again, Gary would have her job on a silver platter. No matter how questionable his story-*getting* ethics were, the story-*printing* had to be ironclad.

Plus, her "in" with Nick was more like an "out" right now, and anyway, she didn't want this story because she knew him. She wanted to be the best reporter for the job.

"I don't know about an angle," Ava said, choosing her words with extreme care. "I've been watching the story like everyone else, and I'm familiar with the facts. I think a spotlight would be a great personal interest piece with a focus on the positive, and an exclusive interview would certainly sell a lot of newspapers, both locally and in bigger markets."

"An exclusive," Gary echoed, jabbing one sausagelike finger in her direction. "You really think you're tough enough to squeeze something useful out of this Brennan guy when he hasn't let out a peep to anyone else?" The only thing more unmistakable than the challenge in his voice was the doubt.

But Ava answered him with even more unmistakable certainty. "I'm confident I know how to work a source to break a great story, yes."

For a second, Gary looked like he was going to argue, but then his expression went cold and flat. "Fine by me if you want to waste your time trying, Mancuso. But if there's a story there, it had better be big, and you'd better be the one to get it. This Brennan guy gives an exclusive interview to another paper? You won't even get a shot to cover a junior varsity football game."

Ava sat in the driver's seat of her Volkswagen, her arms knotted over her chest and her eyes on the Double Shot as if she were three paces away from a shoot-out. Just because she'd spent five hours here last night—to no avail— didn't mean she had to like the place. She normally avoided establishments like the Double Shot at all costs, but right now, the bar was a means to an end.

A really broody, smoldering-in-the-best-possible-way, clearly-still-mad-at-her-for-the-past end.

"Okay." Ava smoothed a hand over her blouse, straightening the green silk beneath her coat before grabbing her huge leather tote from the passenger seat and abandoning the comfort of her car. Gary had given her this assignment, and now her pride *and* her job depended on getting this story. If she had to sit in a bar in order to get a word in edgewise with Nick Brennan, so be it.

But God, did the bitter smell of liquor have to permeate *everything*?

Ava set her shoulders, brushing off the thought as she crossed the Double Shot's gravel-strewn parking lot. Objectively, the place was nicer than most, with its weathered clapboard siding and whitewashed shutters surrounding the gleam of bright, clean windows. Lantern-style light fixtures hung at even intervals along the building's narrow wooden porch leading to the front door, and the tiny white Christmas lights lining the railing added extra glow. Even the polished brass door handle felt warm in her palm from the remnants of slanted sunlight peeking past the pines and evergreens dotted around the parking lot.

"Hey, welcome to the Double Shot!" A cheery blonde greeted Ava from behind the polished mahogany hostess stand. "How many in your party?"

"Just me, but I'd love to sit at the bar, if that's okay." The words felt odd in Ava's mouth, probably because she'd never once spoken them in her life, but if she wanted another shot at talking to Nick, being up close and personal was definitely her best chance.

The blonde's lips curved into a knowing smile, and she tilted her ponytail toward the stretch of dark, glossy wood spanning the restaurant's entire back wall. "You and everybody else."

Ava's eyes made the full adjustment from the over-bright sunshine to the dusky low lights in the bar, and whoa. Both the dining room and the bar area were more than halfway filled with a growing crush of people, servers weaving expertly through the crowd to take orders and deliver drinks amid the rising din of voices.

"Is this normal for four-thirty on a Friday?" Ava asked, unable to hide her shock. Why on earth would a small-town bar and grill be brimming with this many people only thirty minutes after opening?

Unless of course, that small-town bar and grill had a big-time story working behind the counter.

"Nope." The blonde's head shake confirmed both Ava's suspicion and her fear. "I mean, the new menu's great and we've been busy lately, but not like this. Oooh, it looks like you're in luck though. There's one seat left at the end of the bar over there. Feel free to grab it while you can."

"Thanks." Ava zeroed in on the same spot at the end of the bar where she'd taken up residence last night, moving with purpose toward the empty bar stool. The seat was fairly out of the way—likely why it was the last stool standing right now—but Ava didn't mind. She'd chosen it last night for its good vantage point on the rest of the bar. Sometimes gathering facts meant watching twice as much as asking, and even though she'd had only the one brief exchange with Nick last night, Ava had still learned plenty.

He might not have given anyone a story, but everyone in Pine Mountain wanted a piece of Nick Brennan.

"Oh! There he is. There's Brennan!" The excited murmur came from somewhere in the growing crowd, and Ava's gaze shot involuntarily to the swinging door behind the opposite end of the bar. Her pulse tapped out the Morse code equivalent of *yes, yes, yes* at the sight of Nick emerging from the kitchen, falling into step to take drink orders alongside the same tall redhead who had been behind the bar last night. They orbited around each other with precision and an ease that suggested they not only worked well together but were friends, and Ava watched him covertly as he interacted with various customers.

His movements were smooth and decisive, right down

to the stretch of lean, corded muscles over his forearms as he reached for a chilled pint glass to fill it expertly at the tap in front of him. Every motion had purpose, and the unwavering control built in to his stubbled jawline sent a quick streak of envy through Ava's gut. While it quickly became clear from Nick's deadpan expression that there was a reporter or two in the bunch asking questions, he took the attention from the other people at the bar in polite stride.

Until he landed in front of her, anyway.

"You're back," he said, his dark eyes going wide. For just a sliver of a second, there was nothing between them but high-octane intensity, and it shot down Ava's spine in a bolt of pure want.

"I, ah, thought I'd give dinner a try." She held up a menu, trying like mad to remain unaffected by both her mutinous libido and the sudden scowl spreading over Nick's darkly handsome face. He snapped a clean bar towel from a stack beneath the counter, putting it to use on the polished wood between them.

"Have you ever heard the expression *let sleeping dogs lie?*"

Her snort was soft but inevitable. "Yeah, I'm a reporter. I poke the dogs."

"I'm not giving you a story," he said, his tone completely devoid of emotion, but two could dance to that song. It was obvious she was going to have to chisel out whatever leeway he'd give her, and she was nothing if not persistent. Plus, he had a hell of a smile, and damn it, Ava really wanted to see it again.

"Okay. Then could I please have a cheeseburger with waffle fries, hold the tomato, and extra fried onions?"

Nick's brows winged upward, but hell if he didn't step

up to the plate. "Not planning on kissing anybody later, I take it?"

The heat that had flared through her only a minute ago went on a massive comeback tour, but going soft wasn't on her menu of options. "That's kind of a personal question, don't you think?"

Ava got the smile she'd been after, and great God in heaven, the sweet and seductive pull of Nick's mouth could render an otherwise intelligent woman totally useless.

"How's that shoe fit when it's on the other foot, Spitfire?"

A shocked laugh popped past her lips without her brain's permission. "You did not just call me that." The nickname he'd given her seven years ago had settled into the dusty recesses of her memory, but it curved right back into her ear as if it had never left.

"You're changing the subject," Nick said, sliding a scoopful of ice into a pint glass with a *clink*. He'd filled it two-thirds of the way with lemonade before Ava finally conceded.

"Fair enough. Tell you what, then. Why don't we trade?"

"Trade what?" He topped off her drink with the perfect layer of iced tea, placing it on a cocktail napkin in front of her.

"A question for a question," she said. Okay, so it was a wing and a prayer and a whole lot of *hey, what the hell*, but at this point, she had no other options. "I'll answer yours if you answer one of mine. In fact, I'll even go first." After all, what could it hurt to tell him that she didn't have any plans to kiss anyone later? It wasn't like she had to cop to the fact that she hadn't been kissed—truly, properly, felt-it-in-every-corner-of-her-being kissed—in what had to be a century.

Or however long it had been since Nick had last put his mouth on hers.

He paused, and oh my God, he was thinking about it. "Off the record. Nothing about what happened yesterday is on the table. And I answer first." His tone was as immovable as his stare, and Ava jumped in with both feet.

"Done."

"Okay, then," Nick said, his hands hitching just slightly as he wrote up the ticket for her order. "Ask away."

She scooped in a deep breath, but said nothing. She needed to gain his trust here, which was the mother of tall orders, considering their past. But her sudden desire to melt his calm, cool exterior extended past wanting a story, so Ava simply said, "How long have you worked here at the Double Shot?"

"That's your question?" Now Nick's hands screeched to a complete stop. His lips parted, showing just a flash of white teeth against his nearly black facial scruff, but she stood firm.

"That's my question," Ava agreed.

He examined her for a second, as if looking for a trapdoor. "Two years," he finally said.

"Oh." Her brain brimmed with no less than a thousand other questions, but a deal was a deal. "To answer your question, no. I'm not planning on kissing anyone later tonight."

"That's nice, but it isn't my question."

Ava pulled back against her bar stool. "I'm sorry?"

"You said a question for a question. I never specified which question I wanted to ask." Although Nick's expression delivered just the facts, the tiny crinkle at the corners of his eyes was a dead giveaway that she'd been had.

Of all the underhanded, sneaky . . . "You tricked me."

"Yup," he acknowledged, unrepentant. "But you agreed."

Damn it, there was no way she could *not* answer whatever he asked now, and judging by the look still hovering in his eyes, the question was going to be a doozy.

"You're right. I did." Ava squared her shoulders, shoring herself up for a direct hit. "What would you like to know?"

Nick leaned in, so close she could feel the warm puff of his breath on her lips and the hypnotizing heat of his nearness, and in that moment, she remembered exactly how much he didn't disappoint in the go-all-in department.

"I want to know why you left me seven years ago."

Chapter Five

If kicking his own ass wasn't a physical impossibility, Brennan would've polished up his shoes and gone for broke right there behind the bar. It was bad enough that he'd agreed to answer anything Ava had to ask, even if she'd surprised the hell out of him by going totally benign with her question. But any second now, she was going to recover from the shock currently dominating her pretty face, and not even one-upping her was worth hearing her answer.

Keeping his emotions on lockdown was hard enough, thanks.

"You know what, forget I asked. I'll get this in for you." Brennan gripped the ticket with her dinner order hard enough to make his knuckles blanch, but Ava was quicker on the draw.

"Nick, wait." Her hand landed on his, but Christ, he felt it everywhere, and if she didn't move, his composure was going to go up in flames.

"Brennan," he ground out, simultaneously wanting her to let go and pull him closer. He might push himself to the point of pain while he worked, but carrying that over into his personal life couldn't happen. Especially not now.

Especially not with Ava.

She opened her mouth, but before even a syllable could get past her lips, a man in a rumpled blazer and the most hideous tie known to man elbowed his way to the bar.

"Oh hey, are you Brennan? Harrison Frost with the *Rockledge County Examiner*. I was wondering—"

"No comment." Brennan nailed the guy with enough of a glare to stop the flow of his question, and Ava slipped her hand discreetly back over the bar. Before she could say anything else, or worse yet, before the reporter standing next to her could connect the dots and start asking *different* questions, Brennan pulled an about-face. His lumbar vertebrae did their best to blackball the sudden movement, but he forced his cross-trainers over the rubber bar mats in quick, deliberate strides, not stopping until he'd reached the touch-screen register at the midpoint of the back counter.

"What's the matter, Brennan? Pretty reporter got your tongue?" Teagan arched an auburn brow to go with the wry smile tugging at her lips, and Brennan grappled for a slow, steady inhale.

"No." But the baser part of his brain reminded him just what he could do to Ava with his tongue. His calming breath jammed to a stop in his windpipe, and come on—how had he miskeyed a fucking cheeseburger on the register? He had to enter at least thirty per shift.

Teagan was next to him in less time than it took to finish his muttered curse. "Hey, I can kick these pain-in-the-ass reporters out if they're bugging you that much. Just say the word."

Brennan's head whipped up from the register's touch-screen. "Are you crazy? Look at this place." They'd barely been open for an hour, and there had to be seventy people in the bar and restaurant combined, with more flowing in by the minute. "The business is over the top."

"Yes, but it means damn little if it costs me my bar manager's sanity. So really, are you okay?" She measured him with a worried glance that marked the question as rhetorical.

But Brennan would be goddamned if he couldn't get these feelings back under control where they belonged. Being rattled just wasn't his MO, and he hadn't been this out of whack in years.

Two and a half of them, to be exact.

"I'm fine," Brennan said, mashing down on the tightness in his chest once and for all. He'd been through worse than this by the truckload. Facing a few reporters and saying *no comment* for another day or two until some other story caught their attention might be aggravating as hell, but it wouldn't kill him. He just had to focus, breathe, and block everything out. And stay away from the end of the bar, because apparently, the key to blowing his composure was sticking around for dinner instead of going home to get kissed.

Yeah. He needed to get moving and do his job. Right. Now.

"Can I help you ladies?" Brennan asked, leaning in toward two giggling brunettes who barely looked old enough to drink. Triple-checking their IDs, he pulled the two light beers they ordered from the cooler at his hip, gaining slight comfort from the *hiss* and *clink* of each lid as he liberated them from the bottles.

"So, um, my friend Courtney wanted to ask you something, but she's a little shy." The taller of the two women nodded toward her friend, who served up a smile that said she was anything but bashful.

The feeling of ease that had just settled in his chest gave a hard flicker. "Shoot."

"I thought maybe I could get a picture with you. You know, for my Facebook page?" She held up her cell phone, and Brennan exhaled as the flicker burned out.

"Sorry, I'm not a camera guy."

"Oh, please don't say no!" The woman pouted, crossing her arms beneath her cleavage in a not-so-subtle lift. "It's just that living in Pine Mountain, we never get to meet anybody famous."

Brennan aimed for a courteous smile, but the tight pull of his jaw told him he'd missed his mark. "Hate to disappoint you, ladies. I'm just a bar manager. Let me know when you need refills."

He hustled to the kitchen, praying like hell that there were plates to expedite, and thank God, Adrian delivered. But the handful of round-trip loops from the kitchen to the dining room yielded two more requests for photo ops, another batch of cookies, an afghan from the Pine Mountain Knitting Circle, and four polite yet firm *no comments*. Thank God his cell number was unlisted, Brennan thought. At least he had that tiny bit of peace and sanity.

Right up until his sister Ellie sent him a text that read,

Pictures of my wedding dress attached. Mom wants to know if you are bringing a date—call me!

Keeping his head down and eyes forward went from game plan to game over in less than half the dinner rush. By the time they closed the kitchen and transitioned to the bar-only crowd, the phrases *what can I get you* and *no comment* were neck and neck in Brennan's vocabulary, and he was starting to think the whole this-won't-kill-me concept was more fantasy than fact.

"I heard the kids from Pine Mountain Community Center made you enough banana bread to start your own bakery," Adrian said, adjusting his Harley-Davidson baseball hat as he grabbed a bottle of their local brewery's IPA for the guy across from him at the bar. While Brennan recognized the genuine gratitude pouring in from the locals bringing him thank-you gifts, the spotlight of their attention still burned on the back of his neck. He hadn't run into danger to find Matthew Wilson because he was a hero.

He'd done it because he wasn't.

"Yeah. Jesse told me," Brennan said, angling himself toward the cooler in an effort to dodge Adrian's X-ray vision.

But Adrian stepped in to deftly check the movement, his proximity and his lowered tone limiting the conversation to just him and Brennan. "Look, I'm not complaining about the business, but we're even more crowded than last night. This place is busting at the joists with local reporters looking for something to print. You gonna humor one of them?"

"I don't have anything to say." Brennan's shrug dropped off his double-knotted shoulders. Rather than slowing down, the requests-slash-demands seemed to multiply with every *no comment*. "I just want to stay busy," he said, popping the handle on the lowboy fridge nestled under the bar top. "Holy crap, what happened to all the iced tea?"

Adrian's chuckle smacked him right in the sternum. "Your reporter, that's what. She's been down there drinking Arnold Palmers and chatting up Annabelle and Teagan all night."

The door to the cooler snapped shut with a *thunk*. "What?"

"Relax. Nobody here is giving up so much as your shoe size. And anyway, Ava didn't ask. Matter of fact, I think she's the only person in here who *hasn't* asked about you tonight. Looks like she's just hanging out."

"Oh." Brennan paused, sliding a glance toward the end of the bar. Ava's head was tilted down, her attention focused on a stack of papers in front of her, her forehead creased into a V of concentration as she read. She scribbled something on the top page, tapping the end of her pen against the soft divot at the center of her mouth, and story or no story, Brennan had never wanted to be a Bic so bad in his life.

"Anyway." He cleared his throat, shaking off the impetuous heat making a playground out of his gut. "She's not mine."

He turned toward the alcove to grab a box of tea bags from the bottom shelf, ignoring the dark eyebrow that had disappeared beneath the brim of Adrian's hat. Brennan set the tea to brew, filling a handful of drink orders as he made his way toward the end of the bar. If Ava wanted to act like a regular customer, then he would treat her like one.

Even if after seven years of radio silence, there was still nothing regular about her.

"Got fresh tea brewing for you," he said, pointing to her nearly empty pint glass as she looked up from the sheaf of papers on the bar. She blinked in surprise, but her recovery time spanned only a few seconds.

"Thanks. I appreciate it." Ava lowered her pen, shuffling the pages into a manila folder before placing it in her bag. Although her smile was genuine, the shadows smudged beneath her emerald green eyes betrayed her weariness, sending an involuntary ripple through Brennan's chest. Okay, so she'd made no bones about wanting a story on the fire, and yeah, that story was what had propelled her back in front of him after seven long years. But when he'd popped off that stupidly impulsive demand to know why she'd left without a word, he'd seen that same vulnerability layered underneath her wide-eyed stare.

Ava was hiding something.

But before Brennan could run the revelation down the chain of command from his brain to his mouth, a swift flurry of movement snagged his attention from the seat next to Ava's.

"Evening, Brennan. Heard you're playing hardball on giving up a story. I have to admit, I respect a man who knows what he wants."

Years' worth of training to notice the details—even the pretentious-as-hell, squinty-faced ones—placed the guy elbowing his way next to Ava as the Perrier-drinking asshat from last night, and Brennan dialed his expression up to its deadliest setting.

"The only thing I want is to do my job in peace. I still have no comment, Mr. Trotter."

The reporter snorted, shooting the cuffs of his over-starched dress shirt as he settled back on his bar stool. "What if I told you I could get your story on the front page of the *Bugle*, and I do mean above the crease, in addition to complete social media coverage? Plus, if you sign on right now, I've got contacts in TV who would pick up this story in a second."

Brennan blanked the irritation from his voice, but just barely. "I'm not holding out for the best exposure, and I definitely don't want to be on TV. I don't have anything to say, above the crease or anywhere else."

"Nothing at all?" Trotter peered through his glasses in haughty disbelief.

"You mean other than *no comment?*"

The reporter's thin lips pinched into a nearly nonexistent

line. "Is all that silence noble, Brennan, or is there something you're trying to hide?"

Before Brennan could slice out an answer and a *get the hell out*, Ava turned in her seat to peg the guy with a disdainful stare.

"Jesus, Mike. He said no comment. Let it go."

Trotter smiled, all teeth, and Brennan buckled over the urge to use them as target practice for his right hook. "Trying to get me to walk so you can slide in and steal this story? I don't think so, sweetheart. Everyone's got something to say. Isn't that right, Brennan?"

Trotter swung back toward the bar, his eyes narrowing to near slits as he thrust his recording device about two inches from Brennan's chin. Brennan parried out of sheer instinct, gripping Trotter's forearm in a tight hold as the guy struggled to shove the microphone back toward Brennan's face, but Ava's sudden gasp and flinch stole his concentration. In the split-second distraction, Trotter pounced. Using his stool for leverage, he pushed up over the edge of the bar, breaking Brennan's grip on his arm with a forceful yank.

"Hey!" The word fired from Brennan's mouth in a jagged burst, but it was too late. Momentum catapulted Trotter from his seat, his arm whipping back desperately in the panic of lost balance.

His elbow connected with Ava's breastbone in a heavy crack, and she crumpled from her bar stool right to the floorboards.

"Adrian!" Brennan's bellow sliced up from his lungs, and he vaulted over the bar without thought. Indelible instinct reared up from its deep-seated home in his chest, and he pushed past the tangle of limbs and shouts and hard-moving footsteps to hone in on the flash of bright green silk beneath the chaos. Ava lay curled on the mahogany floorboards like a slender question mark, and panic laddered up the back of Brennan's throat.

Focus. Assess the situation. Breathe.

"Ava?" Her name got lost in the din of Adrian's zero-tolerance commands, the sloppy shuffle of feet over hard-wood, and Trotter's sputtering protest growing farther away by the second as the furious chef steered him toward the front door. A stern voice—their waitress, Annabelle, maybe?—cleared a wide berth of space at the bar while issuing a no-nonsense warning against anyone taking photos with their cell phones.

"Ava," Brennan tried again, leaning in. Trotter might have a face like a weasel, but he was built like a damned linebacker, and he'd hit Ava with the full force of his body weight. Although it was uncommon, blunt force trauma to the chest could have nasty implications if the blow landed in just the wrong spot, and Brennan couldn't tell if she'd hit her head during the fall. He reached out for Ava's shoulder to gently pull her upright for a better look.

But the second his hands made contact, she went com-pletely rigid, snatching herself backward as she jerked into an impenetrable ball.

"Whoa! Hey, hey, it's me. Brennan," he corrected, his heartbeat ratcheting higher. What the hell would make her react like that? "I want to help you. Just let me see if you're hurt."

"Oh." Ava blinked, her green eyes going wide, but then realization washed over her face as she clumsily pushed herself up to sitting. "No, no, I'm . . . ow."

"Did you hit your head at all?" he asked, fingers itching to travel over her in search of injuries, but she seemed spooked, so he settled for letting his eyes do the job. She was alert and reactive, although clearly rattled, and Brennan revisited the urge to introduce his fist to Trotter's smug-bastard face.

"No. I don't think so, anyway. I'm fine." One hand fluttered up to the center of her blouse, accompanied by a sigh of pain as she struggled to get her feet beneath her. But looking okay and being okay weren't always the same beast, especially if she might've also hit her head. There were half a dozen injuries that could be lurking beneath her "fine" exterior.

"Do you feel short of breath or dizzy?" Brennan palmed her shoulder to get a better visual on her eyes, and jeez, he felt her trembling all the way down his arm.

"No." She aimed the word at her lap, but it came through loud and clear. "Really, I just want to get up."

The request came at the same time Teagan arrived at Ava's side, her eyes doing the exact same tour for injuries as Brennan's had not twenty seconds before.

"Hey, Ava. I'm a paramedic. I want to take a look at you, just to see what's what, okay?"

Ava's cheeks went from pale to pink in less than a second. "I promise, I'm fine." She shifted to an awkward stand, but rather than stepping back to give her space, Brennan slid his shoulder under Ava's arm to help steady her feet beneath her.

"No LOC, no visible injuries, breathing seems okay, but the jackass popped her pretty hard in the sternum before she fell and she might've hit her head on the way down," he told Teagan, already guiding Ava toward the pass-through to the kitchen.

Teagan's brows shot skyward, but she kept up with him, stride for stride. "All right," she said. "Let's go up to the office so I can do a quick RTA."

Brennan nodded in a single lift of his chin. "Couch'll work." It would be a hell of a lot more comfortable to do a rapid trauma assessment there than on the floorboards in the dining room.

Ava huffed out a breath of protest. "I don't need a . . .

whatever that is. Seriously, I just got knocked down. It's no big deal."

"I know," Teagan agreed, cutting off both Ava's argument and the protest Brennan was brewing to fight it. "An RTA is just an assessment, that's all. I want to take a quick look at your head and the spot where you got hit to make sure your ribs aren't bruised. It's strictly precautionary, but it'll make me feel better. Please?"

"Oh." Ava's breath fluttered against his side as he guided her up the stairs leading to the Double Shot's office, one step at a time. "Well, if you put it that way . . ."

Relief pulsed through Brennan's veins. Although both her tone and her expression had gotten exponentially tougher with each passing second, Ava was still shaking like crazy.

Shit. Maybe that was him.

"Okay, here we go." Teagan's voice threaded past his realization, and Brennan lowered Ava to the bright orange couch cushions. He sucked down a breath, then another as Teagan placed her hands on the crown of Ava's head and started to work her way downward. Taking in Teagan's movements and Ava's ensuing responses with care, Brennan mentally checked off each step in the process, letting the precise order calm him further.

At least until Teagan's hands coasted over the spot where Ava's pale skin met the green silk of her shirt and Ava jumped about a mile off the couch.

"Sorry," she murmured, her black hair spilling over her eyes as she dropped her chin toward Teagan's frozen hands.

"No problem. Can you rate that pain on a scale of one to ten?"

"Oh, um. Not bad. Maybe a two?"

"Are you asking me or telling me?" Teagan slid her

glance from Ava's rib cage to her face, but Ava shook her head, suddenly resolute.

"It's a two."

"Okay," Teagan said. She continued even though her expression said she wasn't buying Ava's assertion, and hell if that didn't make two of them. But Ava sat statue-still, with her hands on the knees of her black dress pants and her eyes locked forward as Teagan asked her a few more standard-issue questions and took a look at the bruise already blooming at the open neck of her blouse.

"You're going to have one hell of a tender spot on your chest for a few days, but other than that, I think you're okay." Teagan stood, taking a few steps to the small refrigerator tucked away by the desk to grab a bottle of water for Ava. "Driving after you've been rattled up probably isn't the best idea, though. Is there anyone we can call for you?"

All the color that had returned to her cheeks disappeared, and Ava took a long sip of water before answering. "No, thank you. I'm grateful for your concern, but really, I'm not rattled up. I feel fine."

"Hmm." Teagan ran her palms down the front of her jeans, flipping a glance at Brennan that broadcast her displeasure. "Why don't you take a few minutes to just camp out here and relax, then? Brennan, can I see you in the hall for a second?"

Murmuring a quick "be right back" to Ava, Brennan followed Teagan to the narrow space in front of the Double Shot's office. He knew Teagan well enough that he could already hear her protest about Ava driving herself home.

So it was a complete and total potshot to his gut when she crossed her arms over her white T-shirt and said, "Would you like to tell me how you know what an RTA even is, let alone all the other medical procedures that go with trauma assessment?"

"Uh," came the only answer Brennan could readily grab. Shit. *Shit*. Of course Teagan would've noticed his instinctive reaction. She'd been just as well trained to notice details as he had, and he'd been too firmly ensconced in go mode to cloak his response to Ava's injury or his default terminology afterward. "It's kind of hard to explain."

Teagan surveyed his face, her gaze sliding to the gently closed office door before she finally shook her head. "Damn, Brennan. You've got a lot of secrets, don't you?"

At least he had her here. "No. I've got a lot of shit in my past that's going to stay there."

"If you say so. Look, I can respect that you want certain things in your rearview. But one of them damn near got seriously hurt in my restaurant tonight. I may not know the details, but between this fire at Joe's, the roomful of reporters downstairs, and the woman sitting behind that door, it looks like your past is coming for you whether you like it or not."

Brennan silently bit out every curse word in the book. Seeing Ava again might sting, but he could manage that well enough.

The rest of his past was a different story. He'd barely lived through it the first time, and he'd been the lucky one. No way was he letting what had happened that night—and everything that followed—back under his skin.

He wouldn't survive it twice.

"I'm straight, Teagan. A scuffle like this won't come back into the bar again," Brennan promised, clenching his fists hard enough to make his knuckles throb.

"It's not the bar I'm worried about," she said, her tone softening. "Now do me a favor and take care of Ava, would you? I meant it when I said she'll be fine, but if she thinks she's driving herself home after taking a slap-shot to the chest like that, she's out of her mind."

Brennan nodded, and Teagan gave his forearm a comforting squeeze before heading downstairs to deal with the crowd. He stood in the hallway, digging for a solution and coming up woefully short.

Teagan was right. His past was coming back to haunt him. Only this time, he could control it. He *would* control it.

There was no alternative.

Palming the handle to the office door, Brennan moved back inside the comfortably cluttered space. Ava sat against the bright cushions, watching carefully as he parked himself on the other end of the couch.

"Hey. How are you doing?" Zero points for originality, but Brennan really did want to know, and anyway, he couldn't exactly avoid being a point-A-to-point-B kind of guy.

"Fine." Ava slumped against the back of the couch just a little too much for the sentiment to stick, and something twisted deep in Brennan's chest.

"Yeah. I know that feeling."

"Really?" One dark eyebrow went up. "You've been knocked flat on your ass in front of all your colleagues recently?"

A puff of humorless laughter escaped his lips. "In a manner of speaking. If it makes you feel any better, I'm certain Adrian wasn't gentle about showing Trotter the door."

"I'm sure I'll go to hell for this, but it kind of does. Guys like Mike Trotter make the rest of us look bad." She paused, her tiny smile fading as she ghosted her fingers over the front of her shirt. "Anyway, I know you're busy. I don't want to keep you."

Brennan's heart took a swipe at his rib cage, but damn it, he really had no choice. Tonight had come within inches of wrecking him, and things were only getting worse every time he said *no comment*.

These reporters weren't going to leave until he gave them a damn good reason to go, and that reason was sitting right in front of him.

"I thought you wanted a story."

Ava's eyes went perfectly round. "I thought you didn't want to tell it."

Understatement of the freaking century. "Considering what just happened downstairs, it doesn't look like I get much say. If I give you the story, the rest of those reporters will go away, right?"

"It depends," Ava said, and he had to hand it to her. She was treading just as carefully as he was. "Reporters won't infringe on each other under certain circumstances. If you really want them to back off, you'd have to offer me the story as an exclusive."

"You'd have to make me a few promises," Brennan countered. The resulting flash of steel-tipped determination in her eyes jabbed at his resolve, but he turned toward her in an effort to hammer the words into place. "They're not negotiable."

"Such as?"

"I'll tell you—and only you—what happened the other day at Joe's. But no printing the boy's name, no sensationalizing what really happened, and absolutely no questions about anything occurring before this week. This story is the only one on the table. Take it or leave it."

She slid forward, close enough for their knees to touch. "Agreed on the boy's name. As far as the rescue at the grocery store goes, the truth is already pretty sensational. I won't downplay that just to please you, but I won't turn it into the script for an action film, either. And regarding events occurring before this week . . . no guarantees."

Holy hell, she'd gotten tougher over the last seven years. And holy hell in a hand basket, it was sexy enough to ruin him right here on the couch. "I mean it, Ava. I'll tell you everything that happened at Joe's. But no questions about anything other than the fire."

"I mean it too, Nick. I want the story, but I won't lie to you about what an exclusive like this entails. I can't promise I'll limit my questions to just the events of the other day, or that I won't press you to answer all the questions that pertain to the story. If past events are part of it, they're fair game."

Their conversation from earlier tonight streamed through his mind, stomping on his composure in one fluid stroke. A white hot thread of uncut intensity surged up from his chest, barging out of his mouth before he could hook it back.

"Fine. You want the past on the table? We'll trade. I'll give you the exclusive, with free rein to print whatever you can find, both past and present. But if I'm dishing up a story, then so are you."

The slender ridge of her shoulders locked into place as she whispered, "What do you mean?"

But Brennan didn't budge. Damn it, after seven years, she could still wreck his composure with one sweet and sexy smile. As much as he hated it, he needed to know why she'd left, if only to finally move on, and the same sharp desire that had pressed the words out of his mouth earlier whipped back tenfold. "If you want me to talk, you're going to have to go first. I want to know what happened seven years ago to put you on that ferry off Sapphire Island. I want to know why you left without a good-bye."

Unlike before, Ava didn't even flinch. "If I tell you, will you give me the story on the fire?"

He nodded, certain this was insane. But Christ, he wanted the other reporters gone, he wanted the truth—hell, seeing how headstrong and serious and totally fucking gorgeous she looked sitting there across from him, he wanted *Ava* too much to care. "I'll give you the only story I've got, which is the one from this week. If you want anything else, that's going to be up to you to find."

"Done," she said, without even flinching. "When do you want to start?"

Brennan stood to grab his jacket from the hook by the office door, equally unflinching even though his pulse was on mile twenty-three of an emotional marathon.

"Well, since Teagan's insistent you get a ride home and I get a break from the bar, I'd say there's no time like the present."

Chapter Six

"Okay, Mancuso. You can do this."

Ava repeated the whisper over and over, letting it melt in with her breath as she stood in the tiled alcove by the Double Shot's back door. The bruise on her chest was already throbbing in time with her rapid-fire heartbeat beneath it, but the deep-seated ache was the least of her worries. As if being manhandled in front of half the town hadn't been mortifying enough, Ava had been so stunned at the long-buried sensation of being knocked to the ground that she'd wheeled away from Nick's touch as if he'd been on fire.

And now she was going to have to explain everything *else* she'd buried seven years ago in order to get the story that would save her career. God, what had she been thinking when she'd slapped out that impulsive, ridiculous *done* in response to Nick's crazy offer? It was bad enough that they had a romantic past—one she had artfully kept hidden from her boss. But now Ava had to trot out said past like a show pony on parade day, all while staying one million percent calm, cool, and professional, because news flash! Brennan wasn't just her sexy, brooding ex-boyfriend. Now he was her source.

Come on, girl. It's time to toughen up and do your job.

"Hey." Nick appeared in the door frame of the pass-through between the now-closed kitchen and the bar, the rush of voices and music and bottles clinking together growing muffled as the swinging door *thunked* shut behind him. "Annabelle grabbed your stuff when we took you upstairs. Everything should be right here."

Ava let out a breath of relief at the sight of her black swing coat and her oversized work tote. "That was nice of her," she said, trying to cage her wince at the streak of pain shooting outward from her sternum as she reached for both items.

The dark flicker in Brennan's eyes told her he'd seen it anyway. He looped her bag over a hook by the alcove, holding up her coat to guide it over her shoulders. "She said she hopes you feel better."

"Thanks, but honestly, I'm fine." Ava slid her arms into the soft wool, a slight shiver taking over for the ache in her chest at the warmth of his breath on the back of her neck. She forced her fingers over the smooth, silver buttons, waiting until Nick was busy shrugging into his own jacket before lifting her bag from the hook.

"That's pretty heavy." A frown dipped at the corners of his mouth as he sent a pointed look from her bulky bag to the center of her rib cage. He took a step toward her in the hushed space at the back of the kitchen, cutting the distance between them to less than an arm's length.

"I'm used to it," she said, tipping her shoulder into a shrug before her torso reminded her in no uncertain terms that using any muscles even vaguely attached to her breastbone was a shitastic idea.

Nick took another step, close enough for her to see the unyielding set of his jaw beneath his shadowy stubble. "Not today."

He slipped the strap from her shoulder with careful precision, the movement surprisingly gentle considering his obvious determination. Testing the weight of the bag with one arm, he ushered her to the door with the other, and despite her distaste for being babied, realization settled deep in Ava's belly.

Beneath the gruff exterior he'd gained over the last seven years, Nick was a good guy. Damn it, as emotionally hairy as this little sharing session had the potential to be, she *could* do it. Yes, she hated the reasons she'd left Sapphire Island, and airing out her past was right up there with back-to-back root canals on her list of *yes, please*. But seven years ago, she'd been too young and too afraid to realize what she couldn't avoid now.

As much as she hated those reasons and how vulnerable they made her, Nick deserved to know the truth. Regardless of whether or not he gave her a story, Ava had cared about him.

Even when she'd gotten on that ferry.

"I owe you an explanation about why I left Sapphire Island without saying good-bye," she said, falling into step next to him as they crossed the narrow stretch of asphalt along the side of the building. Brennan stopped a handful of paces away beside a silver SUV, his breath billowing around his face in the frigid night air.

"Okay," he said, but his shoulders hitched upward beneath his black canvas jacket, negating the word.

"Nick?" Ava leaned forward, staring at him in the silvery light spilling down from the overhead streetlamp. "Are you all right?"

"Yeah. I just . . . might've gotten a little impulsive upstairs. I don't normally force information out of people. I promised to tell you what happened last week at Joe's, and I will. But . . ."

He trailed off, and all at once, the dots connected into a bigger picture.

He felt guilty asking her to return the favor.

"But nothing," she said, the words soft even though her voice was firm. Digging into her past to explain why she'd left him was going to hurt, yes, but if her upbringing had taught her anything, it was how to be tough. It was past time for giving Nick answers. After all, she was asking him for honesty, and as vulnerable as the words would make her, Ava was strong enough to finally tell him the truth in return.

"I agreed to tell you why I left seven years ago. And story or no story, you deserve to know."

Brennan stood across from Ava with his heart in his throat and his libido on fire. She had that gleam in her eyes, the one that had earned her that old nickname in spades, and Christ, she was as determined as she was sexy.

Which meant that if he wanted to maintain any semblance of control around her, Brennan was screwed six ways to Sunday.

After the initial push of adrenaline from making the deal had worn off, a thick layer of guilt had settled into its place. He might want to know what had made Ava leave seven years ago, but emotional extortion so wasn't his thing—hell, emotional *anything* gave him a solid case of indigestion.

But now Ava *wanted* to talk about their past, and that curveball alone was enough to shatter the composure he'd carefully reconstructed over the last twenty-four hours. That she was still fastening him with that bright green tell-all stare on top of it all? Yeah, those shattered pieces might as well be dust.

"You don't owe me any answers," Brennan said, partly because it was the truth and partly to buy a second to recalibrate, but she was already shaking her head to cut him off.

"Actually, I do. But more than that, I owe you an apology. I meant it when I said there were complicated circumstances. But that still didn't give me the right to leave without a good-bye."

Ava's voice canted lower over the last word, revealing just a sliver of the vulnerability beneath her fierce exterior, and it tugged at Brennan's chest.

"Let's get in the truck," he said, sending a covert gaze around the sparsely lit side lot. He popped the locks on the Trailblazer, opening the passenger door for Ava before rounding to the driver's side. He might be taking cautious to a new extreme, but considering how ballsy Mike Trotter had been back in the bar, Brennan wasn't taking any chances of being overheard.

He started the engine, fiddling with the keys as the heat kicked on. "I looked for you," he admitted, his muscles pinching around his spine. God, his PT session three days ago with Kat had barely nicked the surface of the ache, but he dug past his old urges for numbness, letting the pain ground him. "I even went to Virginia Beach, but no one had ever heard of you in Uniondale."

"That's because I'm not from Uniondale," Ava said quietly. "Nadine is."

"Your college roommate?" An image of the pixie-faced redhead whose parents ran the main restaurant at the Sapphire Island beach resort bubbled up in his memory. Nadine had insisted she hadn't known where Ava had gone on the morning she'd disappeared, only that Ava had been fine but had to leave earlier than planned. But eight hours later, Brennan had rushed off the island himself to try to find Ava, and with the summer over and his pride run through the shredder, he'd gone straight home to Fairview two days after that. "I don't understand. Why would you say you were from Nadine's hometown?"

"So I wouldn't have to tell you I was from mine."

Ava's mouth flattened into a pale line, and even though questions rushed at his brain from damn near every direction imaginable, Brennan bit them back so she could continue.

"I told you I'd had a happy upbringing in Uniondale, but I didn't. My brother Pete and I were raised in subsidized housing in Philadelphia. Our parents are alcoholics, and to say they were unkind is a gift. They're terrible people, and they specialized in doing terrible things."

"Jesus, Ava." His pulse thrummed with undiluted shock, chased by a hard-edged realization that made his blood run cold despite the heat now pumping through the Trailblazer's interior. "Wait. Is that why you were so jumpy after you got hurt tonight? Did your parents hit you?"

Her wince was so slight, he'd have missed it if he hadn't been trained to pick up every last detail. "It was a long time ago."

Anger ricocheted through Brennan's rib cage, his fingers cranking into tight fists in his lap. "Is that a yes?"

"I told you, they're terrible people. I had Pete, and we did our best to keep our heads down and stick together, but there wasn't always safety in numbers."

Brennan opened his mouth to let loose a string of upper-level curse words—Christ, the thought of anyone putting their hands on her that way made him sick to his stomach—but Ava pressed on, as if she wanted her words out as fast as possible.

"Everyone else on Sapphire Island came from such happy, well-off families, and I'd lived with other people's pity my whole life. Just once, I wanted to fit in like everyone else, to finally leave that awful life behind for good.

I'd been to Uniondale a few times during semester breaks, and it was easy enough to adopt it as my hometown, so just for the summer, that's what I did. I didn't think it would ever be anything more than a small indiscretion to save a little face."

Brennan forced himself to take a mental step back and focus, but with the images in his head and Ava's tough defenses crumbling by the second, it was no easy task. "So Nadine knew?"

Ava nodded, a swath of dark hair tumbling forward to shield her gaze. "She knew about my parents, yes, and she went along with me being from Uniondale. But she didn't know that I went to my brother's place in Philadelphia when I left Sapphire Island that morning."

Although the parameters of their past were changing with each word, the memory of that day still jabbed at him, hard. "Why didn't you tell her?"

Sadness infused the tiny smile on her lips. "Because I knew you'd look for me, and that Nadine would be the first person you'd ask for help."

Well, hell. She'd had him pegged there. Still . . . "You could've trusted me with the truth instead of running away."

The frustration shot from Brennan's mouth before he could water it down or haul it back. But damn it, they'd spent every waking—and sleeping—moment together for three months. Hadn't that meant anything to her?

"I know," Ava said, stopping his aggravation in its tracks. "At least, I do now. But I didn't run that summer because I didn't trust you, Nick. I ran because I did."

The words, her voice, his first name, all of it hit him like a sucker punch, and he stiffened against the driver's seat. "What?"

"I was twenty-two years old, and had never trusted

anyone in my life other than my older brother. I didn't mean to fall for you, but . . ." She broke off, clamping down on her lower lip hard enough to leave a tiny indent. "I did, and I was scared. It's not an excuse, but it's the truth. I didn't know what to do with all those feelings I had for you, and I panicked."

Recognition flared in the back of his mind, becoming brighter as it took hold and spread out. "So you didn't leave because you wanted to end things?"

"No. I left because I didn't want to end things at all. I was just too afraid to tell you the truth about my parents, let alone face feelings I'd sworn I'd never have. It's not like good relationships are in my wheelhouse." Ava paused to give a humorless laugh. "I'm sure this all sounds ridiculous to you, coming from such a normal, loving family. God, it even sounds crazy to me. But—"

"It doesn't."

The words dislodged themselves from the deepest part of Brennan's chest, shocking him on the way out. He needed to get control of what he was saying, and he needed to do it right now. Yes, she'd just been honest with him, but no way could he tell Ava, who was about to interview him for a goddamned newspaper exclusive, that he knew exactly what it felt like to push back on reality when it gave you a healthy shove. He knew what it meant to panic, to numb the ache with distraction while you fought all the demons that were supposed to dull the pain.

For the last two years, Brennan had known exactly what it felt like to run.

"Look, we were young," he said, tamping down his unease. "I'm not going to say I wasn't mad when you left, or that I don't wish you had told me all of this at the time. But we can't change the past. The only thing we can control is the present."

"That's true." Ava proceeded with caution, but the flash of emotion behind her gaze gave her away. "I don't blame you for hating me."

"I don't hate you." Brennan's hand was halfway over the small console separating them before he could register the movement, but at the last second, he pulled back, letting his arm fall short over the molded leather. She'd been so startled by his touch just an hour ago, and with what he knew now, maybe contact was a bad idea.

But rather than flinch at the movement, Ava lifted a dark brow over her steady gaze, turning toward him in her seat. "You pretty much told me in no uncertain terms to get out of the bar last night," she argued, and wait . . . was that a smile edging up the corners of her mouth?

"Okay," he admitted with a self-deprecating shrug, and holy shit, she *was* smiling. "But you threw me for a hell of a loop."

"I know." Ava's expression softened, the overhead lamplight bathing her face in a barely-there glow. "For what it's worth, I am sorry. For not telling you everything, for leaving without a good-bye. For . . . all of it."

"Tell you what," he said, clearing his throat over the rough-edged words. "Why don't we start with a clean slate? Totally fresh, right now. What do you think?"

Her eyes widened. "You're willing to forgive me, just like that?"

This time, he closed the space between their hands, just enough to touch the backs of his fingers to hers. "I can't lie, Ava. Your leaving like that hit me pretty hard."

"I understand," she whispered. "I know it'll take time to make up for what I did."

"It will. But I know it must've been hard for you too, and in a way, I get why you left." Brennan broke off, trying to stomach the thought of her horrible past. "Think you can be straight with me from now on?"

"Yes. But do me a favor." She pressed her fingers against his, lowering her gaze to the contact. "Please don't treat me differently because of what my parents did. I'm not fragile. I won't break."

Brennan nodded, sliding his fingers against her hand, and damn, a touch this innocent shouldn't feel so freaking good. "Okay. But then you have to do something for me."

"And that is?"

"Call me Brennan. The only people who call me Nick anymore are my sisters, and even then, it sounds weird to me."

"Brennan sounds weird to me," Ava countered, and he rediscovered how cute her little nose-wrinkle maneuver was. "Going by your last name is such a guy thing."

Brennan was tempted to tell her it was a firefighter thing, and that just like every other rookie, he'd had zero say over the nickname he'd been branded with as a recruit. But instead, he nudged her hand. "A deal's a deal, Spitfire. Take it or leave it."

Her groan slid into laughter. "Okay, okay! I'll try to call you Brennan, but only if you call me Ava."

"You drive a hard bargain," he said, extending his hand. "Clean slate, Ava?"

Her fingers were warm and strong as she slid them over his palm and shook. "Clean slate, Brennan."

For a second, they sat there, fingers entwined and eyes locked together, and Brennan wanted nothing more than to lean over the console between them, to kiss her fast and deep and not stop until they were both completely out of air and common sense.

Get it together, you jackass! Ava was about to interview him for a tell-all in the paper, which was the one thing—

the *only* thing—he'd managed to avoid when his life in Fairview had come flying apart at the seams. He needed to pin every last ounce of his composure firmly into place in order to keep his past in the past.

Putting his mouth on hers would ruin him.

"So, ah, how does this interview thing work?" he asked, shifting in his seat to flip on the headlights and finally put the Trailblazer in gear. They had a bit of a drive to Riverside, and having something mundane to focus on might teach his impulsively traitorous libido a lesson.

Ava laughed, as smooth and sweet as warm butterscotch, and hell, keeping his eyes on the road wasn't going to be enough. "It's pretty standard, actually," she said. "I ask the questions, you give the answers. Then I write it all up and the story goes to print."

The teasing lilt in her voice made his sudden unease fizzle out, his chuckle escaping without his consent. "I get that part. What I meant was more like when and where."

"Well, the where part is really up to you. As for the when, this is obviously a little time sensitive. I'll start pulling the questions together as soon as I get home. That way we can do the interview at your earliest convenience."

"Ava, it's Friday night. Plus, you took a hell of a pop from that idiot Trotter." Was she seriously going to throw in that much overtime on this interview, even injured?

"Good stories don't happen on a schedule, and my chest is fine. I can be ready any time after tomorrow morning," she said.

Guess that answered that. Damn, she was tenacious. And double damn, that spark in her eyes still shot right through him, even after seven years.

Brennan coasted to a stop at Pine Mountain's only stoplight, turning to give Ava a full glance in the shadows of the truck. "Monday is my day off this week. What do you think about my place, twelve-thirty?"

The spark in her eyes flashed brighter with the intensity of her smile, and it sizzled right through him even in the soft glow of the dashboard.

"I think it's a date."

Chapter Seven

Brennan rolled to his side, burrowing deep into the warmth of his time-softened bedsheets. Brilliant Saturday morning sunshine filtered through his bedroom window, riding past the curtains on the dappled shadows of glittering, snowy pine trees.

Damn. Even lying down, his back felt as if someone had slammed into it with railroad spikes.

Wincing against the pain, Brennan pushed his way out of bed, quick-tripping it to the bathroom for the requisite date with his toothbrush and a mouthful of ibuprofen before shuffling down the hall toward the kitchen. With three weeks to go before Christmas, winter had definitely settled into the Blue Ridge. Between the near-arctic mountain temperatures and the wringer of physical stress from the fire at Joe's, Brennan's back felt like a haystack just waiting for a stiff wind to blow it all to pieces.

Or maybe that was his composure, because in T minus two days, he was going to sit down with the hottest woman he'd ever laid eyes on and she was going to do her best to unearth every single secret he'd ever wanted to forget.

Brennan jammed a lid on the thought and grabbed a can of Coke from the fridge, letting the sugar and caffeine combo do its thing to wake up his system before flicking his cell phone to life. He rebrowsed the string of texts he'd been unable to deal with in the crush of last night's dinner shift at the Double Shot, his finger hovering over the DELETE button for a breath, then two, before actually making contact.

Damn. He really should eat something if his gut was going to get all mutinous and jab at him like that.

Tossing his phone to the counter with a clatter, Brennan unfolded into a stretch that tested his overtight muscles. A familiar electronic ring tone froze his movements halfway to the pantry, and his gut did an automatic knot-and-drop. Brennan knew from experience that if he ignored enough of his younger sister's calls, she'd threaten to show up in Pine Mountain, and that was a can of worms he had no interest in popping open. Better to do this now, on his own terms, where no one could overhear him, anyway.

"Hello?"

"Oh! Um, hey," Ellie stammered, clearly surprised. "I didn't think you'd pick up. Did I wake you?"

"Nope. I was up," he said, and so far, so good. Of his four sisters, Ellie was the cagiest, though, so no way was he abandoning caution.

"Good. How are you feeling?"

Ah, the million-dollar opener. Brennan had lost hope a long time ago that she'd actually believe his answer, but it didn't stop him from saying, "Fine. You?"

"You're up awfully early." An equal mix of concern and suspicion colored her words as she ignored the pleasantries and went for round two. "Aren't you working really late nights at that restaurant now?"

He'd rather be stuck with a thousand pins than admit to Ellie that he was awake because his back never let him get more than a handful of hours' worth of shut-eye, and anyway, she had enough on her mind right now without worrying about his sleep habits.

Speaking of which . . . "Yeah, Friday is our busiest night, so we're usually slammed, especially over the holidays. Sorry I didn't answer your texts. Dress looks nice, though."

"You think so?" Ellie's voice lifted in excitement. "I mean, you only get one wedding dress, so I want it to be perfect, but I really love it, and . . . damn it, Nick. That's not fair."

Brennan froze, the can of Coke halfway to his mouth. The sound of his first name was odd in his ears, as if it belonged to someone else, and he tamped down the memory of the last person who'd used it.

"What's not fair?" he asked in a last-ditch effort, but of course she was too sharp to fall for the rope-a-dope.

"You used my wedding dress to distract me, that's what! Look, we're all really worried about you. You haven't been back to Fairview once since you left. You've bailed on Christmas *and* Easter twice now—which by the way, even Dad has noticed—and Pine Mountain's really far from home."

"First of all, I had to work those days. And secondly, Pine Mountain is my home." He pulled in a smooth, controlled breath, the composure he wore like a full set of turnout gear locked securely into place. "And there's nothing to worry about. Everything here really is fine."

"Fine." Ellie scoffed, as if the word tasted burnt. "You've been saying that for two years."

"I relocated to make a career change, Ells. People do it all the time, and working at the restaurant isn't a nine-to-five gig, okay? Just because I'm busy doesn't mean I'm not doing all right."

Brennan's tone held just enough please-let's-drop-the-subject to get her attention, and *finally*, he got some latitude. He knew Ellie meant well, but this conversation practically had a script, and the last thing he needed was a come to Jesus meeting with his sister about things that were over and done. "I know you don't think so, but I really am all set here. I promise."

Ellie's silence hung fire for a minute before she said, "I'm not trying to be a pain in the ass, Nick. I love you, okay?"

"I love you too, kid." Brennan cleared his throat, scrubbing a hand over his goatee before taking a long draw from his can of Coke. "So you're serious about marrying this Murphy guy?"

His sister hesitated, but relief pricked at his chest when she gave in with a soft laugh. "The Murphy guy's name is Josh, which I know *you* know full well. And the wedding's in three weeks."

Okay. So engaging in a pointless conversation about the past might not be on his agenda, but a little friendly ribbing with his sister? Now, that he'd dive into headfirst.

"So is that a yes?"

Her laughter grew, and damn, he had to admit, it sounded good on her. "Well, there are going to be five hundred people at Saint Mark's on Christmas Day expecting me to take that little stroll down the aisle, plus I'm kind of insanely in love with the guy, so yeah. That's a yes."

On second thought, maybe not with the ribbing. "Older brother, here. Can we skip the you-in-love thing, please?"

"Sure." A crafty grin crept into Ellie's tone. "So have

you been dating anybody lately? I wasn't kidding about adding a plus-one to the seating arrangements, you know."

Brennan winced, grateful Ellie couldn't see the gesture. He loved his sister, and not a little bit, but he wasn't planning on attending her wedding any longer than absolutely necessary. Even then, his agenda was to lie low and blend into the wallpaper. The last thing he needed was to see anyone he knew in Fairview, or worse yet, for anyone he knew to see *him*.

Check that. The last thing Brennan needed was to worry about a date for the ten hours he'd be fading to black in the town he'd left behind.

"Ugh! Okay, fine," he mumbled in defeat. "You-in-love it is."

Ellie launched into a monologue about bridesmaids and bodices and bustles, and Brennan did his best to play along. The muscles on either side of his lumbar vertebrae reminded him exactly how much time he'd spent on his feet last night after returning to the bar from Riverside, and he parked himself in a heavily cushioned kitchen chair as he cradled the phone between his shoulder and his ear. Ellie was clearly the head spokeswoman for crazy-in-love, and even though he had no frigging clue what a hand-beaded empire waist was, it really didn't seem fair to deny her this excitement.

Even if there was no chance in hell he'd ever follow suit. Falling in love with someone meant opening up, and now more than ever, he needed to keep a handle on his emotions. Letting loose with anything other than precise, logical control only got you burned. Literally. Figuratively. Take your pick.

Brennan wasn't going back there either.

After another ten minutes of easy back and forth with Ellie that may or may not have included the words *ice sculptures*, Brennan ended the call on one last assurance that everything in Pine Mountain was status quo. He had a liquor delivery to oversee, not to mention holiday staff schedules that needed finalizing. While he'd never imagined that managing a small-town bar and grill would headline his résumé, the place meant a lot to Adrian and Teagan. Teagan's father had taken a flyer on him when Brennan had needed a job two years ago, no questions asked, and for that, he owed them a lot. The hard work was the least he could do, and if it kept him moving through the present tense, all the better.

Knocking back the rest of his sugar rush, Brennan padded to the bathroom to go through the motions of lather-rinse-repeat. By the time he'd slung on a pair of jeans and a black long-sleeved T-shirt with the Double Shot logo printed across the front, his back was mostly on board with keeping the rest of him upright, although his stomach wasn't feeling quite so friendly. A quick scan of his pantry told him sneaking in breakfast at work was a moral imperative unless he wanted to chow down on condiments, so Brennan went to grab the keys to his Trailblazer from the drawer where he'd tossed them without looking last night.

Only his gaze made a direct hit on a photograph instead.

A dull ache that had nothing to do with his back thudded all the way through him, and his mind wheeled back to the day he'd stuck the thing in there to begin with.

Brennan had been in such a hurry to leave Fairview that he'd dumped most of his belongings into boxes without looking, figuring he'd just pitch anything he didn't want or need when he unpacked. On the fourth day of slow sorting, he'd unearthed the photograph, staring up at him from beneath his collection of hockey memorabilia and a stash of old T-shirts. Brennan had stood over the kitchen trash

can for ten minutes, then twenty, before stuffing the photo
in that drawer. He hadn't clapped eyes on the damned thing
since, having long ago buried it under a pile of take-out
menus and packets of soy sauce from the Chinese restaurant in Riverside. Only now, the story that went with the
image had a very different ending.

"Screw it."

Before the rational part of his brain could override the
hot impulse daring his fingers to move, Brennan creaked
the drawer all the way open and plucked the picture from
its resting place.

The black and white photo of Ava had faded over time,
although his memory of the day it had been taken was
brass-tack sharp. Glossy black hair spilled down the back
of her white tank top like fresh ink on a page as she faced
the camera from the side, her face tipped up and caught
in deep laughter. Her coal-colored lashes fanned downward, framing her closed eyes and sending shadows over
the apples of her cheeks. Her expression was so sweet, so
totally wide open in her happiness, that she looked as
honest and good as a lazy day in the sun.

Seven years ago, he'd have done anything for her, regardless of consequence or cost. He'd been young enough,
reckless enough, to fall in love with her without even realizing she'd been hiding her past. A past worth hiding, sure.
But if he hadn't been so blindly impulsive, maybe he'd
have been able to see it. To save himself the heartache. To
help her cope.

As if flying by the seat of his pants hadn't already done
enough damage.

The thought rattled Brennan firmly back to reality, and
he snapped into place on the linoleum. All that talk with
Ellie about true love must be making him soft. Okay, so

he'd had a thing—maybe even *the* thing—for Ava Mancuso the summer after college. But she was about to ask him no less than a thousand questions about the one part of his life he was desperate to leave buried in the past.

As hard and as fast as he'd once fallen for her, the best thing he could do for both of them now was to shut her out.

Chapter Eight

Ava's breath escaped from her lungs in a slow leak, the exhale smarting even though two and a half days had passed since her embarrassing-as-hell tumble at the Double Shot. The whack to her sternum had stung nearly as much as the shot to her pride, but it was worth the literal heartache. She'd come clean about her past in a move long overdue, and as much as Ava had dreaded spilling her own story in exchange for Nick's, she'd felt oddly strong giving him the truth he deserved. Add to it the fact that she'd also landed the exclusive that was going to resuscitate her dying career, and truly, she couldn't have asked for a better situation.

Even if her sex drive was in *overdrive* at the thought of spending more time with Nick Brennan.

Oh no you don't. Ava nestled further into the comfort of her armchair, stamping out the memory of the dark, glittering, dead-sexy stare Nick had served up last night in his truck. The second she and Brennan had agreed on the terms of this story, they'd entered a business arrangement Being involved with a source, even on a short-term story, was a slippery slope. Ava couldn't say she'd never heard of anyone bending that unspoken rule, but she could sure as hell see the conflict of interest.

Plus, Gary already thought she couldn't bring home the bacon with a source if he spotted her a block's worth of butcher shops. She simply couldn't lose her focus so close to breaking the biggest story of her life.

No matter how scorchingly hot Brennan's five-alarm stares felt on her skin.

Ava sucked in a breath, low and deep. The soft, late-morning hum of the bakery around her smoothed her jagged nerves and knocked her resolve into place, and she clicked over the document on her laptop even though she'd long since memorized the thing.

Solidifying the facts of the current story had been Ava's first step toward preparing her interview questions for Nick, and she took a minute to cross-reference her notes with the public record from the fire marshal one more time. The official report on the fire at Joe's Grocery pointed to faulty electrical wiring as the culprit, with absolutely no signs of foul play. Although the fire had destroyed more than half the building, both Pine Mountain's and River-side's fire departments had worked in tandem to bravely and efficiently fight the blaze, and the residents of Pine Mountain had already rallied around Joe in an effort to help rebuild the grocery store. The facts of the story made perfect sense, and everything from procedure to progression of events fell neatly into place.

Everything, that is, except for Nick Brennan, who as far as Ava could tell, didn't fit into the story at all. Seven years ago, he'd been on the cusp of going to the Fairview Fire Academy with his best friend, Mason Watts, but clearly, Nick wasn't a firefighter now. In fact, even when she'd returned to her Google search with an all-in vengeance, the only concrete information Ava had been able to unearth on Nick was a half-buried public record stating that he'd attended the fire academy as he'd intended to after their summer on Sapphire Island.

The whole thing left her with way more questions than answers about Nick's past. And damn it, the more questions she turned up about him that had no obvious answers, the more she wanted to discover how on earth he'd known how to find that little boy and safely rescue him from a burning building.

What the hell was he hiding? And more importantly, *why*?

"Oh Lord, spare the masses. No good can come from that hell-bent look on your face."

The familiar masculine voice delivered Ava back to the here and now of the Sweet Life bakery. She reached up to close her laptop with a *snick*, eyeballing her brother Pete with equal parts disdain and affection.

"Please," she said, sliding her laptop into her bag over a pop of much-needed laughter. "Like you don't get passionate about your job, *Chef* Mancuso."

Pete's grin got lost in the uncharacteristic stubble peppering his jaw. "Ouch on the formality. So I like to bake a little. What's the big deal?"

"What's the big deal?" Ava echoed jokingly. "Are you even looking at this place?"

She gestured to the warm, honey-colored walls of the bakery, two of which were fully lined with glass display cases boasting everything from cheesecake to Christmas cookies. The wide-plank floorboards glowed like lush ribbons of melted caramel, and the matching built-in shelves on the far wall brimmed over with books, magazines, and newspapers, all ready to be shared with interested eyes. Thickly cushioned reading chairs dotted the dining area, interspersed with sleek bistro tables and a longer communal barlike counter with docking stations for laptops.

The atmosphere blended flawlessly with the fresh bread and sweet sugar aromas wafting in from the kitchen, and Ava had to admit that the place fit Pete right down to his kitchen clogs. Her brother had run the cozy Main Street storefront with his wife, Lily, for over a year and a half now, and as seriously as they both took the bakery, they were even more serious about each other. Or seriously in love, anyway.

Pain shot beneath the center of Ava's pale yellow sweater in a sudden *whump*, and ugh, this bruise needed to fade out, stat. "Anyway, all joking aside, I've got a huge story in front of me. It's time to go big or go home."

"Mmm. Even when going big means getting knocked down by some moron at the Double Shot?" Pete's normally confident smile slid into something a lot less friendly, his knuckles going pale over the handle of the coffeepot caught in his grip.

Damn it, she knew she should've called Layla for a ride to pick up her car instead of her brother. But Layla would've asked a ton of questions that had sharp and sticky answers, and anyway, even though the protective pit bull routine tugged at her gut, having Pete close after being a little shaken up had been a comfort. Albeit a temporary one.

"That was a total accident," Ava said, modulating her voice to cover her chagrin. "I even got checked out by a paramedic, remember? I'm fine."

"Uh-huh. You'd just better hope Mike Trotter stays out of Pine Mountain." He flattened the words with a hard, green stare that told her arguing would be an exercise in futility, so she didn't.

"Now that I've landed the exclusive on this fire, I'm sure he'll move on to something else." Guys like Trotter

were all about making the biggest splash. Never mind that
the wasted water held all the value.

Pete skimmed a glance over the laptop bag she'd tucked
carefully at her side, his expression easing up a fraction.
"Everyone in town is talking about that rescue. It seems
like one hell of a story."

"That's because it is," Ava agreed. "I might be hell-bent
to tell it, but I'm not apologizing for being ambitious."

"Okay, okay. You win." Pete held up one hand in playful
concession while he leaned in to fill her festive red and
green coffee cup with the other. "You don't have to prove
yourself to me."

"You're the only one," she muttered, just low enough for
Pete to miss it. While Gary had initially given her a brows-
up *no shit* when she'd told him she'd landed an exclusive
interview with Nick, he'd been less than impressed when
she'd hedged about the specifics.

But come on. How was she supposed to tell her boss—
the man who held the power to make or break her entire
career—that she'd spent two days searching for details
only to come up with one nebulous might-have-happened,
and that she'd only landed the exclusive in the first place
by coming clean about her tangled-up past with her
source?

A past so brittle and burnt, it had made her run from the
only man she'd ever loved.

"So." Ava straightened in her seat, pasting a smile over
her face. "What's the special today? I'm going to need
some sustenance before I head over to this interview."

If Pete noticed the swerve in subject matter, he didn't
acknowledge it. "I made a batch of cranberry turnovers a
little while ago, and I think there are still a handful of
pomegranate-pistachio shortbread bars in the display case.

But it's slim pickings today, at least until I can catch up from the breakfast rush."

"Where's Lily?" Ava asked, pushing back from her seat to follow Pete to the counter. The oddity of her sister-in-law's absence hit Ava like a delayed reaction, and she swung her gaze around the shop. Usually Pete and Lily manned the Sweet Life in tandem, especially during the midmorning, when they did the most business. Maybe she was in the back now that lunch was around the corner and the rush had mostly died down. "Is she in the kitchen?"

But her brother shook his dark head as he slipped behind the counter. "Doctor's appointment," he said, dropping the coffee carafe back to its burner with a clatter. "So, ah, this assignment is pretty major, huh? Sounds like that big break you've been waiting for."

Ava switched gears, taking the cranberry turnover from Pete's outstretched hand with a cautious smile. While she and her brother were extremely close, she'd never given him any details about her summer on Sapphire Island. As far as Pete was concerned, Ava had taken a great opportunity to spend a summer with her college roommate's family, making some extra post-college money before she jumped into the workforce and left Philadelphia behind once and for all.

He had no idea how much more she'd left behind when she'd hopped on that ferry.

"Yeah," Ava said, toasting him with her pastry. "This story is definitely a step up from the Turnip Festival."

"Oh, come on. I thought that article was a fine piece of journalism."

"That is because you're my brother," she said, sinking her teeth into one corner of the golden, flaky turnover. The sweet-tart flavor of homemade cranberry jam burst on her tongue, filling her senses with a whole lot of *yes, yes, yes* as it melted into the buttery goodness of the crust. "God, Pete. This is amazing."

"Are you saying that because you're my sister?" he asked, propping his palms against the glass display case with a cocky grin.

"No. Why would I sugarcoat something like that? No pun intended," she added before taking another bite.

"You're hilarious." Pete rolled his eyes, but didn't scale back on his smile. "And you just proved my point. I'm not telling you your article was good because I have to."

"Turnip Festival," Ava reminded him, but they were both made up of the same brand of stubborn, and right now, Pete's was on full display.

"Regardless of the subject, it was a solid, well-written article. You're a great reporter, Ava."

She laughed. "Tell me again once I get a byline on the front page, would you?"

"I'm telling you now." Pete leaned in closer, sending a hard prickle through her chest as his normally confident expression turned serious. "I get that work is important to you, but you don't need a byline to prove your worth."

Ava chewed a little longer than necessary, tacking her armor into place along with a grateful smile. Pete had always been there for her, cheering her on and doing his best to protect her no matter what. He'd even bused tables at a greasy inner-city diner every night for two years to afford a more expensive culinary school, refusing to leave Philadelphia even though their father had kicked him out of the house in a drunken rage the day Pete turned eighteen.

Pete had gone to unbelievable lengths to be strong for her until she could escape to college, and to remain close as her only family after that. The least she could do was show him some of his toughness had stuck and she could stand on her own.

"Thanks." She packed every emotion she had into the small word, hoping like hell he'd understand. "But you don't have to coddle me anymore."

"I don't coddle you," he argued, but his sudden merciless fascination with polishing the top of the display case in front of him outed the words for the lie they were.

Ava's muscles went tight over her breastbone. Damn, she'd really had it with this stupid bruise. "Okay," she said, leaning in to buss his cheek and deftly skip over the brewing conversation. She couldn't afford to get all gooey with her brother right now. She was going to need every ounce of toughness she could scrape together for this interview with Nick.

Which reminded her . . . "Anyway, thanks for the quick bite, but I've got to run. Tell Lily I hope she feels better."

Ava collected her things, giving Pete one last wave and good-bye before heading out the front door of the bakery. Wrapping her red wool scarf a little tighter to ward off the winter air, she aimed her boots down Main Street, gathering her thoughts along with her resolve. Pine Mountain was a lot smaller than Riverside, and even though Ava didn't really frequent any local spots other than the Sweet Life, she knew the footprint of the cozy town well enough to get her bearings. She'd recognized the address Nick had given her as belonging to the small group of apartments where her brother had lived before he and Lily had gotten married, which made getting from Point A to Point B easy enough.

Getting out of the car to actually walk up to Nick's apartment, especially with her lack of solid information on his past and the lingering memory of his ohhh-so-sexy stare?

Not exactly the same piece of cake.

"Stop being a sixth-grader," she whispered, the words riding out on tiny white puffs as she pushed her car door wide. Smoothing a hand over her crisp black pencil skirt, Ava stepped out of the car and made her way to the left side of the two-story L-shaped building. She ticked through the numbers on the pretty brass plates attached to the bricks, the heels of her slim leather boots clacking softly on the neat concrete path until she reached the apartment number Nick had given her. Without giving herself even a second to balk or get nervous, Ava placed a knock in the center of the glossy black door. She was a complete professional. She could do this. She *would*.

Oh, God, the sight of Nick Brennan still grabbed the breath right from her lungs.

"Hi." For a second, he just stood there on the threshold of the door he'd swung open, staring at her with those dark, brooding eyes so at odds with the extravagant lashes framing them. His lean, muscular frame fit perfectly beneath his white T-shirt, his broken-in jeans slung over his hips like they'd been born there, and just like that, Ava's pulse surged with speed and heat.

"It's freezing out there. Come on in," he continued, his gaze detaching from hers to do a quick sweep of the periphery over her shoulder. She turned to mimic the movement, her common sense finally barreling back into place.

"Are reporters bothering you here too?" she asked, swinging forward to follow him into the tiny foyer.

"No. I'm not listed, and none of them got ballsy enough to follow me home from work. At least, none that I know of." He tilted his head toward the hallway, his shower-damp hair falling in an infuriatingly sexy tousle that would look sloppy on nearly anyone else. "But thanks for meeting me here. Reporters aside, Pine Mountain's grapevine is kind of notorious. I figured this way, we'd have a better shot at privacy."

The idea skittered down Ava's spine as she followed him further inside, but she kicked it back with a deep breath. Nick was her source. She was here for the story, period. "I don't mind. It's your interview, so you should be comfortable. Plus, coming to Pine Mountain gave me a chance to visit my brother."

Nick's cross-trainers squeaked to a stop in front of his open-air kitchen. "Your brother lives here?"

"He runs the bakery on Main Street," Ava said over a nod. She slipped a covert gaze around the small but tidy kitchen. Becoming a reporter had taught her to gather information from even the smallest details. Nick's kitchen was sparse enough to offer the bare minimum—mostly clear Formica countertops, small breakfast table with two sturdy chairs by the window, one house plant that had seen far better days—but the realization sent a wash of heat through her belly.

Ava would bet her annual salary he lived alone. Double or nothing he spent most of his time at the Double Shot rather than at home. His dishwasher still had the plastic protective covering on the push buttons, for God's sake.

"Oh." Nick delivered the word with a healthy dose of surprise. "I've been pretty busy at work. I haven't had a chance to go down there and try it out yet."

"Wow, that bar must do a ton of business then. The Sweet Life has been open for a year and a half," she said, unable to keep the smile out of her words. Even though Pete had lived in Pine Mountain pretty much in name only until he'd met Lily and they'd opened the bakery together, the town was more tightly knit than a trunk full of sweaters. Most of the locals definitely knew him now.

Of course, Nick didn't seem to be like most locals. In fact, Ava didn't know anyone who worked as much as he appeared to.

Present company excluded, anyway.

"Yeah." He shrugged, shoulder muscles tightening beneath his white T-shirt as he pulled out one of the chairs at the kitchen table for Ava before turning to sit across from her. "We did a huge street fair about six months ago, and added a new head chef. The Double Shot has been pretty popular since then."

"Oh, right." Recognition pricked at Ava's memory. "I heard about that street fair on the radio. My friend Layla said it was a blast, actually."

"But you didn't come down from Riverside," Nick said, settling back against his padded seat cushion to look at her.

"No." She'd felt guilty for two days about faking the headache that had gotten her off the hook from attending, but it had been better than telling Layla the ugly truth.

A street fair run by a local bar and sponsored by an up-and-coming brewery equaled the sixth level of hell for the daughter of abusive alcoholics.

"So you've worked at the Double Shot for two years." Ava laced her fingers together, pressing the sides of her hands over the cool wood of the table, but Nick's unexpected smile caught her completely by surprise.

"You're pretty good at steering conversation. Changing the subject, that kind of thing."

"I'm not changing the subject," she said, hoping the burn on her face didn't equal a visible blush.

Nick snorted, but his smile didn't fade. "And now you're buying time."

"I'm making small talk," she argued, although she had to fight the urge to squirm. How the hell could he read her so clearly after seven freaking years?

"Gotta hand it to you, it's a subtle tactic. Probably part of what makes you a good reporter."

Shock barged through Ava's veins. "How do you know I'm a good reporter?"

"Because you keep asking all the questions."

"You mean the ones you're not answering?"

She clamped her mouth shut, a second too late, but to her surprise, Nick looked far from annoyed at her brash response.

"Touché," he said slowly, borrowing a page from her buying-time playbook. "I offered you the story on the fire. It only seemed smart to read up on your past work."

Oh God, he was serious. "You've read my articles?"

"The online archives aren't too difficult to access with a subscription to the *Daily*. Nice coverage of the Turnip Festival, by the way. I think it was your best piece."

Indignant heat snapped in her chest, launching a retort on a direct path from her brain to her lips, but she caught the words just short of delivery. The scowl she'd grown accustomed to was suspiciously absent from Nick's face, having been traded in for a black-coffee stare that pinned her with something softer and wide open.

Nick wasn't being hurtful or looking down at her. He was being honest.

"Um, thank you." Ava managed to layer a smile over her surprise. "I take all my stories seriously. Telling them well is important to me."

The corners of Nick's mouth lifted just enough beneath his dark goatee to form a slow and sexy half smile that traveled directly to Ava's belly.

"Guess I picked the right person for the exclusive then."

"I'm glad you feel that way." She held on to their eye contact even though it did nothing to dissipate the heat brewing between her hips, and oh God, she wanted his mouth on hers. His hands, strong and callused and oh so capable, were only inches away on the table, close enough for Ava to feel the heat of them on her fingers. It would take a bare flick of her wrist, just a small hint of movement, and her hands could be on his, tugging him forward, eliminating the space between them in less than a breath.

Her rational voice served up a stern reminder that she needed to say something, to sit up straight in her chair and work this story like a professional. But then Nick leaned forward, his gorgeous dark brown eyes dropping to her lips, and both the story and her professionalism were the last things on Ava's mind.

Chapter Nine

Brennan was going straight to hell if he didn't get a handle on himself and dig up some control right fuck-ing *now*.

"Are you hungry? I can make lunch," he blurted, clearing his throat as he shifted back from the table with an awk-ward *thump*. Christ, he was the worst sort of idiot, but if he didn't change the subject and reboot the rational part of his brain, then he was going to pull Ava right out of her chair and kiss her into next week.

And if he kissed her once, he was going to make up for all that lost time by kissing her again. And again. Every-where.

Without even leaving the kitchen.

"Oh. Um, sure," Ava said, yanking her hand over the table to straighten the already even hem of her sweater. "What can I do to help?"

"Well, it's not glamorous, but I've got some stuff for sandwiches." Brennan sent up a silent prayer of gratitude for a task to keep his mind busy and his dick from doing any independent thinking, then another that he'd had the foresight to stop at the market in Riverside after his PT session this morning. "There's bread in the cupboard over there."

"Got it." Her boots clacked softly over the scuffed but clean floor, covering the space in a handful of strides. He moved around her, pulling some turkey and a container of coleslaw from the fridge, and damn, it felt a little too natural to have Ava in his space.

Food. Plates. Breathe.

"You mentioned your sisters the other night. How are they all doing?" Ava asked, and although the question took him by complete surprise, his answer flowed out with unexpected ease.

"They're good. Carrie, Jill, and Marissa all live in Fairview with their husbands, and I've got three nieces and a nephew between them. Ellie went rogue and moved a whopping ten minutes away to South Valley. She's getting married on Christmas Day."

"Are you kidding me?" Ava placed the bread on the counter between them with a laugh, slipping by him to wash her hands at the sink. "The last time I saw her she was still in high school. How is she old enough to get married?"

Brennan lifted his hands in a nonverbal version of *you got me*, trying to focus on the food in front of him rather than the memory of the weekend Ellie had come to visit Sapphire Island seven years ago. Of course, Ellie had loved Ava nearly as much as Brennan had.

"I have no idea," he said, falling in behind her to wait for a turn at the sink. "But apparently it's going to be the event of the holiday season. Her fiancé is an attorney with the biggest firm in Fairview and he just made partner, so they're socially obligated to invite half the planet."

Because going back to Fairview and seeing his family in person for the first time in two years wasn't going to be hard enough. At least with all the focus on Ellie and Josh, Brennan would be able to stick to the shadows until he could get back to Pine Mountain.

The spotlight in Fairview hadn't liked him the first time around. And God knew he'd learned to dodge it like a pro.

"Oooh. Sounds high profile. And very fancy." Ava stood at the slim stretch of counter space by the refrigerator, shooting him an impressed glance before taking a visual inventory of the ingredients he'd assembled.

Brennan shrugged, but his shoulders felt overstarched and tight. "I guess."

"Still not a suit and tie kind of guy, huh?" Her sassy smile chipped away at his unease, and just for a second, he relaxed.

"What gave it away?"

"Besides the totally pained look on your face, you mean?"

Oh, no. No way was he going to let her get away with teasing him like that, even if it was easing his tension over going to Ellie's wedding. "It's not my fault that most neckties double as torture devices," Brennan replied, pulling a butter knife from the drawer at his hip.

"Mmm." Ava cocked her head at him, her hair spilling over one shoulder. "Spend six hours in Spanx and a strapless push-up bra. Then we'll talk torture."

The thought of Ava's flawlessly round breasts peeking out from a bright red strapless dress at Sapphire Island's end-of-summer beach party invaded his memory, and the butter knife fumbled to the floor with a clatter.

"Shit," he hissed, commanding his eyes to look anywhere other than the seductive curves beneath Ava's body-skimming black skirt.

Too late. Damn, she was still hotter than a six-story inferno in the middle of July.

"You okay?" Ava asked, bending down to retrieve the knife as he tried to erase the hint of lace showing through her thin sweater from his vision, and Brennan nodded just a hair too vigorously.

"Yup! Yes. I'm great." As long as *great* was synonymous with *a total flipping jackass*, anyway. How did he manage to lose his mind so thoroughly around this woman? "I was going to make Rachel sandwiches. Have you ever had one?"

Ava's eyes lit with curiosity. "It's like a Reuben, right?"

"Same idea, different ingredients." Brennan pulled a clean knife from the drawer, putting it to use on the bread and butter in front of him before he could go for round two in the dropping-things department. "They're made with turkey and coleslaw instead of corned beef and sauerkraut."

"Ohhhh." She watched for a minute as he placed a skillet over the small cooktop next to the prep space, letting the blue-tipped flames *whoosh* to life before turning toward the bread.

"Because the coleslaw already has dressing in it, you don't really need a ton of ingredients for these sandwiches. That's kind of the beauty of it. They're easy to make *and* they taste great."

"What about cheese?" Ava asked, nodding down at the thinly cut turkey he'd just layered over the coleslaw and bread.

"There's some Swiss in the fridge. Bet it would be a good match for these."

She took the cheese from the refrigerator beside him, placing two lacy slices on each sandwich before finishing the assembly with the remaining bread. Brennan lowered both sandwiches to the prewarmed skillet with a soft sizzle, the sweet, heady scent of melting butter and toasting bread filling his senses with a whole lot of *hell yes*.

Ava gestured toward the pan. "Looks like you found your calling, working with food. Those smell great."

"Thanks, but as much as I like managing the Double Shot, food isn't my calling." He nudged the sandwiches with a spatula, blanking his expression over the words that had just escaped past his lips.

Of course, Ava was too quick not to catch his slip. "No?" She let the word hang on the unspoken question of what his calling really was, but Brennan just stared at the pan, pressing down on the sandwiches with his spatula even though Adrian always harped about it wrecking the flavors.

"No." Silence threaded through the kitchen, punctuated only by the muted hiss of the bread as it went from pale wheat to deep, golden brown. They might've made some headway with regard to what had happened between them seven years ago, but the later part of his past needed to stay where it belonged.

Some things just couldn't be resolved.

"There are some napkins in the drawer over there," Brennan said, kicking the thought to his emotional curb. "If you want to grab them, these are just about ready."

"Okay, sure." If Ava was bothered by his nonresponse, she didn't show it, and the lack of discomfort in the quiet between them actually put Brennan at ease. *Telling her what had happened at Joe's the other day might not be so bad,* he thought with a mental shrug. If the facts were going to come out regardless, he'd rather Ava tell them than anyone else—he'd meant it when he'd said she was a good reporter. And anyway, once the article was printed and the story was there in black and white, the whole thing would likely die down within a week—this time for real. Then he could put his head down and *finally* get back to normal.

Only half paying attention to the familiar scoop-and-flip

he'd learned ages ago at the Double Shot, Brennan slid the sandwiches onto a pair of simple blue plates he'd pulled from the cupboard, turning toward Ava with a growing smile.

"I hope you're hungry, because . . ."

But the rest of his sentence jammed in his throat at the sight of Ava standing frozen in front of the catchall drawer, her fingers firmly grasping the black and white photograph.

"You still have this?" The paper fluttered slightly in her hand, her lashes swept wide in an arc of shadowy surprise.

"Uh, I . . ." For a split second, Brennan nearly gave in to the protective instinct screaming at him to clam up, to dodge the subject and pack away his feelings. But stuffing things aside was what had gotten them into trouble in the first place. He might not be willing to tell Ava about the career he'd left in pieces or the pain and addiction that followed, but damn it, she'd told him about her shitty home life even though it had made her vulnerable. He could at least give her honesty about keeping the photograph.

"Yeah. I do." Forgetting the plates on the counter, Brennan cut the space between himself and Ava to less than a foot. "Do you remember the day I took this picture?"

"Yes." Her voice was barely a murmur, but she met his gaze without faltering. "We were at Butterfly Cove."

He nodded, calling up the memory as he reached out to run a finger over the top edge of the photograph. "You wanted to see if the place lived up to its name."

Ava laughed, whisper soft. "I thought it was just a story all the guys had made up to get unsuspecting girls to sneak off to the secluded side of the island with them."

"You were definitely cynical," he remembered, and God, he could still picture that look of sheer doubt on her face at the promise of the flower-covered meadow leading up to the lushly private beach cove. "But you've got to admit, I wasn't wrong."

Her nod was barely there, the slight dip of her chin edging her close enough for Brennan to feel the slow heat of her exhale. "You weren't wrong. I've still never seen close to that many butterflies in one place in my life. That cove was straight out of a movie, it was so beautiful."

Something far, far outside his control closed the last breath of space between their bodies, and even after all this time, she still fit against his frame, belly to hips, shoulders to chest.

"Do you want to know why I still have this?" He captured the photograph from between Ava's fingers, placing it face up on the countertop before letting his hand coast over the warm cashmere on her shoulder.

"So you wouldn't forget that night?"

A slow smile loaded with both irony and heat tugged at the corners of his mouth. She hadn't been *entirely* wrong about his motivation for bringing her to that cove, and they'd taken full advantage of the seclusion offered by the exotic scenery. "If I live to be ninety, I'll never forget that night."

"Then why would you keep the picture?" She shivered, and the move sent tiny vibrations over the pads of Brennan's fingers as he slid them up the soft column of her neck and into her hair.

"Because, Ava. After seven years, I still couldn't quite let you go."

Somewhere in the dark hallways of Brennan's calm, rational brain, a voice was telling him that being this close to Ava was a five-alarm recipe for disaster. What he needed was to take a step back, to batten down the reckless want that threatened his ability to think objectively, and give her a nice, tidy interview so they could part ways, no harm, no foul.

Brennan kissed her without hesitation.

His mouth found Ava's in a rush, the contact so warm and downright magnetic, he felt it on every inch of his skin. She melted against him, rising on her toes to minimize the seven-inch height difference between their bodies, and the upward press notched her hips over his with agonizing friction that snapped his very last thread of control. Brennan parted her lips in a bold claim, drawing the sugar-sweet taste of her right back under his tongue where it belonged as the kiss became deeper, hotter, more.

"This is crazy," she murmured, the throaty whisper tumbling over his shoulder as he bent to slide his mouth down the plane of her neck. But Brennan had waited seven fucking years for this. Impulsive, daring, reckless, he wanted Ava right here, right now.

"*You* make me crazy." He opened his lips over her throat, his tongue sliding wildly over her even wilder pulse as he hooked a thumb beneath her chin for better access. Ava's hands tightened on his biceps, the pressure both stinging and sweet.

"Keep doing that, and we'll both be crazy together."

Her mouth was back on his in a flash, her arms so tight around his shoulders that he had to bite back a groan. Everything that had made him want her in the past had grown brighter and multiplied, and when she swept her tongue over the seam of his lips, there was no second thought. Thrusting his hands into the dark spill of her hair, Brennan held her fast against the kitchen counter, relearning the heart-shaped heat of her mouth with his lips and tongue.

"*Oh.*" Her body was angled so tightly against his, Brennan felt the sigh collapse from her chest just as much as he heard the sexy half moan. Breaking from Ava's mouth, he edged his way down her jaw to her earlobe, and sweet Jesus, how could she taste so good everywhere?

On nothing more than wicked impulse, Brennan swung her around to press her back to the nearby wall, his aching cock demanding contact with the cradle of her hips. But before he could reclaim his position all the way against her body, Ava dropped one hand to the tiny fragment of daylight between the lower plane of his torso and her belly. Her fingers coasted over the top of his jeans, sliding across one hip bone to the muscles lining his inner thigh, and holy shit, he was going to explode right here in his kitchen.

"Ava." The word was damn near a growl, but caring about that ranked pretty low on his list of priorities right now. "If you do that, I'm not going to be able to stop."

"But I don't want to stop. I want—"

The ear-shredding sound of the smoke alarm sent them careening apart.

"Damn it!" Brennan's heart vaulted against his rib cage, and he swung toward the cooktop, shielding Ava out of instinct. A thick tendril of white smoke curled upward from beneath the burner he'd used to make the sandwiches, the sharp punch of something on fire knocking through his senses. Three firm strides had him in front of the stove, his brain firing on every last cylinder as he zeroed in on the smoldering offender stuck under the heavy black grate.

Registering the tiny lick of bright orange flame bursting from the coal black chunk of whatever was burning, Brennan kicked into motion. The oversized box of baking soda lurking in his fridge was in his hand automatically, the contents smothering the flames with a decisive flick of his wrist. Pulling an oven mitt from the drawer at his side, he slid it over one hand while grabbing the discarded spatula from the counter with the other. He lifted the metal grate from over the burner with his protected hand, and a quick scrape and toss with the spatula had the burning item in the sink a second later.

"Jeez." Ava blinked, moving in a delayed reaction to fan the air with a dish towel as Brennan doused the mess in the sink for good measure. When he was certain it was good and soaked, he turned to open the window by the entryway, and thankfully, the blaring alarm fell silent with the gust of clean air.

"Part of the bread's crust must've broken off when I took the sandwiches out of the pan. Looks like it got caught beneath the burner," he said, his voice echoing in his head after the deafening harshness of the now-quiet alarm. Okay, so it was an innocuous chunk of food, which had caused more noise than harm, but really—how the hell had he missed the acrid smell now permeating the kitchen, or the veil of smoke drifting toward the window?

How had he let himself get distracted enough to lose control of his surroundings—his safety, *Ava's* safety, for Chrissake?

The answer was currently giving him a wide, green stare with no less than a thousand questions behind it.

"You're so calm. I never would've been able to move that fast, let alone think of using baking soda," Ava said, biting her lip. She was clearly calculating her thoughts by the second, and Brennan's defenses snapped back into place at Mach 2.

"You shouldn't use water in a kitchen fire in case there's grease involved. And baking soda is less messy than a fire extinguisher for flare-ups." He shrugged, but the tension knotting his shoulders made the gesture feel as clumsy as it probably looked.

Ava's brows winged upward as she pointed to his barren

kitchen counters. "You barely have pots and pans, but you have a fire extinguisher?"

Crap. "Well, yeah. Better safe, you know."

"Sure, I guess." Ava paused, her expression becoming hesitant to match his. "Listen, about . . . what happened before the alarm. I want—"

"You don't have to say anything." Okay, so Brennan knew that interrupting her was rude as hell, but he had to cut this conversation off at the knees before it went any further. "In fact, it's probably better if we forget it happened."

"Forget it happened," Ava echoed, taking a step back even though her face was unreadable. But he'd given up every ounce of the composure he damn well needed the second he'd put his mouth back on hers. She made him impulsive—*crazy*—and losing that much control, especially to the point of vulnerability, simply couldn't happen.

Not again. Not after his recklessness had cost his best friend's life.

"Yeah. We got caught up in the past there, but what's done is done. Right now I owe you an interview. So if you want, we can get to business."

A ripple of something Brennan couldn't quite label moved over her face. For a second, he thought she'd argue in that trademark jump-right-in way of hers, and damn it, kissing Ava had been ridiculously stupid, because now all he wanted was to taste her again.

But then she stepped back, and the damage was done.

"Right. The story." Ava dropped one last gaze at the photograph on the counter before she opened the drawer to trade it for a handful of paper napkins. "I'm ready if you are."

She shut the drawer with a firm *snick*, heading toward her seat at the table without looking back.

Chapter Ten

Ava surveyed her absolute minefield of a desk, wondering how on earth she could have so much information without an actual story anywhere in sight.

Unless you counted the fact that twenty-four hours post-interview, she still had an absolute ruckus going on between her thighs every time she thought of the source of her nonstory, and it was only getting stronger by the second. Now *that* was pretty damned newsworthy. Stupid, hot, toe-curling, impulsive kiss.

Oh God, it had been so. Freaking. Hot.

"Good morning, sunshine." The sound of Layla's voice at the entryway to her microchip-sized cubicle made Ava jump, her heart giving her sternum a good, hard *thwack* back to reality.

"Jeez!" Ava blurted, unable to cage her surprise, and Layla's blue eyes narrowed in confusion.

"Sorry. I didn't mean to sneak up on you, but I've got a bunch of proofs from the fire. Since you interviewed the hero guy and the piece is running tomorrow, I thought you'd want to help choose a shot so we can get this article to bed ASAP."

"Oh, right. Sure," Ava said, squashing the prickle of

heat brewing at the base of her spine. If she had any prayer of actually finishing this story without spontaneously combusting, she was going to have to figure out a way to douse the fire threatening to ignite in her drawers at every mention of Nick Brennan.

Although when she remembered how quickly he'd shut down and rebuffed her after their scorching-hot kiss, and how perfunctory their following interview had been despite all her efforts to engage him with her questions, his rejection on both fronts should really have done the trick. After all, she'd opened up her emotional floodgates about why she'd left Sapphire Island, and while the truth about their past had been a long time coming, he'd still slammed the door on returning the favor.

Too bad for him, Ava didn't believe a word of either his personal brush-off or his just-the-facts-ma'am story. She'd felt that kiss in every cell of her body, and despite the seven years that had passed between them, she knew from his expression he'd felt the deeply hot pull of the encounter too. He hadn't saved that picture of her by accident. And with those overly starched one-word answers to every interview question, no way was the whole business-only thing authentic.

Brennan was hiding something about his past, and Ava was damn well going to find out what it was.

Sighing, Ava gave her laptop one last frown before unfolding herself from behind her desk. She scooped up the blue, fabric-bound book where she kept all her notes and story ideas, following Layla down the hall and placing it on the table with a soft *thump* as her friend closed the conference room door behind them.

"Okay, what gives?" Layla's expression went from casual to curious before her butt even hit the seat across from Ava. "And before you even think of insulting me by saying *nothing*, let me remind you that nearly everyone in this building is at lunch, we're behind closed doors, and as one of your closest friends and the person who's working this story with you, you are morally obligated to dish."

Whoa. "Let's not get crazy," Ava said in an effort to wrangle a little time. "I don't think there's anything to dish on."

Layla's snort was borderline unladylike. "You're manipulating the conversation like a true reporter, you know that? You've been making your irritated face all morning, and now you're dodging the question and hoping I won't notice. Pardon me while I fly the bullshit flag with your name stitched to the side."

"Remind me to take you on my next difficult interview," Ava muttered. Her chances at keeping this mess close to the vest fell somewhere between *snowball* and *chance in hell*. She wasn't keen on blabbing about her past, and the impulsive kiss she'd shared with Brennan definitely fractured the rules of propriety. But Layla was savvy as sin. No way was her friend going to let her slide with a garden-variety *I'm fine*.

Ava sighed in defeat. "Okay. So I'm having a little trouble with this article."

"*You* are having trouble with a breakout article." Layla's expression clearly outlined her doubt. "You're the most dedicated reporter at the *Daily*, you nailed an exclusive on Pine Mountain's biggest news event, and you've been dying for a personal interest story like this for the last five years. What's the problem?"

Ava picked at an imaginary thread on the sleeve of her shirt. "The problem is my source."

"The bar manager?" Layla asked, and Ava's thread-picking intensified.

"Yeah. It's possible that I, ah, have met Brennan before this week."

Layla's jaw unhinged. "You know the hometown hero guy?"

Lord, did she know him. Dark, sexy smile, mouth parted over the sensitive skin on her neck, kissing lower and lower . . .

Ava swallowed hard. Yesterday's kiss, though unplanned and obviously mutual, had still been a conflict of interest for Ava. Brennan was her source, at least for the next twenty-four hours. Gary might not care so much about blurred ethical lines, but Ava still needed to be careful about divulging anything that would put Layla in a bad position disclosure-wise.

Even if Ava had no intention of repeating yesterday's hotly impulsive kissing session with Nick Brennan. It was over and done, get your parting gifts at the door.

"Brennan and I . . . worked together right after college."

One look at Layla's crossed arms and sky-high brows told Ava she had no chance of easing into this share-fest slowly, and her friend's response knocked the sentiment home.

"You're a total barracuda when it comes to work. No way just being simple acquaintances in the past would mess with your ability to write a story."

"That's a lovely analogy. Thank you." Ava gave the words an extra coating of sarcasm, tossing a crumpled-up page of blank paper at her friend.

It missed by about three feet. "You're welcome. Now spill it."

Blowing out a breath of defeat, Ava forked over a basically clean and definitely condensed version of the summer she'd spent with Brennan, sticking with a vague summer-fling-separate-ways explanation of their parting. Seven years had passed since anyone had pitied her upbringing, and revisiting that reality made Ava's stomach pinch beneath her gray dress pants.

"Wow. I can't believe you had a summer fling with Mr. Rescue!" Layla said, swiveling her gaze to the photo proofs on the table. "Although kudos to you, because really, he's not hard to look at."

"Focus, Layla." Ava frowned, although she purposely kept her eyes forward. It was hard enough keeping her mental images of Brennan in check. An actual, God's honest photograph might send her overeager libido around the freaking bend, and she had an article to finish. "I've been over my notes a thousand times, and I'm telling you, something about this story is too neat."

"But you've got a lot of facts, right? Enough to write the article you promised Gary?"

"Brennan told me what happened, yes, and I wrote up a preliminary piece based on that." Ava reached for her notebook, the spine giving a timeworn creak as she propped it open. "But the man is the master of the two-word answer. If I strung together every last syllable he gave up about that fire, I'd have half a page's worth of words, max. Plus, there's barely a trace of the guy on the Internet, so all I've got is what little he was willing to tell."

"Yikes." Layla leaned in to look at Ava's notes, which were still slathered in question marks of various shapes and sizes. "Your exclusive doesn't sound very . . . well, exclusive."

"Exactly." Ava snapped the book shut, trying to keep her frustration from bubbling over. "Gary wants a showstopper here. A rundown of the facts will be nice, but he's on the go-sell-newspapers warpath. I promised him the impact story of the year, and I swore to him that I could work a source. *Nice* isn't going to save my bacon."

"Hmm. It is a little weird that Brennan's being so secretive, even if you guys did have a thing once. But maybe he's just a good guy who's kind of private and got lucky rescuing a kid."

"He's definitely a good guy," Ava said automatically. "And the facts back up his right-place-right-time story. But my gut is telling me he's a good guy who was in the right place at the right time . . . who's also hiding something."

"Well, let's see here." Layla sifted through the proof shots littered over the table between them, plucking a glossy eight-by-ten from the pile. She studied the photograph for a minute, squinting her eyes behind the frames of her stylish glasses. "Wait a sec. You said he went to the fire academy in his hometown, right?"

"He was definitely planning on attending right after the summer we were together. And as far as I can tell, he enrolled," Ava said, flipping through her scribbled notes. "I had to dig pretty deep, but I found a public record in the Fairview City database with his name listed as a recruit. The file doesn't say whether or not he ever became a firefighter, though, and when I got anywhere close to the subject during the interview, he totally clammed up."

"I'm not sure you need a public record in order to figure out whether Brennan was ever a firefighter." Layla passed the photo she'd been studying across the table. "Take a look at this and tell me what you see."

The image of Nick, four steps from the burst-open doors at Joe's Grocery, greeted her with a scalpel-sharp pang. His face was smudged with soot and bent in ironclad determination, showing a grimace that looked oddly like pain. Matthew Wilson lay balanced across his back, and although the little boy's face was turned to the side, Brennan carried him with clear confidence, his hands locked tight over the child's wrist and arm as he lunged forward.

Ava scooped in a breath. "I see Brennan rescuing Matty Wilson."

"Right," Layla led. "Now look really closely."

She dropped her eyes to the picture again, forcing herself to be objective, to gather information, to soak in every detail. The solid set of Brennan's torso as he shouldered Matthew's weight, the sense of surety dominating his dark features, the pull of his muscles over the grip on Matthew's much smaller body.

The pieces snapped together in one holy-crap instant. "He's got him in a fireman's carry."

"It's textbook," Layla said. "My brother's a marine, and he used to practice it on me all the time. Firefighters use the same maneuver."

"Okay." Ava paused, trying like mad to remain calm and unbiased despite the full-throttle *I-knew-it!* ricocheting through her gut. Following her instincts was her first rule of thumb when it came to uncovering a story, but she'd learned the hard way that assumptions were a bad idea unless she had the facts to back them up.

And if she botched *this* story, her job would be in the toilet, and the only thing she'd be writing would be obituaries. Starting with the one for her French-fried career.

"It's still not enough."

Layla pulled back in surprise. "But you said—"

"I know what I said, and I know what I think," Ava cut in, with more resignation than heat. "But the last time I let my gut do the talking for an article, the paper almost got sued and I damn near got fired. As much as I want a kick-ass story, I can't print what I can't prove."

"So what are you going to do?" Layla asked, and only

then did Ava realize she'd grabbed her notebook to head for the door.

"Writing this story with what I've got is better than printing a bunch of sensationalist conjecture that I can't back up, no matter how loud my instincts are screaming. I'm going to write up my article with the facts I've got and turn it in to make my deadline. I don't have a choice."

Hand on the doorknob, she paused just long enough to shoot a look of sheer determination over her shoulder.

"And once I put this article to bed, I'm going to get the real damn story on Nick Brennan."

Ava squared off with the Double Shot for the third time in a week, but strangely, the punch of being at a bar didn't rankle as much as it had that first night. Yes, the harsh, invasive smell of liquor still put her gag reflex to the test, but the atmosphere was actually pretty fun, and the cheeseburger she'd ordered the other night had practically given her a foodgasm right there on her bar stool.

Plus, there were answers behind that bar. Answers Ava wanted. Almost as bad as she wanted the man who held them.

Kissing Brennan yesterday might've been utterly reckless, but she couldn't deny the truth. Ava had sure as hell meant it when she'd said she didn't want to stop. Despite her job as a reporter and the apparent secrets in his past, Nick Brennan still turned her on like stadium lights at the Super Bowl.

Ava's heels tapped a staccato beat over the time-polished floorboards as she crossed the Double Shot's dining room and walked over to the bar. The place was busy for a Tuesday, but not nearly as packed as it had been over the weekend. Most of the tables were already occupied with people in various stages of drinking and dining, and if she had to guess, she'd peg nearly all of them as locals.

The atmosphere was casual and comfortable, and Ava sent up a silent prayer of thanks that she'd gone home to trade her work clothes in for a pair of jeans and a gauzy white peasant blouse. The four-inch heels she'd chosen to round out her look might be pushing the limits of casual, but if Brennan got to have that sexy, deceptively soft kiss-me stubble, then by God, Ava could rock a pair of strappy heels in her own defense.

"Hey! Looks like we might make a regular out of you, huh?" Teagan's voice rose above the din of the restaurant, bringing Ava back down to the present tense.

"So far, so good. Looks like things are settling down a little around here," she said, glancing around one last time as she slid into her seat at the end of the bar. She opened her mouth to ask for an Arnold Palmer, but Teagan had the pint glass half full of ice and the lemonade in her hand before Ava could get the words out.

"Quiet is kind of relative when you're running a bar and grill, but yes. This is more our normal speed around the holidays." Teagan grinned, jutting her chin at the bar area. "How's your sternum?" she asked, but the question was so nonchalant that Ava didn't think twice.

"It's a festive shade of faded green, but otherwise, it's fabulous." She capped her sarcasm with a self-deprecating smile. As embarrassing as it was to have been shoved over by Mike-the-jackass-Trotter, Ava had survived worse.

Teagan chuckled softly as she uncapped a beer for a guy sitting a few seats down the bar. "Most people get pretty rattled at being knocked down like that."

Ava took in the veiled compliment with surprise. "I

guess. But getting upset wouldn't have changed anything. The only thing I could control was whether or not I got up, so I did."

Teagan placed the iced-tea-and-lemonade-filled pint glass on a bar napkin in front of Ava, her laugh growing. "Lord, this is going to get good," she murmured under her breath, following immediately with, "I'll tell Brennan you're here."

"What makes you think I'm here to see Brennan?"

One reddish brow arched. "I'm just shooting rubber bands at the night sky here, but I'm pretty sure no woman in the history of the XX chromosome ever wore four-inch heels in December for fun."

Shit. "Fair enough," Ava admitted. "I've got the mock-up of the article I wrote on the fire. I thought he might like to see it before it runs in tomorrow's *Daily*."

"Sure." Teagan shifted toward the door leading back to the kitchen, but at the last minute, she turned to float a glance over one shoulder. "And Ava? Nice pick on the shoes. Definitely cute."

Ava put the nervous energy zapping through her veins to good work, reaching into the bag she'd slung over the ladder back of her bar stool to unearth her copy of the article. Although it was way lighter on emotion than Ava would've liked—and Gary was expecting—she had to admit, the piece in her hands was a solid account of the fire. Ava had managed to add a dash of optimism by detailing the way Pine Mountain's community had rallied around the effort to rebuild Joe's Grocery. All in all, the piece was solid, professional, and thorough.

And despite knowing she'd done the safe thing—the smart thing—in writing the story as it was, Ava *still* couldn't shake the gut-deep notion that she'd barely scratched the dark and brooding surface of Nick Brennan's story.

"I'm surprised you're here." Brennan's voice reached her from a few paces away, where he'd stopped short behind the bar to stare at her with an expression that backed up his words.

"It takes more than a gruff attitude and a serious face to scare me away," Ava said over a tart smile. Okay, so she hadn't meant to tease him, but the startled laugh he gave in response made her glad that her sassy instincts had a mind of their own.

"I'm not trying to scare you away. And I'm not *that* serious."

Ava couldn't help it. She scoffed. "You do own a mirror, right?" She swung an index finger around her face in a circular motion before adding, "Not that being serious is a bad thing. You could probably win a mint in Vegas with a poker face like that."

"So you think I need to loosen up." Brennan moved closer, crossing his arms over the front of his dark blue T-shirt. God, it was an epically bad plan to flirt with him, especially given her recent tendency to kiss first and ask questions later. But the dark-edged smirk tilting the corners of his mouth short-circuited her common sense.

"You said it, not me. But for the record, a little relaxing never hurt anybody."

"Says the woman who's married to her job."

Ava raised his smirk and went all in. "To the man who reinvented the workaholic."

Brennan opened his mouth, then closed it as he folded, still smiling. "Nothing wrong with being dedicated to your job."

"I couldn't agree more. It's actually why I'm here." Ava

swung her legs a quarter turn on her bar stool, sliding the mock-up of their interview from her bag. "Here's your article. I turned in the final copy before I left work, but I thought you might like to read it before tomorrow's paper hits the stands."

Brennan eyed the two sheets of paper as if they'd detonate on contact with his fingers. "I didn't know it was customary to share an article before it runs in the paper."

Ava placed the pages on the bar, splitting the distance between herself and Brennan on the glossy wood. "It's not."

"Then why did you bring this out here?" he asked, his nearly black eyes flaring in surprise.

The truth danced on Ava's tongue, and ah, to hell with it. The piece was done, and as hot as it burned, her curiosity about Brennan's past wasn't the only thing that had led her to the Double Shot tonight. "Personal courtesy. You seemed pretty reluctant during our interview, so I thought maybe reading the article before it runs would put your mind at ease."

"Oh." He paused, but then moved forward to pick up the pages from the bar. "Thanks." A few minutes of quiet passed between them, marked only by the comfortable din of clinking cutlery and the muted twang of the overhead music while Brennan read. Finally, he lifted his gaze. "This is just the facts. All you did was tell the story."

"That's my job," Ava said, gripping the rounded edge of the bar in front of her. "I mean, yes, I also interviewed an eyewitness and incorporated her account to fill in the events that occurred before you got there, and I pulled from the press release from the fire department for some of the technical aspects as well as talking to Joe, but . . ."

Brennan waved her off, stepping in until only two feet

of mahogany and her fading-by-the-second willpower kept them from touching. "No, no. I didn't mean that as a bad thing. In fact, the story is good. Great."

Ava's lips parted, her shocked breath heating the sliver of space between them. "You think the article is great?" Granted, she'd worked her butt off to squeeze every last drop of emotion out of the straight-up time line he'd given her, but still . . .

"You got all the facts just right, and you didn't make the story overblown or dramatic. You told it exactly the way it happened. So yeah, I do." He rocked back on his heels, but only far enough to give the pages he'd placed back on the bar a tap with his fingers. "How come you think you're not a good reporter?"

"Aside from my boss's daily reminders that I can't handle the job, you mean?"

Crap! Now was so *not* the time for her brain-to-mouth filter to completely malfunction. Ava scrambled for something—anything—to smooth over her impetuous admission, but of course Brennan was quicker on the verbal draw.

"Looks like you handle being a reporter just fine to me." He reached out to return the copy of the article to her hands, and she slid the papers back into her bag on a shrug.

"Thanks. But my boss is more of a style over substance kind of guy." She wouldn't be shocked if Gary had emerged from the womb on the hunt for a way to increase his bottom line, the splashier the better.

"No disrespect," Brennan said, kicking his jeans-clad legs into a casual lean against the counter facing both her and the bar. "But your boss sounds like an ass."

Ava paused. She'd already whipped the lid off this con- versation. No sense holding back now. "Well, he's an ass who signs my paychecks, and reporting jobs don't exactly grow on trees. It's a small price to pay, and he doesn't break any rules even though his ethics are a tad questionable."

"I don't mean to be thick, but you're from a pretty big city. Doesn't the news in Philly blow Riverside's current events out of the water?"

"Yeah." She propped an elbow on the bar top, twisting the corner of her cocktail napkin around her index finger. God, her memories of Philadelphia stung, but it wasn't as if she hadn't already told Brennan the worst of them. Plus, even when she'd spilled the details of her nasty past, he hadn't treated her like fragile goods. As crushing as it was, that past had made her stronger. She could handle this.

Ava lifted her chin, looking right into Brennan's black-coffee eyes. "The jobs in Philadelphia are better, sure. But twenty-plus years of crappy memories kind of made relocating a no-brainer for me. I only stayed in the city for four days after I got back from Sapphire Island. Within a week, Nadine and I were living in a loft apartment up the road from my place now."

"In Riverside?" Brennan's gaze flashed with curiosity in the spill of the multicolored Christmas lights strung behind the bar. "I thought she was from Uniondale."

"She is, sort of." Ava waited for Brennan to pop the tops off a handful of beers and send them on their way down the bar before leaning in toward him. "Her parents run the restaurant on Sapphire Island in the summer, so they live most of the year in Uniondale, since it's so close. But her mom's side of the family is huge, and they're all from Riverside. Nadine and her parents and sisters come up to ski and spend the holidays at Pine Mountain Resort every year."

He straightened. "So you came to Riverside for a fresh start."

"It seemed as good a place as any, and it was close

enough to my brother to work out," she said. "Of course he moved from Philadelphia to Pine Mountain after that anyway. Old habits, I guess."

"It's cool that you guys are close. I wish . . ." Brennan stopped short, but damn, his expression was as unreadable as ancient Sanskrit. "So, ah, is Nadine still in Riverside?"

Ava shook her head, the change in subject scooping up her full attention. "No. She got married last year. She and her husband moved to Phoenix for his job. We still e-mail a few times a year though." Her mind shifted, curiosity taking over. "How about you and Mason? Do you still keep in touch?"

"No." Brennan's movements halted so completely that Ava didn't press for more. She understood all too keenly how friends could drift apart, and her relationship with Nadine was living proof. Truth was, even though they weren't nearly as close as they'd once been, Ava still owed Nadine's family a massive debt of gratitude. They'd always included her at holiday gatherings and family get-togethers without question, and even though she'd never quite felt that she seamlessly belonged there because Nadine's family was just so massive, that surrogate support had served as a constant reminder of why sticking close to Pete was so vital.

He was the only family she'd ever have. Staying in the Blue Ridge wasn't just a want for Ava.

It was an absolute necessity.

"Anyway." She chased the word with a swallow of her drink, the lemonade tart on her tongue. "To answer your original question, I've got nearly five years of seniority at the *Daily*, and even though my boss can be difficult, writing stories like yours is what I'm made for. Even if it means putting up with tough hours and tougher criticism."

A look Ava couldn't pin with a name flickered across

Brennan's face, his expression going blank before he said, "Looks like I'm not the only one who could loosen up around here."

"Wishful thinking, I'm afraid. I don't really have time for loosening up." She gestured to her bag, which was currently crammed with enough work to send her on an all-night word bender. Just because she'd turned in the story on the fire didn't mean she was off the hook for everything else Gary usually dump-trucked onto her desk.

"So tell me something." Brennan stopped to fill another drink order before satisfying Ava's ramped-up curiosity. "Does your ass of a boss give you a lunch break?"

"Yeah," Ava said, but it came out way more question than definitive fact. "Although I'm pretty sure the cold PB and J I scarf down over the sink in the break room doesn't count as relaxing."

He shuddered slightly before following up with a half smile. "I'm going to have to agree with you there. I've got something different in mind if you want to blow off some steam, but it's a little unorthodox. You game?"

Realization hit her with all the subtlety of a Mack truck on a downhill grade. "Are you asking me to lunch?"

"I'm asking if you want to do something relaxing on your lunch break," Brennan corrected. "Since according to you, I could use a little loosening up anyway. Plus"—he paused, sinking a thumb through one of the belt loops on his flawlessly worn jeans—"I was kind of gruff yesterday during our interview. It wasn't on purpose." Another pause, and his words arrowed right to Ava's belly. "But I'd like to make it up to you."

"Oh. Well, in that case, sure." The answer vaulted right past her lips, but she belatedly added, "You're not going to ask me to do anything totally weird, are you?" One of these days, she was going to have to do something about her complete reversal of the look-before-you-leap strategy.

But today was not that day, because the unvarnished truth was—potential weird factor notwithstanding—now that she'd turned in her story, Ava really wanted to see Brennan again.

And much to her surprise, it looked as if the feeling was mutual.

"I guess that depends on your definition of weird," he said, following up the words with nothing more than that infernally sexy, stubble-laced smile.

She should've guessed. "You're not going to tell me, are you?"

"Not a chance."

"Give me a hint," came her bold counter, but Brennan just leaned in close enough to fill her senses with the fresh ocean-air scent of his skin.

"No." His smile morphed into a grin, teasing every cell in Ava's body as it traveled all the way to her core.

"Be at my place at noon tomorrow. Wear comfortable clothes, and be prepared to sweat."

Chapter Eleven

Brennan stood in the dead center of his living room, surveying his apartment for obvious dust bunnies and trying to keep his back from going into full spasm. But between the stress of the fire last week and the grueling PT session he'd gutted through this morning, he doubted if he'd have much luck. When Brennan had arrived in the Blue Ridge just under two years ago, his orthopedist at Riverside Hospital had given him a standing prescription for muscle relaxers, which he'd never filled, and another one for painkillers, which he'd torn up before he'd even left the clinic. He'd told his physical therapist in their very first session that the strongest pharmaceutical assistance that would pass his lips would be the over-the-counter variety, and the rest was up to her.

And bless her torturous Zenmaster heart, Kat had manhandled him with alternative therapy ever since. Not that Brennan could knock it, because damn, her approach actually worked.

To varying degrees, anyway.

Satisfied that his apartment was free of any flagrant dirt

or disarray, Brennan scanned his T-shirt and gym shorts to make sure they also passed muster. Okay, so what he had planned for his lunch break with Ava hardly qualified as date material, but he was still pretty sure he wouldn't impress her with workout gear that could stunt-double as a dust rag.

Not that he was trying to impress her *or* ask her on a date. She'd done a decent thing by bringing him the article she'd written before it was printed, and he was just return- ing the being-nice favor. Plus, despite her teasing delivery last night, Ava wasn't wrong. Brennan had endured a hell of a week, and both his back and his brain had let him know it in no uncertain terms. He really could stand to come down a notch.

And from the look on Ava's face as she'd talked about her workload, he wasn't the only one. Their interview was over and done, and his past was staying exactly where it belonged. He'd even dodged the land mine of her question about Mason last night, although the calm required for the job had taken every last scrap of his effort.

Now they had nowhere to go but forward. What could it hurt to spend an hour with her, blowing off steam they could both stand to lose?

Brennan's cell phone clamored for attention from down the hall, and he moved to the kitchen to scoop it from the counter. The caller ID had him both smiling and tighten- ing up, but he tapped the icon bearing his sister's pixie face and answered all the same.

"Don't tell me. You and the Murphy guy eloped to Vegas."

Ellie's drawn-out sigh was tinged with just enough laughter to mark her happiness. "Are you kidding? We're supposed to get married in front of God and most of the universe in two and a half weeks. I'm pretty sure an elopement would make the whole you-may-now-kiss-the-bride thing a little awkward. Anyway, Dad would have a cow and three chickens if Josh and I blew off this wedding so we could tie the knot at the Elvis Chapel o' Love."

Hell of a point. "So I take it the planning rages on."

"Mmm-hmm. You know. Busy, busy." There was just enough vague hesitation in Ellie's answer to make it a non-answer, and Brennan's senses launched into full alert.

"What's the matter, Ellie?" He leaned against the sturdy length of counter space at his hip, splaying his free hand over the cool surface as he braced for impact.

His sister's hesitation became a full-blown hitch. "I didn't want to say anything about this until I was sure," she said, bookending the words with an audible wince. "But you need to know. Alex Donovan and Cole Everett are going to be at the wedding. And so is Captain Westin."

Brennan's blood went subzero in his veins. "What?"

"This wasn't my idea, Nick. *Believe* me, I know what it means—"

"You don't," Brennan bit out, but Christ, he couldn't finish. Because finishing meant telling Ellie exactly what it was like to hear those three names again, unearthed from the place he'd stuffed them on the day Mason had died.

"Look, Josh's firm has played Station Eight in the Fairview softball tournament finals for the last two years. You know that league is the *Who's Who* of the entire city. Josh cocaptained last year's team. He knows everyone in the house, right down to the paramedics." The apology clung to Ellie's voice, ripping further into Brennan's belly, but he didn't stop her from talking. "I wanted to tell him no, but then he'd ask me why. And we're inviting everyone else in freaking Fairview, so I have no excuse."

Her words trickled in, hitting him one drop at a time. "You never told Josh what happened?"

"No, Nick." Ellie's hesitation disappeared. "Josh is my fiancé, and he works downtown, so he's not oblivious to the facts. But you firefighters are like Fort Knox when it comes to details about your own, and regardless of how you left it with them, Alex and Cole are no exception. Josh only knows what everyone else knows. There was a fire, and you got hurt badly enough to warrant a career change. That's all."

Pressure climbed the plumb line of Brennan's spine, intensifying with each upward grab. Hell, he needed to get off the phone. He needed to pack all this shit back into its ugly, broken, fucked-up box so he could get rid of it.

Right now.

"Okay. Thanks for calling me, Ells. I know this isn't your fault."

"Don't do this," Ellie warned, but Brennan was already shaking his head, modulating his voice to betray no emotion.

"I'm not doing anything."

"You can't keep hiding!" Barely a beat of chagrined silence passed before his sister added, "What happened in that fire was an accident. Harboring all this blame is going to ruin you."

Inhale. Exhale. Find control. "I'm fine. Really. Love you."

Two things happened simultaneously as Brennan lowered the phone back to the kitchen counter. A soul-sucking pain claimed all the space from his tailbone to both hips.

And Ava Mancuso knocked on his front door.

* * *

Brennan stood at his kitchen counter, paralyzed by both the irony of his situation and the raging pain playing epic-battle Twister with every last one of his nerve endings. But he knew all too well that the way through a full-blown back spasm was to combine gentle pressure with gentler movement. Sitting still would only give the pain a chance to dig its teeth in deeper.

Even if moving hurt badly enough to bitch-slap the breath from his lungs.

"Coming!" Brennan unwound his death grip from the edge of the tan Formica, sliding his fingers over his lower back to locate the pressure point the way Kat had taught him. Pain shot jagged lines across his field of vision, but he forced his legs to move across the kitchen floor, one and then the other. Spasms like this were few and far between for him now, and though they were meaner than most hardened criminals, their sentence was usually pretty short.

Brennan finally managed to get a decent breath in on step four, and by the time he'd hauled his carcass to the front door of his apartment, he was 98 percent sure he'd live through the pain.

Until he caught sight of a wide-eyed Ava on his doorstep, wearing a cute little fleece hoodie with her dark hair tied into two low-slung pigtails, and then he was pretty sure he was already a goner and she was his last wish.

"Oh!" She took a half step backward, her running shoe scraping the brick in a gruff whisper of surprise. "You're here."

"I invited you over," Brennan reminded her, his focus slipping from the pain to her face. Two tiny, crescent-shaped indents marked the curve of her lower lip, and she smoothed an index finger over the worried crease between her brows.

"I know. I just thought you might have . . . Are you okay?"

The crease returned in all its glory, and hell, he should've known better than to think Ava wouldn't notice he was in pain. She was a reporter, for God's sake. She was trained to notice the tiniest details.

Not to mention that her bullshit detector was very likely concrete reinforced and triple-wrapped in high-grade Kevlar.

"Yeah, I'm fine," Brennan said, although it was a lie. Christ, how had he thought he'd be able to lie low at a five-hundred-person wedding? Ellie's fiancé practiced civil law, but still. He worked for the biggest damn firm in the city, and the courthouse was seven blocks from Station Eight. Firefighters, cops, attorneys . . . Pine Mountain wasn't the only place with a hell of a grapevine.

All the unspoken firefighter codes on the planet weren't going to keep Alex and Cole's hatred from being broadcast loud and freaking clear if the three of them clapped eyes on each other.

The pain in Brennan's back sliced through to both hips, and he crammed down the thought of his former squad mates. Right now he needed to control his pain, or it was going to control him. He focused on Ava, lasering in on the thin silver necklace barely visible at the divot of her throat, and yeah, that would work. "Come on in."

The step he took to gesture her inside sent his muscles right back into lockdown, though, and Ava turned toward him with a frown.

"You look pale." She lifted a hand in an automatic motion, skimming it halfway over his forearm before she seemed to realize the contact. "Oh my God, you're shaking. Brennan, what's going on?"

Her touch unraveled the words from his mouth like a landslide, and he stood there helpless while they spilled out. "I hurt my back. Not recently, but sometimes it acts up. The pain's not usually so bad."

"Except for now," Ava said, not a question in sight. "So do you have any medicine? Painkillers or something I can—"

"No." Shit, that came out louder than he'd intended. He cleared his throat. "I mean, the alternative stuff actually works better for me. I just need a little pressure on it and a stretch or two. It'll be fine."

"You're so full of crap."

Surprise replaced the bone-deep ache slamming through Brennan's veins. "What?"

Only a handful of people knew about his injury, but whenever his pain reared its ugly head, every last one of them responded with varying degrees of poor-you concern. Even Kat, who talked a tough game, got a softhearted sympathy flicker in her eyes whenever his therapy got rough.

But Ava just leveled him with a bright green stare that said she meant business. "You say *fine*, and all I hear is the other F word. I'm assuming it would help to get you off your feet, yes?" Without waiting for him to answer, she slipped a shoulder beneath his arm to guide him to the couch.

"Thanks." Brennan sank to the brown leather cushions with a graceless *plunk*, but man, his vertebrae did a touch-down dance at the decrease in gravity. "I'm really sorry. We were supposed to spend your lunch hour relaxing."

"I made it out of the office. That's really half the battle." Ava sat down next to him, flipping her palms in a *what's next* gesture. "You said something about pressure?"

The question was so straight up and devoid of pretense that his answer was automatic. "Yeah. It helps." He rotated his body in an effort to get some leverage from his palm to his lower back, but she interrupted the movement midreach.

"Wait." In one deft maneuver, she'd repositioned herself on his other side, turning her knees toward his back so they were both sitting sideways on the couch.

"What are you doing?" Brennan twisted to look at her over his shoulder. Having anyone behind him, even someone he knew, sent his hackles into high alert.

But Ava put her hands on his shoulders to gently turn him back around. "Just winging it here, but I can't imagine twisting yourself up like a human corkscrew feels too relaxing."

He bit down on the urge to face her again anyway. "It's not a big deal."

She sighed, but without seeing her face, Brennan couldn't discern whether she was giving in or buckling down. "Are you going to tell me how to do this or not? I really don't want to hurt you by accident."

Right. He should've known better than to think she'd cave. "The pain's in my lower back," he conceded, the couch cushions rustling as he angled away from her fully, abandoning control of his most dominant sense. "On either side of my spine."

"Here?" Ava paused for a second, the word arriving before the whisper-soft connection of her fingers on his back, below his kidneys.

"A little closer in, right around the vertebrae, but yeah."

Despite her light touch, Brennan tensed at the brush of Ava's hands moving over his T-shirt. Not being able to see her, to read her face or even her body language, was bad enough. But her fingers were less than a breath from the scar tissue that spiderwebbed out from his spine, crisscrossing the expanse of his lower back in a gruesome relief map of rods and pins that he'd carry around for the rest of his life.

Except when her hands landed over his scars, the damage obvious to the touch even through the barrier of his shirt, Ava didn't even flinch.

"Okay, got it. So just add some pressure?" She pushed slowly with both index and middle fingers, and despite his uptight idiot brain, his muscles rippled in relief.

"Uh-huh," Brennan said, although it came out as more of a grunt. He pulled in a breath, balancing the racing twitches of pain against the steady strength of Ava's fingers. She shifted her weight, presumably to settle in, and the warm, brown-sugar scent of her skin filled his senses.

"Your muscles are locked up pretty tight." Her velvety voice unfolded over his shoulder, tinged with determination as she readjusted the pads of her fingers to the neediest part of his back. "Does this happen often?"

"Sometimes." Brennan surprised himself with the admission. But the world didn't come crashing down because he'd copped to having back spasms, so he added, "If I do a bunch of back-to-back shifts at the bar or there's stress in my muscles from something else, it can trigger an episode."

Ava tipped her hands upward for better leverage with the side of each palm, and God, it was killing him not to see her. "So you really *do* need to relax."

"Maybe." He let out a breath between his teeth as the pain slid into a dull throb.

"Try definitely." Her breath tickled his ear, making the skin on the back of his neck prickle. "How's this?"

"Better." Truth. "And definitely is a little extreme," he tacked on. Not the truth, but any second now, Ava was going to ask a trillion questions about how he'd ended up like Humpty Dumpty. The best way to fortify his defense was with a good offense.

But Ava simply said, "You know what works for me, when I need to chill out?"

Her hands never faltered, moving steadily over his back, and the tension unspooled with each press and sweep.

"What?"

"Promise you won't laugh."

"You realize that's like saying *don't move* or *don't sneeze*, right?" Of course a smile was already poking at the corners of his mouth. Ridiculous involuntary response.

"Promise," Ava insisted, although the smile in her own voice was audible and sweet as hell.

"Okay, okay. No laughing. I promise."

She slid close enough for Brennan to feel the heat of her body, pressing her palms right where he ached. "This is only for extreme circumstances, mind you, and it's kind of unusual. But I swear it works. You take four graham cracker squares—"

"Like little kids eat?" he asked, totally baffled, but Ava cut him off with a *shush*.

"Stop interrupting, or I won't tell you the rest. You smash up the graham crackers, which is kind of cathartic in itself depending on what's stressing you out. Then you put the crumbs in a coffee mug."

Don't laugh. Don't laugh. Don't . . . "A coffee mug," he repeated, barely stifling his chuckle.

She leaned in, her mouth right beside his ear. "You're interrupting."

"Sorry." For a split second, Brennan was tempted to do it again just to feel the heat of her so close. "So, uh, coffee mug."

"Mmm-hmm. Next, you take a little milk and heat it in a saucepan, just until it's warm. Then pour it over the graham crackers, add a dash of cinnamon on top, stir the whole thing up, and bam. You have the ultimate comfort food."

His laugh was completely inevitable, and it felt shockingly good rumbling up from his chest. "Seriously? I'm not even sure that's a thing."

"Of course it's a thing." Ava scoffed. "It's the *best* thing, even though it sounds weird at first. And you promised not to laugh."

Brennan hiked his hands up in apology, although she sounded far from mad. "I know, but you've got to admit, it's totally off the wall. How'd you stumble across the idea of doing that to poor, unsuspecting graham crackers, anyway?"

"I didn't, actually." Ava paused, her voice going softer as she readjusted her hands. "My brother and I had to fend for ourselves for most meals when we were kids, and a lot of times, improvising was the name of the game. Food has always been Pete's thing, so one night when I was about ten, he got creative and came up with the graham cracker thing. For some reason, no matter how loud our parents yelled or how falling-down drunk they got, that concoction made things a little better. Warm, somehow. The way our home should've been."

Brennan sat, perfectly still and mesmerized by Ava's voice, but even in his silence, she didn't pull back.

"Anyway, it *is* pretty weird, and I guess a lot of people would say it's even gross. But to me, graham crackers and milk taste like total comfort."

For a second, then another, they sat in silence, her hands on his back and his heart in his throat, and everything in his mind begged him to turn around and kiss her until the sadness infusing her words turned to dust.

But then Ava lifted her fingers, breaking the contact between them as she moved to give him space. "Your muscles feel a lot looser. How's the pain?"

Brennan turned to look at her, realizing belatedly that his agony had dwindled to a barely there twinge. "Better. Looks like I owe you a little relaxing, if you're still up for it."

"Are you?" she asked, eyeing him with care. "I mean, you said we were going to sweat."

"No, I said *you* were going to sweat," Brennan reminded her, letting a grin unwind over his face. "And I could still use a good stretch."

He walked to the hall closet by the door, his muscles realigning into normalcy with each careful step. Bending down to grab the necessary items from their usual resting spot took a little more creativity than usual, but he managed to pull it off before Ava tried to swoop in and help.

"Yoga mats?" A giggle pushed past her lips as he handed one over, and she clapped a hand over her mouth even though the damage was done.

Oh hell. He'd had enough serious for one day, plus, it felt really good to flirt with her a little. "Laugh now, Spitfire. In twenty minutes, you'll be begging for mercy."

She frowned, placing a hand on the hip of her snug, black, knee-length pants. "From yoga? Deep breaths, pretzel poses, find-your-inner-light yoga."

"Yes, but the pretzels are optional. Have you ever done yoga before?"

"Sure," she said, her serene smile out of place with the mischievous glint in her eyes. "I'm standing on my head in a triple knot as we speak."

Despite the shot of heat percolating through his blood at the mental image of Ava's limbs curled into sinuous knots, Brennan didn't budge. The point was for her to relax, not feel put on the spot, and she wore her sarcasm like a suit of smart-assed armor.

"It's okay if this is your first time. I know enough to get you through the poses." He nudged his tiny coffee table aside, unfurling his timeworn yoga mat over the floorboards in front of the TV. "I normally practice alone, obviously, but I think we'll have just enough room for both of us."

"Not a lot of guys do yoga," Ava said after a beat, toeing off her bright red cross-trainers to extend her mat alongside his. She stood stiffly on its surface, knees locked and arms rigid, and whoa. Their need to unwind was definitely mutual.

"Not a lot of guys have their lumbar vertebrae fused together with enough hardware to set off a courthouse metal detector either." He heard the words only after they were out, silently cursing himself for dropping his guard even to make a passing joke. Ava was too smart for that.

She cast a sideways glance at him, dark hair sliding over one shoulder. "That sounds pretty major."

It was a lead-in, Brennan knew, but he stuffed it aside along with his thoughts of returning to Fairview for Ellie's wedding. He'd handle that soon enough. Right now, he needed to focus on what was in front of him. Or more specifically, who.

"Maybe when it happened," he said, turning toward Ava. "But the yoga's a necessity, and anyway, it really is relaxing."

"If you say so." She tightened her fists, giving the mat beneath her feet a *let's go* expression. "So what's first?"

Brennan laughed. "You might want to try breathing, for starters."

She crinkled her nose with a full dose of *are you kidding*

me? "I'm pretty sure I know how to breathe, what with my twenty-nine years of experience in that department."

He was next to her before he recognized the movement, the deep, sweet smell of her skin pressing hot in his lungs.

"I'm pretty sure you don't, sweetheart. Now close your eyes."

Chapter Twelve

Ava had to hand it to him. When Brennan had promised to make her sweat, he'd meant freaking business.

"You want me to close my eyes?" She shifted her weight, trying to get nice and comfortable, but her heart still pounded like a jackhammer gone horribly awry. When he'd first asked her to come over, she'd thought they'd dip into something gruelingly cathartic, like a short run or maybe a little kickboxing—both things she'd done before without incident or injury. But yoga required focus, and focus required slowing down. Enough to take a good, close look at everything beneath the surface.

Hence the reason Ava had never set so much as a baby toe on a mat in her entire life.

"You don't have to, but sometimes closing your eyes can help you get started." Brennan shrugged, the strong line of his shoulders lifting easily beneath his black T-shirt, and Ava paused, midbalk. Brennan had said he needed a few stretches to get himself back to normal, and after the back spasm he'd just endured, copping out seemed kind of unfair. She'd already spilled more details about herself today than she'd meant to say out loud in front of anyone, ever, but she'd done it to distract him from his obvious pain. Surely she was tough enough to finish up their lunch with a little breathe and stretch, especially if it would help Brennan out.

God, that injury had to have been devastating. Maybe even as bad as her past.

"Okay." Ava discarded her hoodie and commanded her eyes to shut with a determined nod. She could do this. "Now what?"

"Breathe, remember? All the way in," Brennan added, before she could point out that she'd *been* breathing since before they'd even started.

"How many times?" She resisted the urge to crack one eye open to at least see where he was. The whole in-the-dark thing was unnerving as hell.

"There's no rule book, Spitfire. Just breathe."

"Hey!" Ava coughed out a laugh, unexpected and deep. "That's twice now. You promised not to call me that."

His return chuckle vibrated through her, knocking the tension in her shoulders into a free fall. "I know, but I had to get some decent air in you somehow."

She placed a hand on her belly, the other on her chest, and damn if he hadn't been spot on. "Sneak."

"It worked, didn't it? Now do it again."

"I didn't realize yoga was so bossy," Ava said, unable to rein in her sarcasm.

Of course, Brennan met it toe-to-toe. "Yoga's not bossy; I am. Now, are you going to inhale? Because I'd hate to have to tickle you."

"You wouldn't dare." Ava laughed by default this time, her eyes springing open. Brennan stood less than a foot away, armed with a cocky expression and a stare that glittered like warm, black coffee in the sunlit living room.

"You can either breathe in or try me. How do you like your odds?"

Oh. Lord. Above.

"Um." Her throat worked over a hard swallow. "Okay, right. Breathing."

After a few rounds of deep-bodied inhale-exhale, Ava's heartbeat notched back to a semidecent level. She had to admit, the guided breathing wasn't really so bad, not even when she let her lids drift back down on the fourth round. Brennan's voice melted over her left shoulder, talking her through some simple stretches as he did the same ones right next to her, and the movements sent an unexpected thread of calm around her tap-tapping pulse. The muscles in her shoulders listed gently away from her neck, her breath sliding in and out of her lungs with growing ease, and each pose unraveled the tension in Ava's chest further.

"See? I told you it was relaxing." Brennan pressed his palms together in front of his sternum, bending his knees into a half squat over his worn blue mat. The hard, lean angle of his shoulders flexed snugly beneath his T-shirt, muscles rippling against the cotton, and Ava bit her lip in concentration as she tried to keep her focus in check.

"You also told me I'd sweat," she said, mimicking his movements, only more deeply. She adjusted her bare feet on the floor, triumphant. Yoga wasn't so bad. In fact, she could do this all day, as long as he kept his sexy shoulders and unfair-advantage stubble out of her line of sight.

"Don't be so competitive." Brennan stepped to the front of his mat, gesturing for her to stay in place as he grabbed a bottle of water from the small side table next to the couch. "And if you want to sweat, hang on to that pose for another thirty seconds."

"I'm always competitive," Ava snorted, even though her legs were suddenly starting to feel as if they belonged in a Jell-O mold. "Another thirty seconds is a piece of cake."

She tightened her belly and pulled in a shallow breath.

At the five-second mark, her legs gave a twinge and tingle, and she shifted just slightly to offset the growing burn. At fifteen seconds, her lower body started to quake in earnest, screaming at her to ease up. The muscles in her thighs gripped her bones like survivors on a life raft, and she locked her molars with a determined clack. Brennan had thrown down the thirty-second gauntlet, and she couldn't just leave the challenge dangling in the breeze. Ava was tough enough to manage thirty seconds of anything, and even though her legs were starting to visibly shake, surely she could—

Brennan's hands closed around her waist, fingers tightening into her rib cage in the most merciless tickle on the planet.

"Oh my God!" Ava's shriek of laughter paved the way for her head-to-toe flail, and she threw both arms around Brennan's shoulders. For a split second, he froze to his spot in front of her, both palms locked into place over her thin cotton tank top. But then he slipped his arms all the way around her torso, shifting her back a step to help steady her feet.

"Sorry," he said, his chuckle vibrating against her chest as he set her back into place on her mat. "But I told you, these poses aren't competitive. Keeping score isn't really conducive to positive yoga."

"Oh, but tickling me is?" Ava pulled back, fully intending to nail Brennan with a high-level frown—she'd had that pose in the bag! But the unfiltered honesty in his half smile stopped her cold.

"You helped me relax. I just wanted to return the favor."

"I helped you relax?" The question flew out of her mouth, as unchecked as her shock. She'd unleashed her no-nonsense bedside manner on him when he probably could've used some good, old-fashioned sympathy, then bumbled through a bunch of yoga poses at his side. If anything, Ava would've thought she'd been more *de*structive than constructive, but Brennan didn't let up.

"Yeah. My family and my physical therapist kind of dance around me when my back acts up. I know they mean well, but . . . it was just kind of nice to have someone be cool about it. Like it's not that big of a deal."

Ava had felt the scar tissue the minute she'd put her hands on Brennan's back, even through his T-shirt, and the severity had sent shivers all the way down her own spine. No way was she buying that his injury was anything less than an extremely big deal. Still . . .

"It's tough to field all that sympathy sometimes, even when it's well meant," she agreed. Lord knew that was familiar territory from her past. "I'm just glad I could help."

"You did help. Thanks." His fingers tightened around the bend of her elbow, the friction of skin on skin sending a spray of goose bumps over Ava's arm. Something hot and sweet and deeply good broke free in her belly, and as much as she wanted to downplay the sensation, she couldn't.

Helping him relax, even though it had meant revealing things she normally kept hidden, had felt deliciously good, just like the laughter he'd coaxed out of her.

And Ava wanted more.

"You're welcome. But next time, it's my turn. Meet me on the pier at Big Gap Lake at noon on Sunday. I won't even make you sweat."

Ava slipped past the glass doors to the *Riverside Daily* with her gym bag on her shoulder and about sixteen seconds to spare. Normally, she'd never even dream of cutting her lunch hour so close, but with her article on the fire sitting pretty on page three of today's paper and Gary having been mysteriously absent from work all morning, Ava had figured what the hell.

She'd earned a good, relaxing lunch break. One with a stare as sinful as triple-layer chocolate cake . . . and a mouth just full enough to provoke some really wicked thoughts . . . and a sliver of leanly cut abs, just visible in those arms-overhead yoga poses, that showcased a dusting of dark hair leading all the way down to—

"Oh my God, you had sex!"

Ava jumped about a mile and a half off the commercial-grade carpet lining the main hallway to the newsroom, blushing all the way to the tips of her fingers as she shushed her friend with a hiss.

"Jeez, Layla!" She swiveled a covert glance over both shoulders, relief spiraling through her rib cage at the sight of the empty hallway behind her. "Are you out of your mind?"

"No, but you clearly are, and not in the bad way." Layla's perfectly arched light blond eyebrows breached the narrow rims of her glasses, and she fell into step next to Ava with a grin. "Nobody walks around with that goofy little blush-face unless they're getting laid. It's a proven fact."

"I think you need to check the validity of your source," Ava whispered, ducking into her cubicle while trying to keep her dignity intact.

If Layla had busted her with the I-had-sex face when all she'd been doing was *thinking* about having sex, then it had been waaaaay too long since Ava's bedroom had been used for anything other than catching zzzs.

"Sell stupid somewhere else, sweetheart." Layla slipped into the creaky second chair in Ava's cubicle, propping her elbows on her desk with a knowing stare. "You're lit up like the seventy-foot Norway spruce going up this week in Rockefeller Center. At the very least, your lunch with Captain America was more than just business."

Ava sent one last look around the open-air space of the news floor to make sure no one was within eavesdropping distance. With the long hours logged by most reporters, lunch breaks tended to come later than usual, and today's appeared to still be in full swing. In fact, the only other person Ava could see was Ian, and his sandy brown head was half covered in the same kind of earphones Ava favored when searching the scanners for a story.

"My lunch was more than business, but not the way you're thinking." Finally confident they wouldn't be overheard, she slid into her ancient desk chair and leaned toward her friend. No way was Layla going to let this drop, and clandestine sexual tension aside, Ava's thoughts were whirring now more than ever. "Remember when I told you I thought there was more to Brennan's past than he was letting on?"

Layla's expression went from teasing to thoughtful in less than a blink. "Of course."

"Well, it turns out, I was right." She recounted the events of the lunch break she'd spent with Brennan, glossing over her sappy admission of the graham cracker story but detailing their exchange and his injury.

"Holy crap." Layla blew out a breath as soft as her murmur. "So do you think he was a firefighter after all, and maybe he got hurt on the job?"

"It makes sense. I mean, I'm not an expert, but according to that record, he definitely went to the fire academy, and even he said his injury had been severe. It had to have happened under extreme circumstances, and you and I both saw firsthand that fires definitely qualify." Ava paused, even though her gut screeched that she wasn't wrong. "But I can't be one hundred percent sure. He also could've been hurt in something like a car accident."

"You don't believe that, though."

"No, I don't. I get that most guys are kind of touchy about being injured, especially badly, but Brennan's too secretive. About his injury *and* his past." Ava would bet the bank that if she hadn't walked in on him midspasm, Brennan wouldn't have even forked over the fact that he'd been hurt in the first place. "Plus, he knew way too much about how to get Matthew Wilson out of that grocery store, not to mention he's a virtual ghost on the Internet, like something's been covered up. I'm telling you, he has a story. A big one. But it looks like the only way I'm going to uncover it is if Brennan tells me."

"It definitely sounds like he's hiding something. Now more than ever," Layla agreed.

Ava gestured to the copy of the *Daily* sitting on the corner of her desk, frustration welling in her chest. "I know. I just can't prove it." Maybe Gary was right. Maybe she *didn't* have what it took to work a source and break a really big story.

"Ava, don't." Layla shook her head, adamant. "You landed an exclusive no one else in the Blue Ridge could manage, and your article is a strong account of the facts. It's good, clean coverage of an impressive story."

"Sounds to me like today's article was just the beginning."

Ava whipped around, thoroughly startled by the cold, masculine voice shooting over her cubicle from the narrow entryway. Gary folded his arms over his chest, the buttons on his rumpled oxford shirt straining at the movement.

"Ex-excuse me?" Ava stammered, too taken aback to do anything else. Gary was legendary for having his eyes and ears all over the newsroom. She knew better than to get that caught up in out-loud thought.

Oh hell . . . how much had he overheard?

"In my office, Mancuso. Right now." Gary jerked his thinning comb-over toward the glass-lined space at the head of the newsroom before sending a pointed frown at Layla. "Ellis, I'm sure you have work to do."

Layla darted a startled glance in Ava's direction, but Ava returned it with just the slightest shake of her head. She'd dealt with Gary's disdain by the truckload, and even though she stood by her story on the fire, a part of her had known he'd find fault with the fact-laden article. She followed Gary to his office, noting with a cringe that while he made quite a show of shutting the door, he chose to leave the blinds over the floor-to-ceiling view of the newsroom wide open. Everyone coming back from lunch would bear witness to Gary's obvious disappointment, with only their imaginations as the soundtrack.

He didn't even make it to his desk before he pounced. "It seems you've got an angle on this fire story after all. You *know* this hometown hero guy?"

"I did," she corrected, proceeding with her caution flags on high alert. "When the story broke, I hadn't spoken to him in seven years."

Gary's face bent into a dangerous frown. "And you didn't share this little nugget because . . . ?"

"I didn't think he'd talk to me." The truth burned a path out of Ava's mouth, but she kept to it all the same. "And I didn't want the assignment because I knew him. I wanted it because I was the best reporter for the job."

"Yet even with an in, you couldn't seal the deal."

A hard flush of warmth stole over Ava's face as she stood stiffly across from her boss. "I got the story as an exclusive, just like you asked."

"Sounds to me like you got *half* the story," he said, pressing his palms into his giant monstrosity of a desk to lean in and peg her with a beady stare. "The boring half, that is. You landed the exclusive scoop on Pine Mountain's biggest news event in God knows how long, with a source you know personally, and all you managed to scrape together were a bunch of watered-down factoids."

"You had final approval before the story ran." Ava clamped down on her impetuous tongue, channeling all her effort into smoothing her words. "If you had an issue with my article, I'd have been happy to hear your feedback last night." Not that she could've changed anything, because every shred of what Brennan had reluctantly given up had gone into the piece she'd written. Damn it!

Gary gave an ungracious snort. "You're kidding, right? In case you haven't noticed, we're not here for a tea party. It's our job to sell papers, Mancuso, and I can't do that with dead space. Do you want to know where I've been all morning?"

Ava waited, certain she was going to find out regardless of her answer, and Gary didn't disappoint. "I've been sitting in Royce's office, listening to how our quarterly sales numbers so far have sucked more wind than an F5 tornado."

Shock lanced through Ava's gut. "Mick Royce?"

She'd met the eccentric owner of the *Riverside Daily* a mere handful of times. The only thing that overshadowed the man's odd personality was his reputation as a shrewd and savvy businessman.

"Yes, Mick Royce." Aggravation painted Gary's features, twisting his thin mouth into an ever thinner line as he pushed off from his desk. "He wants to know why we're consistently being outsold by the *Bealetown Bugle*, and when I look at articles like yours, I've gotta admit, I don't have a good answer."

"My story on the fire is the truth." Ava might be on precarious ground, but damn it, she was going to *stand* that ground. "I know it's not as flashy as you wanted, but—"

"But nothing. According to you, it was just the appetizer. Now you're going to get the four-course meal."

Ava gasped at the demand, certain she'd misunderstood. "I don't even know that there's anything more to tell. Not for sure, anyway."

"That's not what I just heard you saying to Ellis in your little pajama party out there. Looks to me like you weren't good enough to get the whole story from this guy the first time around, and halfway doesn't cut it," Gary said.

And of course Ava couldn't argue. She believed in the article she'd written, but she also couldn't deny that her big-story instincts had been howling from the minute she'd laid eyes on Brennan outside Joe's Grocery.

"Okay, yes," she admitted, fiddling with the hem of her sweater. "It does seem like there might be a pretty compelling human interest story beneath the surface. One that I didn't cover in my article. But Brennan wasn't willing to tell it, Gary, and you can believe me when I say that not only did I try my best to engage him, but there are no other leads."

"Well, you'd better be prepared to find some." Gary's sweat-laced brow creased, his beefy face pinched tight with disdain. "You're swimming in different waters now that Royce is on the warpath, and it's about time you *finally* learned how to work a source to get a story that'll sell, no matter what."

Ava's gut pitched with unease, but she had no choice but to go for full disclosure. "I know Brennan. Personally."

The implication hung in the air like laundry on the line, but Gary just looked at her with extreme impatience. "Please. I don't care if you run off to Vegas to marry the guy. A story's a story. As long as it's true, I don't give a shit how you get your information. And trust me, you need all the intel you can get on this guy."

Her spine snapped to its full height. "I'm sorry?"

"You asked for the big time, Mancuso. Now you've got to step up to the plate. Clearly, you've got an in with this guy now, and it sounds like there's a hell of a story somewhere in your hometown hero's past. Judging by how much he hates the spotlight, I'd say it might even be a scandal."

No way. There might be a story there, one worth telling even, but Brennan couldn't possibly be tangled up in anything nefarious. He'd risked life and limb to save a kid from a burning building, for God's sake.

"That's a little extreme, don't you think?" Ava asked, in a last-ditch effort to dissuade her clearly delusional boss.

But his rat-like eyes just narrowed further as he zeroed in on her.

"What I think is that you need to do better than the utterly forgettable article that ran in today's paper. You wanted a blockbuster story—*this* story—and now it's time to deliver. I'm not getting shit-canned before you, and Royce is looking for heads to roll. Either you come up with something better than this before those year-end sales numbers come out in three weeks"—Gary paused to whip a copy of today's paper from the cluttered surface of his desk—"or you can find a job being a substandard reporter somewhere else. The choice is yours."

Chapter Thirteen

Ava slumped into the plush cushions of her favorite oversized chair in the Sweet Life, desperate for comfort that didn't come. Four days had passed since her showdown with Gary, and though he'd steered pretty clear of her after issuing his nasty ultimatum, the sly side glances he shot in her direction were reminder enough.

Get a massive story on Brennan—for real this time—or get packing. With a résumé that would read *I'm not even good enough to cut it at a small-town newspaper.*

But Brennan wasn't talking, and what's more, Ava wouldn't pressure him to. Steamy feelings aside, she'd never believed in shady journalism, and even in the face of Gary's threats, she wasn't about to start now. She had nothing to go on other than her gut, and as desperate as she was for a story, Ava couldn't make one up out of ballsy determination and thin air. She'd just have to find a different story, something else worth telling, to get Gary off her back and her name on the front page.

Even if the most exciting thing she'd been able to turn up all week was the Riverside annual fruitcake chucking contest.

"No offense, but you look like someone just stole your

puppy." Her brother's voice threaded past Ava's grim thoughts as he leaned in to top off the holly-printed coffee mug sitting on the side table between them.

"Have you ever noticed that when someone kicks off a sentence with *no offense*, they're usually about to offend you?" Although she'd meant to deliver the words with a hearty dose of her trademark sarcasm, they came out embarrassingly soft.

Get tough, girl. The sooner, the better.

"Hey, I was kidding. I didn't mean to offend you," Pete said, his dark brows lowering in concern. "Is everything okay?"

Great. The last thing Ava needed was for Pete to worry about her. He'd sacrificed enough of his life doing just that already.

She worked up a smile, albeit a lopsided one, and stuffed down her churning thoughts as best she could. "Yeah, sorry. I've just got a lot on my plate at work."

Not only that, but she was supposed to meet Brennan at the lake in less than an hour. Ava had waffled over the idea of canceling, but she didn't have his number and—surprise, surprise—her online search for it had yielded bupkus. Sure, they'd had an incredible time together earlier in the week, sliding right back into the easy comfort and flirty banter that had made her fall for him seven years ago. But she had fallen then, *hard*, and no matter how good Ava had felt spending time with him in their little yoga session, she had no intention of being that vulnerable ever again. Being around Brennan, with those sexy shoulders and that *really* sexy stare, might just be too tempting. And too dangerous.

Even if the danger was sizzling hot.

"Come on," Pete said, interrupting Ava's dismal thoughts with a grin. "It's a gorgeous winter Sunday in the mountains." He made a grand gesture to the sun-drenched windows lining the mostly empty bakery behind them, the contents of the coffeepot in his hand giving a soft slosh. "You're way too serious. Forget work and live a little."

"Okay, who are you and what have you done with my brother?" Ava laughed, her sassy tone returning to her voice. "You never forget work. Although I have to say, my taste buds are thankful."

She took a deep inhale, letting the earthy scent of fresh coffee and the butter-sweet smell of pastries-in-progress chip at the edges of her stress. As ugly as life got, at work or otherwise, she could always count on Pete to make her feel like things might not be so bad.

"Hmm. There are more important things in life than punching the clock. Even when you love your job." Her brother passed off the coffeepot to the teenager who had been working behind the counter, his expression slipping back to concern as his wife, Lily, muscled an oversized tray of her famous eggnog snickerdoodle cookies past the swinging door from the kitchen at the back of the shop.

"Here, let me get that for you." Pete rushed to slide the stainless steel tray from Lily's grasp, placing it on the work space behind the gleaming glass display counter before steering her over to the couch across from Ava. Wow, Lily must really still be under the weather if Pete was getting jumpy over a double batch of cookies.

Her sister-in-law rolled her pretty blue eyes, planting her kitchen clogs on the mahogany floorboards with a sigh.

"Honestly, I'm fine, Pete. You don't need to—" Lily's protest got lost in the wake of Pete's movements as he nudged her into sitting on the couch.

"Hold that thought. I'm going to grab you a bottle of water."

Ava watched, both bewildered and totally amused as her normally cocky brother blazed a nonstop path to the

built-in cooler behind the main bakery counter. After a
quick murmur to the teen behind the register, he returned
with just as much speed, cracking the lid on the plastic
water bottle before handing it over.

"There you go. Lucas has us covered for a few minutes
so you can take a break."

"At least you're equal opportunity with your coddling,"
Ava said, wiggling her brows playfully at Pete. "Although
really, the couch treatment might be a little extreme."

"Ava's right," Lily agreed, and whoa, come to think of
it, she did look pretty wiped out. She blinked, her lashes
creating even deeper shadows against the dark circles
under her eyes. "If I take a water break after every batch of
cookies, we're never going to get anything done around
here. Especially with Christmas only two weeks away."

Pete shook his head, pressing his palms into his apron-
clad hips with an expression Ava knew all too well. "You
need to take it easy," he said, but Lily cut off his argument
with a good-natured—albeit weak—laugh.

"Are you seriously going to be this protective the *whole*
time? I give you less than a month before you end up even
more exhausted than me."

"Jeez, Lil. How long are you planning on being sick?"
Ava shifted to grab her coffee cup, belatedly realizing that
both Lily and Pete were exchanging twin wide-eyed, oh-
shit glances.

"I told you I wouldn't be good at this. I suck at secrets,"
Lily murmured, pinching the bridge of her nose just below
the frames of her slim red glasses. Pete sat on the couch
next to her, hooking an elbow around her shoulders and
dropping a kiss to the crown of her head.

"Don't worry about it, Blondie. It was killing me anyway."

Ava's pulse pushed tight in her veins. "What's going on,
you two? Lily, are you okay?"

Oh God. Pete and Lily were the only family Ava had,

and Lily really did look exhausted. If something serious was wrong with her—

"I'm pregnant."

Ava jerked upright, her palms growing instantly slick. "With a baby?" she blurted, clapping her hands over her mouth the instant the idiocy had crossed her lips. But holy crap! The moment deserved a little craziness. Pete and Lily were going to be in charge of raising an entire human *being*.

Pete laughed, reaching for Ava's hand to give it a squeeze. "Um, actually no."

She wrinkled her nose, the hard prickle of a blush sweeping up toward her ears. "Okay, okay. I know it was a stupid thing to say, but you surprised the hell out of me. You don't have to make fun."

"I'm not making fun of you, Ava." Pete sat back, brushing his palm over Lily's denim-wrapped knee. "You were right. Lily's not pregnant with *a* baby."

The words trickled in, Ava's brain kicking them over just a fraction too slow. "Wait . . ."

"She's pregnant with two."

"Oh my God, you guys are having twins?" Ava's confusion exploded into a hard shot of excitement in three seconds flat. She might've been too cynical to believe that relationships could end up in true love before Pete had met Lily, but they really were the exception to the rule.

"Yeah." Lily dropped her gaze to the dark green apron knotted over her midsection, starting to giggle. "It's such a relief to be able to say it out loud."

"I wanted to tell you the other day," Pete added, sliding an apologetic glance in Ava's direction. "But we thought we should wait until the doctor said everything's perfect."

Ava couldn't pretend to be mad, not even to give Pete a hard time. She jumped from her overstuffed chair to hug first Lily, then her brother. "Everything *is* perfect! I can't believe by this time next year, you'll be parents. Twice."

"Not only that, but you'll be an aunt, twice." Pete unwound from their embrace, his expression playfully stern. "And believe me, Lily and I are expecting you to take your job very seriously."

"Please." Ava scoffed, although the endearment was more sweet than sarcastic. "Like I wouldn't. I'm going to be so in your face when these babies are born, you'll both be sick of me."

Ava's breath clattered to a sudden stop in her lungs. Gary hadn't minced a single syllable regarding the fate of her career if she couldn't land a high-magnitude story ASAP. Ava had been desperate to stay close to her brother under normal circumstances, but now that he and Lily were starting a family? No way could she leave the Blue Ridge. She needed to be here now more than ever.

And that couldn't happen if she earned herself a pink slip and a résumé full of more holes than a pound of Swiss cheese.

"Whoa, are you okay?" Lily's hand closed over Ava's forearm in a flash. "I know we kind of dropped this on you, but—"

"No, no, no," Ava argued, trying and failing to paste a smile on her mouth. God, she had to get out of here. A killer story wasn't just going to fall into her lap, and her time was seriously limited. "Of course I'm okay. I'm thrilled for you guys. I, ah, just forgot that I've got some loose ends to tie up for work, and I'm on deadline."

"Anything we can do to help?" Lily asked.

The question sent a dual flood of guilt and determination through Ava's chest. She couldn't drop the ball on this assignment and be forced to leave the only family she had.

She wouldn't.

"Nope. I've got to take care of this one on my own. Thanks for the offer, though." Ava shouldered her bag with a swoop, keys jingling against her clammy palm as she plucked them from the outside pocket. "I'll catch you guys later. And congratulations again."

Pete frowned for just a split second before hugging her tight. "Just remember what I said about work. It's not always the most important thing."

Ava's smile was stretched thin enough to ache. "You got it, big brother."

It was the first time in their entire lives Pete had said something Ava didn't believe.

Brennan's gaze did a methodical three-sixty around the marina leading to Big Gap Lake for the twentieth time in as many minutes. His eyes moved carefully behind the cover of his Oakleys, taking in the snow-dusted clapboard covering the tackle shop to his left, then the narrow strip of pavement housing the cluster of wooden benches where he sat, and finally, the weathered, silvery expanse of the pier jutting out into the sparkling dark green water. The hiking trails leading out from the top of the pier were well traveled and clear despite the chill in the air, and the handful of well-bundled fishermen on the far end of the lake proved that the marina wasn't just for warm weather.

Brennan surveyed the place, gathering details and soaking in what little warmth he could from the midday sun, yet all the while, a knot formed low and hard in his gut.

Ava was nowhere to be found, and she was fifteen minutes late.

He should've given her his cell phone number, he thought with a silent curse, or at the very least, gotten hers. But after how freaking easy and good it had felt to flirt with her at his apartment the other day, especially in the face of his sister's guest list revelation and the back spasm that had accompanied it, Brennan had thought this date might end with a sizzling repeat of their earlier kiss, minus the smoke alarm.

What he *hadn't* thought was that Ava might not show up.

Just as it had never occurred to him that she would run out on him seven years ago.

"Fuck it." Brennan pushed to his feet with a hard exhale. Loose gravel from the path in front of him crunched beneath his heavy-soled winter boots as he aimed himself on a straight shot toward the parking area. He and Ava might've shared an incendiary kiss, and yeah, listening to her open up a little—not to mention opening up a little himself—had made him feel lighter than he had in years. But he had to be nine kinds of an idiot to have forgotten that she'd blazed a one-way trail off Sapphire Island seven years ago. She might've had good reasons to run at the time, but they didn't change the facts.

She *had* run. And now she was running again.

Brennan crested the upward slope from the marina to the parking lot, fully intent on getting in his Trailblazer and hauling himself out of Dodge. Adrian had given him the day off, but they still might be busy enough to need an extra set of hands at the Double Shot. He could do a hell of a lot worse than put in a hard night's work, and anyway, head down, eyes forward might give him a chance to finally figure out how to deal with Alex and Cole attending Ellie's wedding. At the very least, an extra shift would exhaust him enough to catch a few hours of decent sleep.

Brennan dug into the pocket of his black canvas jacket for his keys as he approached his Trailblazer from the side, but a scrap of bright color caught his attention from the corner of his eye.

Four spaces down and nearly out of sight, Ava stood next to her car, wearing a cherry red scarf and the most pained expression he'd ever seen on her pretty face.

"Ava?" He took a few steps closer, his pulse going from zero to oh-holy-shit in less than three seconds. She'd said to meet her at the pier, but . . . "What are you doing all the way up here?"

"Hi." She winced, as if she'd been hoping he wouldn't catch sight of her. "I'm sorry I'm catching you late. I, uh, just came to tell you I can't meet you today."

Despite the absurdity of her words and the unease growing behind his sternum at her thoroughly rattled expression, Brennan gave a soft laugh. "But you're here."

"I know." She let out a breath, visibly upset even from twenty feet away, and his internal radar started screeching full bore. "I just . . . I need to write a story, and . . . I really have to work."

Nope. He'd seen enough. "What's the matter, Ava?" Brennan slid his keys back into his pocket, covering the remaining space between them with only a few strides.

"Nothing. Nothing at all. I've got this covered. Everything is totally fine."

Brennan recycled her words from the other day without thinking twice. "You say *fine*, and all I hear is the other F word. You want to try again?"

"No. I've got this. I *do*." Ava closed her eyes, and when she reopened them, they were bright with tears that sent another wave of something-isn't-right through his chest. In the entire three months he'd spent side by side with her that summer, he'd never even seen a hint that she *could* cry, let alone would. Ava wasn't just tough—she was halfway to bulletproof. Whatever was rattling her had to be big.

But rather than giving in to whatever it was, she blinked angrily and aimed her gaze skyward. "Great," she muttered.

"I'm such a mess, I can't even bow out gracefully to write a damned story."

"You're not a mess. And I'm not letting you bow out anyway. Come on." He grabbed her hand and turned toward the Trailblazer, and to his surprise, she didn't resist.

"Where are we going?"

Brennan skated a quick glance over Ava's snug jeans and fleece-lined winter boots. Not ideal, but they'd do. "Someplace you can relax."

She chewed her bottom lip, the doubt on her face clear as a summer sunrise as he unlocked the passenger door on the Trailblazer. "Don't take this the wrong way, but I'm not really in the right frame of mind for another yoga session."

Brennan pulled the door open, but instead of stepping back to usher Ava politely inside, he recklessly cut the space between them to less than a breath.

"Yoga's nice, but sometimes you've got to take your relaxing to the next level. I think I can help you out with that, but you're going to have to trust me. Now what do you say—are you getting in or not?"

Chapter Fourteen

Brennan got three-quarters of the way to his destination before Ava finally broke the silence between them.

"You really don't need to do . . . whatever it is that we're doing. To be honest, I meant it when I said I couldn't meet you."

Christ, she wore her stubbornness more comfortably than most people wore their skin. Too bad he'd gotten a glimpse of what lay beneath it, and he wasn't half bad when it came to being relentless, either. "Actually, you look like you could use a break, so I think I do need to help you out. And I know we already covered this part, but you *did* meet me, remember?"

"Well, yes," Ava said, although the agreement sounded far from a concession. "But I didn't have your number, and it wouldn't have been right to just stand you up. I went to the marina to tell you I couldn't stay."

A ribbon of guilt uncurled beneath Brennan's rib cage. "You met me so you wouldn't stand me up?"

"Yeah." She lifted one slim shoulder into a shrug beneath her coat. "Why, what did you . . . oh." Ava nodded. "You thought I wasn't coming."

He opened his mouth to protest—she was clearly having

a rough day—but there was no sense in bullshitting her when she'd just call him on it anyway. "I thought you might've changed your mind and decided not to show, yeah. Sorry."

"It's okay," she said, in a way that made him believe her. "I guess I earned that with you."

"Maybe seven years ago," Brennan countered, realization popping him in the gut. "But I shouldn't have assumed you'd just ditch out." He turned off Rural Route Four, angling the Trailblazer into a tidily kept parking area he'd come to know like his own reflection.

"It's no big deal, really." Ava's coal-colored brows tugged downward, her seat belt whispering over the wool of her coat as she leaned forward to peer through the windshield. "Are we at your apartment building?"

"Yes. And it is a big deal." Putting the SUV in PARK, he tugged the keys from the ignition and got out to open her door. "You explained why you left so suddenly back then, and we promised to move on. I didn't keep my end of the deal back there, thinking you'd skipped out with no good reason. I apologize."

"Oh." She stared at him for a full ten seconds before sliding out of the passenger seat. "Okay."

"Good. Now that we got that out of the way . . ." Brennan tipped his head toward the perpendicular brick buildings in front of them, working up a smile. "Do you want to go give this a shot?"

"Give what a shot, exactly?"

That streak of vulnerability Brennan had seen on her face at the marina made a flickering comeback, dancing briefly in Ava's emerald green eyes before she crossed her arms over her chest. But as expertly as she tried to hide it,

Brennan couldn't help but see the part of Ava that needed tending to, even if he didn't know the particulars.

And Brennan wanted to help her, the way she'd helped him. No questions asked.

"Look, if you really can't stay, I'll take you back to your car. But something's clearly bothering you. I know a way you might be able to let go of some of it, talking optional. But if you don't want to—"

"No! I do."

Ava brushed her fingers over her mouth as if she was shocked the words had popped out, and hell if that didn't make the both of them a matched set. But she hadn't flinched at his back spasm or the revelation of his injury. Brennan wasn't about to treat her as if she was made of spun sugar, no matter how clearly stressed she was.

"Perfect." He led the way to his apartment, praying like hell he'd remembered to make proper use of his laundry hamper after yesterday's double shift. But a quick visual as he unlocked the door and crossed the threshold told him he was okay, just as long as they steered clear of the bed he damn well knew he'd left unmade this morning.

Right. Because just what he needed were thoughts of Ava in his unmade bed. Relieving stress in a different way than he had planned. Hard and fast and more than once.

"Okay!" Brennan barked, his face heating as if she had X-ray vision on his X-rated thoughts. "So, ah, I guess we can get started."

He turned toward the short hallway opposite the kitchen and living room, hanging Ava's coat in his tiny hall closet before motioning for her to follow. While he'd have to be devoid of a pulse not to notice the long, muscular stretch of her legs, in this particular moment, the observation made him a top-shelf jackass. He'd offered to help calm her down, not rev her up. Any thoughts of sliding Ava's body-hugging jeans from her body so she could wrap those lean, strong legs around his waist would have to take a freaking hike.

Christ, he wanted her legs around his waist.

"So, what is it we're getting started on, exactly?" Ava's straight-to-it question jostled Brennan from his illicit thoughts, and he mentally maneuvered himself back to the task at hand.

"Well, I think you're going to have to lose your boots, but otherwise, this might be more up your alley than yoga." He pushed open the door at the end of the narrow hall, clicking on the light with the flat of his hand. He'd come into this room too many times to count, especially right after he'd landed in Pine Mountain, wound up and pissed off and needing release. There wasn't much to look at in the scant, mostly unfinished space, but then again, sometimes the stuff you needed the most was right there in front of you. Hard work. Good meals. Soft bed.

Hundred-pound heavy bag that took all the anger and frustration and pain you could muster and never hit back.

Ava's lips parted as she caught sight of the black leather heavy bag, specially anchored into the exposed joists of the utility room's ceiling, and she stepped toward it with a look of wide-eyed surprise. "Are you serious? You want me to wail on this thing in order to relax?"

All Brennan did was nod. She might be vulnerable beneath that tough exterior, but she was still tough.

"Yup."

Ava flashed him with a smile both grateful and wicked as she kicked her boots from her feet. "Then you'd better hope your ceiling beams are solid, because I have had one hell of a week."

* * *

Of all the places Ava could imagine spending a stress-busting Sunday afternoon, her ex-boyfriend's glorified closet was certainly not on the list. But the deep layer of dread that had taken root this morning at the Sweet Life had anchored into Ava's chest with frightening fierceness, to the point that she'd planned to do nothing but scour every inch of the Blue Ridge until she turned up a killer story that would save her job. Though she hadn't wanted to ditch out on the lakeside winter hike she'd planned for their afternoon, driving to the marina to offer Brennan a quick gotta-work excuse had been no more than a technicality in Ava's brain. Or, at least it had been right up until she'd arrived, and the feelings she'd jammed down all morning— hell, all week—finally spilled over and cemented her to the parking lot.

The career she cherished was on the line, she was perilously close to having to leave the only family she'd ever known, and damn it, as desperate as she was for a story, she was even more desperate for comfort. Not just any comfort.

The minute Ava had seen Brennan, striding up the snowy hill from the edge of the marina wearing that look of dark, powerful intensity, she'd craved comfort from *him*.

Brennan's mouth tipped up at one corner, bringing Ava back to the here and now. "I hear you, but let's not get ahead of ourselves just yet. Have you ever hit a bag like this before?"

"Oh. Um . . ." A ripple of panic spread out in Ava's belly. As soon as she'd seen the heavy bag hanging from the open-beamed ceiling, she'd been dying to jump right in and pummel away her frustrations. But maybe if she admitted the truth about her lack of experience, he'd think she was too much of a rookie after all and make her take some unfulfilling swings at the air like her kickboxing instructor at the gym had.

Rather than tell an all-out fib, Ava settled for jacking her balled-up fists to chin level and prayed she looked passably competent. "I'm sure it'll be fine." She took a quick shot at the bag to prove her words, letting out an involuntary yelp as the impact reverberated all the way up her arm.

Brennan was next to her in less than a breath. "Are you okay?"

Although she fought it with every fiber of her being, Ava's eyes stung from the unexpected bolt of pain. "Oh my God, do you have bricks in this thing?" she asked, turning to glower at the barely swaying heavy bag.

"A hundred pounds of sand, actually." He grabbed her hand, laying her palm over his knuckles for a closer inspection. "Looks like you'll live, but why don't we wrap you up before you get all yippee ki-yay again?"

"Okay," Ava admitted, albeit without dropping her chin. "I could probably use a pointer or two."

To her surprise, Brennan simply shrugged. "Sure. But something tells me once your hands are protected, you'll be a natural."

He took a few steps back, reaching toward a small wooden shelf nailed up to the vertical frame boards lining the rear wall. Grabbing a pair of what looked like long strips of light blue fabric, Brennan returned to her side, close enough that she could smell his crisp-breeze scent mixed in with one of laundry detergent.

He shook one of the strips out while draping the other over the shoulder of his black thermal shirt. "These are mine, so it'll take some extra wrapping, but it's better than going bare knuckled." Brennan paused to drop a smirk over the hand he'd just recaptured, pushing up the sleeve of her gray V-neck to fully expose her fingers and wrist. "Obviously."

Ava's laugh filled the tight space around them, deflating the stress banded around her rib cage on its way out. "I get it. I was impulsive. So what do I need to do first?"

"You need to hit with more than just your hands."

She wrinkled her nose and looked up from her halfway mummified right hand. "I'm sorry?"

Brennan spiraled the thick cotton all the way over her wrist, tapping it into place with the Velcro at the end before swapping Ava's right hand for her left. "Your knuckles are just the point of contact between you and the bag. If you really want to get cathartic about it, the punch needs to come from your whole body. Like this."

He pulled a beat-up pair of padded, fingerless gloves from the shelf, slipping them into place over his hands as he stood at arm's length from the heavy bag. There was barely enough room for them to stand side by side in the confined space, but no way was she shying away from this now. Ava glued her eyes to Brennan's frame with a determined nod, a twinge of heat pulsing through her veins as he faced off with the menacing black leather. With scissor-sharp focus, he measured the heavy bag with an unyielding stare, shifting his stance over the concrete floor just slightly as all the muscles from his shoulders to his waist coiled tightly beneath his shirt.

The resulting *pop-pop-pop* on the bag turned the heat in Ava's veins into a blast of uncut want.

"Oh," came her breathy whisper. Brennan's body was a study of lean lines and hidden power, quickly reharnessed as he stepped back from the heavy bag to look at her over one shoulder.

"See? You've got to grab that strength and energy from

the ground up and let your whole body do the work. Put your back into it, so to speak."

He rolled his eyes, likely at the jab he'd taken at his injury, and the reference propelled Ava's thoughts right past her already questionable brain-to-mouth filter.

"So letting loose on this thing doesn't aggravate your back?" The rapid-fire string of punches he'd just thrown hadn't seemed to bother him, but clearly, he had hiding his injury down to a finely honed skill.

"Not usually. Not if I control it," he added with a shrug. "You want to give it a try?"

Ava stepped up to the heavy bag, enticingly close to both it and Brennan. "Sure." She folded her elbows upright over her chest, mirroring his setup, and threw a semi-awkward punch that rattled up her forearm. "I thought the point of hitting the bag was to lose control." Ava cranked her brow down low and threw another punch, this time using her shoulder to direct the move. *Nice.*

"Mmm. Shooting first and asking questions later will only get you into trouble. Or hurt." Brennan edged past her, angling his body behind the bag to hold it steady. He watched her throw another punch, then one more before nodding his encouragement. "Hitting the bag requires a ton of focus, even when you do it for release. See the difference between that first punch you threw and these?"

Ava paused to accommodate her rapidly increasing need for breath before leveling the bag with another satisfying *thwack*. "Well, yeah," she hedged. "But the whole point is to let go, right? To take all those emotions and get rid of them by punching the bag?"

"No."

"No?" She pulled up halfway through her swing, tightly wrapped knuckles just barely grazing the edge of the black leather. "Then how is it supposed to relax me?"

Brennan let go of the bag to take a step toward her,

dangerously close. "By letting you control your emotions and turning them into something that'll help you."

"You like control, don't you?"

Ava heard the suggestive slant of her words only after they'd escaped, and her cheeks filled with a heated flush. Brennan angled himself behind her, placing a hot exhale by her ear that said he'd heard the innuendo loud and freaking clear.

"And you still like asking questions," he said, his voice honey over gravel. Ava's heart pounded a wild rhythm in her chest, but before she could point out that he hadn't answered, he finished, "Yes. I like being focused. Now let's see if you like it too."

Fitting his stronger frame over her lithe one, Brennan showed Ava exactly how to throw a jab that incorporated the strength of all her muscles. Guiding her arms tight to her rib cage, he walked her through each move with a fluid ease, and she repeated them with growing enthusiasm. The friction of his callused fingertips on her bare forearms and thinly clad shoulders lit her up and spurred her on, the tension from her terrible day melding in with the all-out stress of her really terrible week.

Ava's unease rose up like a sudden tide, but with each full-bodied punch, she found herself channeling it rather than shoving it away. All the frustration over Gary's ridiculous demands, having to prove herself with a blockbuster story, leaving Pete and Lily—all of it became focus rather than fear, and she poured every last ounce of that laserlike attention into hitting the bag again and again and again.

"Holy crap," Ava gasped, finally stopping to catch the breath she'd long since lost.

Brennan orbited around her, steadying the heavy bag on its shiny silver chains before grabbing a hand towel from the shelf on the back wall. "You okay?" He passed the towel over and methodically removed his gloves, but his eyes measured her the whole time.

"Are you kidding?" She pressed the soft terry cloth to her cheeks and forehead, but hiding her laughter was impossible. Every one of her nerve endings tingled with a rush of power like nothing she'd ever quite felt before, as if she was both energized and serenely calm at the same time. "That was *amazing*. I feel great!"

"You really got the hang of it," Brennan said with a smile, reaching up to unwind the skein of now-damp cotton from Ava's left hand. "I told you you'd be a natural."

"Well, yeah, but only because you showed me how to start. Without you, I never would've made it past that first punch."

"Glad I could help." He gestured to the bag with a tilt of his darkly stubbled chin. "But really, I don't think you need me for getting your frustration out."

Something unspoken and hotly impulsive made Ava curl her fingers around Brennan's, halting his ministrations. In that moment, her mind couldn't deny what her body already knew.

She wanted Nick Brennan. And she wanted him right now.

"I do need you," Ava whispered, sliding her arms over the strong ridge of his shoulders to brush her heated body against his. He stiffened, the plane of his chest immovably firm even through the dual layers of cotton between them.

"Your emotions are all over the place from hitting the bag, that's all," he said, but Ava shook her head, pressing even closer.

"No. My emotions are all over the place from you, Brennan. I want *you*. And I'm tired of fighting it."

Chapter Fifteen

Brennan's mouth was on hers the instant she finished her sentence, and dear God in heaven, Ava felt his kiss rake over every inch of her sensitive skin. Pressing the balls of her bootless feet into the cool concrete, she maximized the contact of her mouth, her chest, her *everything* against Brennan's body as she parted her lips in a reckless request for more.

"Ava." He hooked his fingers into the belt loops on her jeans, thrusting against her hips in one long, sinuous slide before taking an infuriating step back. "We can't just jump into this."

But she reclaimed the space between them in an instant. "Oh yes, we can. It's not like we're strangers." The thought was as foreign to Ava as breathing grape jelly instead of air. "I want this, Brennan, and I think you want it too. Even if it's just for today. Be with me."

He bit out a curse as she strung a trail of kisses down the side of his neck. "You're really killing me here."

Ava shifted to look at him, confused. The rock-hard erection pressing tight to her belly left little guesswork as to his desire, and his kiss had been hungry to the point of need. Still, a tendril of doubt flared deep in her gut. "Do you not want this?"

Brennan's eyes glittered, nearly black beneath the scant light overhead, and something unspoken broke loose as he pinned her with a stare so dark and unrelentingly sexy, Ava lost her breath.

"I want this more than you can imagine." The muscles in his jaw went taut as he dropped his forehead to hers, his mouth barely an inch away. "I want to kiss you until I'm out of air," Brennan whispered, his lips feathering over hers in the barest sweep, and Ava nearly whimpered from the want pulsing underneath her skin.

"Brennan, please, I—"

"Shh." He cut her off with another brush of his mouth, and she exhaled, hard and hot. "Let me finish. Yes, I want you. I want to touch every last part of you until we both scream. Damn it, Ava, I want to bury myself inside you so deep and so sweet, you can't tell where I end and you begin. But I can't."

"Why not?" she rasped, her voice so thick she barely recognized it as her own.

"Because." Brennan's palms slid up her arms, a corresponding shiver climbing the length of her spine. "If we do this, it won't be once. I've wanted you beneath me and screaming my name for the last seven years. This happens"— he paused, his fingers flexing into her shoulders with just enough pressure to make her knees wobble—"and it's not going to be fast. It's not going to be impulsive, and it's not going to be just today. Do you understand?"

Ava's breath caught in her lungs, and she tilted her head to look up at him, catching the intensity in his gaze full-on. "I understand," she said.

But instead of walking away, she kissed him.

"Ava." He ground out her name, the vibration melting

against her lips as he coaxed them open with his tongue. Testing her lower lip with barely there flicks, Brennan explored the sensitive bow of her mouth, tasting and teasing until Ava was certain she'd explode. She tightened the knot of her arms around his shoulders, molding their upper bodies even closer as she swept her tongue over his in a bold push. He responded in kind, cupping the back of her neck with one palm while gripping her hips closer to his with the other. The heat, the friction, the pure, unfiltered desire building like an out-of-control wildfire between them—all of it pushed Ava higher and harder and faster, until finally they broke apart, gasping for breath.

"Come with me." Without waiting for a response, Brennan grabbed her hand and carved a direct path toward the door, but Ava slipped in front of him for another greedy kiss.

"Why?" she asked, nipping his bottom lip. She'd wanted his hands on her for the last nine days. The idea of waiting even nine more seconds felt like an eternity.

"Because the next thing on the list is to touch every last part of you until we both scream, and I'm not making you come in my utility closet."

Brennan had her halfway into the hall before she could process the movement, walking her backward with his arms banded under her rib cage to guide the way. Her shoulder blades bumped against a cool surface, but the easy give and continued motion told her it had to be the cracked-open door she'd seen across the hall on their way into the utility room.

Muted sunlight edged past the stark white window blinds in the new space, surprising Ava with its late afternoon slant. She registered details in tiny clips—the soft carpet under her feet, the brisk, ocean-like scent of Brennan's skin on hers, the sleep-rumpled navy blue sheets

suddenly surrounding her body as he laid her on the bed
in the center of the room.

The way he could make her delirious with nothing more
than a simple touch.

"Christ, I missed you," Brennan said, kneeling in front
of her on the bed. She parted her knees in a wordless bid
to bring him closer, and he angled his hips over her center,
leaning in to frame her face with both hands.

"I missed you too." Ava arched against him, reaching
for the hem of his thermal shirt so she could finally, *finally*
get her hands on his bare skin. But Brennan hadn't removed
the second wrap from her hand, and in the heat of the
kisses that had followed, she'd failed to notice the blue
cotton still keeping her right fingers prisoner.

"Ugh, I want this off so I can feel you." She reached for
the edge of the wrap with her free hand, but Brennan cut
the move short by capturing both wrists in one fluid sweep.

"No."

"I'm sorry?" Ava breathed, her heartbeat ratcheting
higher. The urge to touch his body without barriers thundered
beneath her skin, growing from an ache to a full-blown
demand.

One Brennan refused to let her answer. "I said no. I
promised to make you scream, and believe me, I intend to
be a man of my word."

"You promised we'd both scream," she reminded him,
and he responded by tucking her hands beneath either side
of her hips.

"Sit on your hands if you have to, sweetheart. You're
screaming first."

In the span of Ava's gasp, Brennan covered her body
from shoulders to core, his mouth making a slow, sexy
descent from her ear to the column of her neck. Her fingers
tingled with the white hot urge to leave the spot where he'd

placed them, snug against the denim-covered curve of her ass. But not being able to touch him meant having to slow down and focus, and oh God, the man's mouth was pure magic on the spot where her shoulder folded into her collarbone.

"Ohhh." Ava groaned her approval, bowing her spine from the bedsheets to give him better access, and he smiled into her skin.

"Well, that's a start." Hooking his fingers under the hem of her long-sleeved T-shirt, Brennan relieved her of the garment, returning her hands under her hips as soon as the cotton hit the floor. He picked up right where he'd left off at her collarbone, heating her skin with his tongue and his lips before cooling it right back off with gentle puffs of breath. Each move brought him closer to her aching breasts, until finally he traced the slope of one side all the way down to the center of her breastbone, the following exhale turning her untouched nipples into tightly drawn peaks.

"Oh *God*." The words spilled past Ava's lips even though she didn't remember forming them, and she impulsively pushed upward with her trapped hands, canting her hips against the ridge of his cock.

Brennan froze, one finger beneath the front closure of her bra and both eyes locked on her face. "Ava." The word was a warning, low and rough in the back of his throat, and a tiny thrill of realization snapped through Ava's mind.

"Yes?" she asked, using her hands to press her hips up more slowly this time.

"You need to stop that." He thrust back against her, the cradle of his lower body keeping time with her movements for just a minute before he stopped with a groan. "Now."

"Not a chance."

Brennan's eyes flew wide before narrowing in on her in disbelief. "What?"

Ava shook her head, her hair spilling over both shoulders. "I might scream first, but you're coming with me."

Using her hands to guide her, she moved her hips in a rhythm both slow and full of purpose. It took only seconds for Brennan to match it, pushing back into her as he slipped the straps of her lacy white bra from her shoulders. Her nipples strained with the need to be touched, and he didn't disappoint. Brennan balanced his weight on one forearm at her side as he used the other hand to gently skim her nipple with the pad of his thumb. Three passes had Ava panting, and when he dipped his head to draw the needy tip past his lips on the fourth, she arched up on a cry.

"Better," he said, his goatee rasping her nipple with a delicious glide of pleasure-pain. He shifted his body more tightly to her side, coasting both hands down the midline of her torso to reach for the button on her jeans. Returning his mouth to her already aching nipple, Brennan alternated his attention between both breasts as his fingers made fast work of removing the denim. He snapped up both of her hands, unraveling the second wrap from her wrist, then fingers, in a series of well-placed tugs.

"Not so fast," he grated as she lifted her hands to reach for him. "I like you here." Lacing his fingers through hers on first one side, then the other, Brennan slid her palms back into place beneath either side of her hips. The unexpected thrill of their joined touch under her body sent a shot of damp heat to Ava's core, and it doubled as he dropped his eyes to the swath of her white lace panties.

Brennan released one of her hands, notching his body against her side to drag a fingertip over the crease where her thigh met her body. "Show me what you want, Ava."

His other hand, still wrapped around hers and tucked

tight to the swell of her backside, pushed her palm into motion, rocking her hips along with it. The contact of his fingers on the edge of her panties coupled with the rhythm he created with her hips took her straight from slow burn to screaming need. Brennan tightened the hand beneath her to meet Ava's wordless demand for more, and when he slipped past her panties to test her heat with his fingers, her eyes flew open wide.

"That," she cried, tilting her hips even further off the bed. "I want you to touch me like that."

Brennan's lashes swept downward, shadowing his face in the low afternoon light as he gazed at their intimate contact. "Damn, you are so hot. I want my hands on you all night."

Ava took in his face through her lust-filled haze, slowly registering the hard line of his jaw and the taut flex of muscles pressed hard to her side. The sheer want on his face broke past his waning look of control, and between his expression and his touch, she was lost. Ava's knees fell wide as the rest of her body gripped tight, her fingertips curling into the flare at the back of her hips as she thrust against Brennan's hand.

Together, they built a rhythm both hypnotic and hot, the sheer pleasure mixing in with Ava's bright urge for release. Brennan's movements were unyielding, but he watched her with reverence, his heavy breaths matching hers moan for moan. He slid his thumb past the lacy edge of her panties, stroking the tight bundle of nerves at her center, and Ava jacked her hips all the way off the bed.

"Brennan," she cried, arching into his touch. "Oh God. Please . . ."

The request broke from her chest at the same moment he called out her name, and the ragged sound of his voice sent her right over the edge. Ava unraveled under Brennan's hands, wave after wave of breathless free-fall coaxing her trembling from the inside out. His strokes became gentler as she returned to awareness in slow degrees, until he finally smoothed her panties back into place and returned to her side.

"Ava." Brennan cupped her face to kiss her with just a surprisingly soft brush of his lips. "Show me what you want now."

She met his gaze, fully prepared to give him a sexy comeback, when his expression registered in her brain. His hands were still, one palm cradling her cheek, the other propped beneath him where their shoulders touched. That black-coffee stare that had glittered with openly sensual intention just minutes ago slid into something else, something questioning, and the truth slammed into Ava all at once.

Brennan wasn't telling her to show him something brazen as part of their foreplay. He was giving her a chance to run.

"Brennan." Ava slid fully to her side, placing her fingers over the center of his shirt. She should feel vulnerable, nearly naked while he was still dressed, but she didn't. Slowly, she splayed her hand over his thumping heartbeat, sliding close to fortify the contact with her shoulders and chest.

"I'm sure." She kissed him, the salty-sweet taste of his lips invading her senses and rekindling the ache between her thighs. "I want this. I want you."

Ava reached between their bodies for the hem of Brennan's shirt, guiding it over his head in a swift pull. She took a minute to drink in the corded muscles, the hard, masculine curve of his shoulders, the sinewy fold of his pecs. A dusting of dark hair covered his chest, and Ava followed it with her fingers all the way to the thin trail leading into his waistband.

"You still keep a stash of condoms in your wallet for emergencies?"

Brennan laughed, nipping at her bottom lip. "Yeah."

Her hands landed on the top button of his jeans, sliding it free with a twist. "Good. 'Cause we're going to need them."

The garment hit the floor, and with only one quick pause to grab a condom, Ava returned to the bedsheets with a sassy smile. She ran one hand up the length of his thigh, gliding past the edge of his black boxer briefs. Positioning herself on her side to face him, she angled her hips to his, leaving just enough room for her hand between them. Her nipples tightened at the friction from the crisp smattering of hair on his chest, sparking a fresh burst of heat in her core, and she followed it on nothing but impulse.

"Now it's your turn." Ava wrapped her fingers around Brennan's cock, caressing him over the thin layer of cotton. "Show me what you want."

She thrust her hips against the motion of her hand, using both to recreate the sensual movement that had sent her over the edge. Brennan arched into the curve of her fingers, the push sending his rock-hard length over the damp center of her panties.

"Here," he ground out, his voice mingling with her pleasured gasp. "I want to be inside you, right here." He broke the space between them, but just enough to lower the scrap of lace from around her hips. "I want to fill you up so many times, you lose your mind. I want to be here." His fingers swept between her thighs, sliding home with a thrust that made them both moan.

"Then don't wait." Ava mustered the last bit of her composure to pull off Brennan's boxer briefs, planting a string of kisses over his neck as he slid the condom into place. Rolling her back against the mattress, he pressed her thighs apart with his frame, and she arced up to meet him as he thrust forward to fill her.

"Oh." Absolute bliss collided with sheer, sexual desire in Ava's veins. Brennan levered himself forward to cover her, moving slowly until there was no space between them where they were joined. He started a sinuous rhythm, and she answered every thrust with one of her own until they rocked together so seamlessly, there was simply no boundary between where he ended and she began.

"God, Ava," Brennan bit out, his lips rough against her shoulder. "You feel so fucking good."

Pushing back from her chest, he centered his weight on his knees, gripping her hips and lifting her from the heated sheets to hold her flush with his body as he filled her again and again. The need for release coiled deep in Ava's belly, and she gave in to every impulsive demand streaming beneath her skin. She tipped her hips against the strength of Brennan's movements, the angle bringing him to the spot where she needed him most.

"There," she gasped, her body tightening further in delicious demand. "Oh, God, right . . . *there.*"

Ava's orgasm crashed through her, and Brennan's muscular frame went bowstring tight at the sound of her reckless cries. Desperate for him to lose control, she knotted her legs around his waist to deepen their connection even more. His eyes darkened, nearly black and utterly fierce as his thrusts grew faster, matching the intensity of his gaze. Brennan dug his fingers into her hips, holding her even closer as his motions became deeper and more frenzied.

Sliding one hand to Ava's shoulder, he pressed his chest against hers, covering her with heat and friction and closeness so fierce, her breath flew out on ragged gasps. With one final thrust, Brennan groaned out a curse, calling her name as he locked his hips into hers and shuddered over the edge.

They lay together until their heavy breaths turned into slower draws of air, the comfortable weight of Brennan's body covering hers with sweet familiarity. The sunlight poking in through the blinds had coalesced to the shadows of late afternoon, sending thinly lined patterns onto the carpet beneath the window. He brushed a kiss over her forehead before slipping from the room, returning a few minutes later to lie back down at her side.

"I've got to hand it to you," Ava said, propping herself up on one elbow to look at him more fully. "You *really* know how to relax a girl."

Brennan laughed, his whole face softening as he turned to put them face-to-face. "I'm fairly certain that's a mutual talent, but I'm glad you feel better."

The dread that had overwhelmed her earlier threatened to take another poke at her chest, but Ava dodged it with her battle-tested moxie. *Please, please, just give me this moment.* "I do feel better."

"You want to talk about it?"

The simplicity of Brennan's question had the word *yes* burning hot on her tongue. Reaching out, she wrapped her arms around his waist to pull him close, but when her fingers brushed over the extensive scar marking the skin of his lower back, they both froze.

"Do you?" Ava whispered, concern welling in her chest as her eyes flashed up to his.

"Not really."

The wide-open honesty on Brennan's face marked his answer as the truth rather than a cover-up or an excuse. And as much as she wanted to listen if he needed her, right now Ava understood the need to forget.

"Okay," she said, using the momentum of her arms

around his body to roll him deftly against the warm sheets. "I'm here if you change your mind. But in the meantime, maybe we should explore the true purpose of a Sunday afternoon."

A single dark brow lifted. "And what's that?"

Ava smiled, parting her knees over his hips as she leaned in for a kiss that left no uncertainty about her intentions. "Relaxing, of course. After all, if we're going to chill out, we might as well go all in."

Chapter Sixteen

Brennan flipped through the inventory sheets on the clipboard in front of the Double Shot's walk-in fridge, absolutely unable to erase the crooked smile from his lips. The Monday morning produce order had arrived earlier than usual, but not even the lack of extra downtime could knock his mood out of the oh-hell-yes stratosphere.

After ten hours, three cartons of Chinese delivery food, and one really long, *really* hot shower together, Brennan and Ava had redefined the very nature of the word "relaxing."

"Well. That's not your usual fare." Adrian's gruff voice met him from the alcove leading to the back entrance, and he reached up to swing the brim of his Harley-Davidson baseball hat away from his narrowed eyes. Brennan recognized his buddy's bid for a more thorough examination, but for once, he didn't care how closely Adrian looked at him.

"What?" Brennan asked, adding a whistle to his grin. "I can't be in a good mood?"

Adrian went brows-up. "It's nine o'clock on a Monday morning. In a word, no."

"If you say so." Brennan signed off on the updated inventory, moving toward the drink station at the pass-through to the dining room. He scooped just enough coffee grounds into the filter basket to resuscitate a hibernating grizzly bear, hitting BREW for Adrian before grabbing a Coke for himself.

"Hmm." Adrian raised his scruffy chin in thanks, his expression quickly going sour at the Coke in Brennan's hand. "You know that's not natural, right?"

Nope. Not even a raft of crap from his army tank of a boss was going to flatline Brennan's incredible mood. "What, this?" He toasted Adrian and took a long sip. He'd become so used to drinking soda instead of coffee in the morning, that the quirky habit barely registered with him anymore.

Adrian shrugged out of his leather jacket, trading the beat-to-hell garment for one of the clean aprons hanging on the wall next to the alcove. "Yes, *that*. Have you got something against good, old-fashioned coffee?"

"There's such a thing as too much caffeine, you know." Coffee had always thrown Brennan into overdrive. Which would've been great if he'd worked a nine-to-five, and even better if he'd clocked longer hours on a regular schedule. But doing twenty-four-hour shifts at an adrenaline-soaked firehouse meant getting enough sleep—sometimes at weird-ass hours and always at unpredictable intervals—was necessary to a guy's survival. Brennan had quickly learned to swap coffee for something lower grade. Catching decent shut-eye in a bunk full of jacked-up firefighters was hard enough without the caffeine buzz.

Not that he'd had to worry about it for two and a half years. Then again, his system had seen more than its fair share of chemical manipulation, and Brennan knew all too well that the detox—from both the highs and the lows—was a bitch best left undisturbed.

"I think we're gonna have to agree to disagree on that

one," Adrian said, filling his cup to the brim. "How's your reporter?"

Brennan smiled, welcoming his good mood back with open arms. "That obvious?"

"Seeing as how your facial expressions normally range from serious to scowling, I'd say the shit-eating grin is a bit of a giveaway."

"Why does everyone think I'm so serious?" Brennan argued, albeit without heat. So he had a moderately functioning work ethic. Sue a guy for wanting to be busy.

Adrian snorted, grabbing a frying pan from the open-air wire rack by the cooktop and setting it over one of the burners with a *clang*. "Maybe it's because you do things like supervise produce deliveries at ungodly hours on your morning off."

Okay. The big man had a point. "Fine. But you're serious too," Brennan countered. The only thing Adrian took to heart more than cooking at the restaurant was Teagan, and she went hand in hand with the place, anyway.

His buddy shrugged, knotting an apron over his jeans and T-shirt combo. "Yeah, but I belong right here in the kitchen. Always have."

The implication winged between them before settling in Brennan's gut like a stone. "Are you saying I don't belong at the Double Shot?"

"Fuck, no." Adrian pegged him with a gray green stare that backed up the affirmation 100 percent. "If I thought you weren't solid, you wouldn't work in my restaurant, man. All I'm saying is I get the feeling right here you belong somewhere else, you know?"

Adrian brushed a hand over the brick slab of his chest, his gaze lingering on Brennan's for just a second more before he bent down to grab some butter and eggs from the lowboy at his work station. Brennan opened his mouth to launch the tried and true *I'm fine* he'd relied on since the day he'd landed in Pine Mountain, but the words stopped short on his lips.

He had belonged somewhere else once. And in less than two weeks, he had to face the glaring reminder of what he was missing.

Not to mention what he'd lost.

"Yeah." Brennan's back muscles thrummed with a low, familiar ache. "It's kind of complicated."

"I get it, believe me," Adrian said. "But there's a difference between being serious about what you're made for and being serious about *denying* what you're made for. You're a damned good bar manager, and Teagan and I are lucky to have you. But don't lose sight of the important shit, okay?"

The image of Ava, scantily wrapped in one of his bath towels with her eyelashes still spiky-wet from their shower yesterday, jumped to center stage in Brennan's mind, and the throb in his back eased up by just a fraction. "Okay."

Adrian grinned. "Good. Now do you want some of these scrambled eggs? Because honestly, your breakfast choices so far are giving me the goddamn shakes."

With the tension in his system at a temporary standstill, Brennan took a plate full of eggs up to the Double Shot's office. Though Monday was normally his day off, he'd come in to handle the produce delivery and complete the schedule for the handful of days he'd be missing next weekend when he went back to Fairview. Once the paperwork was complete and in a folder on Teagan's desk, Brennan had just enough time to clock out and change for his PT session with Kat. As tempted as he was to blow off the appointment in favor of catching a much-needed nap, he'd used some pretty rusty musculature yesterday with Ava, and not just once.

Cue the goofy-ass grin. Not even twelve hours had passed since Brennan had taken Ava back to her car at the marina after their evening together, kissing her good-bye three times before she'd actually disentangled herself from his arms just before midnight. Even then, she'd run back for one last lingering kiss, pressing her phone number into his hand and telling him to call her whenever he wanted to relax.

He palmed his cell phone and dialed before he could get halfway across the Double Shot's parking lot.

"*Riverside Daily*, Ava Mancuso."

Jesus, even her voice was brown-sugar sweet. "Morning, Ava Mancuso. How's today's news treating you?"

Her laughter filtered right from the phone line to his sternum. "Well, I suppose that depends."

"On?"

"Whether or not one considers the Riverside Elementary holiday pageant news."

Brennan slung the bag with his jeans and clean sweatshirt into the back of the Trailblazer before sliding into the driver's seat. "Ouch. Your boss still isn't offering up the plum assignments, huh?" Truly, the guy sounded like a grade-A douche bag. The story Ava had done on the fire had been spot-freaking-on. She really deserved more credit than to be stuck with small-time stories.

"I'm afraid not," she said with a barely audible sigh. "But writing an article on the holiday pageant is better than writing nothing. Plus, the teacher in charge of the event has worked hard and the kids were all excited at the idea of being in the paper, so that'll at least make writing the article fun."

"Want to tell me all about it over lunch?" The offer sprang from his lips before he could check it against his normally stalwart voice of reason, but come on. It was an impromptu bite to eat, not a complete loss of composure.

"You want to talk about my coverage of the elementary school holiday show?" Ava punctuated her surprise with a chirp of laughter, but Brennan didn't budge.

"Sure. I'm off work, and I've got an appointment in Riverside anyway. What time do you normally take a break?"

"I could probably make it out of here by one for a quick lunch," she said. "But you really don't have to talk shop with me on your afternoon off."

He flipped the Trailblazer's key to check the clock on the dashboard, and yeah, the timing was perfect. "I know I don't. Why don't you meet me at the medical offices next to Riverside Hospital? There's a great pizza place right across the street. The calzones are insane. What do you say?"

Ava paused, but then Brennan swore he heard the smile break over her voice. "Sure. I'll be there."

"Great." His own smile took over, and damn, it didn't feel half bad to give the expression a little air time.

"It's a date."

"If I didn't know any better, I'd swear you were trying to kill me outright."

Brennan counted out a slow exhale into the cushions on the therapy table as Kat did her level best to dismantle the muscles cradling his lumbar vertebrae. He'd swear she was more four-hundred-pound gorilla than petite five-foot-two physical therapist, but saying so out loud would only make his life exponentially more difficult. Not only was she hot and heavy with the Double Shot's sous chef, Jesse, but she also had Brennan sunny side down on the table, and the main space of the open-air therapy room was empty of any potential witnesses.

"Please. Don't be such a baby," she scoffed, pressing the flat of her palm against his T-shirt-covered back with ease. "It's soft tissue manipulation, not Chinese water torture."

Still, Kat scaled back on the pressure, shifting her weight from her position at the side of the padded table to split the leverage with her other hand on his shoulder.

"You say potato, I say bullshit. Ah, that's good." Brennan relaxed into the firm contact of Kat's fingers, willing himself to open up to the sensation rather than fight it.

"It's not bullshit if it works, tough guy." She paused, assessing his lower back with her hands. "You're actually pretty loose all the way through L5. Whatever exercises you've been doing this week seem to be working."

He coughed out a laugh, pushing himself upright as Kat finished her last round of acupressure. "I'll keep that in mind."

"Hmm." She tipped her head in obvious curiosity, her ponytail showcasing various hues from strawberry blond to gold-toned butterscotch, with a healthy batch of hot pink streaks thrown in for good measure. "How's your pain been this week?"

"Fine."

"You know better," she said, flipping her hand palm up and wiggling her fingers in a *give it up* gesture.

Damn it, he really needed a better default position. "On a scale of one to ten, it's a four."

Kat's expression flickered, likely because she knew in vivid detail what had given Brennan the ten that had set the ceiling of his pain threshold. "Any spasms?" she asked, crossing the open space where the three therapy tables stood to grab a bottle of water from one of the cabinets by the exercise equipment on the opposite wall.

"One." He might not have had a full-fledged spasm in a

while, but that didn't mean he had to get all gabby with his details. The spasm had been easily dispatched. Talking about it wouldn't change anything.

Of course, Kat frowned, and there went his choice in the matter. "Could you pinpoint the trigger? Any sudden change in movement or added stress?"

"Not really," Brennan said, although the words felt like metal shavings in his mouth. The muscles that had just gone lax at Kat's ministrations threatened to seize at the memory of the phone call from his sister, and he inhaled in an effort to relax them.

"You know, the stress doesn't have to be a literal force, like lifting something you're not supposed to or staying on your feet for too long." The armful of beaded bracelets circling her wrists clicked softly as she passed over the bottle of water with a knowing look. "Mental anxiety can contribute to back spasms just as easily as physical duress."

"I know, Kat. But really, I'm good."

She paused. "You've functionally recovered from both a devastating back injury and an addiction to prescription painkillers, Brennan. That makes you more than good in my book. But it's not your body I'm worried about."

Before he could argue, Kat added, "I told you when we started that alternative therapy has to work from the neck up. You don't have to talk to me about it if you don't want to. But you're not supposed to need this on an extended basis—it's my job to get you through flare-ups and provide maintenance therapy, not treat you indefinitely."

Brennan's gut did a slow descent toward his cross-trainers. "I know I torqued things up a week and a half ago at Joe's. But the pain's getting better." Not that he didn't deserve a little pain. Checks and balances, and all that shit.

"Okay," Kat said, tucking her hands into the pockets of her cargo pants. "All I'm saying is it might do you some good to air out whatever's bothering you to someone who makes you feel comfortable. Relax your mind, and a lot of times, your body follows."

The words hooked into Brennan's mind, settling in all at once. Although he hadn't intended for Ava to stumble upon the back spasm in question, he *had* felt comfortable that day they'd done yoga, and that comfort had only grown over the past week.

But telling her he'd suffered a back injury a handful of years ago was one thing. Copping to the circumstances that had led to it—not to mention the out of control need to destroy the pain that had so thoroughly ruled him afterward—was enough to make the most honest man hide.

And Brennan was anything but upstanding. He'd killed his best fucking *friend*.

He wasn't airing that out to make himself feel better, because he damned sure didn't deserve to feel anything other than guilty.

"Anyway," Kat said, breaking the tension-thick silence. "It's just a thought. Want to try one last round of seated direct-contact acupressure for the road? I'll even pretend not to hear you complain about my cold hands. How about it?"

Brennan managed a nod, pulling his shirt over his head to leave him in just his low-slung gym pants. A little extra therapy might get him through the rest of this week feeling less like attic floorboards, and maybe the ease in discomfort would let him stuff his churning feelings about returning to Fairview back where they belonged, under wraps.

"You're the boss," he told her, turning away from her to face the window on the far wall. Brennan sat up as straight as he could, but still his gut knotted, threatening to hunch his spine. Old thoughts burbled up, small scraps of memory knocking hard beneath his ribs. Alex's cocky,

all-American smile as he'd clambered into the back step of
Engine Eight with his helmet under one arm, Mason triple-
checking his Scott pack while bragging about sweeping
their weekly basketball pool. The first streak of concern
when Cole had hollered a gruff *shut up* as the update arrived from dispatch. The hot slash of adrenaline in Brennan's
chest when he'd realized the call was far from routine.

The gravel of Captain Westin's voice at the scene of the
apartment fire as he'd said, "Above all, have each other's
backs."

The memory surged to the surface, gripping Brennan
from blood to bones, and for a split second, he didn't fight
it. But then the images flashed forward, growing darker,
leaving the bitter taste of smoke and screams in his mouth,
and damn it, he needed control. He turned to tell Kat to
forget the last round of therapy so he could get the hell out
of here and breathe, when a very familiar, very feminine
gasp interrupted him from behind.

"I'm so sorry. I didn't mean to intrude." Even in the dead
of night, Brennan would recognize Ava's voice, and it
punched all the way through him despite her hushed tone.

"I apologize, our receptionist is at lunch, and I didn't
see any other appointments booked. Can I help you?" Kat
asked, stepping from the edge of his peripheral vision
behind the therapy table, likely to preserve his privacy by
blocking him from view.

Ava renewed her apology, drawing in an audible breath.
"No, I ah . . . no, thank you."

Her footsteps rushed over the tiled floor, and Brennan
knew in that second he could let her retreat. Kat was blocking Ava's vision, and she might not have even caught a
glimpse of his back, considering how quickly she'd stumbled
into the therapy center from outside. But something flooded

through his chest, outmuscling the dread of his memories with its certainty.

She'd trusted him with her past, and she'd proven she wasn't going to run. She was standing right behind him, seeing what no one—not Adrian or Teagan or even his family—had seen for two and a half years.

And Brennan was sick to death of hiding.

"Wait," he said, turning his chin to look over his shoulder. "Ava's with me, Kat. It's okay if she sees my scars."

Chapter Seventeen

Ava stood on the threshold of the Riverside Physical Therapy Center, wishing like mad for the bamboo floor tiles to rumble open and swallow her whole. She'd been a few minutes early on purpose, not wanting Brennan to think she'd had second thoughts like yesterday at the marina. Given the choice between the therapy center and the adjacent pediatrician's office, figuring out where Brennan's appointment was had fallen under the heading of *well, duh*. She'd walked over to sit in the waiting room for a few minutes, not expecting to catch a direct glimpse of the main therapy room from her spot in the reception area.

She definitely hadn't expected to get an eyeful of the five-inch scar angrily staking claim to the center of Brennan's lower back, or the streak of vulnerability on his darkly stubbled face as he'd said she could stay.

Oh God. What had *happened* to him two and a half years ago?

"Well. You are full of surprises, aren't you?" murmured the painfully adorable blonde standing by the padded examining table. Brennan shrugged, but a smile ticked one corner of his mouth upward, and the woman tipped her head at Ava to reveal a row of tiny silver hoops marching all the way up her ear. "Come on in, then, Ava. I'm Kat, Brennan's therapist. We're not quite done, but if he's fine with you staying, far be it from me to break up a good party."

"Oh." A polite retreat formed on Ava's tongue, but she caught it just shy of launch. Both Brennan and his therapist were okay with her being there, and despite the initial bolt of shock at seeing the evidence of his devastating injury, Ava was far from squeamish. Plus, Brennan hadn't backpedaled when she'd told him about her painful past.

She sure as hell wasn't going to get all soft over his.

"Okay, sure. Can I do anything to help?" Ava shrugged out of her coat and pushed up the sleeves of her fitted white blouse, giving Brennan a look chock full of *you asked for it* as she crossed the floor to stand at the foot of the table.

His half smile stayed in place, and he nodded a quick, unreadable greeting at her before turning to glance at a surprised-looking Kat over his shoulder. "Ava helped me with some of the pressure point stuff when I had that spasm last week."

"Ahhh." Kat's elfin features grew amused as she put her hands on Brennan's back. "Well, it looks as if she's helping you now too."

Ava lifted her chin in confusion. "But I'm not doing anything."

"Au contraire," Kat said, and whoa, she had some crazy muscles in her forearms for such a tiny woman. She grinned down at her fingers, moving them slightly. "All this musculature is telling me a different story. See? It's nice and loose."

Kat shifted a few more times, her expression unchanging and her hands moving with the rise and fall of Brennan's breath. Not wanting to distract either one of them—not to mention being just plain curious as hell—Ava watched quietly as Kat worked. Unlike when Ava had walked in on him last week, Brennan's posture was fluid and easy, even though his face tightened in obvious discomfort a time or two before Kat finished a few minutes later.

"There." She stepped back from the table, tucking a strand of bright pink hair into the mix of gold and light brown behind her heavily pierced ear. "I think that's enough for today."

"You don't have to go easy on me," Brennan argued with a frown.

Kat met it with a snort that belied her sweetly serene face. "And you don't have to keep your lunch date waiting. I'll see you next time." She gave him only enough time to guide his T-shirt back over his head before shooing him from his perch on the table.

Guilt flooded through Ava's belly, and she dug her ballet flats into the floor. "I really don't mind waiting," Ava said, but Kat just pegged Brennan with a knowing look before waving both him and Ava off.

"This is the best session you've had in the last week and a half. I didn't go easy on you. You went easy on yourself. Just do me a favor and think about that homework I gave you. It was great to meet you, Ava."

She offered a bright good-bye to both of them that sealed the we're-done-here deal, waving for good measure as she headed toward one of the doors on the far wall. Ava slid a covert look in Brennan's direction as he grabbed his hoodie from a nearby hook and started walking toward the front door of the building, and screw it. She might've caught him at a vulnerable moment—again—but sugar-coating things had never been her forte.

"You're kind of two for two in the unusual lunch break department," she said, infusing her expression with a teasing disdain. "I'm not sure I can top this when it's my turn to pick."

His pause took barely a second before he flashed her that sexy little half smile that really ought to be illegal. "I don't know. Your holiday pageant recap still sounds pretty exciting."

Ava fought the thudding ache behind her breastbone at the mention of her latest story. God, there had to be something else out there besides kids who could play "Silent Night" on the recorder, even if that *was* a lovely snapshot of the Christmas season.

Nope. Not going there. She might have a paltry two weeks to deliver the slam-bang page-turner that would save her job, but right now, this wasn't about her. "Nice try," she said. "But somehow I don't think that's the story you've got on your mind."

"You're right. It's not."

For a minute, nothing passed between them but footsteps and silence as they bundled up to cross the threshold to the sidewalk outside, and Ava's cheeks flared with the rare prickle of a blush. She might not be an expert in decorum, but pushing Brennan into a conversation he didn't want to have wasn't on her agenda, no matter how much the sight of his scars—not to mention the look on his face—said he had a story to tell.

Only this time, he didn't dodge the question. "Before I moved to Pine Mountain, I was a firefighter in Fairview. I spent almost four years on engine at Station Eight."

"I thought you might have been a firefighter," she said, falling into step next to him. There was no point in skirting the topic, and Brennan wasn't stupid. He had to know she'd made that connection when she'd prepared for their interview last week, even if he'd flat-out refused to answer her questions about it. "You were so gung ho about going to the fire academy after that summer on Sapphire Island."

"Yeah. Being a firefighter turned out to be nothing like I'd imagined, that's for sure." His expression grew wistful, but he wore enough of a smile that Ava bit.

"So the job was harder than you thought it would be?"

His smile morphed into a chuckle, albeit short lived. "Every single day. But being in an engine company was better than I imagined too."

"Sounds like an interesting mix," Ava said, following Brennan's lead as he paused at a small intersection to look for passing cars.

"If by interesting, you mean it kicked every part of my ass while simultaneously showing me exactly where I belonged, then yeah. I'd say that's pretty accurate. But being a firefighter isn't a job. It's a lifestyle, and there are no half measures. You're either in or you're not."

"That makes sense." After all, she couldn't imagine being a firefighter was a paper-pushing nine to five. Not that Ava had any experience with that kind of job either. "It must be tough to get used to the intensity, though, even for the best firefighters."

They crossed the street, their feet keeping comfortable time on the asphalt as Brennan seemed to think about his answer. "I guess it was hard to adjust at first. But to be honest, even though we kept regular hours at the academy, being on shift at Station Eight wasn't always insane."

"So how does it work, with the schedule and everything? I mean, is there a night shift and a day shift, or do you switch, like doctors in an emergency department?" Ava asked, her curiosity snapping through her like a live wire. She'd learned ages ago that making assumptions that hung on face value—or worse yet, stereotypes—was dangerous territory. Better to just voice the questions and get the truth.

And Brennan didn't disappoint. "Scheduling usually depends on the size of the company. Fairview's a pretty big city, so in our house we had three shifts, which rotated. Most of us did twenty-four hours on, forty-eight off."

"Whoa." Ava blinked in surprise. "You worked for twenty-four hours straight, every shift?"

This time, he laughed. "Well, yeah, but the calls aren't constant, so in that way, I guess it is kind of like a hospital. The fire station has bunks and a kitchen, and we basically live there while we're on shift. Sometimes it's dead, sometimes we're slammed. Even then, most of our calls are incidents other than fires or false alarms."

"Incidents other than fires?" Ava slowed in front of the tiny strip mall restaurant tucked between the Riverside pharmacy and a hardware store, gesturing to the red and white awning in a nonverbal *is this it?*

He nodded, pulling the door open and ushering her through with a gentle hand on her back. The flow of their movements around each other was as effortless as the conversation, and it only made Ava's interest burn more brightly.

"Sure. You name it, we've probably seen it. Downed power lines, people stuck in flash floods, pileups on the freeway . . . and before you ask, yes. I've even saved a kitten from a tree."

Ava's laugh escaped in a quick burst. "You have not!" So much for ditching assumptions.

"Cross my heart," Brennan promised, motioning an imaginary X over the front of his sweatshirt with one finger. "I think it was maybe the third call I ever went out on. Rookie always draws the short straw. The cat was fine and the owner was grateful, but let's just say I'm glad we wear gloves."

His seamless use of the present tense yanked at both Ava's attention and her heartstrings, but she stuffed it down. Brennan's crooked little half smile, paired with the total lack of visible tension across the back of his shoulders, spoke of his comfort level with the conversation. If he could handle it, then so could she.

"I bet." Ava inhaled the enticing scent of freshly baked pizza, heading for an unoccupied table by the open kitchen. They took a few minutes to get situated in the small booth toward the back of the mostly empty restaurant, but her menu lay unopened on the polished wood table between them.

"It sounds like you saw a lot while you were there."

"Yeah. Station Eight houses a fire engine, a rescue squad, and an ambulance. Everyone responds to fire calls, but squad goes out on most of the other nine-one-one calls in our jurisdiction, too. For things like car accidents or other non-fire emergencies, a lot of times engine is on scene to assist."

"Okay, you're losing me," she said, trying to organize the information in her brain. "The ambulance, I've got, and I'm pretty sure I'm straight on the engine and the fire calls. But what's the deal with the rescue squad?"

Brennan laced his fingers together, dark eyes glinting warmly as he leaned in toward her. "The training for squad is more specialized, and not every house has one. They don't just go out on fire calls. They go out on *every* call. Hazmat, building collapses, water rescue. They do it all."

"And you guys sign up for this?" Ava asked, only partly kidding. But God, hazmat and building collapses? Even without the fires, it sounded top-shelf crazy.

"Squad's extremely elite. Guys don't just sign up for it.

They bust ass, sometimes for years, just to be considered.
I told you, it's a lifestyle, not a job."

She considered that for a minute. "So it's like Special
Forces in the military?"

"That's a loose interpretation," he said, nodding slowly.
"But you've got the right idea."

"Were you on the rescue squad, then?"

Brennan's slight flinch told Ava he was grateful for the
waitress's timing as she arrived with two glasses of water
and her order pad at the ready. After turning Brennan's
request for iced tea and a sausage and mushroom calzone
into a double order, Ava let loose with the apology on her
tongue.

"I don't mean to be nosy or put you on the spot. The
idea of a rescue squad is just pretty fascinating. But we
don't have to talk about it." She bit her lip in an effort to
keep her churning thoughts limited to the space in her
head, but Brennan caught her gaze and held tight.

"It's okay." His voice was quiet but full of honesty as he
said, "The answer to your question is actually yes and no.
Yes, I was technically a member of squad when I got hurt.
But no. Nobody knew it but me."

Brennan sat, stone still and shocked as shit as he realized the words he'd kept on a two-and-a-half-year lockdown had actually come out of his mouth. He'd never told
anyone about the short-lived conversation he and Captain
Westin had shared just minutes before Station Eight's overhead system blared out the automated request for engine,
squad, and paramedics to respond to that apartment fire. It
hadn't been a secret that Brennan's dedication had pushed
him to want to transition to squad, but he'd been passed
over once before for a firefighter with more seniority. So

when the second opportunity had opened up, he'd kept his transfer request on the down-low.

The unfiltered high of making squad had lasted seventeen minutes. The bone-ripping pain and guilt that had come after? Yeah, that was going to last forever.

"Nobody knew but you?" Ava looked at him, the shadow of confusion in her wide, green eyes totally at odds with the bright overhead lighting and cheery Christmas music filtering through the restaurant. It had been frighteningly effortless to tell her the logistics of being a firefighter, the obvious interest on her pretty face sparking his deep-seated nostalgia for the career he'd loved.

This part? Not so much.

"No." Brennan cleared his throat, but still the words scratched out of his windpipe like sandpaper. "I found out I'd made squad just before I got hurt, so none of the guys on engine knew."

Not that telling them would've been easy. Going for squad was a hell of a lot different from *making* squad. Even though he would've stayed in the same house, the news would've earned Brennan a healthy ration of shit from everyone on Engine Eight. Except for Mason.

Christ, he needed to nail his trap shut. Some things were just too far gone to fix with a little bit of airtime and a whole lot of regret.

"So, ah, then I got hurt and it didn't really matter. Injuries like mine are career enders either way, so I decided to relocate, and here I am." Brennan picked up the laminated card boasting the daily specials, giving it a hard stare even though they'd already ordered. A warm brush against his suddenly cold fingers snapped his gaze upward, and Ava curled her hand over his in a quick squeeze.

"And here you are."

Her expression was so wide open, so wiped free of both

judgment and pity, that Brennan nearly let the entire story break loose. But then their waitress swung by with two napkin-wrapped utensil rolls and their iced teas, and the impulse disappeared like smoke in a windstorm.

"Your physical therapy is a bit different from the norm, huh?" Ava plucked the paper wrapper from her straw, taking a sip of her tea, and the swerve in subject matter kicked Brennan right back into gear.

"I take it you've done conventional PT before," he said, repeating her process with his own straw as she nodded.

"I broke my wrist falling on a patch of ice a couple years ago. But I did my physical therapy over at the hospital. This facility is new, right?"

"They moved over here last year, but I've been with Kat for the long haul." Despite the crap he jokingly gave her, Kat had been the only therapist Brennan had been able to make any progress with. "She's really open to alternative methods of therapy and pain management. It makes things easier."

"It makes things easier," Ava echoed, and hell if he wasn't in for a penny now. But detox had taught him to own up to his need for alternative therapy, even if he kept the reasons that had landed him in PT locked up nice and tight.

"I had some issues with pain management after I got hurt." Brennan inhaled, modulating his words with every ounce of control he could muster. "I started out taking oxycodone for the pain post-surgery. Four months later, I was popping it the way most people do breath mints."

Ava's soft puff of breath was the only betrayal of her shock, but she battened it down with a frown as she pulled back against the leather booth cushion. "You had a substance abuse problem?"

Oh hell. *Hell.* How could he have forgotten she'd been

raised by raging alcoholics? "Shit, Ava, I'm sorry. I've gone a little over two years completely clean, but I didn't mean to bring up a sore topic."

"You didn't." The answer was automatic, and she shook her head as if to punctuate the assertion. "I'm not going to lie and say the subject doesn't sting, because you're not an idiot. You know that's not true. But not everyone with substance abuse issues is like my parents. And you've got two years clean. I'm sure you fought some demons to get there."

"Yeah. It was"—*weak, hideous, well deserved*—"a rough time," he finished. While he never would have lied about it—after all, part of successful rehab was knowing you'd really fucked up—Brennan had also never admitted his addiction to anyone who wasn't a medical professional or a direct relation. But rather than getting all awkward or gooey about it, Ava's brows rose in question, and wasn't that just par for the course.

"So what happened? To make you stop, I mean?"

"Ellie," he said, and funny how the word was enough. "I was really distant, out of it most of the time, angry the rest. She's a social worker, so she figured out pretty quick that I was abusing my meds. Once she called me on it, I agreed to get help."

His sister might be younger than him, but man, she was twice as tough. Brennan had entered a full-time rehab facility twelve hours after Ellie's no-bullshit confrontation. Not that she'd really given him a choice, and he hadn't cared enough about himself at that point to fight her.

"Twenty-eight days of detox will give you a hell of an attitude adjustment," he continued. "But I vowed then and there to do alternative therapy whenever possible. No narcotics. No exceptions. No matter how much it hurt."

Ava studied him for the longest minute of his life, her expression soft but without pity. Finally she said, "Coming off a back injury and finishing rehab with no medication sounds awful. You must've been in a lot of pain."

Understatement of the goddamn century. "It wasn't fun," he agreed. His addiction, as short lived as it was, had just traded four months of his life for the ability to be numb.

But even numb, you didn't forget. And it was better to focus on the pain than the truth.

"So that's why you do yoga?" Ava asked. Not even the gravity of the subject matter could put a damper on her curiosity, and damn, she really was a natural with the Q and A.

"Yes, although it's more for the breathing than the actual exercise. Don't get me wrong—Kat's not about to let me get away without physical exercise, and we do some traditional therapy from time to time. But my injury happened two and a half years ago. At this stage in the game, I only see her when I have pain I can't manage on my own. She helps me work out the kinks so I can get back on track."

"The kinks that you got pulling Matty Wilson out of the fire at Joe's." Ava's fingers tightened just slightly over his on the cool tabletop, as if she'd anticipated the acceleration in his pulse. "If you were in pain, I wish you'd told me. All that hitting the heavy bag yesterday couldn't have been helpful."

The same sensation that had elbowed its way past his hard-core need for control when Ava had walked into the therapy center made an encore performance in his rib cage, pushing the words on a hot path out of Brennan's mouth. "But it was. It *is*. Being with you yesterday was the most relaxed I've been in . . . I don't even know how long. And sometimes that helps more than anything else."

Relax your mind, and a lot of times, your body follows.

"So hanging out together, just doing stuff like this, makes you feel better?"

Ava's velvety lashes swept into a wide arc over her bright green stare, but the question was so straightforward that Brennan simply said, "Yeah. It does."

The smile that broke over her face shot straight to his gut before nestling in for an extended stay. "Being with you makes me feel better too. So I guess that means we should stick together."

Chapter Eighteen

Ava put the finishing touches on her article on the Riverside Elementary holiday pageant at a few minutes past seven P.M., triple checking the copy before clicking SEND on her laptop. Okay, so it wasn't Pulitzer material, or hell, even locally groundbreaking, but she'd meant what she'd said to Brennan when he'd called to ask her to lunch. Writing a small article was better than sitting at her desk, twiddling her thumbs.

Even if she still needed a groundbreaker in T minus two freaking weeks in order to keep her job.

Powering down her laptop for the night, Ava pulled her bag from the space beside her desk, popping it open to make room for the computer. Her fabric-covered story notebook fell out with a *clunk,* hitting the timeworn carpet with a sunny-side-up flutter of pages.

"Damn it." She knelt down low to scoop the book back to the confines of her leather tote when the words in front of her stopped her cold.

Fire @ Joe's, unlikely rescue, reluctant hero. What is Nick Brennan hiding?

Ava's pulse picked a fight with her breathing, both of them speeding up in her ears. The instinct that had drawn her to Brennan's story in the first place had been spot-on, and the more she unwittingly discovered, the more she realized the gut-wrenching truth.

Now more than ever, Brennan was still the story of the decade.

"Hey, Ava. You okay down there?" The masculine voice coming from the entryway of Ava's cubicle startled her despite its gentle delivery, and her head whipped up as she slammed the cover of the book splayed beneath her fingers.

"What? Ow!" *Crap*, that had hurt. "Oh, Ian. You took me by surprise."

"Sorry." The sheepish pull of her coworker's smile suggested he really meant the apology. "I didn't know anyone was still here. I was actually just walking by on my way out. Are you working on a story?"

His eyes dipped to her notebook in a pointed glance, and her gut knotted in an instinctive response.

"Nothing solid, really. Just brainstorming."

"Oh." Ian's face twitched in what looked suspiciously like disappointment, sending Ava's hackles into get-up-and-go mode. "Well, can I give you a hand off the floor?"

Ian took a step closer, arm extended, but Ava jumped up and hugged her notes to her chest in a semiprotective hold.

"I'm all set, but thank you." Of course, from his vantage point at the front of her cubicle, Ian couldn't have read the pages in her book any more than he'd have been able to read her mind, but still. As nice as Ian seemed, he *was* Gary's golden boy. A girl couldn't be too careful.

"Ah. Right, then." Ian rocked back on the heels of his loafers as if turning to make his way through the deserted newsroom, but at the last second, he swung back toward her. "Hey, really nice work on that exclusive you did last week, by the way. It was a great piece."

Wait . . . what? "You read my article on the fire at Joe's?"

"Sure." Ian lifted his sandy brown brows in a nonverbal translation of *why wouldn't I?* "I read everyone's articles, actually. You know, just to be in the loop."

"Oh." Ava lifted her chin in surprise. She thought she was the only person on staff who read the paper cover to cover. "Well, I'm glad you enjoyed the piece."

"I did. I know I seemed kind of negative about it during our weekly meeting. To be honest, I didn't think there was a story there, especially since the source seemed difficult. But you really uncovered a good one."

Oh, Ian. If you only knew. "Thank you," she said, eking out a smile.

"You're welcome." Ian nodded, aiming a glance at Gary's darkened office before lowering his voice to a murmur. "Look, I know Gary can really give you a hard time." He paused, as if the massive understatement had jabbed him in the mouth on the way out. "But you write some really compelling pieces, Ava."

She proceeded with care even though Ian seemed clueless about Gary's latest ultimatum. "That's nice of you to say, but I'm not sure it's the general consensus around here. I mean, I just turned in an article on the Riverside Elementary holiday show." Ava tacked a self-deprecating smile to the words, because truly, if she couldn't laugh, she was going to cry. "As excited as the kids were to sing Christmas carols and recite Hanukkah poems, it's hardly riveting stuff."

"Yeah, but you still treat it as if it is. You respect the story no matter what."

The shock of Ian's straight-up reply rebounded through

her rib cage, and after her third attempt at a response, she finally made something stick.

"Well, sure, but that's just part of the job." She might not take her own achievements seriously, but she always gave her career—and the stories that went with the job—the respect it deserved. Come to think of it, so did Ian.

"I'm not sure that's the general consensus around here, either. But I can tell you're a good reporter. And I just thought . . . well, that someone should tell you." Ian stuffed his hands into the pockets of his work-creased khakis, examining the carpet in front of him as if it had suddenly become breaking news. "Anyway . . . have a good night."

Ava stared after Ian for a full five minutes before stepping back to gather her belongings, her thoughts caught in a rough churn. While she'd made strong storytelling her number one priority since the minute she'd started at the *Daily,* she couldn't help but admit that her screwup nearly five years ago still haunted her more than she'd like it to. Not that Gary's constant reminders were exactly conducive to moving up and moving on, but at this stage in the game, some wholehearted trust in herself might not hurt.

But it might not help, either, because Ava needed the mother of all stories, and if she trusted her instincts, they'd lead her right smack to Brennan's doorstep.

Again.

"No," Ava whispered, shaking her head for emphasis even though no one could see her. She sat back down in her desk chair, nailing her decency back into place with each passing breath. Yes, the rescue squad part of Brennan's story had lit her curiosity like a twenty-pound bottle rocket, and okay, fine, it was possible the rescue squad hero angle would make a brilliant personal interest article, especially given Pine Mountain's tight-knit community.

But Brennan was still clearly on team *no comment* with

regard to the spotlight. He might have opened up about the job itself, and even told her about the situation following his rehab, but he'd clearly still dodged the specifics of how he'd sustained such a devastating injury. Something really massive had to have gone down for him to be hurt so badly that he got hooked on painkillers in the aftermath.

What is Nick Brennan hiding?

Before the movement even registered, Ava had re-planted herself in her desk chair, her heartbeat pulsing to warp speed in her veins. She flipped her laptop open with a *snick*, pulling up the blank tab on her search engine.

"Come on, come on," she whispered, biting her bottom lip in concentration as she tapped one finger against the edge of her keyboard. "I know you're in here somewhere. Talk to me."

Nick Brennan, Fairview Rescue Squad.

A hundred and nineteen thousand results popped over her screen, and excitement flared to life in Ava's belly. But after ten minutes of intense scrolling and even more intense hoping, not one of those results yielded a scrap about her Nick Brennan.

"Damn it." Okay, so it wasn't entirely a shock, considering he'd barely made the rescue squad before getting hurt. But it was going to take a whole lot more than ten minutes of fruitless searching to knock her off her game. This story was worthy of being told. If only she could *find* it.

Fairview, VA, firefighter injured on the job.

"A-ha!" Ava's cheeks prickled with triumphant heat. "Getting warmer."

Except after a quick yet thorough scan of the archives of the local paper and the public records from the Fairview City database, the omission of names within each article became glaringly apparent. Not entirely uncommon in news articles where either firefighters or police officers had been injured, but God—the details of each blaze and the injuries sustained by the men and women who fought them outlined in vivid detail just how dangerous being a firefighter really was.

And just how brave you had to be to make it not only your job, but your passion.

Ava sat back in her chair, her thoughts moving nearly too fast to harness. The rescue squad had snagged her undiluted interest ever since the two words had passed Brennan's lips at lunch today. The brand of high-level devotion, the extensive training, the pure intensity that had to go with the jobs those firefighters performed—all of it rattled and echoed and whispered in Ava's mind.

Just because Brennan had been injured and didn't think he was a hero didn't mean the rest of the world would agree. He'd saved a little boy's life with limited regard for his own, and after what she'd uncovered today, Ava would bet the bank that the rescue at Joe's was far from Brennan's first. These rescue squad guys were trained to run into danger, headfirst and hesitation free, when no one else could help. Sometimes at the cost of their careers, even their well-being.

The whole thing—with Brennan sitting front and center—had all the makings of a truly engaging, high-impact story. One that Ava knew all the way to her marrow she could tell with poignant respect. Just like it deserved.

If only she could convince Brennan that in spite of all he'd lost to his devastating injury, he was worthy of the airtime.

One hour, seven Web sites, and sixteen handwritten

pages of groundwork later, Ava's cell phone sounded off from beneath a pile of printouts on her desk. After a swift excavation, she flipped the thing into her palm to check the caller ID.

Her full-face grin was as instant as it was involuntary, but she scaled it down to a flirtatious smile before tapping the icon to accept the call.

"I must say, you're taking this whole stuck-with-me thing very seriously, Mr. Brennan."

A dark and sexy chuckle rumbled over the line, and Ava clasped the phone tighter in an effort to keep both the sound and the sentiment close. "As you so eloquently pointed out last week, I'm quite good at taking things seriously, Ms. Mancuso. I don't see the purpose in half measures. If I'm going to do something, I'm going to do it right."

"I'm shocked to hear you say that," Ava teased, her tone balancing out the lie. Everything about Brennan screamed *all in*, from his intensely decadent stares to his hotter than hellfire kisses.

Oh God. Ava wanted to be all in with him. Right now.

"Speaking of serious . . ." Brennan trailed off, his voice rich with suggestion that shot right between Ava's thighs. "It's way past time for you to leave work, don't you think?"

Her eyes flickered over her fabric-bound notebook, and she snapped it closed with a sweep of her hand. "What makes you think I'm still at work?"

"Aren't you?" he asked, the question catching her point blank in the chest.

"Well . . . yeah." She laughed in soft admission. "I guess I don't see the purpose in half measures either."

"Maybe you should redirect all that seriousness into something else."

Ava's pulse thrummed with instant heat. "Like what?"

"Like me."

She let out a breath full of desire and surprise, her eyes dropping to the notebook under her fingers. "Nick, I—"

"I miss you," he said, and just like that, all her thoughts jostled to a halt.

"What?"

"Look, I'm not very good at this, so I'm just going to say it. For seven years, I wondered what we could've had. Now that I have the chance to find out, I don't want to screw it up by not being honest. I can't make any promises about what will happen down the line, but right now I miss you. I want you to come over, and I want you to stay. Be with me, Ava. Tonight. Right now. Be with me."

For a second, Ava couldn't even think, let alone speak. But the truth in his voice replaced her shock with realization.

Brennan might keep his feelings close to the vest, but he was a good man. A worthy man. A man she wanted right now more than her next breath.

And Ava needed to show him.

"Stay right where you are. I'm on my way."

Ava pulled up to Brennan's apartment building, her eyes zeroed in on his door from a hundred yards away. A bitter wind whipped across the parking lot, nearly knocking the breath out of her chest as she strode over the concrete walkway, but Ava didn't care. She didn't waste a single step as her feet measured the distance along the cheerily decorated thresholds, her heart in her throat as she finally stopped to place a knock dead-center on Brennan's door.

"Hey, that was . . . Jesus, Ava!" Brennan barked, pulling the door wide. "Where's your coat?"

She stepped inside the apartment, propelled by an unknown force she couldn't fight even if she'd wanted to. "In my car." Her arms flashed around Brennan's shoulders, her mouth capturing his surprised laugh as it escaped.

"Are you out of your mind? It's twenty degrees outside," he murmured, the vibration of the words making her lips tingle.

She kissed him again, long and deep. "Mmm-hmm. Coats take time."

"You're crazy." The affirmation came out hushed and reverent, melting over her skin.

"Your fault. Come here."

Ava slid her hands up the back of his neck, thrusting her fingers through the just-messy-enough fall of his hair to hold him close. Brennan's body stilled against hers, nothing moving but the rapid rise and fall of his chest, and oh God, even fully clothed, the contact sent her into a full-body buzz.

She slanted her mouth upward, meeting his lips again in a kiss brimming over with want and greed. A groan broke loose from his throat as he let Ava kiss him, let her explore his shockingly soft lips with bold, hard sweeps of her tongue. Brennan gave her the lead she craved, and she took it without thought, parting his mouth even farther in search of more.

Anchoring his heated palms over her hips, he swung her into the softly lit apartment, letting his back absorb the harsh chill from outside as he kicked the front door closed.

"You're freezing," he said, dipping his mouth to cover the bare stretch of skin between her ear and the open collar of her blouse. "Let me warm you up."

Ava's sigh of pleasure pushed past her lips, her nipples tightening beneath her satin bra as Brennan guided her through the foyer without easing his hold on her waist. They fumbled their way past the living room, too tangled up in each other to be graceful but too turned on to care.

Brennan's hands skated from her waist to her shoulders, sliding around to cup her face. He parted her lips with his, nibbling, tasting, sucking, until finally the kiss became so hot with suggestion, Ava's knees nearly buckled.

Oh, no. No way. Brennan might be able to make her scream with little more than a touch, but Ava refused to go weak. Not now.

Not when she was supposed to be showing *him* how she felt.

Ava dug her feet into the floorboards, stopping their forward movement in the shadows of the hallway. Brennan's brows punched downward in concern, but she coasted a finger over the spot between them to cancel it out. Angling his frame against the sturdy expanse of the wall beside them, Ava notched her hips over Brennan's with a thrust.

"What are you doing?" His eyes darkened, nearly black and glittering with lust as he wrapped his fingers around the tailored edge of her dress pants to return the movement. But as unbelievably promising as his cock felt pressed against her belly, this moment wasn't about taking pleasure.

It was about giving it.

She bit her bottom lip, refusing to break eye contact as she lowered her hands to the top button on his jeans. "I'm warming *you* up." The button popped loose with one deft tug.

"Ava."

The word was a warning and a prayer, and she thrilled at both. "Brennan."

Ava freed another button from its mooring in the denim, and his reply became lost on a moan. Brennan's head tilted back, pleasure etched over his face as he dropped his hands to give her full access to his body. Desire pulsed through Ava's limbs, curling down her spine, tingling hard in the damp space between her thighs as she pulled at the remaining buttons.

Through dark, lowered lashes, Brennan watched her movements one by one, until finally—*blessedly*—Ava slipped the last button free. Her fingers ached from wanting to touch him, starting at the line of silky black hair leading into his boxer briefs and diving lower, sweeter. He canted his hips off the wall as if seeking the same contact Ava was starving for, and she reached down with every intention of giving it to him until they both lost their minds.

Brennan reversed their positions in less than a blink.

Ava's breath rode out on the hard edge of a gasp. Although he'd captured her wrist with one hand to swing her back to the wall, both his motion and his grasp were far from forceful. Brennan stepped toward the cradle of her body, his eyes tracking lower as his lush, wicked mouth curved into a grin.

"Sorry, Spitfire. Ladies first."

Chapter Nineteen

Brennan wanted nothing more than to slow down. He wanted to spend an hour tasting the sweet, hidden spots on Ava's neck that would make her cry out, to undress her stitch by stitch so he could discover every inch of her with his hands, then slowly rediscover the best places with his mouth. But from the minute she'd walked through his front door, determined and headstrong and so goddamn beautiful, Brennan had fought a losing battle.

He wanted her more than anything. And she made him crazy enough to take her, fast and hard and standing in the hallway.

"Brennan—"

He cut off her protest with a punishing kiss, sliding his tongue over hers until she sighed against his mouth. Reaching to the tight stretch of space between them, Brennan lifted her shirt from the top of her dress pants, unfastening the closure on the black wool with an economical twist.

Ava's hands found his in the shadows twining their bodies, but rather than trying to slow him or turn the tables, she urged him faster. Her pants whispered to the floorboards at their feet, and Brennan followed their downward motion with his hands.

"Step out." Christ, just the hint of her bare skin so close to his was enough to make him want to come.

She reached for his waist, sinking her fingers around the open denim. "After you."

"No."

Ava stilled. "But I want to make you feel good too."

Something Brennan had no name for broke loose in his chest. He stepped forward in a rush, covering Ava with his lips, his shoulders, his hips.

"Don't you get it?" he grated, exhaling hard and hot over her ear. "You make me feel *everything*. Right now, the only thing I want is to have you under my hands so I can make you scream. You want to make me lose my mind? Step out of those pants and let me touch you."

Ava toed her way from first her shoes, then the garment, hands pressed over his chest for balance. Brennan was certain she could feel the slamming of his heartbeat beneath the thin cotton of his T-shirt.

But then she was wearing nothing from the waist down but a pair of tiny blue panties, and Brennan couldn't make himself care about anything other than the sight of her.

"God. Look at you." Instinctively, Brennan dropped to his knees, wrapping his palms over Ava's hips to keep the ice blue lace directly in his line of sight. She froze in place, her body bowstring tight beneath his hands, and all at once Brennan realized how vulnerable she was in this moment.

And yet, she made no move to hide.

"Ava." He lifted his gaze, pinning her wide-eyed stare with one of his own. Her coal black hair spilled over her shoulders, a sultry contrast to the white of her blouse in the shadows. Her nipples stood in sweet relief behind the sheer fabric, cresting higher with each rapid breath. But it was her skin that tempted him the most, the scent of brown sugar and desire making his cock unbearably hard as he skimmed a touch over the indent where her thighs met her core.

"Look," Brennan repeated, silently commanding her eyes downward as he angled his shoulders between the cradle of her hips. Her eyes lowered without closing, and he felt the intensity of her watching his every move. He shifted toward the incandescent light filtering in from down the hallway, placing a kiss below her navel. "Look at what you do to me."

Without warning, he hooked his thumbs beneath the lace riding low on Ava's hips, tugging it over her thighs to reveal her sex. Holy hell, she was stunning, all wet and wanting and perfect, and it was all Brennan had not to rip the lace off her rather than guide it the rest of the way down.

Even completely bare and laid out in front of him like a lush and wicked banquet, Ava didn't hide.

And as much as he knew he should, Brennan didn't wait.

Pressing both palms to the space where her legs joined her body, he met her heat with his mouth, pleasuring her with bold strokes and brash kisses. Each motion drove him harder, daring him faster and farther, and he refused to relent. His cock ached with a bolt of pleasure-pain, demanding attention, but he tamped it down. There was nothing in this moment but Ava, her taste, her openness, her pleasure.

He was giving it to her. Only her. Right now.

She dropped a hand to his shoulder, fingers sliding up to cup his face, and the gesture unlocked him from his frenzied haze.

"What are you doing?" Brennan's pulse slammed through his chest as Ava tipped his jaw upward while lowering her other hand.

"You said to watch." Her voice was honey and velvet

and a thousand other things, but all of them escaped him when she dipped her fingers to the center of her body.

"But I want you to watch too."

The sound in his throat was more growl than groan, but Brennan didn't care. He swept back against Ava's core, following her lead for only a second before taking it along with her. Her gasps became moans, her grip on his shoulder tightening as she rocked against his mouth, his lips, his tongue. She led him to every sweet spot, drawing him in with her fingers and her breathy sighs, until finally she started to tremble.

"Oh . . . oh *God*. I . . ."

Brennan punctuated the incomplete thought with one last thrust of his tongue. Ava's free hand dug into his shoulder, clutching his T-shirt as she came undone around him. Her trembles grew into a full-bodied quake, her voice, her climax, all of it vibrating through him in lust-fueled waves. Slowly, he softened his touches breath by breath, pulling back just enough to catch her boneless body midslide down the wall.

"I've got you. Come on." Brennan swung his bedroom door wide with one arm, wrapping the other around Ava's rib cage. Christ, his bed had never looked so good.

But even as he led her right up to the edge of it in his moonlit room, Ava didn't sit or lie down as he expected.

Instead, she turned his back to the bed, pushing him to sit before she took a step back.

"Ava—"

"Shh." She leaned toward him just enough to brush her fingers over his mouth, refreshing her taste on his lips. "I might have come first, but you're not done watching."

Ava retreated just out of reach, dropping her gaze to the deep V of her shirt. The silky edge fluttered low over her thighs, offering a tantalizing suggestion of her nakedness beneath. She worked the buttons slowly, each one making him harder and more desperate to be inside her. As if he'd broadcast the thought out loud, Ava paused to shake her head at him in the shadows, and *hell* . . . how was he supposed to keep his hands to himself when she bit her bottom lip like that?

"You are gorgeous," Brennan whispered, nearly choking with relief as she finally stepped back to the open angle of his hips. He reached out at the same moment she closed in, pressing him back over the mattress in a tangle of long legs and hot, fast intention. His T-shirt never stood a chance, and the rest of his clothes followed on a quick trip to the floor. Ava shifted to her side in the pool of dark bedsheets, propping herself up on one elbow with a sexy grin.

"That's a two-way street." Her eyes coasted slowly downward, and she followed her gaze with a light trail of her fingers. The contact shot through him in a greedy push of want, his cock jerking against her palm as she stroked him with perfect pressure. "Let me show you."

"Ah. Ava," Brennan swore, and damn it, he couldn't wait. Grabbing her hips, he rolled her beneath him, kissing her deeply before pulling back to grab a condom from his bedside table drawer. Ava parted her knees in a wordless proposition, and Brennan answered by filling her with one smooth thrust. A hundred sensations sizzled under his skin, tightening at the base of his spine to send his hips into instant, ungentle rhythm. Every thrust tempted him deeper, each retreat calling him back to her sweet, slick center with more speed, and Ava's velvety sighs urged him recklessly into both.

Christ, she was stunning, wild hair spilling over her shoulders, lithe body matching his movements, pulse for pulse. Ava dared him harder and faster, until finally, she locked her hands around his waist, pulling him in to cover her fully.

"Brennan." The word broke from her mouth, her muscles growing so taut he could feel his own release threatening in the lowest, darkest part of him. Her hips moved even wider on a cry, and he hooked a hand beneath her knee, scooping upward to fill her completely.

Ava's eyes flew wide, her release riding out on a pleasure-soaked moan. The sound snapped Brennan's waning control in half, pushing him over the brink. His orgasm flashed all the way through him, sudden and powerful, and he gave in to it with a curse and a shout. Raw sensation dominated his body, locking him against Ava's hips as he came in wave after wave of pure, intense pleasure.

For long seconds, Brennan forgot how to breathe, but then slowly, surely, he filtered back down to reality.

He was gripping the back of Ava's thigh with one hand, pinning her in place on the bed.

Hard.

"Jesus," Brennan hissed, jerking away from the frame of her body as if she'd burned him. A punishment he'd have full-well earned, for how he'd just lost control. "I'm sorry, Ava. I—"

"Stop." She stilled, but her expression held no hesitation or fear. "You have nothing to apologize for."

"I got carried away." He gestured to her leg, but she propped herself up over the covers and cut off his argument with a laugh.

"I should hope so, seeing as how I seduced you the second I walked in the door."

Still, he couldn't give in to impulse like that. What if he'd lost control and hurt her?

Brennan opened his mouth to renew his protest, but Ava shifted to claim the space he'd put between them.

"This is mutual, Brennan." She paused, pressing forward to brush a kiss over his lips. "It might be a little impulsive, and maybe a little more crazy, but that's okay with me. As long as that part's mutual too."

"I didn't hurt you?"

"No," she said, without pause. "Because if you had, I'd have told you. I want this, just the way it is."

A vulnerable flicker mixed in with the honesty on Ava's face, and he realized again that she'd had the chance to hide her feelings, or worse yet, to run.

And once more, she hadn't taken it.

"Just the way it is, huh?" Relief eased through Brennan's veins, doubling up at her throaty giggle as his return kiss became a gentle nip of her bottom lip. He couldn't deny the attraction between them, and more importantly, Ava was genuine, *and* genuinely okay. "I guess I can live with that."

"Good," she said, her sassy smile flashing in the moon-lit shadows of his bedroom. "Now do you think you can live with taking a break for dinner? I'm all for seduction over sustenance, but at some point, a girl's gotta eat."

A quick visual inventory of his fridge told Brennan he was going to have to dig for a whole bunch of culinary prowess if he wanted to feed Ava something other than chili from a can. But working with Adrian for the past eight months had taught him a thing or two about food, not the least of which was that chili from a can should proba-bly be outlawed.

"Pickings are kind of slim," Brennan apologized, sending a sheepish look over his shoulder. "I kind of asked you over on the spur of the moment."

But rather than get awkward, Ava simply grinned at the mention of his spontaneous invitation. "I'm glad you did.

Sorry I'm not much help in the kitchen, though. The only thing I know how to make really well is a mess."

"You want to learn?" The question launched from Brennan's mouth before he could stop it, but the spark of interest in her emerald green eyes made him glad as hell he'd asked.

"You'd teach me how to cook?"

"I'd teach you how to scramble eggs," he clarified, sliding the cardboard half carton from the refrigerator. "It's not that hard."

Ava gave a mock shudder, but padded over to the cook-top nonetheless. God, she looked cute with his borrowed T-shirt covering her to midthigh and her hair piled on top of her head in a semimessy knot. "You're giving me a whole lot of credit there."

"Or you're not giving yourself enough."

"Mmm. You should probably reserve judgment until *after* you've seen my appalling cooking skills."

"You don't believe in yourself much, do you?"

As soon as the words had crossed his lips, Brennan silently cursed his utter lack of brain-to-mouth filter. Ava hadn't had a set of parents who'd believed in her or encouraged her efforts the way his had. And now, with her douche truck of a boss following suit and knocking her career, there was little wonder Ava was light in the self-credit department.

Her expression shifted, so slightly he'd have missed it if he hadn't been trying to read her. "You're talking to a woman who thinks graham crackers mixed with milk is a culinary delight, remember?"

"How could I forget?" Brennan paused, putting the eggs on the counter so he could slide both arms around her waist. "I still wish you'd give yourself some credit."

"What about you?"

Her return question was more wide-eyed interest than

reporterly intrusion, but Brennan still sidestepped it out of instinct.

"What about me?" He pulled back, crouching down low to slide his lone skillet from the cabinet next to the cooktop. Of course Ava was waiting for him with an expression reading *really?* when he stood to place the pan on the burner.

"You saved a little boy from a burning building, Brennan. Don't you think that deserves some credit too?"

Brennan blew out a breath. Instinct had the answer on his tongue even though his defenses whispered in no uncertain terms that he should clap his pie hole shut. But come on. He wasn't airing things out to Mike freaking Trotter. This was Ava, for God's sake.

Ava, who had come right over when he'd called, no questions asked. Ava, who had just shuddered and screamed beneath his hands, who'd made him shudder and scream right back.

Ava, who had just looked at him with nothing but pure, sweet honesty as she'd asked *what about you?*

"I don't know," Brennan admitted, balancing his words against the emotions flinging themselves around in his head. "I get that most people think what I did at Joe's is heroic." He countered her brows-up shock with a shake of his head. "And yes. In a way, it is. But I didn't become a firefighter for the recognition. All the fanfare feels unnecessary."

"Hmm. So for you, even something big like risking your life to save someone else's is all just part of the job." Ava tipped her head, her nearly black bangs sweeping down over one eye as she processed his words and watched his movements at the cooktop. She took in both with such natural interest that the words just kept tripping out of his mouth.

"Exactly. It's important, but it's also what I was trained

for." He grabbed a carton of milk from the fridge, bare feet *shushing* over the floor. "I mean, wouldn't you feel weird if people made a huge deal every time you wrote a story? It's what you do."

Ava laughed. "Come on, Brennan. Saving Matthew Wilson from a burning grocery store is a far cry from me writing about the Riverside Turnip Festival. It's not even apples and oranges. More like apples and . . . well, turnips."

"On the surface, maybe. But let me ask you this. Do you ever think twice about a really difficult story? Or did you treat the Turnip Festival the same as you did the story on the fire?"

"Stories are stories. They're all important," she said, emphatically. "It wouldn't be right to pay attention to only the big ones."

"Right." Brennan cracked a few eggs into a bowl at the counter, adding just enough milk and some salt and pepper before passing it to Ava. "Being a firefighter is the same. Whether I'm running into a five-alarm fire or pulling a kitten out of a neighborhood oak tree, it all matters. And it's all part of the job."

"Have you ever been to a five-alarm fire?" she asked, and God damn it, he'd waltzed right into that one, hadn't he?

He yanked the refrigerator door open, willing his hand to stop shaking. *Breathe. In. Out.* "Once."

Ava clutched the bowl to her chest, her delayed realization obvious. "I'm sorry. That was a really stupid question. What, um, what do you want me to do with this?"

She plunked the bowl to the countertop in front of her and started rummaging through his utensil drawer in a clear bid to divert the subject, and a flare of guilt twisted behind his sternum.

"It's okay. You're kind of programmed to ask questions,"

he said, his arm brushing against hers as he reached in to scoop a fork from the drawer.

Ava paused for only a second before taking it from his fingers. "Just like you're kind of programmed to dodge them, huh?"

The words held no accusation, and hell, it wasn't as if she was wrong, anyway. Firefighters rarely got loose lipped about the darker parts of the job, with each other or anyone else.

When the shit hit the fan, Brennan had been able to count on the firefighters at Station Eight for two things. To always have his six, and to never say a single syllable after a tough call.

He hadn't spoken to Cole or Alex in nearly two and a half years.

"There are parts that are hard to air out, yeah," Brennan admitted, the rest of his past grinding to a stop in his throat.

"I understand," Ava said. "None of my friends here in the Blue Ridge know about my parents. Nadine was the only one, and even then, we never talked about it before she moved. I don't think either of us quite knew what to say. But . . ."

She broke off, shifting her weight from one bare foot to the other before exhaling in a wordless *here goes nothing*. "Just because the past is painful doesn't mean it's all bad. Don't get me wrong—growing up with abusive parents was pretty horrible. But if I forgot my past completely, I wouldn't be who I am. As crappy as it was, my past makes me stronger in the present. Sharing the truth with you made me realize that. So I guess what I'm trying to say is, sometimes stories are worth telling. Even if they're difficult."

For a second, Brennan stood completely poleaxed on

the linoleum. Yes, he'd give anything to forget that fateful, awful night that he'd climbed into the back step of Engine Eight for the last time. But it had never crossed his mind that stuffing back the past also meant forgetting who he'd been, things that had been sewn into his very fabric, not just as a firefighter, but as a person.

Losing the past would mean forgetting Mason. And *fuck*. Brennan was supposed to have had the guy's back. He owed his best friend so much more than that.

Even if it meant Brennan would have to spill his secrets in order to man up.

"I got hurt in an apartment fire," he said, the words tasting rusty in his mouth. Brennan reached for the bowl Ava had set on the counter, desperate for something to focus on other than the memory welling up in his mind like a gut-wrenching wound.

Ava nodded, passing the fork back over as if he'd broadcast his need for control, even over something as inconsequential as scrambled eggs. "Sounds like a big call," she said.

"The fire started out small enough, but the building was old." Christ, the speed with which the flames had rolled over every surface, unrelenting and eerily graceful, had damn near stunned him into place in that first hallway. "We had to get everyone out before we could even think about containing the flames. Even with squad on scene too, it was rough. The building was one of the biggest in Fairview. Plus, it was the middle of the night, so nearly everyone was home and in bed."

Brennan stopped, measuring his breaths along with the soft *clink-clink-clink* of the fork as he whisked the eggs. His heartbeat slammed in his chest, pushing a rush of white noise through his ears while the muscles in his back knotted over, one by one. But Ava stood firm beside him at the counter, and her quiet presence sent more words fumbling past his lips.

"We do searches in pairs, but visibility was nil after only a few minutes. A lot of tenants managed to get out on their own, but some needed help, especially as the fire spread."

"I'm sure they must have been frightened," Ava said, and he nodded in return.

"That's an understatement." The sharp sound of a mother's voice, desperately begging him and Mason to find her son, echoed through his mind, and damn it . . . he couldn't do this. If Brennan unleashed the entire story, he wouldn't be able to control his anger, his grief.

His guilt.

Above all, have each other's backs.

Ava slid the bowl from his unsteady hands, allowing him to laser in on both his waning calm and the skillet he'd left perched over the dormant burner. He cleared his throat, grabbing the butter he'd taken from the fridge along with his resolve.

"Everyone inside the building was pretty much in a full panic. No one could see, and even getting from apartment to apartment was tough going after a few minutes," he continued. "But when the rubber meets the road, that's when we've got to be the most calm. It's against human nature to want to run *into* a burning building. But I was trained to do the things that scare the hell out of most people. And everything I'd ever trained for came down to that call on that night."

"God, Nick. I can't even imagine how hard it must've been." The honesty glinting in Ava's bright green eyes hooked directly into Brennan's chest, pulling the memories from his mind to his mouth.

"To be honest, even with the countless calls I'd been on before that, and all the rescue squad training on top of it, I couldn't have imagined it either. For every person we got to safety, two more popped up in their place needing help. Between the smoke and the darkness, we might as well have been blindfolded and shoved inside a pressure cooker. Keeping accurate track of which spaces we'd already cleared was damn near impossible."

Brennan had never admitted out loud how gut-twistingly overwhelming that fire had been—it wasn't like there was room to show fear or, hell, anything other than balls to the wall certainty when a call got really hairy. But Christ, the fire that night had slashed into them with a thousand razor-sharp teeth. There hadn't been time for hesitation, let alone fear. Not until after, and then it was too late.

"But you still helped those people get out. They wouldn't have been able to escape that fire without you," Ava said. She reached out to brush her fingers over his forearm, and the touch was so simple and strong and downright vital that it steadied him despite the gut reactions ricocheting through his veins.

"Yes." All of them save one, and of course that one would stick in his ribs for the rest of his life. Damn it, he really *couldn't* tell Ava this part. As much as Brennan wanted to respect Mason's memory, the impulsive decision he'd made to lead his best friend up to the third floor to look for that little boy was Brennan's burden to bear. He didn't deserve to lessen the load by airing it out.

He needed to carry the weight, forever. End of fucking story.

"Anyway, I got hurt when part of the floor collapsed. The injuries were a career-breaker, and you know the rest."

Brennan waited, mentally doubling down for the detail-seeking questions Ava was sure to launch in his direction.

Only, she didn't. "I'm really sorry you were hurt," she said, capping off the words with a no-nonsense dip of her chin. A second later, she reached for the bowl on the counter, picking it up like business as usual, and damn, she couldn't have thrown him for a bigger loop if she'd started belting out show tunes right there on the linoleum.

Scooping up the fork, Ava started whisking the eggs, but her lack of kitchen experience sent a splash of the mixture over the edge of the bowl and onto the hand he'd planted over the counter.

"Shit," she whispered, her gaze yanking up to his. "Sorry."

The flush on her face, so natural and sweet, smoothed out Brennan's emotions. "You really weren't kidding about making a mess in the kitchen, huh?"

"At least I warned you," she said, biting her lip as she grabbed a paper towel from the counter to help wipe up the spill.

"You did."

For a minute, the only thing that passed between them was the click of the burner and the heady scent of butter melting in the skillet, and the quiet allowed Brennan to recalibrate. He might not want to stitch his entire heart all over his sleeve, but talking to Ava about his past, even if only a little bit, hadn't been as bad as he'd expected.

He slid her a glance, and yeah, still freaking sexy, even in his T-shirt. "So do you want to try again with the eggs here?"

"Seriously?" she asked, although the question was oddly devoid of her trademark sarcasm. "You don't have to humor me to save my feelings. I'm clearly not chef material."

Damn, she was tough. More on herself than anything else. Too bad for her, Brennan had her number. "It's scrambled eggs, Spitfire. Not rocket science. So are you going to do this or not?"

Ava chirped out a laugh that shot all the way through him, ushering away the last remaining scraps of his unease. "Did you just *dare* me to cook?"

It took every ounce of Brennan's self-control not to turn off the stove, chuck the eggs, and have Ava for dinner instead, right here on his kitchen counter. "Yup."

She plucked the spatula from his hand, pointing it at him with a sassy, sexy smile as she took his challenge head-on.

"Careful what you wish for, Nick Brennan. You just might get it."

Chapter Twenty

Ava stared at the screen on her laptop so hard, it was a wonder the damn thing didn't cave in from the pressure. The pages of her faded blue notebook were crammed with so much information that the notes spilled over into the margins, bursting with ideas and quotes and Web site references on first responders. Layla had eagerly pitched in by looking for photos to back up Ava's findings, cherry-picking the best ones to go with Ava's notes. Ian had offered up the name and number of a lieutenant friend of his in Bealetown when she'd reluctantly admitted to him that she'd been working on the piece, and even Gary had essentially left her alone while she poured herself into all things hero.

She'd spent the last six days up to her chin in research on firefighters and rescue squads, determined to write Nick Brennan's story in a way that would show the entire Blue Ridge how deserving he was—how deserving *all* these men and women were—of praise and respect.

Because the minute he'd told her the heartbreaking details of how he'd been hurt in that apartment fire, it had hammered home what she already knew. Brennan *did* have a story beneath his dark and broody exterior, and it was one worth telling. Ava was dead-set on showing him how worthy he was despite the damage that had been done.

The best way she knew how to do that was with words.

"Wow." Ava's sister-in-law Lily's voice snagged her out of her work-induced twilight zone, bringing her back to the soft lights and mouthwatering smells of the Sweet Life. "That must be one hell of a story. You haven't even touched your cookies, and those linzers are your favorite."

Lily gestured to the side table at Ava's elbow, where a plate brimming with delicate jam-filled sweets gleamed up at her like tiny stained glass windows.

"They are," Ava agreed, her chest twingeing with re-morse as she slid a cookie from the plate. The flaky, rich butter cookie combined with a hint of strawberry tartness on her tongue, and holy cow, her brother was a culinary rocket scientist. "I guess I lost track of time."

"That's what Sunday afternoons are for. Especially around here." Lily's gaze swiveled over the cozy interior of the empty dining room as she plopped down next to Ava on the well-cushioned sofa. "So, tell me about this article that's got you all wrapped up."

"Uh." The ungraceful grunt was all Ava could manage around the sudden trepidation boomeranging through her veins. Yes, she was certain her rescue squad story deserved to be told, and double yes, she knew beyond any and all doubt she could tell it poignantly, with an emotion that would impact everyone who read it.

But Ava had spent a week's worth of nights chasing away the chill of winter in Brennan's bed, and her sex life wasn't the only thing getting hotter by the millisecond.

Which was more than a little problematic, seeing as how she'd kept her jaded, cynical heart locked in an ice age for the last seven years.

"I'm writing a personal interest piece," Ava said, dipping her toes back into the conversation with care. As much as she wanted to keep her story under wraps until it ran, right after Christmas, putting Lily off altogether would be rude.

"Ooooh." Lily's eyes sparked with interest, and she rubbed the tiny baby bump over her apron with one hand. "Better than the holiday pageant? Because those kids were really cute."

Ava bit back the urge to wince at the mention of her last assignment, turning the expression into a smile over Lily's genuine enthusiasm. "Yeah." She hesitated, not sure if she should say more, but oh, screw it. Brennan's story was going to save her career, and the truth was, Ava was two degrees from exploding with excitement over writing it. "Actually, I'm putting together an in-depth article on firefighters."

"Wow. That story you did a couple of weeks ago on the fire at Joe's must've really sparked your creativity, huh?"

Biggest. Euphemism. Ever. "Ahhh, yeah. I'd say that's pretty accurate."

"Ava." Lily drew the word out like warm saltwater taffy. "This wouldn't have anything to do with your exclusive peek at a tall, dark, and totally secretive bar manager, would it?"

"Why would you think that?" Heat prickled all the way to Ava's temples, but Lily offered no quarter.

"Because he's completely good looking, your blush matches those poinsettia plants over there, and you just answered my question with a question. I know you're a reporter and that makes you naturally inquisitive, but come on, sweetie. I didn't just fall off the apple cart. Plus"—Lily paused to nudge Ava's knee with her own—"if I'm not mistaken, you're covering up yesterday's shirt with a Double Shot hoodie that's three sizes too big for you."

Well, crap. Ava should've known her meticulous sister-in-law would notice her idiot blush and her best-effort stab at recycling her couture. But really, it wasn't Ava's fault that Brennan had seduced her into staying at his place all weekend long. A girl only had so much willpower.

"Okay, okay," Ava said, ducking her chin into the ocean-scented black fleece, and great—now she was grinning too. "Brennan is the key to the article I'm writing, and he and I have been spending a lot of time together lately. But it's not that big a deal."

"Oh yeah, I totally got that from your Cheshire cat impersonation." Lily snorted, although the gesture was more playful than rude.

"Just because I'm enjoying myself doesn't mean things are serious," Ava said, sliding the plate of cookies between them on the couch. "Let's face it—I'm not exactly a shining example when it comes to stellar relationships with the opposite sex."

Lily picked up a cookie, nibbling the edge. "Do you want to be?"

Ava's pulse took the slingshot route through her veins. "What do you mean?"

"You just seem happy, and I've never seen you grin like that over a guy before." Lily popped the rest of the cookie into her mouth before adding, "Being serious about someone you really like isn't such a bad thing. Even for cynical you."

Ava paused. She'd never made any bones about her views on relationships, and it wasn't like Lily was wrong about her current state of happiness. At least her sister-in-law had nailed two of the three.

"My hanging out with Brennan *isn't* really a bad thing," Ava finally said. "But we're keeping things casual. Also, let's face it"—she aimed a pointed glance toward the door leading back to the Sweet Life's kitchen—"Pete is just a smidge overprotective as it is. If he finds out I've spent every night this week at Brennan's place, his response would be anything but laid back."

"Please." Lily bit into another cookie, pausing for only a minute to let a blissful *mmm* eke out before she added, "You can take my word for it. Pete's no saint in that department. He may mean well, but he has no room to get uppity."

"Argh!" Ava barked out a laugh, even as she resisted the urge to jam her hands over her ears and start belting out *la-la-la* to block out the image parading across her brain. "Look, I get that you two didn't get pregnant via Immaculate Conception, but come on. That's my brother."

"Exactly," Lily flipped back, shifting against the over-sized leather couch cushions to pin her with an I-mean-it stare. "He's your brother, not your keeper. He's protective of your well-being, and he's got good reasons for that." What her words lost in edge, they picked up in emotion as she gave Ava's hand a quick squeeze. "But you're twenty-nine. If he can't handle the concept of you having a little hot, mutually exclusive sex with someone you like . . ."

"Jeez, Lil. You're not pulling any punches, huh?" Ava hooked her arm over the back of the sofa, making triple-sure her brother wasn't around to overhear them. She should've known matter-of-fact Lily would throw it all out there as is.

"I'm sorry," Lily said, her expression telling Ava she meant it. "I didn't mean to embarrass you. Or pry."

Ava paused, fiddling with the zipper on her borrowed hoodie. Ah, to hell with it. "You're not prying. And you're also not wrong." The admission tasted decadent on her tongue, spurring her to share more. "But you and Pete are all I've got, and the last thing he needs right now is to worry about my relationship status."

"And your relationship status is . . . ?"

A pang unraveled in Ava's belly, but she couldn't deny the kernel of truth nestled tightly beneath it. "My relationship status is pretty freaking enamored with Nick Brennan."

In hushed tones, she offered Lily the story of how she and Brennan had originally met. Being well versed in both Pete's and Ava's past, Lily's gaze flashed with understanding as Ava explained her hasty departure from Sapphire Island, then lit with sisterly happiness as Ava copped to how seamlessly she and Brennan had gotten reacquainted over the last couple of weeks.

"Oh my God, sweetie. You really *do* like him."

"I don't know," Ava said, going for the full-on confession even though her defenses were screaming at her to toughen up and go the no-big-deal route. "I mean, okay. I do like him. But as amazing as I feel when we're together, the whole thing scares the crap out of me too. I don't want it to get serious."

Lily's blond curls bounced off her shoulders in an adamant head shake. "Ava, listen to me. You have a good heart. I understand why you're feeling wary, but don't run just because you're scared this thing with Brennan might not work out."

"But what if . . ." Ava stopped, her heart pounding an unsteady rhythm as the rest of her words rushed out on a whisper. "What if I'm scared things *will* work out? I fell in love with him once, Lily, and I screwed it up enough to lose seven whole years. What if I fall for him again and I lose even more than that? Or worse yet, he does? I just can't risk it."

"Yes, if you take the risk, you both might lose everything," Lily said, sending a streak of shock between Ava's ribs.

"What?" Was she serious?

"I love you, honey, but your brother taught me a long time ago not to bullshit a bullshitter, so I'm just going to give it to you straight. Deciding to be with somebody *is* a risk, and with a past like yours, it's a pretty scary one. Sometimes, relationships don't work out and hearts get broken."

Ava dropped her forehead to her hands. "If this is supposed to be a pep talk, we need to work on your rah-rah skills."

"I'm not done," Lily argued, albeit without heat. She scooped up Ava's fingers, looking her directly in the eyes. "You wouldn't listen if it was *all* hearts and giggles, now would you?"

Ooookay. So Lily had a point. "I guess not."

"I know not. While some relationships don't work out, some do. I get that I'm about to border on total sapdom here, but I'm a firm believer that if you take the leap for the right person, they'll catch you. Even if you surprise them by jumping."

All the deep breaths in the world couldn't temper the *holy shit* coursing through Ava's veins. "Did Pete catch you?"

Lily's face broke into an ear-to-ear grin. "Right after I was done catching him. We kind of padded each other's landing."

"And you weren't afraid he wouldn't?" Ava asked, but Lily's total lack of hesitation squashed the flare of doubt lurking in her brain.

"Maybe at first. But once I realized how I felt, I knew I'd do whatever it took to show him what he meant to me."

On second thought, *holy shit* didn't even begin to cover

this. Ava hadn't thought twice about diving into Brennan's story—she'd known all along how much it deserved to be told.

But diving into his arms—to stay this time——felt like a whole different ball game.

"Did you ever think putting yourself on the line like that with Pete might be the biggest risk of all?"

"Hell yes." Lily's laugh echoed between them, strangely knocking Ava's tension down a notch. "I tried to beat him in a widely publicized TV baking competition, remember? But it was *how* I tried to beat him that made the difference."

"I'm sorry," Ava admitted, and really, there should be a handbook for all this relationship stuff. "I don't understand."

"I stayed true to myself, and I did what was in my heart. If you do that, everything else has a way of falling into place."

Ava blinked in a desperate effort to tame her swirling thoughts. But the longer she sat there, the louder and more insistent her gut instinct became.

If she stayed true to herself—deep down true to her roots—she'd jump into Brennan's arms just as fast and as sure as she'd jumped into his story.

No matter how vulnerable it made her. No matter how uncharted the territory.

No matter what the risk.

Brennan was up to his elbows in an unremarkable Monday post-dinner shift when his cell phone started doing the jump-and-jangle in the back pocket of his jeans.

"What the hell?" he murmured, sliding the thing from its usual hiding place. Less than a half dozen people had the number, and nearly all of them were sharing the same space with him right at this very moment.

Except his sister, whose smiling image greeted him like a gut punch from the screen of his caller ID. Brennan's eyes did a quick tour of the Double Shot's bar area, merrily lit with strings of tiny colored bulbs, and he reluctantly sent the call to voice mail.

Christmas—and Ellie's wedding along with it—was five days away. Less than a week from now, he'd be lurking in the shadows of Saint Mark's Church, watching his sister rehearse her way down the aisle and trying like hell not to think of the last time he'd been in the place.

Damn it, he missed his best friend.

"Hey. You okay in there?" Ava's voice threaded past the sudden squeeze of both his memory and his back muscles as she emerged from the hallway leading to the restrooms, and he stuffed his phone back into his pocket with a nod.

"Sure," Brennan said, trying not to wince at his heavily slanted version of the truth. At least he felt better now that she was in front of him. *Inhale. Breathe.* "You doing okay down there?"

He tilted his chin in the direction of Ava's regular seat at the end of the bar, and she laughed. "I am. Although I think you're going to have to cart me out of here in a wheelbarrow later. That shepherd's pie was unbelievable. I had to restrain myself from licking the plate."

Brennan returned her satisfied expression with one of his own. They'd spent every one of her nonworking hours together over the last week, and each passing minute had felt more and more right with Ava nearby. She'd trusted him with her past, and listened sympathetically when he'd told her what he could of his. They were picking up where they'd left off seven years ago, and Brennan couldn't deny how down-to-his-bones good he felt when they were together.

Even in the face of this impending wedding.

Brennan shook off the thought, tacking a smile to his face despite the mountain of effort required for the task. "Glad you enjoyed your dinner. I'll pass on your compliments to the chef, even though it'll go right to his overinflated head."

He reached out to grab Ava's pint glass so he could freshen up her drink before she returned to her seat, but she caught his hand before he could make contact with the bar. Pressing her frame over the rounded curve of mahogany, Ava leaned in as she tugged him close to plant a kiss right on his mouth.

"What was that for?" he asked, even though his dick sent up a big, fat *who cares?!*

"That was a preview," she said, her eyes unwavering as she leaned in to kiss him again. "Of my compliments to the bar manager."

Something Brennan couldn't tag with a name rushed up from his chest, and he loosened the words before his nerve could take a hike. "Come with me to Ellie's wedding."

"What?" Her green eyes widened under the soft glow of the candy-colored Christmas lights overhead, and she pulled back to reseat herself on the customer side of the bar.

"I get that it's Christmas, and you normally spend the holidays with your brother. Of course I'll understand if you can't go. But . . ." Well, shit. No sense in scaling back now that the jam was out of the jar. "I'm sure Ellie would love to see you, and I'd like to take you as my date. It's short notice, I know, but—"

"Yes."

"Huh?" Christ, could he be any more ineloquent?

But if Ava noticed his bumbling, she didn't let on. "I said yes. Of course I'll go with you to Ellie's wedding."

"Even though it's Christmas?"

Her smile moved all the way through him, taking ownership of even the smallest places as she said, "Absolutely. I wouldn't miss it."

As he watched her move back toward the spot she'd so thoroughly claimed at the end of the bar, laughing with Teagan and Annabelle and looking downright irresistible in her wide-open honesty, Brennan knew that if he wasn't careful, he was going to lose his heart.

And as reckless as it was to fall for Ava again, Brennan wanted her too much to care.

Chapter Twenty-One

Ava sat in the passenger seat of Brennan's Trailblazer, death-gripping her sides with both hands and gasping for a desperate breath.

"Oh my God, stop!" A fresh round of laughter welled up behind her breastbone, spilling past her lips in an unrepentant peal at the mischievous grin bracketing the corners of his goatee. "You put Kool-Aid powder in the poor guy's gloves the same day he had a date with a model?"

Brennan's chuckle wound through the SUV, a deeper, sexier version of the smile that always leveled her, and Ava scooted a little closer to the console between them as he answered.

"Yup. Worked like a charm too. Our next call was a kitchen fire. As soon as my buddy put on his gloves and started to sweat, bam! Instant rainbow."

"You used more than one color?" Ava asked, oscillating between being totally incredulous and highly impressed.

"I'm equal opportunity. One red glove, one purple. The dye lasted all the way till the next shift. But that's what he got for waking me up at six A.M. to the soundtrack of a chain saw."

Finally, Ava managed a full round of inhale-exhale.

God, she couldn't make this stuff up if she tried. Brennan had just spun an hour's worth of anecdotes to prove it. "Did you guys pull pranks like that often at the firehouse?"

"Are you kidding? We had the combined maturity of a twelve-year-old boy. Those two practical jokes don't even make the greatest hits list." Brennan sat back to adjust his sunglasses, his easy expression tightening a shade as he turned off the main road and onto a smaller side street.

"Brennan?" A hard streak of worry claimed Ava's smile in one quick gulp, and she pinned him with an assessing head-to-toe. They'd been road-tripping to Fairview for nearly five hours now on no more than a ten-minute bathroom break. Even though they were obviously close to their destination, the trip couldn't be a joyride for his back. "Are you okay?"

"I'm fine," he said, lifting a hand to counter the protest that must've been visible on her face. "It's just . . . before we get to my parents' place and things get crazy, you should probably know that a couple of the guys from Station Eight are going to be at the wedding tomorrow."

"Is that a bad thing?" Judging from the way his shoulders were suddenly strung like a circus tightrope beneath his black canvas jacket, her intuition was spot-on. But God, according to the stories he'd just told, Brennan and his former squad mates all seemed tight. Like brothers, even.

He looked out the window at the passing residential scenery before answering. "I didn't leave under the best of circumstances. Things might be a little tense."

A frown pinched at the edges of her mouth, tasting even more bitter than it felt. As she'd pieced together the story, now sitting safe and snug on her laptop in Pine Mountain, she'd read more than one research article exploring the psychology of how the grave injuries of one firefighter affected everyone in the house. Most guys were sympathetic and supportive.

But firefighters compartmentalized in order to survive. And sometimes that meant shutting people out.

Even the people closest to them.

"You think things will be tense because you were hurt?" Ava did her damnedest to stamp the irritation from her voice, but God, the thought of the literal insult and injury really burned her toast. Hadn't he been through enough?

Brennan reached for her hand, his shoulders descending slightly against the driver's seat as he laced his fingers through hers to hold on tight. "I think I'll do my best to have a good time with you and hang out with Ellie before we go back to Pine Mountain on Sunday. I doubt we'll even talk to anyone from Eight."

Although a tiny part of her burned to push past his bid to kill the subject, Ava snuffed out the urge. It couldn't be easy for Brennan to return to the city where he'd lost so much, even if it was just for two days. As badly as she wanted to be a sounding board for him if he needed one, she'd come to respect the fact that he wasn't always a tell-all kind of guy. If he needed her, he'd say so, the same way he had last week in his kitchen.

And if he needed her, Ava would be there.

"Right." Brennan cleared his throat as he guided the Trailblazer to a stop in front of a cozy-looking brick colonial. "Speaking of Ellie, I guess I should warn you. It's been kind of a while since I've been back home to see my family."

Ava blinked, trying to process his words. "But you're all really close."

He and his sister had seemed as tight-knit as Ava and

Pete the weekend Ellie had visited Sapphire Island, and that was truly saying something in Ava's book. Plus, Brennan had always talked about his parents and sisters so easily. Anyone with two eyes and half a brain could see they were a Hallmark card waiting to happen.

"Yeeeeeah. That's where the warning comes in." Brennan slid from the driver's seat, making his way to her side of the SUV to meet her on the pavement. "Your brother's your only family, right?"

"Yes," Ava said, although the thought of her parents didn't kick as hard as she'd expected. Brennan knew the score with her past, and he wouldn't treat her any differently for it.

"My family is pretty big, and when we're together, not one of us specializes in subtlety. Weddings and holidays are usually a gigantic production. Roll them both together and add in every last branch of the Brennan family tree, and it's like a genealogical version of the perfect storm."

"Seriously?" Ava eyeballed the house in front of them, complete with pretty pine wreaths on each window and two—make that three minivans parked at the top of the gently winding driveway. How bad could a gathering of people who loved each other really be? "You make it sound like a natural disaster."

Brennan's expression was a fifty-fifty split between humor and apology as he guided her up the cobblestone walkway to stop at the front door. "You said it, sweetheart," he said, pulling her tight against his chest just long enough to place a kiss on the crown of her head.

And then everything around them detonated into complete and total chaos.

"Nick! Oh my God, I *knew* I heard you. Jill, Carrie, Marissa! Nick's home!" A petite brunette with familiar features let out a twenty-decibel squeal as she whipped the front door wide on its hinges. But rather than waste another second on pleasantries, the woman dragged Brennan into the foyer, launching herself at him in a full-body hug.

"Oof! Hey, Ells." Brennan grunted in surprise before returning the embrace. "It's nice to see you."

The woman—whom Ava belatedly recognized as Brennan's sister—stood back to pin him with a stern expression, although her dark eyes twinkled too happily for it to stick. "Are you kidding me right now? You haven't been home in two years, it's Christmas Eve, and I'm your *sister*. You'd better come up with something more than a cookie-cutter *nice to see you*."

"Would you rather I say it's not nice to see you?" Brennan asked, all smart-ass and no heat. But clearly there was safety in numbers, and another voice chimed in from over Ellie's shoulder.

"Nice to see you? You need to work on your intro, little brother. That charm of yours is seriously rusty." A second pretty brunette jumped in to give Brennan a long hug while Ava's maybe-I-underestimated-this meter took a sky-high spike from her spot on the threshold.

The damn thing nearly exploded when a third voice entered the fray.

"You actually said that, Nick? You need some new material before Mom gets down the hall. After all, it's only the biggest holiday of the entire year *and* the night before your baby sister's wedding. We're not a bunch of strangers, no matter how long you stay away."

By the time Brennan's fourth sister appeared to give him grief in the hallway, Ava realized she was about a thousand nautical miles out of both her league and her comfort zone.

"Okay, okay! You missed me, I get it." Brennan laughed, and at least he seemed at ease with all the sisterly ribbing.

"But in my defense, it is really good to see you guys. Even if you gang up on me when I compliment you."

"*Nice to see you* isn't a compliment among family, it's . . ." Ellie trailed off, her gaze locking on Ava's in the doorway. "Ho-ly shit, you brought a date," she whispered, taking a step backward in the crowded foyer. "Wait . . . Ava? Is that you?"

Every eye in the entire room zeroed in on her, and for a split second, Ava's defenses hollered that she was too far out of her element to survive. That this big-family dynamic was about two tons more than she'd bargained for. That her horrible, abusive past made her too jaded and closed off to know how to cope with a functional, loving family.

But then Brennan grabbed her hand, and suddenly, none of Ava's past mattered.

"I'd say it's nice to see you all, but I hear that line's been taken."

Brennan sat back in an armchair by the fireplace, surveying his parents' family room as if it were ground zero at a nuclear testing facility.

Considering the complete insanity of the last three hours and what the room looked like as a result, the analogy wasn't entirely a stretch. But as crazy as it had been to sit through the riotous rush of opening presents and having a preholiday lunch with his huge, boisterous family, Brennan couldn't deny that returning to Fairview had felt far less stressful than he'd expected.

Starting the second he'd grabbed Ava's hand on the threshold.

"Hey!" *Speak of the sweet and sinful devil*. The way she made him so hot and so happy with one easy smile was just not right. "There you are."

Ava waded through the ankle-deep piles of discarded wrapping paper covering the floor, passing over the Coke she held in one hand before shaking out the trash bag in the other. "Your mom said you might want this. She's setting all the kids up with a movie in the rec room while your sisters start getting ready for the rehearsal."

"You don't have to clean up. Here, let me do that." Brennan stood, leaning in to take the trash bag from her. Aside from the fact that it was impolite as hell to let her tidy up solo, his mother would evil-eye him right into next week for letting a guest do cleanup duty.

But Ava just plopped jeans-first to the middle of the carpet and started hauling in the crumpled paper with a shrug. "Everyone's busy with last-minute wedding stuff, and I really don't mind. Although I've got to admit, I'm not sure one trash bag is going to cut it."

"There are no half measures around here, especially on Christmas," Brennan agreed, sliding in next to her to double-team the mess. "Normally, we'd wait until tomorrow to exchange gifts, but with the wedding, I guess my mom thought this would be easier. Sorry if it was a little intense."

"Well, I did lose track of the presents somewhere around the nine-dozen mark, but it was pretty fun to watch everyone open their gifts, especially when it came to your nieces and nephew." Ava uncurled from her cross-legged position to cover more ground, and the move revealed a bright red and green pedicure in place of the socks she'd been wearing only an hour before.

"Whoa. That's, um, festive," he said, and holy hell. Were those neon-colored Christmas trees on her big toes?

She laughed, the throaty sound vibrating all the way through Brennan's chest. "You like that? Josh's niece needed a guinea pig for the new mani-pedi kit Ellie gave her, so I volunteered my feet for the cause."

"You let my not-quite brother-in-law's thirteen-year-old niece paint your toenails for practice?"

"Sure, why not?"

Brennan slung a covert gaze around the room to make sure it was empty before wrapping his fingers around the curve of her ankle to draw her close. "Because," he murmured, leaning in to press a kiss to her neck, "I can't say this with one hundred percent accuracy, but I'm fairly certain you now glow in the dark."

"Oh, come on. It's not . . . so . . . bad." The last word spilled from Ava's lips on a sigh, and she loosened her grip on the trash bag in favor of threading her hands through his hair.

"You may be right. But still," Brennan hedged, running his tongue around the shell of her ear in a feather-light flick before adding, "I think we should test the theory in our hotel room later. For purely scientific purposes, of course."

"You're pushing it, Brennan." Still, she didn't let go.

And Brennan didn't want her to. "Well, I am trying my best." Jesus, she was killing him, all brown sugar skin and sweet, sassy attitude. Finally, though, he couldn't avoid the reality that any one of about fifteen various and sundry family members could walk right in and stone cold bust them making out beside the Christmas tree. As hot as Ava was, Brennan would *never* live that down.

He dropped a kiss to her temple, reluctantly pulling back to stuff more wrapping paper into the bag. "Anyway, I really am sorry about the chaos."

Ava's mouth ruffled in amusement, which did nothing to block his illicit thoughts of her. "It's wrapping paper, not ruination. I think I'll survive."

"I didn't mean just this." He gestured to the dwindling

piles of gift wrap, along with the snowflake-printed tissue paper and the handfuls of gold and silver confetti ribbon strewn beneath the tree. Although the warning he'd given Ava earlier was partly in jest, his supersized family was overwhelming on a good day. She was tough, sure, but . . . "I know you're probably not used to such a big production."

For a second, the only thing between them was the quiet rustle of paper. "I'm not. But everyone's been so nice. Ellie jumped right in and told me all about her new job downtown, and Jill and your mom showed me how to make the Brennan family recipe for the glaze on the honey-baked ham. Even though my kitchen skills are still on the wrong side of embarrassing."

"Hey, you made kick-ass tuna melts the other day," Brennan reminded her. "Don't forget."

Ava tossed a ball of wrapping paper at him, although her laugh threw her aim way off base. "No, you made kick-ass tuna melts. I just flipped them when you told me to."

"It's the hardest part." Brennan scooped up the last of the mess around him before propping his back against the side of the sofa for a good, relaxing stretch. "Anyway, I'm glad you're okay, being here instead of with Pete and Lily."

Ava didn't hesitate with either her smile or her words. "I told you, I wouldn't miss this. And not just because your sisters gave me the lowdown on your teenage years while we were organizing the place cards for the wedding either."

His head jacked up, pulse thrumming to the tune of *shit shit shit*. "Just remember, all stories have two sides."

Damn it, Carrie loved to tell anyone who'd listen how he'd accidentally backed their father's Chrysler over the mailbox twice in the same day. It was bad enough that Jill and his mom had cornered Ava in the kitchen when she clearly didn't like to cook. Poor woman was probably drowning in familial overkill right now.

"Mmm." She cocked her head at him, dark hair tumbling over her shoulders in soft waves. "It's just like you not to want to take credit for saving your neighbor's prized candlestick collection."

"Ugh, they told you that story?"

Damn, he'd all but forgotten about the night he'd gotten up for a midnight snack and caught sight of a robbery in progress next door. Probably because it hadn't been one-tenth as big a deal as it sounded.

But Ava wasn't about to let him off the hook. "Of course they told me! Not that I'd have ever heard about it otherwise. Did you seriously tie up the thief with bungee cord and sit on him until the cops got there?"

"Only after it was clear the intruder was an amateur." And unarmed. And about thirty pounds lighter than Brennan had weighed at the time. Brennan might've been a little impulsive to interfere, but he also wasn't an idiot. "It was just a small-time B and E, and the guy was more nervous than nasty. He didn't even put up a fight after I caught him trying to run."

"It wasn't small-time to your neighbor," Ava argued, slipping in next to him to give him a playful nudge. "Marissa said some of those candlesticks were family heirlooms."

"I don't even know that the guy would've had the smarts to steal them. It all turned out fine," he said, nudging her back before sliding his fingers through hers. While he'd always shied away from the retelling of that story— all he'd really done was grab the guy and hold tight for seven minutes until the cops got there—it definitely wasn't the worst thing his sisters could've pulled out of the archive. Plus, sharing stories with Ava was different from airing them out with the entire universe. She didn't just listen, although the genuine interest with which she heard him out always put him more at ease.

Ava saw him. She fit into his life, even the crazy and difficult parts, and she *got* him.

To the point that he thought maybe, finally, he might be able to forget the rest of his past and move forward with her.

"You're pretty incredible, you know that?" Ava nestled in next to him to place their entwined hands over her out-stretched leg, and Brennan chuffed out a laugh.

"Funny, I was just thinking the same thing about you."

"Come on. You nab candlestick thieves and save kittens from trees. You're a regular hero."

His muscles stiffened without permission from his brain, but Brennan tugged in a deep inhale to offset the squeeze. "That's kind of a stretch. And the kitten thing was just part of my job."

"I know," she said, her tone marking the words as the truth. "But that job is part of who you are. You've got to have a certain brand of dedication to be a good firefighter. You even said that yourself."

"I'm not a firefighter anymore, Ava." And in the end, his actions had erased any hint of *good* from his résumé.

"Yes, Nick. You are." Her palm slid over the front of his sweatshirt, coming to a stop over his slamming heart. "Right here, where it matters, you are. And I know that having been hurt makes this hard for you. But you're a good person, with a good story. It's not so bad to let that be a part of you."

She slipped her arms around him, fitting herself against him hip to hip, head to shoulder, and the simplicity of how right she felt canceled out the blowback of her words. Their breath melted together with the far-off sounds of his family in the rest of the house, the soft light and brisk scent of the Christmas tree, the familiar comfort of a home he'd truly missed. But rather than mash back all the emotion bubbling beneath the steely surface he'd created to keep it in, Brennan inhaled, true and deep for the first time in two and a half years.

Ava saw him. She got him. And even if he didn't know it on his own, when she told him he was worthy, he believed it was true.

Chapter Twenty-Two

Ava propped her elbow against the elegant stretch of the brass and mahogany bar at her side with a smile she felt all the way to her four-inch heels. She'd been on her own for the last couple of hours, with Brennan and his immediate family all involved in wedding party duties leading up to the ceremony, then picking up right where they left off after Josh and Ellie's *I do's*. But being in the church with his family, sharing all their joy and helping out with small tasks whenever needed, had sent an unexpected shot of warmth all the way through her chest.

While her old friend Nadine's family had invited Ava to spend Christmases with them in Pine Mountain, she'd always felt just one step outside the family circle when it came to the festivities. But from the minute he'd scooped up her hand in his parents' front hallway yesterday, Brennan's family had naturally folded Ava in, as if there was not only room for her, but the day wouldn't be quite the same without her there. When Ellie had snuck an excited grin-and-wave combo at Ava from the back of the church, then when Josh broke protocol to meet Ellie partway down the aisle because he just couldn't wait any longer, their pure, radiant excitement slipped past Ava's cynical safety net to nestle directly into her heart.

But it wasn't until Brennan locked eyes with her at regular intervals during the ceremony, twining their gazes over a smile that read *are you okay out there?* that the comfort in her heart became the foundation for something far, far deeper.

She hadn't just felt invited. She'd felt necessary. Treasured.

Loved.

"Bride or groom?" A smooth, masculine voice delivered Ava right back to the luxurious reception room on Planet Country Club, and holy *GQ* model on a stick, the guy in front of her was blond-haired, blue-eyed, broad-shouldered gorgeous.

Even if his demeanor shouted loud and freaking clear that he knew it.

"Oh! Um, bride." Ava slid her fingers around her glass of club soda, grip going slightly tighter on the hand-cut crystal as *GQ* ordered a Jameson on the rocks. "You?"

Was it her imagination, or did those Caribbean blue eyes just go a shade colder at the innocuous question? "Groom. I don't believe we've met. I'm Alex Donovan."

"Ava Mancuso," she said, offering her hand for a perfunctory shake. "It's nice to meet you, Alex."

His smile amped up like a toothpaste ad on steroids, although it seemed more cocky-guy playful than cheesy or menacing. "Pleasure's mine, I assure you. Sorry if I·snuck up on you a bit. It didn't seem polite to let you stand here by yourself when everyone else is mingling, but if you'd rather not have company . . ."

Ava sent a furtive glance through the crowd, zeroing in on the wide hallway leading out to the grand foyer. The occasional silvery flash filtering in over the paneled wood walls told Ava that Brennan was still knee deep in family photos. Holding her own with a little small talk wasn't the worst thing in the universe, and cocksure demeanor aside, Alex seemed nice enough.

"Not at all. This place is so beautiful, I guess you just caught me daydreaming a little."

"Not necessarily a bad thing." He paused to give the bartender a thank-you nod at the delivery of his drink, swishing the ice cubes around with a muted *clink*. "So tell me, Ava. What do you do? Besides daydream, I mean."

She had to hand it to him. The charm was something else. "I'm a newspaper reporter."

Well, *that* took the edge off his smirk. "Not here in Fairview," Alex said, covering his brows-up surprise with a sip of his drink.

Ava fought back a shudder at the hard-edged scent of the whiskey, her curiosity triple-timing through her veins. "No, but how did you know that? Do you work for the *Sentinel*?" She'd read dozens of articles in the *Fairview Sentinel*'s archives. Just because she didn't recall Alex's name in a byline didn't mean he didn't have one.

But his laughter answered the question even before he backed it up with words. "No, I don't think I'd make a very good story jockey."

Right. Come to think of it, she should've guessed as much from his callused handshake. "It's definitely one of those professions you've got to be made for."

"Now you're singing my tune. What's your home paper?"

"I write for the *Riverside Daily*. It's a smaller publication based out of the Blue Ridge Mountains."

"You live in the Blue Ridge?" His shoulders jacked up into a hard line beneath his charcoal gray suit jacket, and he took a more substantial sip of his drink before setting it down on the gleaming stretch of the bar.

"Ever since I graduated college," she said, confusion narrowing her stare. Why would her current home take such a swipe at his expression?

"And how is it that you know Ellie Brennan, living all the way out there in the mountains when she's lived here in Fairview for her entire life?"

Nope. No way. His smile had done a one-eighty too quickly, and she knew fishing-for-info questions when she heard them. She was a reporter, for Chrissake.

"I'm here with her brother, Nick. How is it that you know Josh?"

Alex tossed back the remainder of the amber liquid in his glass before lifting his chin at the bartender for a replacement. "We play in the same softball league. Josh plays for his law firm, and I'm on the team where I work."

"And that is . . . ?"

"Fairview Fire Department. Station Eight."

Ava's heart crash-landed somewhere around her knee-caps before springing back up to a defensive position in her chest. "So you know Nick well, then."

Alex's laugh came out covered in barbed wire, edgy and sharp, and it matched the whiskey on his breath as he leaned in toward her with a humorless smile. "Better than you do, I'd bet."

Just like that, Ava's impulse control left the building, and she smiled back with every one of her teeth. "Don't put your money down on something you know nothing about."

To anyone casually chatting around them, they likely looked like just another couple socializing during cocktail hour. But even though Ava would never dare to make a scene at Ellie's wedding reception, she also wasn't going to field any attitude from some guy she'd barely met.

"I think that lack of knowledge is a two-way street,

sweetheart," Alex said, although his brows-up expression was back with a vengeance. Before she could pop back with exactly what *she* thought, another guy arrived at the bar, splitting his olive green gaze between them.

"Hey, Teflon. You're looking a little serious for your surroundings. You okay?"

Alex's laugh was more of an ironic snap as he took a step back to gesture formally in her direction. "Oh, I'm great. Just chatting it up here with Brennan's girlfriend, Ava."

The new guy's exhale translated to a nonverbal *well, that explains a lot*. Still, he extended a hand in polite greeting. "Cole Everett."

She took it, although warily. "Let me guess. Station Eight?"

He nodded, one economical rise and fall of his light brown crew cut. "For the last eight years. Alex and I came up in the class before Brennan. It's . . . been a while since we've seen him."

"I get the feeling that's on purpose." Ava's cheeks prickled with heat at the thought.

"It's complicated," Cole countered, cutting off whatever Alex looked eager to add by tacking on, "And not the right place or the right time to air this out."

Alex mumbled something about it being far past time, but then he softened his scowl at Ava. "Look, you seem like a smart woman. All I'm saying is, you might want to look long and hard at the company you keep."

Seriously? All this posturing over an injury? What the hell?

She was putting an end to this, right now. "I am a smart woman, and I like keeping company with Brennan just fine." Ava planted her black patent leather heels into the floorboards and stood up as tall as her spine would allow.

"What I don't like are arrogant, life-sized Ken dolls whose special of the day is to kick a good man when he's down."

"A good man," Alex said, low and bitter. "Is that what he told you?"

"It's what I know," she countered, making sure both Alex and Cole saw it in her stare.

"In my book, a good man looks out for his own. So maybe you should get the whole story on *your* man, directly from the source." Alex's bright blue eyes met hers and held for just a breath before he shifted to look over her shoulder.

"What do you say, Brennan? You up for telling your girlfriend the truth?"

Brennan's back muscles seized in conjunction with his lungs, making both movement and breath impossible as Alex stared him down through the soft lighting in the cocktail lounge. Ava swung around on a gasp, her wide eyes still full of the conviction he'd overheard her leveling at Alex.

Conviction he was about to turn into a pile of ash. Christ, how could he have let her think he was in any way decent? What's more, how could he have thought he'd escape a return to Fairview without an in-your-face reality check?

His best friend had been buried under three stories' worth of burning rubble because Brennan had been impulsive. Overconfident.

Wrong.

"We're not doing this here," Cole murmured, sending a pointed look around the guest-filled room. It was just like the guy to be a traditionalist and stick to the unspoken rule that firefighters dealt with their laundry in-house, no matter how dirty. Only problem was, Brennan didn't *have* a house. And he sure as hell couldn't go back to Eight. He hadn't been there since the night of the fire.

No matter how desperately he ached to put his feet on the path leading back to that firehouse, if only to take what he knew he had coming, he couldn't. Brennan had made the decision to lead Mason out of that stairwell for one final sweep to find that kid. He'd known it was a risk, that the fire was fully involved with the potential to come crashing down around them.

Brennan had forfeited his right for forgiveness when he'd kicked in that door anyway. Now what he needed was to smash that night back into the dirty little hole in his chest and get the fuck out of here.

"There's nothing to do," Brennan finally managed, the words scraping his throat raw on their way out. He turned on his heel, heartbeat sledgehammering through every last pulse point in his body, when Donovan's reply nailed him right between his shoulder blades.

"Go ahead and keep walking away like always, Brennan. Whatever helps you sleep at night."

Before he could even process the fact that he'd moved, Brennan wheeled back around, his emotions becoming the air in his lungs as he lowered his voice with deadly intention.

"You think I sleep at night? That I don't replay what happened at that fire on a continuous goddamn loop in my head? I haven't slept for the last two and a half *years*, Donovan. I doubt I ever will."

Cole moved forward, placing himself between Brennan and Alex as he took a few steps toward a more private alcove beside the bar. "Look, we were all rattled by what happened, and there are some things that never got resolved. But—"

"But *nothing*," Alex interrupted, irritation rolling off his frame in waves. "You're really going to boil it down to something that simple? Let's not sprinkle sugar on this bullshit just so we can call it candy."

Cole's brows winged upward, and oh hell. Just what they needed was for the calmest guy in the house to get pissy. "I'm not downplaying any of what happened." The look on his face dared Alex to argue, which he didn't. Unfortunately for Brennan, Cole also didn't back off the subject. "But clearly there's a lot left unsaid."

Dread leaked through Brennan's limbs, his palms going slick as he curled them into fists. "What do you want me to tell you?"

Alex jumped into the answer with both feet first. "How about that you fucked up, and because of that, we lost one of our own? We're supposed to have each other's backs, Brennan. All the time."

Just like that, all the grief and anger and blame that Brennan had clutched inside himself for two and a half years came slashing to the surface.

"Do you think I don't know that? I was there! I wasn't just on scene, or in another part of that apartment building. I was *there*, right goddamn next to him when that floor collapsed. I made that call. *I* led the way, and I'm the one who got hauled out on a stretcher instead of in a body bag."

Cole opened his mouth, stepping forward with concern etched hard around his eyes, but the words kept barging past Brennan's lips without his brain's consent.

"You want me to tell you what I told the investigators? That I'd never seen a fire that brutal in my life, that I thought there was a kid trapped inside?" Damn it, he heard the terror in that mother's voice every single night, felt the weight of it every time pain shot through his back.

He barreled on. "Or do you want me to tell you that Captain Westin called the fire only seconds after we finished our sweep, and we were turning around to fall out when the floor caved in?"

Memories hurled themselves through Brennan's mind, as vivid and real as if they'd happened a minute ago, even though he'd kept them hidden for so long.

"I made a judgment call to go down that hallway to look for that kid. I knew the risk, and I took it. I'd love to tell you that what I did is killing me, but it isn't. I get to drag myself out of bed every damn day, and instead, what I did killed someone else."

Grief clawed all the way through Brennan, spilling over everything inside the way it had for the last two and a half years.

"And I'm going to live with that for the rest of my fucking life."

This time when he turned to walk away from Alex and Cole, he didn't look back.

It wasn't until Brennan got all the way through the lobby, past the set of heavy oak doors and onto the frozen sidewalk beyond them, that he realized Ava had been right behind him the whole time.

Chapter Twenty-Three

"Brennan, wait."

Ava's voice slid past the waves of emotion doing a spin-cycle through his gut, but Brennan was too far gone to turn her words into anything that would stop his one-way trip down the sidewalk and all the way back to Pine Mountain.

Her footsteps quickened, heels sounding against the pavement in a rapid-fire *clack-clack-clack*, and she planted herself in front of him, gentle but unmoving. "Wait."

He stopped, bracing himself for the onslaught of her questions. But instead, Ava just reached up to cup his face with both palms, guiding his eyes to the anchor of her clear, green gaze.

"I'm going to tell Ellie you're not feeling well, and that I'm taking you back to the hotel."

Shit. Ellie's wedding reception. Jesus, he was the worst brother in the history of siblings for ditching out on his sister's celebration.

The sentiment must've been plastered all over his face, because Ava pressed up to her toes, keeping her no-nonsense stare level with his. "She'll understand, and you already did the pictures. I just don't want her to worry."

Brennan promised to wait for Ava to return, although the five minutes her trip took did nothing to soothe the trepidation that had migrated from his gut to his chest. He never should've come back, never should've let himself have the comfort of being back in Fairview, with his family, where he'd once belonged so thoroughly.

And now Ava, who'd held him close and told him with all that honesty that he was a good person, with a good story, knew beyond a shadow of a doubt how wrong she'd been.

"Okay." She arrived back at his side, her cheeks flushed from the winter air and her breath billowing around her face in puffy white wisps. "I had to promise to text her later, but we're all set."

Brennan nodded, slipping his suit jacket off his shoulders in order to circle it around Ava's.

"Aren't you cold?" she asked, indicating his black dress shirt as she slid her arms through the wool.

If only the cold was the worst of what he felt. "No. I'm fine."

The lie hung between them as they walked the three blocks between the country club's neatly landscaped grounds and the elegant hotel where they'd spent the night before. Brennan auto-piloted his way past the lobby, the elevator, the threshold of their room, until finally, he and Ava stood face-to-face in the cozy sitting room of their suite.

"I think we both know you're not fine," she said, wrapping her arms around herself with a shiver. His suit jacket swallowed her trim shoulders, the only thing standing between her thin silk dress and the frozen chill of their walk, and Brennan crossed to the small gas fireplace to flip the switch.

The irony of the move wasn't lost on him.

"I will be," he corrected, watching the purple blue glow

of the pilot light at the base of the gas-powered flames. "As soon as I get back to Pine Mountain."

"Are you sure that's what you want?" Ava's eyes glinted in the firelight, the stubborn lift of her chin betraying her obvious opinion that leaving things as-is was not Brennan's best plan.

"What I want is to change things that happened two and a half years ago." If only he'd waited mere minutes, if he'd assessed things even a little bit differently . . . if . . . if . . . if . . . "But I can't."

"No," Ava said, shocking him with her straight-up agreement. "You can't."

Whether it was the way he'd already uncorked the truth in front of Alex and Cole, or the thick rush of emotions still churning hard in his gut, or hell, the pure honesty on Ava's face as she'd delivered the truth in a way that didn't sugar-coat—or worse yet, pin him down—Brennan couldn't be certain. But he took a step toward her, breathing in the sweet scent of her skin, and damn it to hell's basement, he trusted her.

Ava saw him. She got him. Even when he'd told her about his injury, his addiction, all the other bits of his past, she'd never catered to his vulnerability or his pain. He might not be the man she thought he was, but right now, in this moment, he needed to tell her the truth.

All of it.

"Firefighters always work in pairs. It's like the buddy system, so someone's always got your back." *Inhale. Exhale. Breathe.* "When we arrived at that apartment fire, no other first responders were there yet, so everyone from Eight broke off into teams. A couple of guys from squad went up to vent the roof, to give the fire a place to go so we could try to manage it. But there were so many people trapped inside, most of us went in for search and rescue."

"Like you," Ava affirmed. Her face remained neutral, drinking in his words in that trademark Ava way, and her lack of drama or overdone sympathy guided more of the story right out.

"Like me." God, the building had been so dark, so suffocatingly hot, that finding anyone had been a freaking miracle after the first few trips inside. "My partner and I worked our way up, carrying out a few kids and people who'd breathed in too much smoke, ushering out the rest. But the fire spread so fast. Even with all our equipment, visibility was for shit."

All of a sudden, Brennan was right back in that apartment building, the weight of his turnout gear hanging heavy and familiar on his frame, the tight seal of his mask pressing hard to his face. Even with the aided breathing from his Scott pack, the air had still been palpably thick with ash and heat and other things he refused to contemplate, even now.

His throat clenched, threatening lockdown, but he pushed past it, welcoming the discomfort. "We were on the street, passing someone over to triage, when a woman came up to us, frantic. She couldn't find her son."

Ava's fingers curled around the bottom of his jacket sleeves, dark lashes sweeping wide. "Oh God."

"The building was getting dangerous at that point, but she was desperate, trying to go back inside. It took two paramedics just to restrain her. Their apartment was on the fourth floor, so we went up for a sweep. We knew our captain was going to call the fire at any minute, and we were running out of time."

At the tiny tug of confusion in her brows, Brennan added, "When a fire gets to a certain point—too dangerous to fight from the inside—Captain Westin makes the call for us to fall out and fight things from the outside."

"But you went back up even though you knew he was going to call the fire." The words weren't a question, although Brennan answered Ava regardless.

"We did, but it turned out to be worse than we thought up there. Even getting down the hall was a job and a half." He'd been so sure, *so fucking sure* that his rescue squad training would get them past the danger, that they'd find that kid and get the hell out of there, that everything would end up the way it was supposed to and not the way it had, that he'd recklessly kicked past all the burning debris without a second thought.

Brennan struggled for breath, remorse vibrating under his skin as he pressed on. "We swept the apartment as best we could, but there were literally seconds on the clock, and we came up empty. The ceiling was coming down around us, floorboards groaning with every step. Our captain made the call, but we didn't want to leave without the kid. I . . . thought I could look one more time, just for a second, so my partner and I turned back for one last shot."

Despite her steel-girded demeanor, Ava's eyes glittered with unshed tears in the firelight. "Oh, Nick," she whispered, one hand ghosting up to cover her lips.

He opened his mouth, wrenching the rest of the story from the deepest part of his chest. "It ended up not mattering. Before we could even get to the back room in that apartment for a second sweep, the floor collapsed. I fell about two stories and landed feet first on the second-floor landing. The impact crushed two of my lumbar vertebrae." The pain had reverberated up his spine, shredding a liquid-lightning path all the way to his teeth, and Christ, even then it was nothing compared to what spilled out of him right now. "The . . . guy who was with me . . . had it worse. . . ."

Ava's tears breached her lids, tracking silently down her face, but still, she held steady and strong, just listening.

"He fell the whole way, sustaining multiple injuries. One of them to the head." Brennan's heart crumpled behind his rib cage, and he sucked down a sloppy breath. "He died at the scene."

"I'm so, so sorry." Sadness claimed Ava's features, followed a moment later by questioning fear. "What about the little boy? Was he in the apartment with you?"

Her stricken expression begged Brennan to say no, and at least in this, he wouldn't disappoint. "No. He'd gotten out through another exit, and in all the chaos, his mother just couldn't find him."

Ava rushed forward then, her hands finding his shoulders so he had no choice but to look her in the eye. "What happened that night isn't your fault, Brennan. You had no way of knowing that boy was outside."

"But I had every way of knowing the situation was too dangerous," he argued, trying to step back. Brennan had made the call to go down that hallway, and Mason had followed without question. It had been a less-than-split second choice.

Only his best friend—not Brennan—had paid the ultimate price.

Ava shook her head, holding firm. "Of *course* it was dangerous. You were fighting a fire. It doesn't mean you're to blame."

"I was the one with the more extensive training. I should've been smarter about going into a room so heavily involved, and I should've had my partner's back."

"You're a good man who was doing his job," Ava said, and damn it, her ironclad belief in him was written all over her stubborn, beautiful face. "You were trying to save a little boy."

Brennan broke from her grasp, delivering the piece of the past that he knew would change her mind about everything.

"And instead, I killed my best friend. The firefighter next to me was Mason, Ava. I made the judgment call that ended his life."

For a second, Brennan's words made no sense, as if he'd spoken another language with unfamiliar words Ava couldn't string together.

And then the dots connected, like a series of high-powered magnets, clicking into place with enough gravity to force the breath from her chest in a sharp *whoosh*.

"Mason?" An image of the sandy-haired guy who had been Brennan's best friend that summer they'd all spent together on Sapphire Island flickered through her brain. "Mason Watts was a firefighter with you at Station Eight?"

Ava's gut pitched all the way to her shins. Brennan and Mason had been inseparable, best friends since grade school. Going to the Fairview Fire Academy had been all the two of them had talked about the entire summer they'd worked as a group at the beach café.

Of *course* Brennan and Mason hadn't drifted apart like she'd assumed. And they'd both been side by side in that horrific fire? God, how had she missed something so huge?

"Yeah. Eight is a big house, so we both landed there after graduating from the fire academy." Grief slid over Brennan's face, shadowed deeply in the scant firelight of the sitting room, and Ava's heartbeat sped up.

To feel he'd been at fault for anyone's death would've

hurt him horribly. To believe he'd been responsible for the events that had killed his best friend, and keeping that guilt chained beneath the surface for the last two and a half years?

Brennan must have been dying inside.

"No." Ava closed the space he'd just created between them on legs she couldn't quite trust, but she forced strength into her voice. "You didn't. You didn't kill him."

"I did. I led him down that hallway, Ava. If I hadn't—"

"Was he a good firefighter?" Ava interrupted, and Brennan seemed so startled by the question that his answer flew right out.

"One of the best."

"Then even if you hadn't led him down that hallway, he'd have elbowed his way around you to try and find that kid. You were doing your job, Nick. Both of you. And that means not backing down."

Brennan shook his head in a broken movement. "The fire was too big. I had more training than Mason. I should've known . . . not to be so impulsive."

"You weren't impulsive. You were decisive." Ava cupped his cheeks, bringing her face in a direct line with his, only inches away. Her heart ripped open at the tragic belief stamped over his face, but she refused to stand down or back away.

"You thought there was a child trapped in that fire, and you both did all you could to try and save him. Mason was a good man. And you are a good man."

"I'm not. I'm—"

"No." Ava pressed her fingers against his face to keep him with her, guiding his forehead down over her own. "You're a good man, Brennan. You're brave and strong and kind."

Her lips brushed over his, the intimate contact anchoring

the truth between them. "What happened in that fire isn't your fault."

Brennan's breath escaped in a soft puff against her lips. "Ava—"

"It's not your fault," she insisted. "You didn't hesitate, because if you had, you'd have lost precious seconds trying to save the little boy you thought was stuck in that apartment. You didn't hesitate because it was your job to act, even in the face of risk and danger."

Ava lifted up on her toes, maximizing the contact between them as if she could infuse her conviction into his body through touch.

"You didn't hesitate because you're a good man, Nick Brennan. Nothing you can tell me will make me think otherwise. And I'm going to do whatever it takes to make you see it."

Brennan's eyes buttoned shut, his frame shuddering against hers. "I miss him so fucking much."

Although her insides were screaming with heartache, Ava refused to give in to the sadness. Brennan needed to know he was worthy, and she was going to show him.

"I know. But you didn't kill Mason. None of this is your fault."

He grabbed onto her in one uninterrupted rush, locking his arms around her waist in a fierce grip. Their mouths touched together in a vital connection, and a desperate sound issued up from Brennan's throat. She ignored the tears pricking the backs of her eyelids, holding steady even though she felt anything but.

"It's not your fault."

Ava cradled Brennan's face more gently, but kept her intention front and center. Lifting up as high as she could onto her toes, she used her four-inch heels to her advantage as she kissed his forehead, the thrumming pulse points on his temples, the lashes cast down over his cheeks. His breath pitched against her in bursts, as if oxygen was at a premium, yet still, she didn't let go.

She studied Brennan's face, taking in every nuance and shadow cast by the orange gold glow of the fireplace. Sliding her fingers from his cheeks to his hair, she moved a trail of kisses over his jawline, repeating the process on the other side. Rather than eliciting passion, as all their other kisses had up until tonight, Ava kept her movements soft and reverent, trading desire for intimacy. Each soft brush of her mouth had Brennan's fists growing tighter and tighter over the wool covering her dress, his exhales pushing out of him in ragged need.

Need Ava was fully prepared to fulfill, in any way she could. "I want to show you what I see when I look at you. Please." She placed both palms over his wildly beating heart, canting her gaze up to meet his nearly black eyes. "Let me in."

Brennan slanted his mouth over hers in a kiss so needful and pure, Ava felt it resonate in every part of her. But he didn't push, didn't pursue or take control. Instead, he pressed his lips to her mouth, relaxing his chest against the front of her borrowed jacket, letting his hips melt in with the seam of her body. He wordlessly stood in front of her, letting her deepen the kiss by degrees, parting his lips to grant her access to the warmth of his mouth, his tongue.

Ava took her time, reveling in the fresh, crisp taste of him. She kissed him languidly, as though time just didn't exist for them and this moment, right now, was everything she'd ever wanted or known. Pausing to capture his lower lip between her own, Ava teased and stroked and sucked. She tested the heat of his mouth again and again, until finally, she pulled back on a breathless sigh.

"I love the way you fit against me," Ava murmured,

shifting back from Brennan's body just far enough to separate the edges of the coat around her shoulders. The cool air of the room felt welcome on her skin as she shrugged out of the garment, leaving her in nothing but her thin-strapped, green silk sheath. She raised her fingers to the hard plane of Brennan's chest, loosening his tie and freeing his shirt buttons one by one.

"Ava." Whatever else he'd thought to say got lost on the tide of his low moan as she reached down to slide her hands beneath his now open dress shirt, pressing past the T-shirt under it to find the warm expanse of his skin.

She countered his moan with one of her own. "I love the way you say my name." Her hands traveled up, the friction of skin on skin sending a deep pulse of want directly between her hips.

Brennan's head dropped back as he said her name again, and oh God, Ava wanted everything about him.

"I love the way you sound when I touch you." Greedy to illustrate the point, she pulled his dress shirt off his body, tugging the thin, cotton T-shirt that remained over his head and to the floor. The soft dusting of hair on Brennan's chest lay at odds with the hard angles of his shoulders, and he shivered as she moved her fingers over first one, then the other.

Fueled by the open pleasure building in his dark, hooded eyes, Ava stopped at his biceps, squeezing tight. "I love the way you like to watch."

His breath cut out on a round curse as she reached for the hot sliver of space between their bodies, the corded muscles of his inner thigh jumping under her whisper-light touch. Brennan's gaze never left her hands, both busily working his belt buckle, and Ava couldn't fight the lust spinning up in her core.

She paused for just a split second, closing the barely there distance to fit herself to his chest. The dizzying heat of his bare skin tightened her nipples to stiff points, a reaction he clearly felt if the rock-hard erection pressing into her belly was any indicator.

"I love how you feel," Ava murmured, her voice throaty from the unchecked need making her breath unsteady and her panties damp between her thighs. But what she wanted was so much less important than Brennan's need, and even though it took willpower she hadn't known she had, she broke from his touch to hold only his glittering stare.

"You're the only person who ever made me feel perfect, even when I didn't deserve it. I love you, Brennan. I love you."

His eyes widened, but she lifted her fingers to his mouth, coasting them over his kiss-swollen lips.

"You don't have to say anything," she whispered, and she meant it. The words made her vulnerable, yes. But they were the truth no matter what, even if he didn't say them back.

"I know." Brennan kissed the pads of her fingers one by one before placing her hand over the center of his chest. "But I want to. I love you too, Ava. I have from the minute I saw you standing in the Double Shot. In fact, I don't think I ever stopped."

They joined in a passion-filled kiss she felt in every fiber, all the way down to her most fundamental parts. With a few swift movements, Ava undressed him until he was bare. Her body, her mind, her heart, every part of her begged to have him inside of her until they both came undone, only so they could start from the beginning and do it again.

Brennan's hands rode the length of her thighs, forging

a path of tingling demand as he moved higher over the silk of her short hemline. A moan lifted up from her chest when he paused at her breasts, creating blissful friction between the ultrathin fabric and the purposeful movement of his thumbs.

Unable to wait even another second for him to touch her naked skin, Ava swung around in his grasp, so close that the heat between their bodies hypnotized her with raw suggestion. She dropped her chin toward her aching nipples to give him access to the zipper on her dress, looking over her shoulder at him without hesitation.

"Please. Take this off and take me to bed. *Please.*"

The taut muscles of Brennan's chest flexed into her shoulders and back, and he seamlessly threaded his fingers through her hair, guiding the zipper of her dress down to the small of her back. Ava sighed with both relief and yearning as the dress floated to the floor with a *shush*, and Brennan tightened his grasp on her hips as he pulled her even closer from behind. His cock pressed into her back, and she arched to meet him, his mouth and hands moving over her now-bare skin just slowly enough that she thought she'd scream.

His palms flashed over her shoulder blades, moving around to test the weight of her breasts from behind before sliding his hands down to the flare of her hips. She rocked against his arousal hard enough that he dug his fingers into the ribbons holding her panties together, and she did it again just to take in his involuntary exhale over her shoulder.

Together, they made their way to the bed on the far wall, the firelight reaching for them in strains of amber and gold. Brennan stopped only for a brief second to take a condom from the bedside table drawer before joining Ava on the soft sheets.

"Hey." He lay down next to her, their bodies side by

side, and brushed a kiss over her mouth. Everything about the moment, from the rasp of his goatee on her lips to the slide of his fingers under her chin as he held her close to kiss her again, made Ava feel beautiful and brand new.

"Hey." They parted for just a breath, forehead to forehead, chest to chest. But the desire drawing them together quickly became too strong to ignore, and Brennan put on the condom with a few circumspect movements. As soon as he finished, Ava slipped out of her panties, guiding his back to the bedsheets and pushing him prone to straddle his hips.

"Jesus, Ava. I want you so much." Brennan tipped his body up, fitting his cock against her slick entrance, but she didn't rush. The scent of brisk oceans and pure need filled up her senses, and she gasped as he rocked into the cradle of her hips, slowly filling her body as well.

"Brennan." She leaned forward, framing his shoulders with both hands and saying his name as if no other words mattered. Brennan kissed her neck, twisting his fingers through her hair to reveal more skin, more want, more everything as he slid his tongue over her. They moved together in slow, suggestive thrusts, but all too soon her body demanded more.

Brennan surged beneath her, arching up again and again until they were joined so completely that she had to let go. His hands wrapped around her hips, lifting and lowering in gorgeous rhythm. Ava surrendered control of her motions, gripping the sheets with tight fists and leaning all the way over his chest as Brennan led her higher, tighter, faster. His eyes never left hers, and when he hooked both hands over the curve of her backside to open her even wider as he thrust, Ava shattered on a ragged cry.

"I love the way *you* sound when I touch you," he said, bringing her back to earth with a series of soft kisses and shallow movements. Need rekindled under her skin, but it wasn't desire for her own release.

It was desire for his.

"Like this?" She moaned her approval of Brennan's touches, his left hand still firm on the swell of her ass, his right doing wicked things to the spot where their bodies joined. His ministrations intensified with her gasps, his own voice blending in with pleasured groans until finally, on one last thrust, he went completely taut beneath her.

After a portion of time Ava couldn't measure, they shifted apart, but just long enough to quickly clean up, then resettle against the sheets and each other. The gas-powered firelight draped over the bed, providing just enough illumination for Ava to catch Brennan's gaze.

"It's been a long day. Let's get some sleep," she whispered, gathering him close. Although it wasn't terribly late, he looked exhausted, and the words he'd spoken earlier sprang into Ava's heart with a jolt.

I haven't slept for the last two and a half years. I doubt I ever will.

With one hand on his chest and the other holding tight beneath his shoulder, she waited until Brennan's breathing evened out into long, deep pulls. When his face went totally lax with the mark of deep sleep, she kissed his temple and slid from the bed.

Ava dressed quickly in jeans and a long-sleeved T-shirt, scooping up her bag with carefully planned moves. She padded into the hall, closing the door with a near-silent *snick* before flipping her cell phone into her palm to send Ellie a quick all-is-well text.

She'd deal with the fact that it was a bald-faced lie later. Right now, Ava had bigger things on her plate.

Namely, the newspaper article sitting spring-loaded and

ready to deliver to her knuckle-dragging overlord of a boss first thing Monday morning.

The hotel lobby was empty, not exactly a shock considering it was Christmas. All the guests were likely there for Ellie's wedding, and by now, the late dinner reception had to be in full swing at the country club.

Ava slid into the damask wingback chair standing sentry by the computer reserved for guests, tapping the keyboard to life. Her fabric-bound notebook lay nestled in the bag at her feet, but she left it there, unopened. A few swift keystrokes had her on the home page of her favorite search engine, and with her heart lodged firmly in her throat, she typed with shaky fingers.

Mason Watts, Fairview firefighter.

The screen exploded with results, and each article made her heart break for Brennan that much more.

She couldn't add to his grief with another one, even though she believed in every word of the story she'd written. Turning in the piece she'd done—no matter how well intentioned and well delivered—would rip his old wounds right back open.

And this time, the pain just might ruin him.

Chapter Twenty-Four

Brennan blinked back the momentary displacement of waking up in a bed other than his own, blearily calculating the details of the night before. The muscles strung across his lower back threatened their usual mayhem, and he very nearly gave in and gritted out the pain.

Until he realized Ava was snuggled up next to him, wearing nothing but a bedsheet.

"Mmm." She stirred slightly, turning away from the morning sunlight slipping past the curtains on the far wall and further into his chest. "How'd you sleep?"

His muscles held tight, but the pain didn't double like usual. "Okay." In truth, he'd slept harder than any night in recent memory, although he felt more restless than revitalized.

Ava was the first person in two and a half years to know the full-blown truth about his past.

And she was the *only* person on that very short list who thought he was a good man in spite of it.

"You barely moved all night." Ava peered up at him, her sleepy-sweet expression kicking his unease down a notch.

All night . . . damn it! "I missed half of Ellie's reception." Brennan pushed up from the bed, his pulse three steps ahead of him, but Ava calmed his burst of panic with just a simple touch.

"I talked to her after you fell asleep. Twice, actually."

Confusion replaced the unease darting through his gut. "You did?" Had he been that out of it, that Ava had talked to Ellie twice and he'd had no clue?

"Mmm hmm. I went out in the hallway so I wouldn't wake you. She said, and I quote, 'Tell him to get some rest, and to stop worrying about missing the damn reception.'"

Okay, so his sister had his number, big time. "I feel bad that I wasn't there for her."

"You *were* there for her. For as long as you could be." Ava paused, tucking the sheet beneath her arms as she sat up to look at him. "I think she feels bad that Alex and Cole were at the wedding."

The panic he'd just gotten rid of returned tenfold. "Did she see me talking to them last night?" They'd kept their words quiet, sure, but any idiot would've been able to see the tension on their faces if they'd been standing close enough to that alcove.

Ellie was far from an idiot.

"No," Ava said, and a single syllable had never sounded so good in Brennan's ears. "There were five hundred people spread out over three rooms at that cocktail hour. I don't think anyone saw you. Not to notice the conversation, anyway."

"Good." Brennan reached for the basketball shorts he'd discarded in a heap by the bed yesterday morning, skinning into them before letting his feet hit the floor. "We can get on the road as soon as you're ready. I'll call Ellie when we get back to Pine Mountain this afternoon. She and Josh aren't leaving for their honeymoon until Monday."

"Are you sure you want to leave so soon?" Ava asked,

no less than a thousand other questions banked in her wary, emerald stare.

Brennan should've known she'd hop the inquisitive path sooner or later. As much as he knew she was trying to help, he wasn't changing his mind. Not about this. "It's the only choice I have, Ava. I need to leave Fairview, the sooner, the better. It was stupid to think I could avoid a blowout with Alex and Cole."

"Then maybe you shouldn't."

Her words arrived soft and sure, without indictment, but they still hit him like a flathead ax. "So you think I should just what? Go back to Station Eight and tell my side of things like it's no big deal? You know what happened that night."

"Yes." Ava slid from the bed, the sheet rustling as she pulled it from its mooring in order to reach the spot where he stood. "But do Alex and Cole?"

"They were there," Brennan said, desperate to tamp down his churning emotions even though he couldn't force himself to swallow the rest. "They had their radios on just like everyone else, and . . . they helped pull both of us out after the floor caved in. Believe me, they know *exactly* what happened."

"After what I heard last night, I don't think they do."

Brennan cursed. "I was heavily medicated right after the fire. My first surgery was only a day later, to relieve some of the swelling and start to repair the damage. Our captain came to see me, and at first the guys were there too. But I couldn't face them after . . . Mason."

Her chin snapped up. "So you refused to see everyone?"

"Not everyone. I saw my captain. And anyway, I meant for it to be temporary," he argued, fighting more with himself than Ava. "I felt guilty, and I guess part of me wanted them to hate me the way I hated myself."

"You thought you didn't deserve their support, so you pushed them away," Ava said, understanding starting to break over her words.

"I saw Captain Westin twice. He tried to convince me to at least talk to Alex and Cole, because we'd been the closest. I wanted to, but . . . any time a firefighter dies in the line of duty, it's standard procedure for there to be an internal investigation. None of us had ever been part of one before, and the whole thing really messed with everyone's head space. Reliving the fire, with all the details right there in the open . . . that made it even harder to face any of them. So I shut them all out."

Ava stood in front of him, her forehead dipped in thought, and Brennan opted for a preemptive strike to end the conversation. "Before you ask, Mason's death was ruled accidental."

"Then why don't Alex and Cole think so?"

"Because I never talked to them to tell them otherwise. The investigation report goes into a closed file, so they only knew what they saw and heard that night. By the time I got out of the hospital, I was already eating painkillers instead of three squares a day. My best friend was dead, and the career I lived for was an afterthought. Everything I'd ever known had been run through the shredder. I spent four months locked in my apartment, ignoring everyone's phone calls and trying to go numb. Once I got my reality check courtesy of detox, it was too late. All I wanted was to get the hell out of Fairview."

Ava's lips parted, the last piece clicking into place. "So you left right after rehab."

"And I never went back. Clearly, Alex and Cole would've preferred that I had kept it that way."

"Don't you think it's time you guys hashed things out?"

Ava clamped her bottom lip between her teeth. "I'm

sorry. I know that's easier said than done." She stepped in, defusing the argument brewing on his tongue. "But it's been two years. I get that sometimes the past makes the present hard to deal with. But I also know that once you *do* deal with it, moving on is a whole lot easier."

She stepped in, warming him instantly as she brushed her fingers over his cheek. "Brennan, you deserve to move on. You deserve to tell them your side of the story."

For a single second, Brennan's gut panged in agreement. Christ, he wanted nothing more than to look Alex and Cole in the eyes and tell them the truth—the real truth—about everything that had gone down. How he'd been devastated not just to lose Mason, but the career he'd been made for. How he missed everyone at Eight horribly even though he'd been the one to walk away. How, as much as everyone at the Double Shot had welcomed him, he was dying to return to his family.

His home.

"There's nothing to deal with," Brennan said, slamming the door shut on the possibility. His chance at forgiveness had come and gone ages ago, and he'd been the one to walk away from it. The only thing he could do now was put his nose back to the grindstone and move forward in Pine Mountain. "I know you're trying to help, Ava. But Fairview's in my past."

She opened her mouth to argue, and damn it, he just couldn't do this. "I can be ready to go in twenty minutes. If that works for you," he said, hating the frost on his words even as he did nothing to thaw it.

"Oh." Ava swallowed hard, her feet tangling in the bottom of the sheet as she took a stutter-step backward. Her chin jerked up in that tough-girl defense mechanism she always relied on, and Brennan hated himself with a little extra venom for bringing it to life.

"I'll be ready in fifteen," she said, then walked to the bathroom to shut the door.

Ava blinked back the heavy doses of Monday-morning sunshine blasting their way through the parking lot at the *Daily*, shielding her eyes with one arm as she auto-piloted through the front door. At six-forty A.M. the day after Christmas weekend, the office was a graveyard, with only two other cars in the parking lot for the entire building. But sleep had pretty much laughed in Ava's face ever since Brennan had told her the entire truth about the night he'd been injured.

If the heartbreak of his revelations hadn't been bad enough, the sting of him shutting her out so thoroughly after she'd suggested he try to talk to Alex and Cole had sure done the trick. They'd spoken maybe seven words to each other on the trip back to Pine Mountain, after which they'd picked at an early dinner and chastely kissed before parting ways.

Oh, toughen up, girl. You've got bigger worries than a broody boyfriend.

Ava blew out a breath as she scanned the newsroom. Every cubicle in the place bore zero signs of life—other than Ian's, of course, but she was pretty sure he lived here anyway. As much as she hated to admit it, her inner voice had a point. Telling Gary they couldn't run the hometown hero story was going to suck, and not a little. But Brennan's gut-wrenching admission, plus the additional research she'd done Saturday night in the hotel lobby to fill in what details she could of Mason's death, had locked all the pieces into place.

Brennan's name had been kept from public records to

protect his privacy because he'd been injured. Ava just hadn't realized he'd been hurt in more ways than one.

"Mancuso."

"Oh!" Ava launched into an ungraceful flail, her leather tote pitching from her shoulder to the foot-worn carpet in front of her cubicle with a muffled *thunk*. "God, you scared me to death."

Gary lifted an unimpressed brow as she scrambled to scoop up her scattered belongings. "Your head needs a better swivel. I swear you'd miss a story if it fell right in your damn lap."

"You're never here this early," she said in her defense.

"Royce will be here for year-end meetings in two days. Believe me, he's not going to impress himself. Speaking of which." He jerked a thumb over his shoulder, his expression so flinty and cold that Ava had to bite back the temptation to ask who'd died. "My office."

Ava's stomach did a shift-and-drop that would've made most roller coasters proud, but she nailed her shoulders into place around her spine. She was going to have to come clean to Gary about her story at some point today, anyway.

Might as well do it when the newsroom was dead and no one would catch sight or sound of the fallout. Except maybe Ian, and it wasn't like the guy didn't already know the score.

"Actually, I need to talk to you about the story I've been working on. The firefighter piece," she started, but Gary cut her off with an impatient wave.

"I *told* you that hero guy had dirty secrets." He whipped a computer printout off his desk, thrusting it into Ava's shocked hands.

"What are you talking about?" She scanned the pages in front of her, a chilled spray of goose bumps washing over her skin. Oh God. This couldn't be. . . .

"That is an official investigation report conducted by the Fairview Fire Department. Seems your golden boy has quite the past out there in Virginia. It's no freaking wonder he wanted to come out here to the sticks and lie low."

"How did you even get this?" The investigation had been done internally, just as Brennan had said, and none of the specifics were a matter of public record. Ava hadn't been able to find the report, not even when she'd searched on Saturday night with Mason's name and all the other particulars Brennan had told her attached to the search.

If Brennan hadn't trusted her with his crushing retelling of events, she'd never have connected all the dots. And she definitely got the feeling firefighters kept to themselves with their personal stuff.

No way would one of them talk to Gary, of all people.

"You'd be amazed at the doors that open up when you know how to work a source," he said. "Let's just say I found someone at the fire marshal's office who was amenable to incentives."

Her mouth dropped in disgust that she had no hope of covering up. "Bribing a source is completely immoral." Although it wasn't illegal, which Gary knew full well.

Apparently, he was also well versed in covering his ass. "No one said anything about paying anyone, Mancuso. I simply came up with information. Information *you* couldn't wrangle out of a source you've been working for weeks."

The implication reeked of innuendo, and Ava's palms curled into clammy fists. "In the interest of full disclosure, I told you Nick Brennan and I have a personal relationship."

"You think I give a rat's ass about what you do in your spare time? As long as the story is true, I don't care how you get it. But the fact remains that you didn't."

"Wait . . ." Gary's words tickled at the back of her brain

before sliding into focus. "How do you know what's in my article? I haven't turned it in."

He threw his arms in the air, sending the buttons on his too-tight shirt into red alert. "Jesus, you really are green. Who do you think owns your laptop? I'll give you a hint, sweetheart. It's not you."

Ava's jaw unhinged. "You *hacked* my laptop to read my story?" This couldn't be happening.

"Like I said, it's not your laptop. Anything you write on that baby is property of the *Daily*. And there's no chance I was going to leave you completely to your own devices after your last dud. I need a showstopper, and I needed it five minutes ago."

Her heart sank like the anchor on an ocean liner. "You can't run this story, Gary."

"Well, you're finally right about something."

Hope flickered, sweet and low in Ava's chest. But then Gary stomped it out with a thin, humorless smile.

"You have twenty-four hours to get me a story on this guy that will *sell* papers. I want all of this"—he gave the report in Ava's fingers a hard tap—"included as part of the deal. And believe me when I tell you your job *is* on the line here."

"I won't do it." The words vaulted from her mouth automatically, and Ava backed them up with her stare. She'd just signed her own walking papers, she knew, but she didn't care. Yes, she believed Brennan's story deserved to be told. But not like this.

Not when it would do more harm than good.

"What did you say?" Gary asked, but no way was she backing down now.

"I said, I'm not writing the article. A firefighter from Station Eight died in this apartment fire, and it tore the whole house apart. I refuse to sensationalize a tragedy for the sake of selling papers or saving my job." Ava gripped the report in her hand hard enough to put a dent in the pages, her entire body filling with strength she'd had no clue she possessed. "I did all the research. I know all the facts. And I won't write it."

"Oh, I think you will," Gary said, slithering in for the deathblow. "Because if you don't, *I* will."

Panic stole the breath from Ava's lungs. "You can't."

Of course, they both knew she was wrong. Gary hissed, "I can, and I will. Granted, it'll be a monumental pain in the ass to root through all your goody-goody research to find anything I can really use, but one way or another, this story is happening, Mancuso. And it's happening today."

He stalked past his desk, serving up a stare that marked his words as all truth and no bluff, and in that moment, Ava knew she had no escape.

"It's up to you which one of us gets to tell it."

Chapter Twenty-Five

Brennan stared holes at the touch-screen on the Double Shot's bar register without seeing a damned thing. He'd been back in Pine Mountain for just over twenty-four hours, working without pause for nearly half of them, yet he couldn't calm the restless ache at the bottom of his gut. He knew this place like his own reflection, could run the front of the house from a sleep state, even in a busy dinner shift. The work was a constant barrage of go-go-go, just the way Brennan wanted it.

So why the hell couldn't it calm him?

"Who pissed in your Post Toasties?" Adrian's question took Brennan by surprise, although judging from the big guy's comfortable lean against the alcove behind the bar, he'd clearly been there for a minute or two.

"Straight to the point, as always," Brennan said, his attempt at sarcasm sprawling flat on its face between them.

"And you're dodging the question. As always." Adrian folded his arms over his parking lot of a chest, and damn it, Brennan really wasn't in the mood for this.

"Now that the dinner rush is over, I'm going to check on inventory." He ducked his head to slip out of the alcove, only to meet an immovable expanse of chef's whites and surly attitude.

"You already did that twenty minutes ago. You want to try again?"

Damn it. It figured Adrian had seen Brennan check the walk-in as soon as the shift had slowed. "For the record, it's kind of creepy how Big Brother you are in this place."

Adrian rolled his eyes, waving his meat hook of a hand in a *give it up* type motion, and Brennan caved.

"Fine. I'm just trying to stay busy, okay? It helps me sort shit out." Usually, anyway. Tonight, the whole routine was just making him restless.

"Why don't you stay busy by bringing your reporter a refill? She's working really hard, and it looks like she's had a rough day. Bet she could use the sugar rush."

Brennan followed Adrian's gaze to the spot where Ava sat, halfway across the restaurant. She'd passed up her regular spot at the end of the bar in favor of a private booth off the beaten path, explaining her change in location with a tough deadline and a tougher article. Her beautiful face was shadowed by weary frown lines as she dropped her chin to read the notebook in front of her, and Brennan's conscience slapped him with a double serving of guilt.

She might be lost in work right now, but Ava was also as tough as they came. Just because she hadn't admitted that he'd hurt her feelings yesterday didn't change the fact that he'd probably done so.

Brennan hadn't meant to push her away when she'd suggested he work things out with Alex and Cole. The knee-jerk reaction of trying to forget the past had just shoved the response right out of him. His frustration over not being able to change any of it had done the rest.

He might not be able to change what had gone down, but talking about it with her wasn't really the worst idea.

Maybe that's what would help him move on, once and for freaking all.

Brennan snuck a glance across the Double Shot's sparsely populated dining room. The dark circles smudged beneath Ava's normally sparkling eyes betrayed her, and he exhaled, hard. God, he was an ass. An ass who owed her an apology and an explanation. Which Adrian had clearly picked up on, even though he didn't know the particulars.

"Thanks for the advice, you old softie," Brennan said, one corner of his mouth lifting in the approximation of a smile. Adrian returned the favor, clapping him on the shoulder before taking a step back.

"You're welcome. But if you ever call me soft again, I'll end you, brother."

"And they say you have no heart."

Adrian muttered a semi-audible suggestion involving different body parts, but Brennan caught the guy's smirk as he turned to walk back toward the kitchen. Grabbing a clean pint glass from the shelf next to the register, Brennan poured the now-familiar combination of iced tea and lemonade.

"Oooh, are you taking that to Ava?" Annabelle made her way behind the bar, keying in an order at the register while fishing a bottle of Budweiser, then another from the cooler at her hip.

"Sure am."

Annabelle's bottle opener clinked against the glass as she treated each lid to an expert lift and flick. "Can you drop these with Jackson and Shane at table seventeen first? I've gotta run to the kitchen to see if their wings are up. Last *Monday Night Football* game of the year, you know?"

Brennan shot a gaze at the oversized flat screen on the

far wall. "Can't let the natives get too restless," he said, taking the bottles from her fingers. "I've got your back."

Seventeen was only two tables away from Ava's booth, and anyway, just because he owed her a sorry-I'm-a-knucklehead-I-screwed-up didn't mean his work ethic could take a complete hike.

He delivered the beers and a couple of hey-how-are-yas to the pair of regulars with polite efficiency before excusing himself to finish his rounds with Ava's drink. The detour had put him at her back, her dark head and the knotted line of her shoulders the only thing visible as she hunched over the papers on the table in front of her.

"Hey," he said, pulling up with a sheepish smile when her head whipped around and her eyes went as round as dinner plates. She closed the notebook in her fingers with a downward tug of her brows, and hell . . . he had some making up to do. "I thought you might like a refill."

"Oh. Thanks." She dropped the book to the stack of papers in front of her as if the fabric-bound cover had scorched her fingers, and screw it—he wasn't a beat-around-the-bush kind of guy.

"You're welcome. Listen, I owe you an apology."

"No, you don't."

A fresh layer of unease flashed over her features, making him all the more insistent. "Yes, I do. I know you were just trying to be helpful yesterday. I shouldn't have shut you out. The stuff with Alex and Cole . . . I guess it just gets to me."

"Brennan, really. You don't have to explain. It's fine."

Her choice of words sent a prickle of dread down his spine. "It's not fine." Impulse screamed at him to reach for her, kicking his hands into motion. He realized just a breath too late that he'd been so intent to get his apology out and talk to her honestly about the guys at Station Eight, that he'd forgotten about the drink still wrapped in his grip.

"Ava . . ." Brennan shifted his torso to put the pint glass across from her at the table, but at the same time, Ava planted her feet to stand. His free arm bumped hers in an awkward tangle, and he looped his hand beneath her elbow to steady her.

"Whoa! Hang on." Brennan plunked the glass on the pine tabletop to avoid dropping it, but the move upset his already questionable balance. Scrabbling for purchase, he tried to guide her back to the safety of the bench seat behind her, only to knock her book and a bunch of papers to the floor in the process.

"Damn it. Ava, I'm sorry." Brennan knelt down low to scoop up the pages, and Ava catapulted into action beside him.

"No! No, no, it's fine, just . . ."

Not even her panicked tone could rip through the confusion taking root in his brain.

"What is this?" He stared, unblinking, at the printout in his hands even though the bold-lettered title beneath the horribly familiar city seal couldn't possibly be right.

CITY OF FAIRVIEW . . . OFFICE OF THE FIRE MARSHAL . . . OFFICIAL INVESTIGATION, FAIRVIEW LAKES APARTMENT FIRE.

Brennan's blood turned to ice in his veins.

The date stamp in the corner of the printout was today's.

"Why are you reading the investigation report on the fire that killed Mason?" Hell, Captain Westin had called in so many favors to make sure the details remained under lock and key, getting that report had to have taken some seriously creative legal judo.

Or possibly a bribe.

Brennan riffled through the pages he'd gathered, the

chill in his veins reaching the center of his chest as he got to the fourth piece of paper in the pile.

RESCUE SQUAD HERO STARTS OVER IN PINE MOUNTAIN.

"Are you . . . is *this* the big story you've been working on?" Brennan swallowed back the bitter aftertaste of the question, staring at printout after printout as he snatched them from the floorboards. Archived news articles from Fairview's local paper, reports from the fire marshal's office, training requirements for rescue squad applicants—*fuck*, she even had the wet-behind-the-ears file photo of him as a recruit at the academy.

Ava had been writing a story. About him. About *this*. The whole goddamn time.

"Brennan, I can explain—"

"I asked you a question."

Ava flinched at the serrated edge he'd put to the words, but she didn't drop her gaze as she answered. "Yes. I've been putting together another article about first responders and firefighters."

"About me?" he asked, and her stare filled with tears.

"Yes, but—"

"But what, Ava?" He exploded to his feet, anger brewing deep and hot in his gut. "I trusted you. I told you things nobody knows, not even my family. Goddamn it, I fell in love with you—again—and for what? To find out I'm just a notch in your fucking byline?"

Her shoulders snapped against the back of the booth in surprise. "No! Brennan, this is a lot more complicated than it looks."

"How long have you been writing this story?"

She blinked, two seconds too long. "Two weeks."

Brennan straightened, every last flicker of hope dying out in the depths of his chest. "Then it doesn't look complicated from where I sit."

"Please," Ava said. "This isn't what it looks like. You have to believe me."

Christ. All the nights she'd brought work into the Double Shot over the last few weeks, all those curiosity-filled questions he'd answered, thinking she'd been genuinely interested. All the emotions he'd unloaded on her about his past. His career. His loss.

He'd believed her when she'd said he was worthy. But she'd only said those things so she could use what she learned in a newspaper article.

Yet again, Brennan had risked his stupid, trusting heart for a false version of Ava Mancuso.

Only this time, he wasn't going to let her smash it into bits.

"No, actually. I don't have to believe you." Brennan inhaled, snuffing out every last emotion he possibly could before releasing his breath over a stone-cold stare. "When is the story going to run?"

"The day after tomorrow."

"And is this fire part of the article?" He held up the investigation report, every dirty little secret he'd ever wanted to bury reduced to four pages of eight-and-a-half-by-eleven paper.

Ava's chin lowered in a broken nod. "Yes."

The tears she'd held at bay finally tracked down her face, and Brennan had to admit, the timing was perfect. She really had the whole yank-on-a-guy's-heartstrings thing down cold.

He ran a palm over his sternum before dropping his hand to his side in disgust. "Right. So I guess we're done here, then."

"Brennan, please," Ava whispered, moving out of the booth until she stood less than a foot away. "Let me explain. I don't have a choice."

Her wet eyes glinted with honesty, and for a single,

traitorous second, Brennan paused. Hope ignited, bright and sweet in his chest, reminding him who she was, daring him to believe, to trust her.

But he'd been burned too many times by that spark of hope. The best thing—the safest thing—was to snuff it out.

For good.

"You know, all those times you said my story was worth telling, I should've known you were just trying to justify using it to your own ends, and that all you wanted was a scoop. But it doesn't matter. You know what? Tell it to the world, Ava. Shout it from the goddamn rooftops if you want. But don't—*do not*—sit there and tell me you have no choice. You might not like the options in front of you, but you sure as shit have them. Just like I have mine. Difference is, you're just not tough enough to make a smart call."

Brennan reached down low to swipe her faded blue notebook off the floor, slapping the papers on top of it as he handed them all over without expression.

"Now get out of my bar."

Chapter Twenty-Six

Ava got all the way to the threshold of Pete and Lily's cozy lakeside cottage before her good old-fashioned cry became an out and out grief quake.

"Holy shit, Ava. What's the matter? You sounded awful on the phone. Are you hurt?" Her brother tugged her gently over the frost-covered boards of the porch, worry blazing in his green eyes. He followed his top-to-toes visual assessment with a gentle sweep of his hands over the arms of her thin wool sweater. "And where the hell is your coat?"

God, she hadn't even felt cold. Not from the weather anyway. "I, uh . . . I don't know. And, no. I'm not hurt."

The lie scorched a path past her lips, but Pete looked panicked enough as he brushed the sleep out of his eyes to give her a third look-see in as many minutes. No matter the provocation during their rough and rocky upbringing, Ava had never let Pete—or anyone—see her cry this hard. Not when she'd accidentally broken their father's favorite beer mug and he'd "accidentally" broken her arm in return. Not when she'd spent holidays with Nadine's huge, loving family only to yearn wholeheartedly for one to call her own. Not even when she'd watched the sun break over the horizon from the deck of that early morning ferry on the day she'd left Sapphire Island seven years ago.

The bone-deep pain that had replaced everything in her chest when Brennan kicked her out of the Double Shot had put all that other hurt to shame before she'd even made it to her car.

Ava stuttered out a sigh. "I'm really sorry. I know it's nearly ten, and you guys get up so early to open the bakery, but . . ."

Pete cut off her apology with a wave, leading her down the hall to his brightly lit kitchen. "Lily sleeps like a prize-fighter going down for the count. She barely even budged when my cell phone rang. And I don't care about the bakery."

Ava's lips parted over no sound, and her brother shook his head as he pulled a high-backed farmhouse chair from the table in invitation. "I mean, don't get me wrong. Running the Sweet Life means a lot to me. It's the career I always wanted. But it's a place, Ava. People are more important."

Hell if *that* didn't prompt a fresh round of tears from her mutinous eyes.

"Yeah." She slapped at her cheeks with the back of one hand, forcing herself to get it together as she tucked her legs beneath the cranberry-colored tablecloth. "I might've missed that memo."

"I'm sorry." Pete sat across from her, scrubbing a hand over his five o'clock shadow. "But I'm afraid you lost me."

Ava inhaled a rickety breath, and exhaled the pocket version of her life's events over the course of the past few weeks. While gabbing freely about her love life with her overprotective and under-restrained brother had never ranked particularly high on her list of sure-let's-do-that, Ava hadn't thought twice about calling him tonight. She'd done enough damage in the past by keeping her feelings inside, and she had to admit, Pete was a surprisingly good listener when he wanted to be.

"Jesus," he murmured, blowing out a slow breath across the table. "What happened after he told you to leave?"

Ava slumped in her chair, but didn't deny the truth. "Well, since my menu of options had exactly one crappy selection, I left. To be honest, it all happened really fast. I didn't mean for him to find out the way he did."

She'd been waiting to tell Brennan about the story—and Gary's subsequent ultimatum—until after they left the Double Shot for the night. Upsetting him at work wouldn't have helped matters, plus, she'd thought maybe if she had a little time to really think about it, she'd come up with some way to make things right.

But then she'd been so mired in looking for a Hail Mary in that damned report that Brennan had taken her by surprise, and yeah . . .

Now they all knew the unhappy ending to that story.

Frowning, Pete eyeballed the fresh round of tears clinging to her lashes. "Do you want me to go down there and break his legs?"

Ava coughed out an involuntary laugh. Okay, so maybe Pete wasn't *entirely* a calm, cool listener. "Thanks, I think, but no. If anyone deserves blame, it's me."

"I'm not sure that's quite true." Pete pushed back from the table, moving over to the stove with practiced, comfortable strides.

"Please." Ava's heart twisted against her breastbone, but it was past time to face the truth. "For the last two weeks, I've been writing a story about the one thing he's been trying to hide for the last two and a half years. I should've told him."

"Maybe. But you wanted to write the story to show him

what he meant to you. Telling him would've defeated the purpose."

Before Ava could open her mouth to argue, her brother gave her a dead-certain look that told her he knew of what he spoke. "Trust me on this one. Sometimes stories need to be shown. And you had no way of knowing everything that happened at that fire. You didn't intend to hurt him."

"I still stand by the story I wanted to tell. Brennan is . . ." *Amazing. Courageous. Gone.* "Worthy of the recognition," she choked out. "But he went so far as to leave his hometown to try to get away from what happened there. And now everyone will know about his past."

"Hmm. I'm no expert," Pete said, pulling a carton of milk from the fridge, "but it seems to me that hiding from your past isn't usually the best plan for coping with it. Especially if it's tough."

And didn't they both know that firsthand? After all, leaving Philadelphia sure didn't kill the demons that had been born there, either for her or her brother. Still . . . "Yeah, but he's not some dirtbag covering up a scam or a scandal. Exposing him like this isn't right."

Pete tipped his head in a nonverbal *okay, you've got me there*. "What about your original article? The one you wrote before you knew about Mason? If you stand by it like you said, maybe it wouldn't be the worst thing to let Gary run it."

Ava's mind clicked back to the piece she'd spent the last two weeks fitting together, bit by meticulous bit. "I *do* stand by it. Or I did. I don't know. But it doesn't matter anyway. Gary wants more sensationalism. He wants the dirty details of that fire front and center on page one, and he won't settle for anything less."

"Now there's someone whose legs deserve to be broken.

Asshole," Pete muttered, sliding a deep-bellied coffee mug from the cupboard at his shoulder.

"Asshole or not, he's got me by the hair. Either I write this article with all the gory particulars right there for the world to see, or he will." The trembling she'd been able to keep at bay worked its way back into her chest, rising up to claim her voice as she continued.

"At least if I write it, there's a chance I can help Brennan save a little face. Anything Gary churns out will be astronomically worse. Even if he has to work his ass off to get it done."

At least she had a tiny bit of leverage there. It would take all of Gary's questionable brainpower to get a story like this done in twenty-four hours from scratch. His code of ethics might be anorexic, but he still had to research and fact-check just like everyone else.

"What about Brennan?" Pete asked, coming back to the table with a mug in each hand.

Ava's eyes filled with tears, and seriously, she was never going to get anything fixed with her idiot face leaking like this. "What about him?"

"Any chance he'll hear you out once he's calmed down?"

"No." Her heart ached at the admission, but hating reality didn't make it any less true. Or any less deserved. "I never meant to hurt him. But I still did. I only wanted to stay close to you and Lily, and to tell Nick's story with integrity. He's . . ." Her throat clenched, but she willed the words to life. "He deserves nothing less. I just didn't know that telling it would do more harm than good."

Her brother placed the mug full of milk and graham crackers in front of her at the table, fixing her with a bittersweet smile. "You're always going to be close to me and Lily, Ava. We don't need to be in the same place for that."

Ava nodded. Despite the two years Brennan had spent

in Pine Mountain, he and his sisters had slid right back into place as if the distance didn't matter. And when family truly cared about each other, and loved each other no matter what, the distance really *didn't* matter.

She and Pete were too close to let anything come between them.

"I know," she whispered. "People are more important, right?"

"Now you're catching on."

Ava dropped her chin, and not even the spicy-sweet scent of warm cinnamon and rich milk could comfort the ragged hole in her heart. "I just wish I'd slowed down long enough to realize that before it was too late."

Pete leaned in to kiss the crown of her head. "You'll find an answer with this article. You always respect the story in front of you."

The words trickled into her brain, and God, that phrase was so familiar. . . . "Say that again?"

"What? You'll find an answer with this article?"

Ava cranked her eyes shut, grasping at voices, memories. "No. The other part."

"Oh. You always respect the story," her brother said. "I mean, I know your choices for this one kind of suck, but . . ."

You respect the story. No matter what.

Ava's memory kicked to life in a single, beautiful instant, and she stood up from the table in a rush of impulse and absolute certainty.

"My choices might be difficult, but Brennan's right. I *do* have them. And it's far past time that I made the right call on this one, once and for all."

* * *

Brennan had never wished for a crush of pre-New Year's Eve revelers—or better yet, a raucous bachelor party for a double wedding—so hard in his life.

Of course, it was closing time, and the Double Shot was painfully empty. Just like every ounce of space in Brennan's chest. Two days from now, everyone in Pine Mountain would know exactly who he was. His job. His secrets. His past.

And there wasn't a damn thing he could do about it.

"Here." Adrian's voice delivered Brennan back to the Double Shot, the familiar *clink* of glass on wood snagging him back behind the bar.

"What's this?" Brennan slid a skeptical stare at the two shot glasses full of whiskey lined up neatly across the wood, the half-full bottle of Crown Royal sitting next to them like a bookend with really bad intentions.

"For a bar manager, you kind of suck at this. But we can work on your skills later. Right now, you look like you could use a stiff drink."

The words *I'm fine* spun up from the defenses long programmed into Brennan's repertoire, but he bit them in half as he picked up one of the shot glasses. "You're the boss."

The whiskey burned a straight path from belly to balls, lighting up all five of his senses like the Fourth of July before settling in a hard tingle at the back of his neck.

Brennan shuddered in an effort to recalibrate. "Shit."

"Yup." Adrian placed his now-empty shot glass on the bar without missing a beat. "Teagan locked the front door on her way out, and Jesse just took off for the night. So are we talking about this?"

"No." Bitterness that had nothing to do with the whiskey flooded his mouth, and hell—some defenses never died.

"Okay." Adrian poured another round, but Brennan's hand fell just short of the glass. As tempting as it was to literally drown his sorrows, he'd learned a long time ago that going numb didn't take care of his problems.

Brennan paused. "There's a lot of stuff you don't know about me. It's all going to hit the fan in a couple of days, and I'm not sure how it'll play out."

"Does it have anything to do with this?" Adrian held out a crumpled printout, the title blazing, RESCUE SQUAD HERO STARTS OVER IN PINE MOUNTAIN, and sweat dotted Brennan's brow.

"Where did you get that?"

"I found it on the floor under Ava's table after she left. Two minutes after you inventoried the walk-in. For the third time tonight."

Ah, fuck. There was no sense in trying to get out of this now. Adrian was the most freakishly intuitive guy he knew. Except maybe for Captain Westin.

Brennan ran a finger around the shot glass, but opted for pouring himself a Coke instead. "I used to be a firefighter."

"Something tells me that's not quite past tense, considering how you pulled Matthew Wilson out of Joe's Grocery a few weeks ago."

"I was injured on the job," Brennan said, although it was a hell of a sugarcoat. "And I left under bad circumstances. So, yeah. There's no going back."

"You know I respect you, right?" Adrian tossed back Brennan's shot of whiskey without breaking eye contact, and Brennan nodded without thought.

"Yeah."

"Good. Because you're full of shit."

"Excuse me?" Okay, so it wasn't smart to pick a fight with a guy who had just done two rapid-fire shots of whiskey and was the size equivalent of a Sherman tank, but come on. Brennan couldn't just leave that alone.

But rather than rise to the throw down in Brennan's voice, Adrian softened both his stance and his tone. "Don't get your shorts in a knot. I'm trying to help you."

"It's not working," Brennan snapped, feeling like an instant dick. He amended, "I don't think anything can help this now."

"Christ, you are a pain in the ass." Adrian shook his head, adjusting his black and silver Harley-Davidson baseball hat with one hand. "Did you even read this?"

"I don't need to read it." So much for not being a dick. "I lived through it once already."

As loaded with emotion as Brennan's words were, his buddy didn't even blink. "Well, it looks like your story's coming back for another round, like it or not. So the question isn't whether you want people to know it."

Adrian took the page off the bar, placing it between Brennan's fingers.

"It's how you're going to change things so you can live with them the second time around."

Chapter Twenty-Seven

Brennan's eyes burned as if they'd been hand polished with lighter fluid and set out to dry in the midday sun. He parked himself at the last booth in Scarlett's All-Night Diner and ordered a Coke, relearning the place with a couple of furtive glances. The restaurant had been standing at the corner of Fairview and Church since Brennan could remember. Between the laid-back atmosphere that felt like an old pair of jeans, its location two blocks from Station Eight, and the owner-slash-cook's easy affinity for slinging together some of the most killer food on the eastern seaboard, Scarlett's was a local favorite among firefighters.

"Well, well. You are a sight, son. I'll give you that." A familiar, raspy voice surfaced from two and a half years in Brennan's memory banks, and hell if it wasn't more comforting than anything else.

Damn. He'd missed this place.

Brennan stood, running a hand over his hair to no avail. Nothing short of a shower, a shave, and a hot date with a hairbrush could hide the three hours of sleep he'd put on top of the five-hour, middle of the night drive into town. "You don't have to pretty it up, Captain."

Captain Westin smiled, his light brown eyes crinkling into age lines at the corners. "Well, then. You look like shit, Brennan. But it's still great to see you."

He extended his hand, clapping Brennan on the shoulder as they shook, and shock rippled outward from Brennan's gut. "Thanks. How are things?"

"Ah. Let's see. My daughter, Zoe, is back in town, heading up a new program with the city. I love the girl, but she's giving me more fits than any one man should have."

The radio clipped to the thick strap on the shoulder of the captain's uniform let out a crackle and squawk, and he reached up nonchalantly to listen first, then lower the volume. "And Chief Williams is passing a kidney stone over a sudden vacancy at the academy. One of his best instructors just up and ran off with a Vegas showgirl, which of course is now the problem of every captain in the city."

"A showgirl, huh? That's interesting," Brennan ventured, but he knew both Chief Williams and the way things worked in the FFD well enough to know the score. Shit always rolled downhill in Fairview, and it picked up speed and velocity as it went.

"It's a train wreck," Captain Westin corrected, pausing to ask a passing server to fill the double-sized coffee cup he'd flipped over. "We're rotating men from all three shifts over there as best we can, but you know how it is. Qualified instructors are hard to come by."

Although Brennan had had a handful of great instructors at the academy, most guys who knew their shit and were jacked up about being firefighters were . . . well, firefighters. "Well, I know you're on shift right now. Thanks for coming to see me."

Captain Westin nodded, a quick dip of his gray blond head. "I heard your trip into town was a quick one. I'm sorry I missed you at Ellie's wedding."

Well, looked like they were going to get right to it, then. "Yeah. I'm sure Alex and Cole mentioned that we, ah, spoke."

Firefighters might keep their opinions in-house, but that didn't mean they didn't have them. And from Alex's no-bones-about-it confrontation, he'd looked to have enough for everyone at the station combined.

Westin said, "Two sides to every story. But I've told you that before."

"Yes, sir." Brennan took a deep breath, and—screw it; Adrian was right. He'd come too far and hurt for too long to do this the wrong way twice. "Thing is, I'm thinking maybe my statute of limitations has run out on second chances."

Captain Westin sat back, swirling his spoon through his cup of coffee even though he hadn't added milk or sugar. "I pulled a copy of the official investigation report and showed it to Donovan and Everett the day after your sister's wedding."

Brennan's glass hit the Formica tabletop with a clunk. "You . . . what?"

"First off, let me assure you that I still run a tight house with even tighter rules. As captain, it's up to my discretion to share certain details with my men. I only do so when I deem it necessary, and this situation fit the circumstances."

"But why would you do that now? It's been two and a half years."

"It has," Captain Westin agreed. "And it's been a long time since Cole or Alex has brought up what happened that night. But seeing you again changed that, and as captain of Station Eight, it's my job to do whatever I need to in order to get my firefighters right. Losing a brother is a hard thing for all of us, Brennan." He leaned in, his serious-as-hell stare paving the way for the words that followed. "But they didn't lose one that night. They lost two, and it was far past time for them to know why."

Brennan tried to swallow, but nothing got past the grief still lodged in his throat. "I didn't think it would hurt anybody but me if I took the blame and disappeared."

"I'll tell you now what I told you then. Mason's death was a tragedy, and there is no way around that. He was a good man, and he is sorely missed. But the golden rule is a tricky one when you only take it at face value. You're a bit overdue to look past the surface, Brennan."

All the breath vanished from the room as the sentiment that had pinned Brennan's self-blame into place for two and a half years suddenly took on new meaning in his mind.

Above all, have each other's backs.

Brennan had left Fairview to take the blame for Mason's death, but he'd never stopped to think that Cole and Alex wouldn't want him to. That they'd have his back if he told them what had happened.

That he'd shut them out instead of letting them help.

"Shit."

"I see we're making progress." Captain Westin chuckled over the rim of his coffee cup, but Brennan shook his head.

"I can't believe I didn't get it. It's been so long." God, how had he been so blind all this time? And more importantly, why was it all so clear *now*?

You're a good man, Brennan. You're brave, and strong, and kind. . . .

No. No way had Ava led him here. She'd wanted a story, plain and simple.

"Brennan." Captain Westin leaned in, nothing but truth in his eyes. "When I said it's my job to keep my firefighters straight, I meant all of you. You've been carrying around a lot of guilt for the past few years. Now what do you say we put this to bed, once and for all?"

Brennan nodded, pushing back to toss enough cash for their tab on the table before following Captain Westin out the door and onto Church Street. His boots felt strangely light on the winter-chilled pavement, as if each step was finally taking him back where he belonged.

He hitched for only a second as they rounded the last corner, his breath sticking in his lungs at the sight of the tall, unassuming building he'd called home for four years. Morning sunlight colored the bricks in shades of red and brown, glinting off the gold-stenciled sign reading FAIRVIEW FIRE DEPARTMENT, STATION EIGHT, which stood proudly across the top of the building. The automatic doors on two of the oversized triple bays on the front of the house were closed, but the clang of equipment over concrete and the masculine laughter that accompanied it were a pure indicator that some things never changed.

Hell. Maybe it *was* too late for this. After all, it wasn't like he could come back, anyway. Not the way he wanted to. His vertebrae were like an old jigsaw puzzle, all missing pieces and busted edges. Active duty would never happen again, not even with all the forgiveness in Fairview.

Brennan stood, mired in doubt and cemented to his spot next to Captain Westin on the threshold of Station Eight, when a familiar item in a decidedly unfamiliar spot caught his attention and grabbed on tight.

Hanging directly over the center of the middle bay was a helmet bearing the Fairview Fire Department crest and Station Eight shield, the back edging clearly marked in silver lettering.

IN MEMORY OF MASON WATTS. FIREFIGHTER, BROTHER, FRIEND.

Looked like Mason had Brennan's back too.

"If you need me for anything, I will be in my office," said Captain Westin as he left Brennan.

He walked to the open bay, inhaling the heavy smell of diesel from the bright red engine and the blue and white ambulance lined up by the automatic door. A handful of guys Brennan didn't recognize stood in various stages of hard work, pulling the equipment from Engine Eight's storage compartments for inventory and safety checks. Each of them wore the standard-issue navy blue firefighter's pants the captain always insisted on, along with either long-sleeved T-shirts or thermal tops emblazoned with the FFD crest.

"O'Keefe, you slacker. Don't you have inventory to do in that big old box of yours? Band-Aids to count, or something?" Alex slung a Scott pack over one shoulder, dodging a friendly shove from Station Eight's paramedic, Tom O'Keefe, as Cole joined in and said something that made both men laugh.

Their laughter faded in short order the second they saw Brennan standing in the doorway.

Ever the peacekeeper, Cole was the first to recover. "Didn't think we'd see you again," he said, not inviting Brennan in, but not kicking him out either.

Alex knotted his arms over his chest, his expression as closed off as his stance, but Brennan refused to let it rattle him.

"I thought about what you said, and you were right. There's a lot we never talked about."

"Yup. There is." For a minute that went on for an ice age, Cole split his gaze between Brennan and Alex. Finally, he jerked his light brown head toward the equipment room. "We were just putting this gear away. Why don't you come on back?"

"I don't want to get in the way," Brennan said, hating every ounce of being a bystander.

Cole laughed, shrugging his Scott pack over one arm in

a well-practiced lift. "Then don't. It's not like you don't know your way around here."

O'Keefe took a step back, offering Brennan a deferent nod and a wide berth so he could follow Cole and Alex to the equipment room off the garage bay. Although the layout was a little different and the names on the individual stalls were more new than familiar, Brennan still knew exactly how many footsteps it would take to get him to the spot that used to house his turnout gear.

Alex dropped his Scott pack to the shelf labeled DONOVAN, the heavy clang of metal on metal grating the air space between them. "How come you never told us what happened that night?"

"Way to ease into things, Al," Cole said, but Brennan didn't flinch or hold back.

"No, he's right. I should've talked to you, and I didn't. I had good reasons . . . at least, I thought I did. But I was wrong."

There might be only a single-digit number of things that would put cement shoes on Alex Donovan's larger-than-life attitude, but hell if Brennan hadn't just bull's-eyed one.

"You were wrong." Alex stared, and it was all the lead-in Brennan was going to get.

"Yeah." His back muscles jumped in anticipation, but he smoothed them out with a long draw of air. "At first, I didn't want to see you because I was too screwed up. Losing Mason and my career and all that surgery. It was just . . . easier to push everything away. I'm not proud of it, but that's the truth."

Cole nodded, sitting down on the wooden bench in front of them and bracing his forearms over his thighs. "Understandable."

Alex shifted his weight from one heavy-soled work

boot to the other, the look on his face reading an unspoken *I guess*. "That was at first. What about after?"

"I didn't realize it until recently, but I guess I didn't come back after that because we always take care of our own. I knew eventually you'd all get each other straightened out, but . . ." Brennan broke off, the words clotting together in his mind.

"You thought you didn't deserve that too," Cole finished.

"I felt guilty," Brennan said, and damn, the admission pulled up on his shoulders as it tumbled from his mouth. "And then I just wanted to forget."

Going for full disclosure, Brennan told them how he'd made rescue squad just before the apartment fire, as well as revealing the details about the four months he spent in his post-injury stupor and his twenty-eight days in detox. Just putting his past to words made Brennan feel lighter, the irony of everything he'd tried so hard to avoid growing stronger with each breath.

The story really was worth telling.

"Jesus, Brennan." Cole ran a hand over his crew cut, coasting his palm over the back of his neck. "Being hooked on painkillers is no joke. I wish I'd known how bad you needed an ear."

Shock had Brennan's head snapping up. "I wouldn't have talked," he argued, but Cole parried that with ease.

"It doesn't matter. I should've tried harder to get you to. After Mason died and you wouldn't talk to anybody, we all spent a lot of time not knowing what to think. It was easy to jump to conclusions and blame you for walking away. But I should've known you wouldn't just bow out without a reason. I should've pushed."

Alex pressed his lips into a thin line, but he nodded in agreement. "Me too." He pushed off from the edge of the equipment stall where he'd been leaning, uncrossing his arms to extend a hand to Brennan. "I'm sorry for what I said at Ellie's wedding. I knew you didn't have anything to do with what happened to Mason. Any one of us would've led the way to that apartment to try and save that kid, exactly like you did, Brennan. You've gotta know that."

"I do now," Brennan said, startled to finally discover that it was true.

"Westin showed us the fire marshal's report." Cole stood, repeating the handshake Alex had just shared with Brennan. "It kind of put things in perspective. Although hearing your side of the story has helped a lot more."

"Yeah." The feeling of dread that had made a home in the pit of Brennan's gut resurfaced. "Well, Westin isn't the only one with access to those files, and someone leaked them to the press. This story's about to get a whole lot more public than any of us would like."

"Does this have anything to do with your reporter girlfriend?" Alex asked.

Ah, hell. Brennan was going to have to face this tomorrow anyway. He might as well give it a practice run.

"She's not my girlfriend. But yes. She's running a story in tomorrow's paper in Riverside." Brennan recounted the events that had gone down at Joe's, and how he and Ava had reconnected, then *dis*connected over the story she'd written and the one she was about to let loose.

"Hold up." Alex lifted a hand. "Writing a story about you without letting you in on the deal is uncool, I'll give you that. But I'm not sure I buy that she bribed someone downtown to sell you out. This is a woman who totally went to bat on your behalf, dude. Not to mention, she's tremendously fucking hot."

Cole shook his head, looking a little bit shocked and a whole lot amused. "Don't be a dick, Teflon."

"Why not? I'm great at being a dick. And come *on*,

Everett. You saw the woman in question. I'm just asking what we're both wondering. Are you sure there isn't something else to Ava's article that you're not seeing?"

"Uh, no. I mean, yes. I don't know how else she'd get a copy of that report," Brennan finally managed, the words crowding past his shock. "What do you mean she totally went to bat for me?"

Alex opened his mouth to answer, but Cole cut him off with glee. "Donovan got a little uppity with her about being there as your date, and she called him an arrogant, life-sized Ken doll."

The laugh that popped past Brennan's lips was completely against his will. "She said that?" Damn, she really was a spitfire.

"Didn't even skip a beat. In fact, as much as I hate to admit it, I've got to agree with Alex," Cole said. "Ava seemed pretty convinced you're a quality guy. She wasn't shy about airing it out, either."

Alex snorted, his feelings stitched to his sleeve just like always. "The woman is a total cherry bomb." The affirmation was tied up tight with approval. "You really sure it's not going to work out? She was in your corner just forty-eight hours ago."

Admiration and want collided in Brennan's gut for just a breath before he tamped them back into the past, where they belonged. "Well, she's not now. She's going to run the story to prove it tomorrow."

"My bad," Alex said, lifting both hands in genuine apology. "You know we've got your back if there's any local fallout from the article."

"Thanks. I appreciate it, man." Brennan gestured toward the door, shooting straight for a change in subject. "So does the oven in the kitchen still only have two temperatures, or did you lame-asses finally sell enough T-shirts to replace the thing?"

"Why don't you come find out, Fryboy? Word on the street is that you can cook circles around all of us now."

But even as Cole slapped him on the shoulder and welcomed him back into Station Eight with open arms, a part of Brennan's heart still sat empty in his chest.

Chapter Twenty-Eight

Brennan backhanded the sleep out of his eyes as he trudged through the fresh layer of snow in the Double Shot's parking lot. After round-tripping it to Fairview with only a twenty-four-hour turnaround time, he was bordering on total exhaustion. But he'd been away from the bar for too long lately, and even though yesterday's trip to Fairview had ended with the promise that it would be the first of many, Brennan owed Teagan and Adrian no less than six double shifts to make up for his time away from work.

Starting with today's.

Brennan palmed the building keys from his back pocket, letting himself into the empty restaurant. He did a quick visual, checking over the receipts from the night before and updating the numbers in the computer system before turning to take the bar stools off the counter.

The one on the end slipped out of his hand with a clatter.

"God damn it," Brennan hissed, righting the leather-backed stool with a decisive flip. It was just a stool. They had twenty of them. He was going to have to get over the fact that this one would be empty from now on.

Even if someone else sat in it every single night for the rest of time.

He forced his feet back to the bar, shrinking down lower in his canvas jacket to ward off the chill still permeating the air. Another fifteen minutes' worth of tasks didn't warm him, and oh, what the hell—at least doing freezer inventory would keep him awake.

"Whoa." Adrian's gravelly voice hit Brennan point-blank in the holy-shit region of his chest, and the big guy didn't pull any punches from his spot at the pass-through. "You look like shit in a shredder."

"Thanks, Gigantor. You're a peach." No point denying the truth, and anyway, how he looked was a step up from how he felt. Not that Brennan would admit that out loud.

"You seen today's *Daily*?" Adrian asked, kicking a thin layer of snow from his boots. He tossed the paper to the stainless steel counter behind the bar, just within Brennan's reach.

"No." No need to lay eyes on a train wreck to know it was going to be bad. "Look, I'll do a better job handling the publicity this time, even if it's negative. But really, I—"

"What publicity?"

Seriously? "From Ava's article."

Adrian snapped the paper wide, raising a brow over the top edge. "There's no article, Slick."

"But she's a reporter. Why wouldn't she run the story?"

Brennan racked his brain, turning over every possible scenario until . . .

She was in your corner just forty-eight hours ago. . . . You really sure it's not going to work out?

You're a good man, Nick Brennan . . . and I'm going to do whatever it takes to make you see it.

What if she really *hadn't* had a choice about writing the story? Knowing her boss, it would mean her job, but what if Ava's version of proving what she believed meant she'd chosen to do nothing at all.

What if she loved him enough to pull the story, even
after he'd told her in no uncertain terms to get out of his
life.

"Can you cover me?" Brennan dug through his pocket
in a frantic search for his keys, yanking them from his
jacket in a rush.

Adrian's brows rose. "Sure. Where are you going?"

"I need to find Ava before she leaves Riverside," he
said, rushing toward the door. "I can't let her get away
twice."

Ava tossed the last of her personal items into a cardboard box and closed her desk drawer with a *snick*. She
handed the box off to Layla, scooping up its twin from
the chair in her cubicle.

Make that her *former* cubicle.

"I can't believe how different it's going to be around
here without you," Layla said, a mournful pout shaping her
mouth. The *Daily*'s newsroom was caught in all the usual
midmorning rush, although the place sure had seen its fair
share of extra buzz over the last twenty-four hours.

God. Ava was going to miss it here.

"You'll have plenty to keep you busy," she told Layla,
her chest thudding with a heavy ache despite her ironclad
efforts to stay tough. "Anyway, I can't stay."

Layla nodded, dropping her gaze to the box in her arms.
"I know."

"Come on. It's time to go."

Ava turned, casting a long, last look over the newsroom
where she was about to leave five grueling years and one
hard-fought career.

Her eyes landed on a very disheveled, extremely wild-eyed, and utterly breathtaking Nick Brennan.

"Ava!" Brennan strode down the stretch of carpet in the newsroom's main corridor, and she blinked, certain the emotions of the last few days and the four cups of coffee she'd thrown back this morning had just sent her over the edge of reason.

Nope. He was still right in front of her. And he looked *furious*.

"Where's your boss?" Brennan's eyes moved over the box in her grasp, his expression dropping briefly into something she couldn't label before hardening back into anger. "Where is he *right now?*"

Ava opened her mouth three times before she could coax anything intelligent past her vocal cords. "Technically, in his office, I guess, but he's really not—"

"He's not firing you, that's what."

Brennan charted a course for the glass-walled office at the front of the newsroom, and Ava jostled her box to the floor as she renewed her protest.

"Brennan, wait."

Nope. No go. Holy crap, he was going to burn a path in the carpet.

"Brennan . . ."

She rushed after him to no avail, and okay, now it was time to get serious.

"Nick."

He screeched to a stop just shy of the office door.

"A lot of changes have gone down here at the paper since Monday night, and yes, I am leaving the *Daily*. But before you go barging into that office, you should know that nobody fired me."

"But your stuff is in boxes," he argued, gesturing to the spot where she'd plunked down her belongings.

"I know. I put it there when I resigned."

"You *quit?*"

Ava nodded, certainty welling in her chest.

She knew Nick Brennan's story. It was time he learned hers.

"I should have told you from the beginning that I was working on an article about firefighters, and that I wanted to use your story as part of the piece. I only meant to show you that you're worthy of recognition, but just because I think your story is worth telling doesn't mean it's mine to tell. I was wrong, and I'm sorry."

"Ava, wait."

"No, you deserve to hear the rest. I wrote my article as a personal interest piece, but Gary wanted more. He'd been pressuring me to write something splashier, to increase the bottom line. I don't know how, but he got his hands on the investigation report from the night you were hurt. He said if I didn't use it in my story, he'd write the piece himself."

Brennan's hands curled to fists at his sides, and she rushed to continue before he went all commando again. "But you were right. I had choices. I knew printing those details wasn't right, so I called the owner of the paper to file a formal complaint against my boss. My fellow reporter Ian backed up my claims, but I couldn't risk the article being run the way Gary wanted it run, no matter what."

"Ava . . ."

She shook her head, adamant. If she didn't get this out now, she wouldn't have another chance. "So I quit. The research that was on my laptop stayed here, unfortunately, but I knew Gary couldn't piece anything together without my extensive personal notes."

Her mind flashed quickly over the tattered blue note-book she'd tossed into Big Gap Lake yesterday morning. "And because I no longer work for the paper, he couldn't make me share them. I know it'll never make up for what I did—"

"Ava—"

Ava's throat threatened to tighten, but she stood firm. "No. I needed to be strong enough to stand up for what was right. Not for me, but for you. You deserve your integrity no matter what the story is, and it's my job to give it to you regardless of cost. Not just because I'm a reporter, but because I love you. I know it's crazy, and I know you're still furious, but I love you. And—"

"Spitfire."

The rest of her words crashed to a halt on her lips, and the edges of Brennan's mouth ticked slowly, beautifully upward.

"It is crazy, and I was furious. But you were right. The story is worth telling. It just took me a while to figure that out."

Ava's heart sped up. "It did?"

"It did." Brennan bridged the distance between them in three brisk strides. "But I think I've got it now, thanks to you."

"But it's not my story," she said, confused.

"You're right. It's my story. But I'm trusting it to you. You had my back when I thought no one else did, and you believed in what you knew. I want to give you exclusive rights to write the story your way, but only if Gary gives you your job back. It's what *you* deserve."

"Gary can't give me my job back."

"Oh yes, he can." Brennan renewed his efforts to reach the front of the newsroom, but Ava placed a hand directly over his heart.

"He can't, because Mr. Royce fired him. Gary doesn't work here anymore."

Brennan shook his head. "But neither do you."

Ava smiled, the irony playing on her lips. "Mr. Royce asked me if I'd reconsider. And with Ian as the new managing editor, I thought about it. But in the end, I decided to try freelancing for a while. It's past time for me to take hold of my career, my way."

"So you could still write the story. From anywhere," he said, dropping his gaze to the hand Ava still had across the center of his chest.

Oh . . . God. "Only if you want me to."

In less than a breath, Brennan's hands cupped her face, drawing her close. "I want you for more than a story, Ava. I love you. I want you forever."

He captured her mouth in a kiss she felt all the way to her toes, and Ava kissed him back with equal measure.

"Well, good. Because you just professed your love for me in front of a room full of reporters. I'm pretty sure there's no way you'll stay out of the news."

Brennan flicked a glance at the twenty or so faces staring at them from the utterly quiet newsroom, but the spotlight didn't rock him one bit.

"Let 'em talk," he said, and then he kissed her again.

Chapter Twenty-Nine

Two weeks later

Brennan held the envelope stamped with the official seal of the Fairview Fire Department between shaky fingers, inwardly cursing himself for not having the balls to just open the damn thing and get it over with.

"Is that what I think it is?" Ava's bright green eyes sparkled above her mischievous smile, and she leaned over the bar from her perch in the very last seat.

He leaned back to steal a quick kiss despite his nerves. Damn, he loved this woman. "Yeah."

"Adrian! Teagan! He got the letter," Ava called over Brennan's shoulder, and he coughed out a laugh in her direction.

"Traitor." Within seconds, everyone on the Double Shot's staff gathered behind the bar, with Lily and Pete keeping Ava company on the customer side of the wood.

"What are you waiting for, Slick?" Adrian tilted his stubble-covered chin at the envelope. "Do the honors."

Brennan looked around the bar, his heart taking up residence in his windpipe as he stuck his finger into the seam of the envelope with a big, fat *here goes nothing*.

Dear Mr. Brennan,
   We are pleased to offer you the position of
instructor at the Fairview Fire Academy. . . .

Holy. Shit.

After three trips to Fairview, two interviews, and one hard-as-hell exam, he'd done it.

Brennan was going home.

"Well?" The look on Ava's face suggested she already knew the answer, and God, not even a fully loaded tanker truck would crush her belief in him.

"I, uh. I got the job."

The room exploded into excited cheers and raucous applause, and Ava flung her arms around him from her side of the bar.

"I knew it! I'm so happy for you."

He let her kiss him for a minute—after all, he wasn't an idiot—before pulling back to give her a questioning look.

"You're sure?" he asked, turning to add Pete and Lily to the conversation.

Ava didn't even blink. "We've talked about this. The editor at the *Fairview Sentinel* has already agreed to run the rescue squad piece, and I've got a line on a few other stories for them too. Fairview's not up the street from Pine Mountain," she said, pausing to let her brother squeeze her arm. "But places aren't as important as people, and the person I belong with is you. If you're going back to Fairview, I'm going with you."

"I'm really going to miss you guys," Brennan said, reclaiming the attention of everyone at the bar. The place might not be a firehouse, but the people in it had accepted him, no questions asked, for the last two years.

"You're a tough act to replace, hero." Adrian tipped a beer in his direction. He slung an arm around Teagan's shoulders, his smile as natural as breathing, and hell if Brennan didn't get the emotion behind it, once and for all. "Make sure you don't forget us little people."

Brennan laughed, reaching for Ava's hand and knowing that second chances really did exist.

"I've got your back. You can count on it."

You met the guys at Station Eight in
ALL WRAPPED UP.
Now get to know them in

RECKLESS,

Rescue Squad Book One,

coming next February.

SOMEONE'S BOUND TO GET BURNED ...

Zoe Westin may be a fire captain's daughter, but feeding the people in her hometown of Fairview is her number one priority. Running a soup kitchen is also the perfect way to prove to her dad that helping people doesn't always mean risking life and limb. But when she's saddled with a gorgeous firefighter doing community service after yet another daredevil stunt, the kitchen has never been so hot.

Alex Donovan thrives on adrenaline, and stirring a pot of soup doesn't exactly qualify. He's not an expert at following the rules either, not even when they come from the stubborn, sexy daughter of the man who's not only his boss, but his mentor. Determined to show Zoe that not every risk ends in catastrophe, Alex challenges her both in the kitchen and out. One reckless step leads to another, but will falling for each other be a risk worth taking, or will it just get them burned?

Praise for Kimberly Kincaid and her novels

"An author on the rise."
—RT Book Reviews

"A sweet and sexy treat!"
—Bella Andre

"Smart, fun, and heartwarming."
—Jill Shalvis

Two things in firefighter Alex Donovan's life were dead certain. The first was where there was smoke, you could bet your lunch money there was going to be fire. The second was wherever there was fire, Alex wanted in.

No contest. No question.

"Okay, listen up, boys, 'cause it looks like we've got a live one," Alex's lieutenant, Paul Crews, hollered over the headset from the officer's seat in the front of Engine Eight, scrolling through the confetti-colored display from dispatch with a series of *clacks*. "Dispatch is reporting a business fire, with smoke issuing from the windows at a warehouse for a chemical supply company on Roosevelt Avenue. Looks like the place has been abandoned since the company went under last year."

"Is that down in the industrial park by the docks?" His best friend Cole Everett's tried-and-true smile disappeared as he reached down from the seat next to Alex to yank his turnout gear over his navy blue uniform pants, and yeah, this wasn't going to be your average cat stuck in a tree scenario.

"Yup. Nearest cross street is Euclid, which puts it four blocks up from the water and smack in the middle of In-dustrial Row." Crews looked over his shoulder and into the back step of the engine, jerking his chin at the two of them in an unspoken *get your asses in gear,* and hell if Alex needed the message twice.

"Pretty shitty part of town," he said, his pulse jacking up a notch even though he reached for the Scott pack in the storage compartment behind his seat with ease that bordered on the ho-hum. Not that his adrenaline wasn't doing the hey-now all the way through his system, because it sure as shit was. But getting torqued over a promissory note from dispatch without seeing the reality of flames only wasted precious energy. He'd learned that well enough as a candidate nine years ago.

Plus, there would be plenty of time to go yippee-ki-yay once shit started burning down.

"Does it matter that we're headed into Fairview's projects?" Mike Jones asked from Alex's other side, yanking his coat closed over his turnout gear with more attitude than anyone with three weeks' experience had a right to.

Hello. The candidate has a sore spot. Not that it would change Alex's response, or his delivery. Sugarcoating things was for ass-kissers and candy store owners, and neither title was ever going to go on his résumé.

He fixed Jonesey with a hard stare. "It does when there are probably squatters inside the building, Einstein. How do you think a fire starts in an abandoned warehouse anyway?" Even money said the place hadn't seen working electricity in a dog's age. With the city still in the hard grip of winter, there was zero percent chance this call site had nobody home.

"Oh." Mike dropped his chin for just a split second before picking up the slack with the rest of his gear. "Guess I wasn't thinking of it like that."

But Alex just shrugged. He'd never been one for getting his boxers in a wad, let alone keeping 'em that way. Especially over the small stuff.

After all, life was too short. And hell if he didn't know *that,* up close and personal.

"Gotta use it for more than a hat rack, rookie." Alex tossed back the emotion in his chest like a double shot of Crown Royal, and it burned just the same as he slapped the kid's helmet with a gloved hand. "You'll learn."

Crews eighty-sixed his smile just a second too late for Alex to miss it, the wail of the overhead sirens competing with the lieutenant's voice over the headset as he blanked the momentary blip of amusement from his face. "There's no reported entrapment, but Teflon's right. An abandoned warehouse in a neighborhood like this is ripe for squatters, even in the daytime. Plus—" Crews broke off, the seriousness in his voice going full-on grim. "We don't know what kind of chemicals might've been left in the place. We need to go by the book on this one. Thirteen's already on scene."

"Outstanding," Cole muttered, tacking on a few choice words to the contrary about their rival house, and Alex's gut nose-dived in agreement.

"Those guys are a bag full of dicks." Not to mention their captain was a douche bag of unrivaled proportions. Alex might not stay mad at most people for long, but he sure as hell knew a jackass when he laid eyes on one.

"I mean it, Teflon." Crews's warning went from dark to dangerous in the span of half a breath. "I don't like those ass-clowns at Thirteen any more than you do, but a call's a call. Head up, eyes forward."

"Yeah, yeah. Copy that." Alex took off his headset, his mutter falling prey to the combination of Engine Eight's growl and the rush of noise that accompanied the final prep for a real-deal call. He went the inhale-exhale route as he triple-checked his gear, monitoring his breath along with his time as they approached the edge of town leading into Fairview's shabbier waterside neighborhoods.

"So, um, how come your nickname is Teflon?" Jones

shifted against the Scott pack already strapped to his back, the heel of one boot doing a steady bounce against the scuffed black floor of the engine.

Alex's laugh welled up from behind his sternum, and what the hell. The rookie might be ten pounds of nerves stuffed into a five-pound bag, but at least he was curious, too. "I guess you could say it's because I've got special talents."

Jones's head jerked back. "You cook?"

Cole flipped the mouthpiece of his headset upward, tugging the thing off one ear to interject. "Hell no," he said, although his tone coupled with his laugh to cancel out any heat from the words. "Clearly, you didn't partake in dinner last week when he was on KP."

"Hey," Alex argued, although he had a whole lot of nothing to back it up. He was a single guy who'd lived all by his lonesome for twelve years. Sue him for not being a gourmet chef. "Dinner wasn't that bad."

"Dude. You fucked up spaghetti."

"Italian cuisine can be extremely tricky." He tried on his very best cocky smile, the one that got him out of speeding tickets and into the panties of every pretty woman he set his sights on, but of course, Mr. Calm, Cool, and Buzzkill just snorted.

"The directions are on the freaking box." Cole lifted a hand to stop Alex from going for round two, turning his attention back to Jonesey. "To answer your question, Donovan here got his nickname for exactly what you just witnessed."

The candidate's blond brows lifted upward, nearly disappearing beneath the still-shiny visor on his helmet. "Which is . . . ?"

"He's slick enough to sell a cape to Superman. No matter what he gets himself into—and believe me, I've seen him get into some high-level shit—he talks his way right out of it. Trouble always slides right off him."

"Ah." Understanding dawned on Jones's face, and he swung his gaze from Cole to Alex. "Nothing ever sticks to Teflon."

"Nope," Alex said with a grin. Going through life on a bunch of should-haves and maybes was about as appealing as a prostate exam with a root canal chaser. If he wanted something, he did it without hesitation. Dealing with consequences was for after the fact, and despite Cole's smart-ass delivery, he wasn't wrong. Alex could handle anything that came his way, no matter how big, how bad, or how dangerous.

And he tempted all three on a regular basis.

GREAT BOOKS,
GREAT SAVINGS!

When You Visit Our Website:
www.kensingtonbooks.com
You Can Save Money Off The Retail Price
Of Any Book You Purchase!

- All Your Favorite Kensington Authors
- New Releases & Timeless Classics
- Overnight Shipping Available
- eBooks Available For Many Titles
- All Major Credit Cards Accepted

Visit Us Today To Start Saving!
www.kensingtonbooks.com

MAY -- 2016